HR MOORE

LEGACY OF THE MIND

Titles by HR Moore:

Legacy of the Mind

Origin of the Body

Design of the Spirit

www.hrmoore.com

*****

For Chris and for Alice.

*****

CHAPTER 1

'You won again.' It was a statement, not a question as Cleo knew what the answer would be.

Anita inhaled, lines appearing on her forehead as she raised her eyebrows, two graceful dark wings framing impatient grey eyes. She had entered and won every challenge since she was twelve years old. First she'd won all the junior challenges, then, when she was fifteen and competing at a pace none of the adults could keep up with, people started to care more about who came second, as that's where the real competition was.

'So nonchalant.' Cleo teased.

'It's hard to get excited about winning when you know you're going to win.'

'I don't know, Bas has got pretty close to you a couple of times,' said Cleo, mischievously, her eyes glinting as she threw her long, silky, black hair over her shoulder.

Cleo on to her favourite topic of conversation so soon, that must be some kind of record, thought Anita. She half smiled and raised one lofty eyebrow. 'Bas. Beat me?'

Cleo smirked. 'No, I suppose not'.

'Come on, we'll be late if we don't get a move on, and I'd be happy not to be late to our Mind class given how terrible I am at it.' Anita was very definitely a Body; she could take anyone on when competing in Body disciplines. She suspected there may be a fair bit of Sprit in her blood too, but Mind had always been a challenge. She didn't really understand why everyone had to continue with these ridiculous classes for years after school anyway. She was 25, but formal weekend education had to continue until 30, the age when the 'Centre comes together', whatever the bloody hell that meant. Allegedly, at the mystical age of 30, one's Mind, Body and Spirit blend into one, and from that point, developing any one skill becomes more of a challenge.

Anita found Mind enough of a challenge anyway and seeing as nobody she knew had morphed into some new magical being at 30, she suspected that it was all just propaganda anyway. The Descendants and their Councils had always had a passion for the theatrical. However, today was not the day to challenge the Descendants' vision and she really didn't want to have to play chess for hours on end with a Councillor, the punishment for being late, so it was best to be on time.

*****

'Oh look who's here,' said Cleo, playfully, shooting a sly sideways glance in Anita's direction as they approached the Temples. Anita looked around and saw the cause of Cleo's sudden excitement; she'd clocked Bas' tall, muscular frame, angular features and short sandy coloured hair. He exuded his normal relaxed demeanour, leaning back against the base of a large oak tree soaking up the sun's hot rays, legs half bent in front of him, arms resting easily on his knees. 'He seems to be looking for someone...I wonder who that could be.' Cleo was in her element, mincing her sparrow-like legs, boyish hips sashaying gleefully as they approached.

Anita shoved her roughly, putting an end to the strutting, but knowing all this would really do was encourage her. 'I see him every day at the Observatory. He's probably looking for that girl we saw him with last week,' she said, a little too defensively, because not very deep down Anita knew Cleo was right. He was waiting for her like he always was. She could feel his energy perk up every time he saw her, a sharp intensification that directly corresponded with the wide, endearing smile that would spread across his face. Thank the Gods not everyone could feel energy and nobody knew she could. It was usually a skill reserved for the Spirits, and usually, only those that had spent a very long time studying, but she had always been able to do it, ever since she could remember.

*****

They rotated through their classes. First was Mind, where today the aim was to move an object using only the energy of one's mind. This everyone thought was ridiculous; nobody had ever known anyone who could do it. Not even the Councillor leading the lesson could do it, so it all seemed pretty pointless. Some girl in the back had a hysterical moment when she swore she'd managed to move the flower in front of her a little, but seeing as she couldn't repeat the feat, everyone lost interest pretty quickly. Anita wasn't a fan of the Mind Temple. Its gothic features made it oppressive, like the walls contained secrets and the doors might suddenly slam shut, locking you in, never to let you go.

They escaped the gloomy space and moved onto their next class, Spirit. Anita had always loved the Spirit Temple. It was so lofty and light, sunlight streaming in through enormous slit windows that extended up its clean lines to a spired point towering acres above. The flowers everywhere were free and wild and flitted about spontaneously in the light breeze that always seemed to play across the colossal open expanse of the Temple's floor. Whereas the Mind Temple had a number of closed off, secluded areas, full of dark corners where it was easy to hide, conspire and observe, the Spirit Temple was one enormous open space, sectioned loosely into areas by the soaring columns that seemed too few and too high to effectively hold the walls in place. Obviously, Anita was most loyal to the Temple of the Body, but she had always felt an inexplicable pull towards the Spirit Temple.

The lesson focused on joint meditation, where two people sit opposite one another and meditate together, the two peoples' energy working together to take them both to a shared mental space in one or the other's mind. Here they have a shared experience that is invisible to the outside world. This again had seemed ridiculous until several months ago when Anita and Cleo had been paired. Whilst meditating, they had each been in a boat on the sea. Although they hadn't seen one another there, through much in depth comparison, they'd found that the details of the boat, the weather, the sea, had all been identical, so they usually tried to be paired with each other to see if they could get any further. Today, however, Bas had jumped in before Cleo and Anita could pair up, so Anita spent a couple of very uncomfortable hours trying to ignore Bas' soaring energy and closing herself off to anywhere he wanted to meditate to.

It wasn't that there was anything wrong with Bas. He was gorgeous; tall, athletic frame, olive skin, classic good looks. He was a kind, loyal friend – Anita's only real close friend apart from Cleo. He usually came second to Anita in Body challenges, not to mention that he was intelligent, in an academic sort of way, ran the energy Observatory, and came from a well-connected Council family. But Anita had just never seen Bas as anything other than a friend. She could see the girls all swoon when he walked by. Most of them would have swooned just because of his family connections, social climbing rife amongst Empire's well to do. Mothers with nothing better to do spending their days plotting how to marry their daughters off in advantageous ways. In addition, Bas was handsome, clever and didn't have a big head about his background, making him target number one. But his energy never shifted with any of their daughters like it did with her. Anita made it pretty obvious she didn't see him that way, but he never quite seemed to take the hint.

Next up was Body class, where people were taught how to use their energy to influence the actions of their bodies. This afternoon was all about shooting, but seeing as Anita was a better shot than any of the Councillors, she was allowed to skip the lesson. In fact, she hardly ever went to Body lessons, unless something like yoga was being practised, and this was only because there was a cross over with the Spirit disciplines. She usually went for a run or a ride during this time, meeting up with Cleo and Bas afterwards to walk home, but today she decided to stay in the Spirit Temple to meditate; she hadn't exactly had a productive session with Bas after all.

*****

After two long hours of not being able to concentrate, having spent most of the time running her hands irritably through her shoulder length brown hair, Anita was thinking maybe she should have gone for a run after all, when she felt a sudden surge of energy in the Temple. She looked up, and from where there had been a circular stone in the floor, in the centre of the Temple, moments before, there was now a hole with a man emerging from it. Like Bas, the man was tall and athletic, but whereas Bas was thick set,

4

this man was lean. He must be a Councillor, Anita mused, almost losing interest, but as he turned, Anita's breath caught involuntarily in her throat. He was exquisite; ruggedly handsome with broad shoulders and tanned muscular forearms. These were just visible under his heavy, red, floor-length cloak, protruding from a loose white shirt with casually rolled up sleeves.

His mind was somewhere else, the stone sliding closed unnoticed behind him. His face was angled towards the floor, brow furrowed, deep in complex thought as he started walking towards where Anita sat, transfixed, at the back of the Temple. When he walked, he seemed weightless, moving apparently without effort, yet purposefully, with the grace of a highly trained dancer. He looked up and Anita's blood seemed to stand still in her veins. His eyes were a bright, piercing blue, with both a depth that could have been a century old, and a life that hinted at a rebellious intelligence. His face was framed by tousled blond hair, neat enough not to be outlandish, but messy enough not to be conformist. His jaw was locked, lips a little pursed and twitching, betraying his all-consuming concentration.

Much to her confusion, Anita felt her energy start to bubble uncontrollably inside her. She felt it rise rapidly, as though riding on the back of a bird, frantically flapping its wings, thrown upwards from her stomach to her chest. Here, she could contain it no longer, and it burst free with a force so strong that Anita feared she might find an actual hole, not that she could muster the will to tear her eyes from the form in front of her and look down. He snapped out of his thoughts and looked immediately alert, his radiant energy rapidly diminishing as he tracked Anita's energy back to its source. His eyes found her without difficulty and ran searchingly over every contour of her body, taking in the potential threat before his shocking blue eyes locked with hers. Anita couldn't begin to read what she saw there. Confusion? Aggression? Wariness? Intrigue? It was all she could do to hold his gaze with her own inquisitive eyes, her energy shamelessly betraying her emotions as he considered her from afar.

He stood stock still, she sat spellbound, each considering their next move, when a crisp, impatient voice rudely shattered the silence. 'Alexander,' it said, as a second man strode confidently into the Temple.

Alexander? Surely not? Anita's energy changed; she turned defensive and panicked, and Alexander smiled, intrigued by her reaction. 'I'm coming Marcus,' he responded, not taking his eyes off Anita for a second, 'is Gwyn ready?'

Shit, it is them, Anita managed to compute, unhelpfully diverted by Alexander's voice, which was rich and smooth like melted chocolate. She struggled to regain some composure. Why are they here, she questioned, dimly, as she gathered the tremendous strength required to tear her eyes from Alexander to take in Marcus' form. She was completely unprepared for what she found. Holy Gods, he too was perfect. He was as tall as Alexander, but his thinner form made him seem somehow more refined. Whereas Alexander was wearing a loose shirt, slacks and beaten up soft leather mules, Marcus was impeccably dressed in expensive, well cut attire. Everything seemed flawlessly in place, from his shiny leather brogues, to his pressed white shirt and expensive gold knot cufflinks, to his perfectly quaffed, short, dark, hair and chiselled cheekbones. His eyes were dark and opulent and contrasted with Alexander's for reasons more integral than just colour. Marcus' contained none of the grounding of Alexander's. Instead, they flitted playfully, looking for something, anything of interest. They were impulsive, giving the impression that most of life bored him. Their sole occupation was to find something entertaining, to supply at least a small diversion before life returned to its usual dull monotony. He too sported a floor-length red cloak, but he wore it with a different kind of authority, an audacious authority. Whereas Alexander seemed to flow when he walked, Marcus was more overtly commanding, arrogant almost, with clipped, impatient strides. His energy was the most potent she had ever felt, and as it flowed over where she was sitting, it had a drug-like effect on her. Once again, Anita felt the pressure in her chest build, knowing, like a bottle being filled from a tap, there was nothing she could do to stop it from erupting without the source being shut off. Given that Marcus remained where he was, it once again poured out of her. Alexander turned casually back to look in her direction, the side of his mouth twitching almost unnoticeably, raising one, infuriating, mocking eyebrow as he flicked his impertinent eyes over her once more.

'Come on. We haven't got all day,' came what must have been Gwyn's voice from the entrance. It was curt and officious. Anita couldn't see her, but she sounded horrendous. Wow, thought Anita, you haven't even seen what she looks like yet, let alone talked to her, and already you're insulting her. You're a total bitch, she thought, as she struggled vainly to get her energy under control.

Marcus spun briskly around, striding past Anita to join Gwyn outside, without sending as much as a glance in her direction. Alexander followed him out, but stopped as he came close to where she sat. 'You should learn to control your energy,' he said, in a voice soft and low but commanding, 'with energy that strong, you are a very desirable asset.' With that he flowed out of the Temple, leaving Anita dumbfounded, head spinning, drained and empty, wondering what in the world had just taken place. That he could obviously read her energy was horribly embarrassing, but why did her energy rise like that towards both Alexander and Marcus? That had never happened to her before. Her energy was usually so static, unless of course she found a new challenge. Was this a challenge? How? What did Alexander mean about her energy being so strong? And what did he mean about her being an asset? Most of all though, why were the Descendants in Empire? They usually lived in Kingdom so they could be close to the Grand Temples, and very rarely came out here.

Anita spilled out of the Temple and almost ran headlong into Bas and Cleo, who had just finished their Body lesson. 'Oh my Gods, did you see her?' Cleo practically sang. She was bristling with delight, swishing wildly the ends of her thin cotton scarf; Cleo's equivalent of rubbing her hands together with glee.

'Yes, I saw all three of them in the Spirit Temple. Alexander appeared out of the centre, and then Marcus came in, and then Gwyn called for them from outside. So I suppose I only actually saw two of them, but oh my Gods, what are they doing here?' Anita blurted out in a jumbled rush.

'All three of them?' said Cleo, jealousy clear in her tone. 'We only saw Gwyn. She appeared from the centre of the Body Temple, all flowing golden locks and cloak,' she said, cattily. Anita was glad to see she wasn't the only one reacting badly to Gwyn. 'What are Alexander and Marcus like? I bet they're gorgeous, just like everyone says.'

Anita could feel Bas' jealousy at the mention of their names, noting that boys seemed to have the same negative reaction to Alexander and Marcus as girls did to Gwyn. Given she wasn't sure she could find the words to adequately describe them, even if she tried, she changed tack. 'More importantly, why are they here?'

'Don't know. Nobody in our class knew either. Well, the Councillor probably did, but he wasn't letting anything slip,' Bas replied.

'It'll give me something to find out at work then,' said Cleo. 'If there's any gossip to be shared, then The Island's the place. I'll see you there later?'

'Yep, sure, see you later. Have fun at work,' said Anita, shooting Cleo a knowing smile. Cleo was about to be in her element; fun was an understatement.

Cleo worked at The Island, a bar on an island, in the middle of the river, on the outskirts of town. It was pretty much the only place to socialise in Empire, so that's where everyone went, and Cleo used her place of work to keep abreast of anything and everything that might be going on. She wasn't above slipping a few free drinks across the bar to help people on their way, and she was incredibly persuasive, so she was right of course, the quickest way to find out why the Descendants were in town was through Cleo, at The Island.

CHAPTER 2

Bas decided to go back to the Observatory and tried to persuade Anita to go too. He'd been paying close attention to the energy since Philip's death and wanted to see if there had been any movement in the last few hours. Interested as Anita was to see the effect this was having on the energy, she wanted to mull over what had happened at the Temple, so opted for a run by the river instead. She agreed she would stop by the Observatory and pick up Bas later and they could head to The Island together.

After her brief encounter with the Descendants, Anita felt like a wound spring. She was angry at herself for her uncontrollable and embarrassing energy, and Alexander's cryptic comment about her being an asset had left her feeling vulnerable. She didn't understand why they were here, but the whole thing had left her deeply unsettled. Anita felt out of control, and she didn't like it.

She ran for miles along the river, her long, muscular legs eating up the ground. The shallow, meandering water usually took her mind off whatever she was preoccupied with, but today it was no help. She ran faster and faster, but this just seemed to make it worse. She was more frustrated by the end than she had been at the beginning, and by the time she got to the Observatory, she was in a foul mood.

'So are you going to ask her?' asked Patrick, Bas' runtish lab assistant, with floppy brown hair, blotchy, almost translucent skin and exceptionally bad fashion sense – although he obviously thought he was the height of cool. He had been probing about this for weeks.

'Maybe,' Bas replied, feigning exasperation, but he was fooling no-one, least of all Patrick. Patrick, like everyone else, saw the way Bas looked at Anita and knew there was nothing Bas wanted more than for her to want him too. Patrick, frankly, had always thought Bas was crazy. He could have his pick of any other girl in Empire, and it wasn't like they didn't throw themselves at him (much to Patrick's annoyance), but Bas only had eyes for Anita. He just didn't get it. Anita was alright he supposed; she was quite good looking, had a cracking body – if you liked the toned, athletic, slightly menacing look – but she was unpredictable and stubborn, she did not suffer fools, and was used to winning everything. In truth, Patrick found Anita intimidating and unfathomable. Maybe that's what the attraction was, that she was mysterious.

A light started flashing on the dashboard in front of Bas, indicating there was a spike in the energy in the immediate vicinity. The Observatory usually used this measure to keep tabs on when a Descendant was coming, but strangely, Anita had the same effect; her energy was so strong that it set off the alarm. Patrick saw the light too. 'Well, now's your chance to *maybe* ask her. I'll make myself scarce. See you at The Island later.'

'Hi Patrick,' said Anita, as she clunked up the metal spiral staircase into the room. Anita had no idea why Patrick always seemed to be leaving just as she arrived. Obviously she knew why he was going, Cleo and Patrick really should compare notes, but how was his timing always so impeccable?

'Hi Anita,' he replied, sensing her bad mood, which made him both doubly glad he was leaving and a little sorry for Bas. 'I'm just off to The Island. See you there later?'

'Yep, sure,' she said, in a terse voice; the last thing Anita wanted was to be left alone with Bas. Patrick turned and grabbed hold of the express exit, a pole through the floor, and winked annoyingly at Bas as he slid out of view.

The Observatory was an incredible building. It had been commissioned by the Descendants four generations back, as they had wanted to keep tabs on the energy. Bas' family, who had been in charge of the Archives for centuries and were known for their study of the energy, had helped design the building. They'd been put in charge of research from the start, earning Bas' ancestor a position as a Councillor, a position his father now held and that Bas would hold in the future.

The building was over three levels. Downstairs was a large, perfectly round, midnight blue pool of water that was always eerily still, as it helped to absorb any background energy 'noise'. The middle floor contained all the dashboards that provided readings of energy levels in various locations around the world, gently humming as it processed the energy flows, dials whishing backwards and forwards and lights flashing in a way that would seem meaningless to the uninitiated. The top floor contained the instruments that actually recorded the energy waves, and this level was Anita's favourite. There were multiple instruments up there, each trained in a different direction and all with golden receiver dishes attached that were shaped like the energy waves themselves. The receivers were of various sizes so they could pick up different frequencies of energy from different distances, with the biggest so large it had to rest on the floor of the roof. Anita loved to lie on this one and stare up at the stars, feeling the large, lolloping energy waves reverberating through her and off to be recorded in the dashboards downstairs. Of course, this affected the readings, so Bas wouldn't let her do that at a time like this, but she climbed to the roof anyway to look out over Empire.

Empire had a regal look about it, sort of understated yet effortlessly elegant. It was balanced, embraced and contained by the docile looking river, with several beautiful, arched, red brick bridges stretching across the meandering waters to connect the wealthy centre to the other side. The less desirable areas there were hidden from view from the Observatory by the bulk of the town. The centre of Empire spanned an area about the size of a square mile, built in an era before anyone saw a need to put walls up, the imposing spires of the Temples dominating the skyline, seeming to watch over and protect the buildings around them. Surrounding the Temples sat a number of well-to-do areas with fully stocked food markets, jewellery shops, clothes shops, perfumers, stationers, restaurants that always served an array of new and fantastical concoctions. And then, of course, there were the lovely, large, red brick houses with eccentric gardens full of climbing plants that seemed perfectly at one with their overstated owners. The most desirable houses, lived in generally by Councillors, along with properties owned by the Descendants themselves, tended to sit on the outskirts of town or in the surrounding countryside. They usually sat atop imposing hills or nestled on the side of one of the ancient woodlands, all gloriously picturesque, secluded, and with spectacular views.

Empire had once been the world's premier city, where trade was done and Gods were worshipped, however, Kingdom, a much more impressive, imposing metropolis had long since claimed that title. Empire now felt like it was in retirement, basking in previous honours and glories, living out a dignified and well thought of old age.

'I'll never get tired of that view,' said Bas, coming through the window to the roof behind Anita and nodding towards the lit up town. 'I like it best at night.' Anita moved slightly further onto the roof, so Bas wasn't standing quite so close, and sat down on one of the pipes that connected the receivers to the dashboards downstairs.

Bas stood easily, leaning against one of the receiver dishes, and Anita appraised him as he struggled with some internal debate; the muscles around his mouth clenching uncharacteristically and a tension filling his torso and powerful arms. 'So, are you going to the ball?' he blurted out quickly, trying to make throwing caution to the wind sound casual. Anita turned away so she could hide the look on her face. The only light on the roof came from inside, so she hoped Bas couldn't see.

'No, I don't think so,' Anita swiftly replied. 'The ball isn't really my thing. Sucking up to the Councillors, watching everyone make idiots of themselves in front of the Descendants, having to pretend to fawn over every word they say. It isn't my scene.'

'Oh,' Bas replied, his energy immediately tumbling. Anita felt bad, maybe she'd gone too far, Bas was, after all, going to be a Councillor one day, but there was nothing she wanted less than to go to the ball with Bas, and she wasn't very good in situations like this. Aside from the obvious, that it would give him the wrong impression, she didn't want every girl in town to hate her. People already thought she was weird for winning all the challenges; she didn't want to be loathed too.

'Found anything new with the energy?' she asked, hoping the change of subject would lift Bas' mood.

'No, nothing yet. There was a small downshift when the announcement was made about Philip's death, but it seems to have come back up again. I'm expecting Alexander's Crowning to lift the energy further; it's always exciting to have a new ruling Descendant.' Philip, Alexander's grandfather, had recently died, and a high-profile death was always a cause for concern around the energy. 'It's Christiana's death I'm really worried about, what with the unconventional bloodline.'

'Well, hopefully we won't have to worry about that for a while. We Body types are generally stronger than we look.' She shot Bas a smile that was supposed to at the same time say 'sorry' and 'chin up', but she wasn't sure that was quite how he took it.

Bas smiled optimistically. 'I know. I am one, aren't I? Shall we go?'

*****

The Island was nothing more than a shack really, strips of wood thrown precariously together decades before to form a building initially intended as a warehouse for traded goods. Since then it had been embellished inside and was now laid out over two levels. There was a short, stubby bar on the lower level to the right, bottles of all kinds of mysterious looking liquids balancing perilously on the uneven shelves behind. This level also had a private room behind the bar, ample space for standing, a couple of tall tables, and ledges here and there to place drinks on. One of these ledges jutted out awkwardly, partially obstructing a shady looking passage to the back door, leading to wooden decking and benches overlooking the river beyond. To the left of the door was a set of three squeaky wooden steps that groaned agedly every time a pair of feet touched them. They led to a raised seating area with a series of booths and rough wooden tables that afforded varying degrees of privacy, the walls adorned with weird and wonderful trinkets from those who had ventured into the Wild Lands to trade.

The place was packed. Clearly the news that the Descendants were in town had spread like wildfire, and everyone wanted to know why. Luckily, Cleo had grabbed a booth when her shift had ended, and Bas and Anita pushed their way through the crowd to join her. 'Before we get into the gossip, let me get you a drink,' said an overzealous Cleo, by way of a greeting. She flagged down one of the other bartenders and ordered a bottle of Ginger Champagne.

'What are we celebrating?' asked Bas, surprised. Ginger Champagne was pretty rare and usually only saved for special occasions. Luckily, being friends with the owner's favourite bartender and only daughter meant they never had to pay for such luxuries, but still, this was an extravagant move.

'We're celebrating my brilliance at extracting the gossip I am about to tell you from one of the Councillors,' Cleo replied eagerly, carefully annunciating each word to make sure they could all hear and therefore marvel at her achievement. Three glasses were placed on the table and filled with champagne.

'The gossip mill comes up trumps again,' Anita commented, wishing that Cleo would just get on with it, but knowing there wasn't the remotest chance of that. But the promise of gossip seemed to lift her mood a little.

'Indeed it does,' said Cleo, taking a moment to build some suspense, savouring the attention that was now being paid to her, before beginning her story. 'So, we know so far that the ruling Spirit Descendant passed away a couple of weeks ago, meaning that Alexander, Philip's grandson, will succeed to the throne soon. We also know that Christiana, the ruling Body Descendant, is getting on a bit.' Cleo paused, the silence pregnant. 'What we didn't know until tonight, is that Christiana is more than getting on a bit,' she took a deep breath, 'she's dying.'

'What?' Bas and Anita blurted out together.

'That's going to have a significant effect on the energy,' said Bas, livid. 'They have got to prepare people for news like this.'

'But why would the Descendants all come here if Christiana is dying?' asked Anita.

Cleo looked smug. 'Why indeed?'

'Cleopatra, we know you're brilliant, and for that we're eternally grateful, but we're dying over here. The suspense is literally killing us.'

'Alright, alright. They've brought Christiana here to die. There's something here she wants to make peace with before she goes, but nobody knows what it is. All they know is that she's currently on her death bed below the Temple of the Body and that Austin is fuming about the whole thing.' Austin, Marcus' father, the ruling Mind Descendant, had a reputation for being venomous. He, as with most Minds, thought himself superior to everyone, including the other Descendants, so it wasn't surprising that he was cross at having to be in Empire at the whim of another.

'They're going to hold the Chase, the Crowning and the ball here instead of in Kingdom. They're going to hold off for a couple of weeks, as the likelihood is it'll be a double Crowning with Peter succeeding Christiana.'

'They're going to let him rule?' asked Bas. 'Surely it would make more sense to pass straight to Gwyneth?'

'Nobody knows if either of them is eligible to rule, given that Christiana has no direct female heir. The bloodline could be broken anyway, and the prophecy could already be dead,' Anita chipped in, trying to take in the magnitude of what she had just heard.

'Well Gwyn certainly doesn't act like it's dead, given the way she was strutting across the Temple earlier,' Cleo retorted.

'So they're having the Crowning here? But where will it take place if not by the relic?' asked Bas.

The three Temples were always built as triangles, with three tips, one from each Temple, meeting at a point in the middle. In Kingdom, the main parts of the Grand Temples were open to everyone, had a central triangular section that only the Descendants were allowed to use, and the joined tips, which housed the relic, were also open for everyone to visit. Crownings usually took place by the relic so that everyone could see them, but in Empire, the layout was slightly different. The Temples were open to everyone, but underneath each Temple were chambers that only the Descendants were allowed to use. Underneath the joined tips was a sacred area, but nobody, apart from the Descendants and a few select Councillors, was allowed to know what was there. The area of the joined tips was closed off to everyone but the Councillors, who used the hexagonal chamber inside to host Council meetings when in Empire.

'The rumour is that most of each Crowning will take place in the public centre of the relevant Temple. The Descendants will then go to the sacred centre underneath the tips to perform some part of the ritual, and then will come back up to complete the ceremony.' Cleo really had excelled herself this time.

'And the Chase? Where and when will that take place?' Anita asked, as offhandedly as she could.

Cleo and Bas smiled. 'Bet you can't wait to get your teeth stuck into that one,' said Bas. 'See if you can't beat the Descendants.'

Luckily, at that moment, there was a ruckus across the bar, and Anita took the distraction as an opportunity to evade a ribbing and head to the bathroom. But what Cleo had failed to mention, was that the young Descendants had been in the back room of the bar, and the commotion was a result of them deciding to leave. Anita found herself trapped in their path to the door, a mass of bodies having closed ranks behind her to gawp at the Descendants as they

15

passed, so she couldn't go back the way she had come, and she couldn't go forwards, or she would run right into them. There was nothing she could do to avoid them apart from duck her head and try to be inconspicuous.

Gwyneth came first. Cleo was right, she did have flowing golden locks, her long blond hair seeming to glimmer in the light. She was tall and thin, unpleasantly thin. Her floor length silk dress and red cloak made her look the part, but she had the air of someone trying just a little bit too hard. Nor was she that pretty, her nose a bit too long and eyes set a little too close together. Gwyn walked past Anita without so much as glancing in her direction. Unfortunately, the same luck was not to be had with the next Descendant, Alexander. As soon as she saw him, her energy lifted. She did everything she could to try and suppress it, but Alexander's head turned slowly, carefully, so he could see where the energy was coming from. Here we go again, thought Anita, desperately trying to curb her energy, his piercing blue eyes looked down at her, this time only a metre away. He didn't say a thing, looking intensely into her eyes. She held his gaze and wished she knew what he was thinking, but his expression gave nothing away. People had started to turn and watch them now, but Anita was determined not to break first. He might have an effect on her, but she wasn't going to let every victory be his. By now, Marcus, who had been talking to a couple of Councillors at the bar, had noticed something was going on, and sauntered over to see what was happening. Alexander felt him coming and moved on, following Gwyn out of the bar.

'Well, that was interesting,' Marcus drawled, standing very close and looking down at her with flirty eyes. He smelt of soft vanilla, and as it wafted over her, she inhaled greedily, momentarily disorientated as her pulse reacted, quickening, her energy singing, colour rising to her cheeks. She told herself to snap out of it, exhaling sharply, trying to get a handle on her out-of-control emotions. 'Alexander doesn't usually deign to interact with anybody. And even if he didn't talk to you, I would call that an interaction, wouldn't you?'

'I'm not entirely sure what I would call it, other than weird,' Anita shot back, a little too sharply.

Marcus smiled. It wasn't every day a girl spoke to him like that. 'We're heading back to my family's residence just outside of town. Why don't you join us?' Anita recognised a challenge when she saw one. If she knew anything, she knew she did not want to take on the Descendants all at once, and certainly not on their territory. If Anita had had a social climbing mother, what she was about to do would be cause for disinheritance, but seeing as she didn't, and that, to Anita, winning was more important, she had to say no.

'I'm terribly sorry, but I have a prior engagement,' she said sweetly, looking up at him through her lashes, matching his flirty tone, 'excuse me.' And with that she left through the back exit, leaving everyone in the bar staring at Marcus as he turned indifferently and strode out to join the others.

'Holy Mother of the Gods,' Cleo exclaimed, bounding out of the bar after Anita, 'what were you thinking?'

'It was a challenge,' Anita shrugged, exasperated, as though this should be enough to explain everything.

'You have just committed social suicide.'

'Social suicide? How?' Anita spat at her. 'Where exactly was I in the *social standings* anyway? They're just people Cleo. People like you and me, but they just happened to be born into a different bloodline.'

'They're powerful Anita. You need to be careful.'

Alexander's earlier words came back to her, 'you are a very desirable asset', and it halted her tirade. She knew Cleo was right. 'Look, I know I shouldn't have done it like that, but I couldn't go to Marcus' 'residence' and be their plaything for the evening.' Cleo nodded. At least Anita hadn't made a complete swooning idiot out of herself like most other girls would have. 'Look, Cleo, I think I'm going to head home. Thanks for the champagne and say bye to Bas for me?'

'Sure, no worries,' said Cleo, blankly, shaking her head as she turned and went back inside.

CHAPTER 3

Alexander got up and made his excuses. There was only so much of Gwyn and Marcus proclaiming they were masters of the universe that he could take. He had never really liked spending time with them, but since Philip had died, he found them tedious at best. He decided to go back to the Temples and see how Christiana was doing; she was always a sound source of advice, and maybe she could help him understand why the Body girl was having such an effect on him. He, unlike her, was able to control his energy, so no-one would know, but he couldn't stop thinking about her. Maybe it's just her energy, he thought, as he descended through the centre of the Temple of the Spirit into the lower chambers; it's totally raw and unrefined, she has no idea how powerful she could be. But he knew that wasn't all it was, images of her pale lips, hypnotic smoky eyes, slender hands, delicate creamy skin, dark shiny hair, the dip between her collarbone and neck, the curve of her toned arms, for some reason kept invading his every thought. For some inexplicable reason, his mind kept drawing him back to her.

Alexander descended into the plush private chamber that now belonged to him underneath the Spirit Temple. His spacious accommodation consisted of a study, a bedroom, a bathroom, a sitting room and a small kitchenette. His grandfather, Philip, had had the whole place overhauled when he had ascended to rule, but Alexander hadn't even thought about changing it when it had been passed to him; he didn't see the need. It functioned perfectly well, and Philip had made it quite comfortable. Alexander pushed a small square at the side of the worn wooden panelling covering the wall at the back of his study, the only wall not covered in bookcases laden with pile after pile of Philip's dusty manuscripts, and a secret door sprang open. He ducked through the opening into the gloomy corridor behind, lit only by the occasional lantern, and began to follow it towards the chambers underneath the Temple of the Body.

Alexander's mind wandered as he walked. He barely noticed the twists and turns he had to navigate, his feet seeming to follow their own path, rousing from his thoughts only as he approached Christiana's chambers and picked up the sound of muffled voices. The only people allowed down here were the Descendants, a small handful of trusted and very well paid servants, and occasionally a Councillor, accompanied by a Descendant. Alexander immediately recognised Austin's harsh tones and Christiana's weak replies, felt the unsettled energy from both of them and knew something was wrong. Deciding it best to observe for a bit before wading in, he snuck forward as far as he dared without risking discovery, hid behind an ornate grey granite pillar, from where he could see what was going on, and listened.

'I've got to find her. I have to tell her Austin. I know she's here. What we did…'

'You're going to tell her?' Austin spat. 'I thought you just wanted to find her and see her. What good can telling her possibly do now?'

'The energy. Once I'm gone, who knows what will happen. Only the Gods should have the power that we took. I'll always regret it.'

Alexander felt what was going to happen next. Austin's malicious, negative, energy rose to unprecedented levels. Christiana felt it too; she had surprising Spirit skills for a Body. 'Austin, she will find out. The prophecy will one day be fulfilled. The true bloodline will be restored.'

'No, she won't,' Austin sneered, unpleasantly, brushing Christiana's words aside. 'We're the only two left that know the truth now Philip's gone. And soon it will just be me,' his voice a terrifying mix of wistful longing and startling cruelty. Austin reached down and put his hand on the pillow next to Christiana's head, his brutal intention plain. Christiana didn't fight, she had accepted what was to come, her face relaxed, her energy calm, unconcerned with the predicament she now found herself in.

'The true bloodline will be found Austin,' Christiana repeated, her voice soft but insistent, like this was so obvious an observation that anyone would be a fool not to see it. 'This is bigger than you. It's in the hands of the Gods,' she said, pausing and looked openly up at Austin, her eyes still sparkling, full of life, a smile playing around her old lips, lined with age. 'The Gods who you are about to help me join.' Austin's eyes flew open. He knew it. He had always suspected that she was a reader. It explained a lot. Austin grabbed the pillow and furiously covered Christiana's face, using all his weight to hold it resolutely in place. Christiana didn't struggle. She lay totally still until Alexander could feel her energy no longer. He could have intervened. Should he have intervened? But being a reader, she would have known he was there, and she hadn't appealed to him. He was more likely to be able to help fulfil her final wishes if he wasn't at war with Austin, but now he knew exactly what Austin was capable of and it made him sick. He turned and left, quickly navigating back through the black corridors. He rushed into his chamber, swinging the panel swiftly and firmly closed behind him before retreating up into the Temple and out into the night. He vomited violently as he reached the cool night air, still not quite able to believe the act he had just witnessed. He left the Temples and somehow stumbled to the river before letting his legs give way, sinking gracelessly to the hard ground of the river bank. He sat all night, not feeling the cold or the damp that penetrated his clothes, feeling nothing, feeling numb, barely even hearing the gurgling of the river passing by. Eventually, as the sun started to rise, a greyish light beginning to illuminate the water, tears trickled their way down his cheeks as he held his head in his hands, staring into nothing, a deep sense of loss beginning to grow inside him.

Hours later, when the sun was fully in the sky, but blocked out by determined black clouds, casting a gloomy light over Empire, he got up and returned to his chamber, full of questions. What had Christiana meant about taking the power of the Gods into their own hands and about the bloodline and the prophecy? Did Christiana have a female heir? Was that who Christiana had wanted to find? What had they done and why? Was Christiana the rightful heir? Philip knew something and had never told him? Had Philip been involved in whatever this was? There were too many questions to answer all at once, but Alexander knew the place to look was in the

Archives, which, luckily, were kept in Empire. An examination of the birth and death records was the best place to start.

*****

Ever since the encounter at The Island a few days before, Anita had been restless. People were gossiping about her and why she had attracted the Descendants' attention, and she would rather just fade into the background. She had gone to the Observatory every day and had been sullen and moody with Bas and Patrick, and for that, she felt bad, which made her even more frustrated. All she could think to do was turn to Body pursuits, but no amount of riding, sailing, climbing or swimming could seem to lift her mood. What was really annoying was that the Descendants had gone quiet since that night at The Island. Nobody had seen them or heard from them, and even Cleo had nothing to share. They could be anywhere, they could have left Empire, nobody knew. Anita desperately wanted to understand why she reacted to the presence of Marcus and Alexander, and how she could 'control her energy' as Alexander had suggested she should.

Today's Body pursuit to try and lift her mood was a run by the river with her grandmother's springer spaniel, Thorn. She hoped maybe the combination of exercise and playing with Thorn would do something to pick up her spirits. She was preoccupied with thoughts of embarrassing displays in bars when she felt someone with powerful energy coming up behind her. She was instantly wary. This had been her automatic reaction to most people since Alexander's words in the Temple, so she was guarded as she spun around to see who it was.

Her energy immediately lifted when she saw Marcus' blissful form coming towards her. For Gods' sake, get a grip Anita, she said silently to herself, but this just seemed to spur on her energy's disobedience and once again she felt like she might explode. Luckily, Marcus didn't seem to have Alexander's reader skills, so that should save her one embarrassment at least.

'Well hello,' came Marcus' drawl as he approached. 'Fancy seeing you here.'

'Hmm,' Anita replied, feigning disinterest and calling to Thorn.

'Mind if I join you?' Marcus asked.

'Umm…' Anita was trying to think of a suitably offhand reply, when Marcus said, 'great,' smiling a cheeky smile that reminded Anita of a naughty five-year-old.

'Right,' she said, rolling her eyes as she set off at a fair clip across the field. Marcus kept pace with her, but he wasn't in any state to make casual conversation, and Anita smirked as she increased the pace. They reached the fence and Anita jumped straight up on the stile, making to climb immediately over into the next field, but Marcus reached out a long, surprisingly strong hand, grabbed the back of her top, and pulled her roughly back down.

'I think that's enough of that for the moment,' he gasped, dryly, trying to catch his breath. 'You've made your point.'

'I'm sure I don't know what you mean,' Anita retorted, playfully. The run had improved her energy no end, and now she was in a mischievous mood. She liked the way this encounter was going.

'I think you've got a fair idea,' Marcus fired back, seeming to have recovered enough to assume his usual, superior stance. 'How did you get so fast?'

Anita shrugged. 'I don't know,' she said, softening a bit. 'I've always been fast and strong and able to beat anyone I've competed against. At first people thought I cheated, but now they just think I'm weird.'

'Well, I know what that feels like.'

Anita snickered. 'What you feel is adoration and envy and jealousy. Nobody thinks you're weird.'

'What's so different about how people treat me? People stare at me, they talk and point, they treat me differently…'

'…ahh, the poor little Descendant…' Marcus exploded forward so his face was inches from Anita's, the smell of vanilla invading her lungs once more.

'You think it's funny? You haven't got a clue.'

Bloody hell, his energy was more up and down than hers was. Anita was intrigued. 'Then enlighten me,' she said, in a soft voice, starting to feel him infecting her emotions.

The side of Marcus' mouth curled into a smile. He took a step forward, and Anita instinctively stepped backwards, her route blocked by the tree behind her, her back now flat against its bark. There was nowhere for her to go, and Marcus placed his arms either side of her to pin her in place. She was trapped and her pulse quickened. Marcus leaned his head forward to look straight into her eyes; he was enjoying this. He was back where he wanted to be, and, to her surprise, Anita quite liked it. Marcus relaxed and the mood between them shifted. There was a tension in the air as they waited for what seemed like forever to see what would happen next,

but Austin wouldn't listen, and obviously he's the only Descendant with any legitimate power at the moment.' Bas paused again, struggling. Anita felt useless, desperately wanting to help, but with no idea how to. 'We told him that we would see this. A sudden, dangerous drop, and then, who knows what, but it's unlikely to bounce back like it did with Philip. People think it's over. They think we'll never be free from the Gods now, that we'll be slaves forever. We've never seen anything like this, and we still don't really understand the way the energy works. We could start to see any number of things happen.' He paused, Anita sensing that they were about to get to the crux of Bas' rambling. 'We failed to stop it.'

The words hit Anita like a train, and her reaction was immediate. 'What?' she said, with such force it surprised even her, but Bas smirked and looked away. Anita shuffled around so she could see more of his face and put her hand on his arm. 'You can't be serious?' she said gently. 'You did everything you could. You stood up to Austin, and he doesn't exactly sound like a bundle of joy, and we can still find a way to bring the energy back up.'

'How are we going to do that?' said Bas, as though Anita were a naïve child. 'All gather round and politely ask the Gods if they would mind very much leaving us alone, so we can all live happily ever after?'

Anita was more than a little shocked. She had never seen Bas like this, and he had certainly never spoken to her like that. She dropped her hand back to her lap and turned back to face Empire, until finally, a logical argument popped into her head. 'So, the energy didn't start to fall until the announcement?' Anita questioned.

'Yep, it exactly coincided with the speech. You saw the dashboards,' he said, pithily, taking a deep, loud breath like he was humouring her, but she had better get to the point soon.

'But Christiana died several days ago, Austin said so himself, in which case, it wasn't Christiana's actual death that sent the energy plummeting, but peoples' reaction to the news.' She was getting excited now. 'Which means that there is at least a chance we could find a way to bring the energy levels back up. If we could find a way to make people believe that we can still get rid of the Gods, then we might not be headed for destruction.' Bas wasn't biting. 'Come on Bas, you know I'm right. As you've suspected for some time, it's not the actual events that cause energy fluctuations, but peoples' emotional responses. It's people that control the energy, which means there's still a chance we can turn this around.'

'Even if you're right, you think Austin's going to let us interfere? He's dead against any intervention. He thinks we just need to accept the inevitable and get on with our lives.'

'I didn't say it would be easy,' Anita replied, her tone reflecting the irritation she was starting to feel at Bas' uncharacteristic negativity, 'but I'm yet to find a challenge that I want to turn down, and I'm afraid this one is not going to be first on that list. So you can either help me, which would make my life a lot easier, seeing as you're the energy expert, or wallow in your depression and help to pull the energy down further.'

Bas knew she was right. The more people that gave up, the worse it would be. He inhaled again, this time resigned. 'Alright. Count me in,' he said, rolling his eyes, but his energy betrayed him, and Anita threw him a victor's smile. 'You can be really annoying sometimes you know,' he said, petulantly, hiding and fighting the involuntary upward turn of his lips.

'Thanks. I'll take that as a compliment,' she grinned.

*****

Bas sat outside the chamber in the centre of the Temples. He was staring into the mid-distance and thinking about what he was going to say to the Grand Council (preparation had never really been his strongest suit), when his father came out and put a heavy hand on his shoulder.

'We're ready for you,' said Alistair, Bas' mid-height, grey-haired father, who looked almost lanky next to Bas, although his shoulders were really quite broad, 'are you ready?' His kind, perceptive eyes searched Bas', trying to tease out his inner feelings, not that his son's feelings usually needed much teasing; he was pretty up front about his emotions.

'As I'll ever be,' Bas replied, giving his father a knowing look. As Bas and Alistair walked into the chamber, every pair of eyes turned to look at them, but Bas ignored every single one. He was always fascinated by the layout of this room. The Councillors from the three Temples sat along three of the walls at the edges of the hexagonal room, with the Descendant for each Temple sitting in the middle of their wall of Councillors. On the floor, in the middle of the room, was a circle that nobody was allowed to walk over, the area directly above whatever sacred thing lay below the Temple points. Opposite the middle wall of Councillors was a lectern, to which guests such as himself were summoned to give presentations and updates to the Grand Council.

Bas made his way purposefully to the lectern. The last thing he wanted to do was let them intimidate him, so he didn't rush, he tried instead to move across the room as though this was where he was born to be. He wasn't sure whether he succeeded or not, but was extremely glad to reach the safety of the lectern, where he could bring up the illustrations of his results and encourage everyone to focus on those, instead of him.

'Good morning, Descendants, Councillors. It's a great honour to be here today to present to you,' Bas started, noticing that the chairs for both the Body Descendant and the Spirit Descendant were empty. Alexander and Peter were each sitting to the side of the chair, that in a few days, would be theirs, presumably, Bas thought, because Austin had insisted that they could not sit in the Descendants' chairs until after their Crownings. He wants to make sure everyone knows he's the only one with any real power, thought Bas, as though anyone had any question in their mind. 'As you can see,' Bas continued briskly, using an energy wave to bring up a projection of a graph in mid-air, 'the world experienced a significant and instantaneous negative response to the news of Christiana's death. The moment Austin's speech concluded, the energy plummeted to unprecedented levels, and it continued to drop for three consecutive days. It finally slowed and levelled out last night to where it is currently, here,' he said, pausing to let everyone take in the dramatic drop, pointing to a place on the graph that matched his words.

'To put it bluntly, we have no idea the effect this drop in energy will have on our world. However, it is likely to have a profound impact on our agriculture, fish stocks, weather, and most importantly, on the mood of our people. This last point is the most important, as this is something over which we can exercise at least a modicum of control. Three days ago, before Austin gave his speech on the steps of the Temple of the Body, Christiana had been dead for several days already, however, there was no impact at all on the energy as a direct result of her death. As soon as Austin told the world that Christiana was no longer with us, there was an instant and dramatic decline. This obviously indicates that it is our perception of events and the state of the world, and not actual events and the real state of the world that have the most profound effect, indeed, any effect, on the energy. This means that if we can find a way to positively influence the general populous, if we could

31

give them hope and make them feel like there may yet be a way to free the world from the Gods, then we could stand a chance of bringing the energy back up to more normal levels, to save our world from what, frankly, could be destruction. If we don't do this, there's a chance that the mood will get worse as a result of the negative effects, which will, in turn, drag the energy down further, in a vicious and destructive spiral.'

At this point, Austin, who looked like Bas had just casually sauntered over to his chair, slapped him in the face, taken a bow, and then strutted back to the lectern, took to the floor. He looked down at Marcus, who was sitting to his right, before theatrically addressing the Grand Council. 'Councillors,' he said, in the same buttery tone that he had used for the radio broadcast, and coming across as a great deal more pompous in real life than he had over the energy waves, 'let me start by expressing my gratitude to Bas for coming and speaking to us today.' He declined to address the other Descendants directly, self-righteous idiot, thought Bas. 'I'm sure it is a daunting task for one so…young,' he drawled, in a way so condescending that Bas had to fight quite hard the urge to punch him. Instead, he looked over to his father, who gave him a 'we knew this would happen' kind of look, before turning his head back towards Austin.

'Now, it would be easy for us all to jump to conclusions at a difficult time like this, when we are all still grieving the loss of one as great as Christiana. However, we simply cannot try to keep alive the hope of freeing the world from the Gods,' he said, pausing for dramatic effect, 'when that hope is now gone.' He said each word in staccato to emphasise his message, and as the words left his mouth a cold silence rippled across the chamber, every person holding their breath. 'We have seen energy dips before,' he continued, seemingly oblivious to the effect he had just had, 'and it has always bounced back when people have come to terms with the events that caused it. In a few days we have the Chase. This is a high-spirited event that is known to boost the energy, and after that, we have a double Crowning and ball. These, I am sure, will lift the energy, and I am confident there will be no…,' Austin looked pointedly at Bas, '…*destruction* for us to worry about.' The way Austin lingered over the word destruction made it sound like a challenge, something along the lines of 'prove me wrong if you dare'. There was nobody in the room who had the power to challenge Austin. Even if Peter and Alexander had been crowned already, it was unlikely they would want to take on Austin this publically so early on in their Descendancies, so everyone remained silent, stunned at what they had just heard. Bas nodded towards Austin, his time clearly up, and retreated towards the door. One of the Councillors' aides opened it for him, and he walked out into the sunshine, weather which didn't exactly reflect his mood.

Well, that went just as expected, Bas thought to himself as he waited for his father. The energy update had been the last topic of the day, so they would walk home together.

Alistair came out of the chamber with a collection of other Councillors, and he said his goodbyes as they reached where Bas was standing. They walked a short distance in silence before Bas could contain his emotions no longer. 'Well that was a complete waste of time, and to top it all off, Austin made me look like a total idiot.'

'You can believe that if you want Bas, but you know as well as I do that most people in that room knew you were talking sense.' Alistair's soft, reasonable, yet authoritative voice had its usual calming effect. 'Austin knew you were talking sense too. The question is, why is he so set against trying to drum up a little positive energy,' said Alistair, musing as they walked. 'Anyway, we will continue to monitor the energy and provide reports to the Grand Council. If crops start to fail, as they inevitably will, he will have to do something, unless he wants to deal with an uprising.'

'That would be a sight I wouldn't mind seeing,' Bas smirked, 'apart from the bit where there are food shortages. Not sure that would suit me.'

'Who knows, maybe the new Descendants will see sense,' said Alistair, but both he and Bas doubted it. It wasn't that they wouldn't agree with Bas, rather that they wouldn't want to disagree with Austin. Alistair smiled, 'but before anything else, the Councillors need to organise a Chase,' he chuckled, 'it was news to everyone in that room that the Chase will take place before the funeral. You should have seen James' face! I don't think he'll be getting much sleep over the next few days. They'll start with an announcement early tomorrow I should think, so make sure you're watching the energy. Anyway, enough of all that, shall we pop in on Anita and Cordelia on the way past?' Alistair monitored his son's reaction closely as he mentioned Anita's name.

'Yep, sure, why not,' Bas responded flatly. Alistair didn't know, but could guess what was wrong. He didn't probe directly.

'Do you think the Chase and ball will have any meaningful effect on the energy?' Alistair asked instead, pretending that it was an unconnected, casual comment.

'You think I can't see right through you?' Bas replied, resentfully. 'You're so obvious it's painful. No, I'm not going to the ball with Anita. She isn't going to the ball. Says it's not her thing. And no, I don't want to go with some desperate, vacuous Councillor's daughter, which is what you are about to suggest, thank you very much.'

'You've got to take somebody, and Missy is very nice. Not vacuous at all.'

'Firstly, what kind of a bloody name is Missy, and secondly that you focused on the fact that she isn't vacuous means that she is desperate, which means that she probably looks like the back end of a bus.'

'Very well. Have it your way,' Alistair said, trying to hide his exasperation as they reached Anita's house, 'but you've got to take somebody.'

'Oh sod off would you,' said Bas, angrily, but Alistair smiled inwardly, knowing there was no real fire behind his words.

*****

Cordelia's house was, in fact, a small and ramshackle cottage covered in white climbing roses. It was a perfect chocolate box cottage from the outside, with a beautifully maintained garden, four pretty little windows and a sweet winding path to the slightly run down looking front door. As usual, Bas and Alistair veered off the path and made their way round the side of the cottage to the back door, which was wide open. They could hear voices inside, so knocked half-heartedly as they walked straight in with an upbeat 'hello?'

'Hey,' came Anita's happy response as she recognised the voices and came to greet them both with a brief hug. Anita knew Alistair well; he was a longstanding friend of Cordelia's, which is why she and Bas had met in the first place. He had given her the job at the Observatory and she saw him a lot; he often popped in to see how the research was going and to offer his opinion on any fluctuations.

Cordelia had also heard who it was and shouted, 'tea?' from the sitting room. Without waiting for an answer, she put the kettle on top of the wood burning stove that was roaring in the hearth. It was the end of Autumn, still hot outside, yet Cordelia always liked to have the fire burning. She said it made her feel safe and it gave the house a cosy feel. Alistair plonked himself down into a well-worn armchair, and Bas dropped onto a sofa that had seen better days before they accepted steaming cups of tea and a piece of homemade chocolate and beetroot cake from Cordelia.

Anita looked around as she sat down next to Bas, curling her feet up under her, thinking how different Cordelia's house was to Alistair's. Cordelia's was small, dark, cosy, well-worn and a total jumbled mess of stuff, whereas Alistair's was light and airy like the Observatory. Alistair had filled his house with antique energy meters and devices, everything with its place, and his furniture was old and comfortable, yet smart. It was a curious mix of antique and modern, and Anita, who normally felt poised and in control, always had the feeling that she was on the edge of breaking something priceless when she was there. They seemed quite at home here though, she thought, helping herself and Bas to their second pieces of cake.

As Anita listened to Alistair and Cordelia's meandering conversation, she suddenly realised she had no idea how they had become such good friends. Cordelia must be about 20 years older than Alistair, and there was no obvious reason for their friendship. In fact, Anita couldn't think why she hadn't asked them how they had met before. 'How did you two meet?' she blurted out abruptly.

Cordelia and Alistair turned around and looked at her in surprise, Cordelia giving her a sad, wistful look and neither immediately responding. 'Oh I don't know,' Cordelia eventually ventured, her voice delicate and decisive, containing a subdued, yet sharp edge of warning that made people think twice before disagreeing with her, 'it was so long ago I can't think exactly how we met now.' And with that, Alistair changed the conversation to focus on how Anita and Bas had hated each other when they'd first met, when Anita had come to live with Cordelia at the grand age of three. He started recounting embarrassing stories of how, through Bas' unwavering determination, they had finally become friends.

At last the torture was over and Alistair and Bas headed for home, but Anita couldn't help thinking about the look that her grandmother had given her and about how Cordelia and Alistair had met. She decided she would do some digging and drop it into conversation again at some point soon.

Cordelia came back from showing them out and as she sat back down, an intriguing smile meandered across her face. 'So, I hear rumours that somebody wants to take you to the ball.'

What? A look of panic shot across Anita's face, a rush of adrenaline coursing through her veins. How could she possibly know? How did anyone know? She looked questioningly at Thorn before inwardly chastising herself for being totally ridiculous. 'I don't know what you're talking about,' Anita said, too quickly, trying to brush the comment aside.

'Well, the whole of Empire seems to be talking about it.'

'Talking about what?' Anita questioned, confused. Had Marcus told everyone?

'Whether you'll say yes obviously,' Cordelia laughed back, shaking her head, bewildered.

'I haven't decided yet,' she blurted back, barely able to form a response.

'Well, that's a turn up for the books, Bas must be thrilled.'

'Huh? What do you mean?'

'That you didn't say no outright,' said Cordelia, looking at Anita like she might have just hit her head.

'Oh,' Anita finally twigged what her grandmother was on about. 'Bas and I are just friends, and will only ever just be friends. I don't want to give him the wrong impression.'

'I see,' Cordelia replied, frowning in puzzlement. 'In which case, who were you talking about?!'

Cordelia was really interested now, but Anita was furious at herself and got up to leave. 'I'm going for a swim, see you later,' she said, throwing the words back over her shoulder as she hurried away, leaving Cordelia staring bemused after her. Now that was interesting, Cordelia thought to herself.

CHAPTER 5

Two days later, Anita made her way to the river bank opposite The Island, to where the congregation of Chase contestants had gathered. She spotted Bas and made her way towards him, hoping he wasn't still in a bad mood. They had announced the Chase yesterday, the day after Bas had presented to the Grand Council. However, this had caused practically no shift in the energy, and he had been in a foul mood ever since.

'Hey,' said Anita lightly.

'Hi,' Bas responded, visibly perking up at the sight of her. 'Ready?'

'I was born ready,' she said cockily, but today she was a bit nervous, not that she would ever admit that to anyone. She had never before competed against the Descendants, and she didn't want to think how she would react if bitch-face Gwyn beat her. For the sake of the Gods, be nice, thought Anita, inwardly chastising herself.

A Councillor appeared and ushered the contestants away from the rapidly growing crowd towards the top of the nearest hill. When they reached the summit, they found the Descendants were already there, cloaks on, looking regal, all standing in a line behind three boxes, Austin in the middle. Austin beckoned to James (the Councillor who'd had to hastily organise the Chase), who brought him an energy speaker so he could project his voice to both the contestants in front of him and to the crowd below.

Austin reminded Anita strongly of Marcus, but with a few notable differences. He was older, grey hairs rippling through his dark locks, his face more tanned, with lines both from age and too much time spent out in the sun. He was a little broader, a lot fuller, taking far less exercise than he used to, and had not a hint of Marcus' fun-loving disposition, radiating instead a menacing authority, enhanced by cold eyes that confirmed her suspicions; he was just plain mean.

'Descendants, Councillors, contestants, children of the Temples of the Mind, Body and Spirit. We are here today to celebrate the beginning of an historic and momentous occasion, the Crowning of Alexander, son of Anthony, and Peter, son of Christiana. As is customary, according to our traditions, those Descendants not currently in power will compete with any and all challengers who put themselves forward to become the Chase Champion. The Chase Champion will also open the dancing as guest of honour at the ball. I am thrilled to see such a turnout to compete here today,' he said, pausing as he surveyed the contestants, 'and I do hope we have a competitive and fair Chase.' Austin eyed Bas suspiciously, obviously sizing up Marcus' competition. It's not him you need to worry about, thought Anita, smiling to herself. 'Contestants, please take your positions.' With these words, Alexander, Marcus, Gwyneth and Peter all took off their cloaks with a theatrical flourish and handed them to a waiting Councillor. Marcus is pretty hot, Anita thought, as he handed over his cloak. Focus Anita, focus, she said to herself and forced herself not to look in his direction until this was over. She would need her wits about her if she were to win today; she suspected the 'fair' part of Austin's speech would almost certainly be disregarded.

The contestants lined up behind the Descendants, who were now in front of the boxes, facing down the hill towards the crowd below. The boxes contained homing pigeons, each with its home in a different location. Austin would pick one box at random, so that, in theory, nobody would know which way the pigeon would fly. He would then release it and the contestants would chase it to its home. Here, the winner would claim their prize, which was normally just the glory of winning, but today included the privilege of being guest of honour at the ball. Homing pigeons were used as it was easy to track their energy. Each contestant would be given an energy meter that they would lock on to the pigeon's energy, the idea being that they could then use the meter to track the pigeon. Often contestants had to drop out right at the start if they couldn't lock on quickly enough, as they were left with nothing to follow, however Anita found this easy, probably something to do with being a reader. I must watch Alexander, thought Anita, he'll no doubt be off to a flying start too.

The other problem contestants often ran into was blindly following their energy reader, instead of also thinking about the best route to take. Contestants might end up at the top of a vertical incline with no easy way down, or swimming across a river without realizing there was a bridge fifty metres downstream. At least she was on home turf, thought Anita, that should be an advantage.

James was moving around handing out energy meters, and Anita took her small golden box as it was handed to her. Here we go, she thought, as the metre sprang to life in her hand and she took her place behind the Descendants at the brow of the hill.

'In the interest of fairness, I shall choose a contestant to pick the pigeon you will chase,' said Austin, motioning to a girl standing beside Bas to step forward. 'Which box shall it be?' he asked.

The girl looked a little dazed at having been picked, but pointed at the left-hand box, saying, 'that one,' in a small voice, before stepping back into line with the other contestants.

'Splendid,' proclaimed Austin. 'Contestants, please ready yourselves,' he ordered, reaching forward and unhooking the latch on the box. 'I declare this Chase…open,' he roared, as he flung the lid open and a pigeon launched itself into the sky.

Anita watched the pigeon in what seemed like slow motion as it paused for a split second in mid-air. She used this opportunity to point her energy metre at the bird and lock on to its energy before hurtling down the hill with the rest of the contestants. About half way down she felt someone shove her forcefully sideways. She stumbled and almost fell as she saw Gwyn whip past her. Bitch, thought Anita. Now she felt justified in hating her. Two can play at that game, she thought, as she launched herself off a ledge at the bottom of the hill. She felt like she was flying. Not missing a beat, she landed, completed a forward roll, and picked up her pace again. The stunt gave her a bit of a lead, as most other contestants, including Gwyn, she noticed smugly, were taking the path all the way to the bottom, and were stuck in single file as the path narrowed. Anita knew that Bas would follow her though, and the other Descendants had been behind her, so who knew what they'd done. She pelted at full speed across a rickety bridge over the river into the dense woodland the other side. Anita could feel someone coming up behind her. She knew with energy that strong that it would be one of the Descendants, she just didn't know which one, and it would waste time and energy, not to mention require risking running into a tree, if she turned to take a look.

She soon got an answer. As she landed her vault of the fence at the far side of the woods, she saw Alexander's delicious form recover from his own leap and race away. Anita picked up her pace to match Alexander's, not quite believing how fast he was for a Spirit. They flew across the open field, easily jumping the stream that ran through its middle, and leapt at the steep incline the far side. Anita felt totally exhilarated. This was the first time she'd ever been truly challenged in a race, and that spurred her on to new depths of determination.

They reached the hill's summit and picked their way down the other side back to the river. 'You could at least pretend to use your energy metre,' Alexander jibed. 'I've already warned you once.'

'You seem to have a callous disregard for your own safety, whilst being particularly precious about mine,' she shot back. 'Any specific reason for that?'

'I'm the Spirit Descendant; people would mock me if I couldn't read energy. You, on the other hand, are a Body, with, as it turns out, exceptional Body skills, as well as significant Spirit abilities. You are not what you might call normal, and this is a dangerous climate in which to stick out.'

'Well you seem to have remarkable Body skills for a Spirit and seem to be fine, so I'll take my chances,' retorted Anita, as they reached the river and started jumping from rock to rock to cross it. The next group of challengers, including Gwyn, Bas and Marcus had reached the summit behind them, and Anita made a show of holding up her energy metre as she crossed the river and pointing in the direction that the pigeon had flown. 'Happy now?' Anita called over her shoulder as she launched into a sprint along the river bank the other side. Alexander pelted after her, a bit pissed off now. He'd recently been getting used to people doing whatever he said, and Anita's disobedience was infuriating.

They carried on at full speed for an hour, going up hills, down the other side, across the river, over fields, through woods, until at the summit of a small hill, Anita's energy metre started playing up. It was indicating that she should head east, when she had seen the pigeon (and could feel its energy) heading north. 'That's weird,' said

Anita, as they ran down the slope the other side, 'my energy metre's telling me to go east. What does yours say?'

'It says to head north,' said Alexander, showing Anita his metre, 'and I can feel its energy heading in that direction.'

'I can too,' she said, as Alexander's face hardened.

'Austin,' Alexander spat.

'Um, why?' Anita asked, as she started to run north after the bird.

'He must have tampered with the metres because he wants a Descendant to win,' he said. 'Energy metres don't just pack up. They lock on to one source of energy and don't change until they're given a new target. You didn't accidently set it to a new target?' Alexander asked.

'No, of course not. I'm not stupid,' she said, indignantly. 'I work in the bloody Observatory; I know how to use an energy metre.'

'You work in the Observatory?' Alexander asked, surprised. 'So you're an energy expert too?'

'Well I wouldn't go as far as expert,' she said, upping the pace a little, 'but I work with Bas and help him monitor the energy.'

'Brilliant,' he said sarcastically. 'So you're an energy reading Body who also knows all about energy. It doesn't get much worse than that.'

'For the sake of the Gods,' Anita fumed back, 'are you always such a pessimist?'

'You've got to lose the Chase.'

'What?' Anita laughed back. 'You're off your rocker if you think I'm going to lose.'

'You've got to. Austin will know you're a reader if you win.'

'How? I'll just say I saw the pigeon head north and that your metre was pointing north, so I headed north. It's not entirely untrue.'

'And what about when we get to the end? How are you going to explain how you actually find the pigeon?'

'I'll get lucky.'

'You'll get lucky? Yeah, sure, no one will suspect a thing.'

Anita had had enough. 'You stay here and keep spouting doom and gloom if you want to, but I'm going to get a move on, or else this little disaster of yours will be entirely hypothetical anyway.' Alexander relented and picked up his pace. He would just have to make sure he got to the pigeon first.

Two hours later, both Anita and Alexander could feel that they were nearly there. The pigeon had stopped, and its energy was getting closer. As they leapt over a style into the next field, a beautiful farmhouse with several rickety old barns came into view, along with a massive crowd of people who were all intently watching an energy projector. As was normal for a Chase, the crowd had been told where the pigeon was heading as soon as the contestants had left, and they had been transported in energy trains to the finish. Energy trains ran on an energy cell and hovered above the ground as they travelled. Energy cells had been an invention of Bas' grandfather, who had worked out a way to capture and consolidate energy waves so they could be used as a power source. The energy trains that had been used for the Chase were exquisite examples and almost certainly belonged to one of the Descendant families. They had plush velvet seat covers and heavy, luxurious drapes along the sides.

As they raced across the field, a cheer went up from the crowd. All eyes turned towards them as they fiercely competed to take the lead. As they reached the courtyard, Alexander was slightly in front. They felt the pigeon's energy behind them at the same time, and both whipped around immediately, turning in perfect unison, like dancers performing a routine. They headed for one of the barns, Anita now slightly ahead, having benefitted from the sudden change in direction, and as she entered the barn, she saw the pigeon sitting on a low stack of rectangular hay bales. She could feel Alexander's energy immediately behind her, so strong that it felt like it might envelop her, but she reached out and snatched the scroll at the pigeon's feet just ahead of his long, muscular hand. She somehow managed to leap on top of the bales to avoid directly colliding with them and skidded to a clumsy halt. Alexander, however, had no option but to do the same, and bowled into Anita with such momentum that he pushed her off the other side, landing on top of her and leaving them in an awkward heap on the floor, luckily not totally in view of the growing crowd of people in the barn.

'Happy?' Alexander hissed at her as he pulled himself to his feet.

'I will be when you get off me,' she retorted. 'You know there's nothing worse than a sore loser.' Alexander looked spectacular, in a terrifying kind of way, as he stalked out of the barn trying to regain his composure.

Anita got up as gracefully as she could to find herself face to face with the fearsome Austin. 'Well, that was interesting,' he said, in a sing-song voice, but pinning her with cold and dangerous eyes. 'Congratulations…um…'

'Anita,' Alistair said, coming to the rescue, 'congratulations. A startling performance as ever. Austin, this girl has won every contest she has ever entered, and she hasn't disappointed again here today. Well done Anita.' Thank the Gods for the wonderful Alistair, though Anita. She must remember to thank him properly later. 'The presentation Austin?' prompted Alastair.

'Yes, of course, follow me,' he commanded, and Anita followed Austin out of the barn, with Alastair stuck firmly to her side. As they emerged into the courtyard, Anita saw most of the other contestants had also finished, with only a few stragglers still making their way to the farmhouse. She briefly caught Bas' eye; he was sporting both a huge grin and an enormous graze down one of his legs. Anita gave him a questioning look. He inclined his head in the general direction of Gwyn and Marcus, and Anita was glad she hadn't had to deal with them on the Chase. Poor Bas. Alistair ushered Anita after Austin, who was giving off extremely strong negative energy. Maybe Alexander was right; maybe she should have kept a low profile. Well, too late for that now, she thought, as she stepped up in front of the crowd.

'Descendants, Councillors, contestants, children of the Temples of the Mind, Body and Spirit. Today we have witnessed a spectacular, competitive Chase, with our worthy contestants having battled for three long hours, over difficult and varied terrain, to get here. But, as is always the case, there can only be one victor and today, by an excruciating margin – better luck next time Alexander – the victor is Anita, of the Temple of the Body.' A roar went up from the crowd when he said her name, much to Anita's surprise. Normally everyone was indifferent when she won. They must just be happy that someone other than a Descendant had finished first, thought Anita, as Austin continued. 'As is customary for a Chase of this importance, we have a spectacular prize for our winner. Along with being guest of honour at the Crowning Ball, and leading the ball's first dance, I present to you, Anita, a vintage energy meter from my own private collection.' The crowd gave another roar as Austin took the energy metre from James, who had been nervously hovering with it at the side of the stage, and handed it to Anita, looking pained as he did so. Anita was gobsmacked. This she had not been expecting. She caught Bas' eye again, who was looking

43

longingly at the metre in her hands. Bet he can't wait to get a look at this, she laughed to herself, as Austin ushered her off the stage.

'Well, that concludes today's festivities. I trust that you all had an enjoyable day and I thank the contestants for playing their part. Please make your way to the energy trains which will return you to Empire.'

As the crowd was dispersing and Anita was making her way towards Bas and Alistair, she felt a hand close around her arm. She turned to see Austin, who looked like a small boy about to pull the wings off a fly. 'Of course, our champion cannot travel back with the crowds. Please, join us in our carriage,' he said, in his horrible, over-the-top voice, pulling Anita towards a floating golden carriage that looked like it was worth more money than there was in the world, with plush, overstuffed red velvet seats. The carriage already contained Marcus and a driver. Great, thought Anita, I'm sure this won't be awkward at all, her energy already rising at the proximity to Marcus she was heading for.

As they approached the carriage, however, as if things couldn't have got any worse, Alexander blocked her entrance. 'Allow me to help you,' he said, in his charming, chocolate voice, taking Anita's hand and moving aside to help her climb the steps into the carriage. 'Austin, I thought I would ride back with you, I trust that will be okay,' he said, climbing in behind her without waiting for a response.

'Of course,' Austin snarled, as he too climbed into the carriage. 'Let's get a move on then,' he barked at the driver when he had settled himself down. He sat beside Marcus, opposite Alexander, who had taken the seat next to Anita.

They travelled in awkward silence for several minutes, Anita looking out into the countryside to avoid looking at her travelling companions, hoping this would be enough to keep her energy under wraps, before Austin broke the silence. 'That was quite a show Anita,' he said dangerously, his hard brown eyes glinting as he stared menacingly at her. 'Very impressive.'

'Thanks,' she smiled back at him, warily, in the sweetest, most innocent tone she could conjure. 'I've always had a knack for Body contests.'

'I see,' he drawled.

'Yes, congratulations,' interjected Alexander. 'It was close at the end there, but the best contestant won,' he said, in what seemed like a sincere way. Marcus was sizing up Alexander like he was about to launch himself towards him, Anita pondering why as Austin resumed his campaign.

'It was especially impressive how you turned so quickly at the end, when you both realised that you were heading in the wrong direction.'

Anita looked him straight in the eye, saying as naively as she could, 'well, as you know, we Body types are prone to having lightening reactions. When I saw Alexander start to turn, I did the same. When I turned round, I saw the open entrance to the barn, took a punt, and got lucky. You see the strangest thing happened in the middle of the Chase; my energy metre broke. Luckily, I saw the pigeon heading north and, of course, could see Alexander was still heading north, so I continued that way, but it's such a strange occurrence for an energy metre to go wrong like that. Have you ever heard of one breaking?' she asked in a sugary voice, still holding Austin's now murderous gaze. She could feel his energy turn from playful boy to hostile animal and felt Alexander's defensive reaction, as he stiffened slightly beside her. Anita felt her energy intensify, but it wasn't focused on Austin, it was on Alexander; she liked that he was defending her. She felt Alexander's energy soften slightly, but only for a moment, as he felt the impact he had had on her.

Bloody hell Anita, she said silently to herself, as, to everyone's surprise, Marcus interjected, 'you probably just accidently reset the metre to track something else. It happens.'

Marcus, knowing the best way to deal with Austin was not head on, was trying to soothe the situation, and looked at her with a slight plea in his eyes. 'Yes, probably,' Anita replied, trying to pull herself together with a slight shake of her head. 'Luckily I was with Alexander, and I could follow him. Otherwise I would have been out of the race, and given how competitive I am, that would not have been an attractive sight,' she laughed enthusiastically, hoping self-depreciation would help move the conversation to safer territory.

'Well luckily you did have Alexander to follow, and we now have the good fortune of your beauty on our journey home,' said Marcus, again taking everyone by surprise. Anita went bright red, thinking instantly of the kiss in the field and Marcus' invitation to the ball. Shit, she thought, please don't bring that up now. This time it was her who sent Marcus a pleading look. Mercifully, Alexander came to her rescue, obviously feeling her energy shift. He asked Austin about the history of the energy metre that Anita had won. Anita knew Alexander would now suspect something was up with her and Marcus, but she would take that over Marcus bringing it up in front of Austin any day.

Austin, glad the attention was once again back on him, launched into a story about how the metre had belonged to his father, Tobias, a story which lasted all the way back to the city. Anita zoned out pretty quickly, watching the countryside whip past, thinking about the ball, the Chase, the antique energy metre she now owned, why Austin had tampered with her race metre, and why Alexander was so concerned with her being 'careful', whatever that actually meant. She was horribly confused and couldn't have been happier when the carriage pulled up outside Cordelia's cottage, where she could say goodbye and retreat to a place where there were no readers to scrutinise her energy, nor spectacular specimens to cause it to spike.

*****

Anita headed to The Island later that night to see Cleo. It felt like ages since she'd seen her. She walked into the bar and heard Cleo before she saw her, 'I knew she would win. I told you. She's never been beaten yet, and she wasn't going to let a few Descendants stop her.'

'Hey Cleo,' Anita called across the room, waving at her best friend. She made gestures which hopefully meant 'I'm going to get a drink, I'll come over in a minute', and headed to the ugly little bar to place her order. The Island was packed full of people who'd been at the Chase, both those who'd been in the crowd and contestants, but thankfully the Descendants didn't appear to be around. At least that gives me more time until I have to give Marcus an answer, thought Anita, suddenly unsteadied as an overexcited Cleo yanked her sideways. She'd bounded across the room to wrap her arms around Anita in a frenzied hug.

'YOU DID IT!' Cleo squealed. 'WELL DONE!'

'Thanks. It was a bit close for comfort this time, but I just about managed to get to the scroll first.'

'Well, I knew you would do it all along. Now, let me buy you a celebratory drink.' Anita put her hand up to protest, but Cleo shot her a warning look so ferocious that she backed down immediately.

'Thanks. I'll have an Empire then please,' a cocktail made of a curious mix of spirits that Anita had never quite managed to determine. This Cleo seemed pleased with, presumably because the drink was both extremely potent and suitably extravagant. Cleo called the order to the bartender, who said he would bring the drinks over, then dragged Anita back to the table where she'd been sitting. Cleo shooed the guys she'd been talking to away (this always amazed Anita) and leant in conspiratorially; clearly there was something Cleo wanted to discuss.

'So,' she started, still totally over the top, 'I've heard a rumour.'

'Oh, a new and different past time for you. I'm thrilled you're branching out...'

'Sarcasm is the lowest form of wit you know.'

'No?' Anita replied sarcastically.

Cleo gave her a chastising look, but couldn't contain herself any longer, so pressed on. 'I've heard that Marcus is inviting someone outside his usual circle to the ball.'

'Really?' asked Anita, feeling a slight flutter of panic. 'How do you know that?'

'Well, you know James, the Mind Councillor who organised the Chase?'

'Yes.'

'His son Henry has invited me to the ball!'

'Congratulations,' said Anita, with genuine feeling, internally slightly surprised, although she didn't know why; it was exactly the kind of thing that Cleo always managed to engineer.

'Thanks,' Cleo shot back, looking smug, 'we can discuss how I pulled that one off in a minute, but anyway, he came in to see me last night for a drink, and we drank a little too much Island Punch. He started saying that Marcus' friends had all been teasing him about not having a date for the ball. Pretty much everyone else in their circle has a date, most of them with each other, obviously, apart from Marcus, Henry, and one other notable exception,' said Cleo, eyeing Anita deviously, 'some girl called Missy, who will be attending the ball with Bas.'

'What kind of a name is Missy?' laughed Anita. 'And who is she?' she asked, feeling both relieved and a tiny bit jealous, if she was being totally honest with herself. She didn't want to go out with Bas, but she felt a bit possessive over him anyway.

'She's the daughter of some senior Councillor. It was probably orchestrated by their parents if you ask me...but anyway, Henry said they'd all been teasing Marcus about it yesterday, and he said he had options outside the normal crowd. Apparently, he said he wasn't going to tell anyone who he'd decided to take because he wanted it to be a surprise on the night.' Anita sat very still, not saying a word. Should she tell Cleo? It would be good to talk to someone about it. But before she got a chance, Cleo was already speculating as to who it could be. 'I think it's that girl in our Mind class; the useless one who thinks she's practically a gift from the Gods. Or maybe the girl that Austin chose to pick the pigeon this morning. Maybe he's in on it too. I can't imagine Austin would like it if Marcus turned up at the ball with someone outside their circle unless he knew about it first.'

'Cleo,' Anita said quietly.

'Uh huh,' Cleo replied, at the same time as thanking the waiter for the drinks he'd put down in front of them.

'There's something I need to talk to you about,' she said slowly, 'outside.'

Cleo looked worried. 'Is everything alright?'

'Yep, just something I want to talk to you about, but it's a bit crowded in here.'

'Okay,' said Cleo, as they picked up their drinks and headed to the back door. They sat down on a bench overlooking the river and Anita took a sip of her toxic cocktail.

'Delicious, as always,' she stalled.

'You didn't bring me out here to talk about cocktails,' replied Cleo, anxious to find out what Anita wanted to talk about; she could practically smell the gossip.

'No,' said Anita, wondering how to approach this. 'You know the other week when I turned down Marcus' offer to go back to his with the others?'

'No,' gasped Cleo, 'you went?!'

Anita smirked and shook her head, 'no.'

'Oh. Sorry, carry on.'

'The following day, I was running by the river, when Marcus ran up behind me. He asked if he could join me for a run, so obviously I put him through his paces.' Now Cleo smirked. 'We got a fair distance before he wanted to stop for a break, and we chatted for a bit.' Cleo's face was frozen in a look of open-mouthed disbelief, and Anita had to stifle a laugh as she continued. 'And he asked me to go to the ball with him. Well, it was more of a command than a question really…'

'…so you're the one he's taking to the ball?'

'Well, I'm not sure.'

'You're not sure? What do you mean you're not sure? Presumably you said yes?'

'Um.'

'Um?'

'Well, I told him 'maybe'.'

'You told him 'maybe'?' Cleo repeated, in a disgusted voice.

'Yes.'

'Right.'

They sat there in dumbfounded silence for a minute before Cleo piped up again. 'As you know, this doesn't normally happen to me, but I'm basically speechless. You've got to go to the ball with him.'

'Why?'

'Why?! Because he's a Descendant and can you imagine the look on bitch-face Gwyneth's face if you do?'

'That's probably the best reason I've thought of so far,' laughed Anita. 'But other than that, I just don't know if it's a good idea.'

'Why not?'

'I don't want to draw attention to myself.'

'You didn't stop to consider that when you won the Chase this morning.'

'I know.'

'Even so, why not? A bit of attention can be fun you know.'

'Hmmm.'

'And you have to lead the first dance, so it may as well be with someone who'll look good, and by the relic, he looks good.'

'That makes it even worse. Everyone's going to be looking at me leading the first dance anyway, but if I'm dancing with him, everyone will be looking at me and speculating what's going on between us and why he chose me.'

'Let them speculate and enjoy the attention. That's what I'd do.'

'Yes, well you've always been better than I have at that.'

'You should go with him. Enjoy it. Put two fingers up to bitch-face Gwyn. I saw her shove you at the start of the Chase. You know you want to.'

'I'm still thinking about it. Don't worry, you'll be the first to know what I decide. But in the meantime don't you dare tell anyone.'

Cleo looked hurt. 'Me? Gossip? Never.'

'Come on, let's go back inside. I think I need another drink.'

CHAPTER 6

The following day was Christiana's funeral and Anita walked to the Temple of the Body with Cordelia, Alastair and Bas. When they got to the Temple, Cordelia and Anita found seats in the open section at the back and Alastair and Bas walked the seemingly endless distance to the front, where they had seats reserved for them with the rest of the Councillors and their families. As was customary, those belonging to the Temple of the Body were given first priority over the newly laid out seats, and those belonging to the other Temples took any seats left over, or stood at the back. The Body Temple didn't have the same colossal, open, expanse as the Spirit Temple. As opposed to sky-high pillars holding up the roof, the Body Temple had a series of high arches splitting the space into distinctly separate, but still relatively open sections. Every Temple had a clear run from at least one entrance to its altar. In the Spirit Temple, pretty much every entrance had this, but in the Body Temple, many had to sit in side chambers with views obstructed by the intricate brickwork. The Mind Temple was a total nightmare for large public events, as the spaces were so closed off that only a very fortunate few ever got to see anything, but that's how the Mind Descendants liked things; small and elitist.

Twenty minutes later, all the seats were taken, and a massive crowd stretched out behind the ropes that had been erected to keep a pathway clear for the coffin. Christiana had been extremely popular, mostly for her fairness and generosity, and many people had travelled from Kingdom to be there.

Music wafted back through the Temple from a harp at the front, bouncing around the arches and up to the spire above, vibrant yet haunting music that made the hair on the back of Anita's neck stand up as the procession of the coffin and the Descendants began. Everyone turned round in their seats to watch the coffin, carried by six Body Councillors, enter the Temple, with Peter and Gwyn following immediately behind. They were both wearing black cloaks and Gwyn had a black birdcage veil across her face, with small white flowers in her hair. Very theatrical, thought Anita. Behind them was Alexander, also with a floor-length black cloak, his dishevelled hair looking a little more tame than usual. He had his usual regal-yet-rugged look about him, like some ancient knight about to wield a sword in the pursuit of the righteous. Anita noted that his energy seemed to be less prominent than normal and wondered how he was able to mask it as he did.

Finally, Austin and Marcus entered the Temple, both also in black cloaks, but theirs with a red trim running around the edge. They can't even show her respect at her funeral, thought Alexander. As he entered the Temple, Alexander unintentionally inclined his head in Anita's direction, feeling her brazen energy. She really needs to learn to hide that, he thought, noticing he was a little riled as he moved on.

Austin was in front of Marcus and looked every inch the evil dictator as he sauntered into the Temple. Marcus, however, looked regal, his chiselled features as glorious as ever as he strode after his father. He spotted where Anita was sitting and looked directly at her, locking his eyes with hers as he ascended the steps. Anita held his gaze and hoped people hadn't noticed. He neared where she was sitting and broke eye contact to keep from having to turn his head, continuing up the aisle to join the rest of the Descendants. Cordelia looked sideways at Anita but didn't say anything. She knew Austin and Marcus had given Anita a lift home after the Chase, but after that look, she wasn't sure if that was all that was going on.

The funeral was short but emotional. Austin gave the opening speech, which most people thought a little strange. He explained it away by starting, in his normal, cloying, voice, 'as the only current reigning Descendant...' Anita rolled her eyes as he said it. There were several moving tributes to Christiana and the spectacular Body feats she had achieved during her life, along with accounts of her generosity to those of all Temples. Peter gave a gripping insight into life as the child of someone so exceptional, however, the most moving account was the last, from Alexander.

'...and at the age of five, when I had recently lost both my father, in a tragic fire in this very Temple, and my mother, of a broken heart just a few months later, it was Christiana who guided me. Over the years she was a source of unparalleled council. She was a leader but not a dictator, she was competitive, proud, stubborn, but above all compassionate. She observed the world around her, striving not to control, but to understand. She was a source of hope, believing in honesty and doing what was right, even when this path was the most difficult and dangerous of all. But Christiana's mortality was part of what made her great, and her time had come, as it will for us all. Our deep and painful loss is truly the Goddess Tatiana's gain.'

At the end of the funeral, the Descendants and Councillors processed out with the coffin. Christiana's body would be transported back to Kingdom where it would be buried alongside her ancestors. The crowd started to disperse as soon as the procession had left the Temple and Cordelia turned to Anita and fixed her with a curious look. 'I didn't realise you and Marcus were such good friends,' she said pointedly.

'We're not,' replied Anita. 'Why do you say that?' she asked, offhandedly, hoping to throw Cordelia off the scent as she got up and filed out of the Temple with everyone else.

'You know just fine why I say that. We can talk about it later,' she said, having just spotted Alistair and Bas. Anita was following in her wake, totally preoccupied by thoughts of Marcus' alluring gaze, when she felt someone's presence block her path. She looked up to see Marcus and her energy immediately responded. Get. A. Grip. Anita. She counselled inwardly.

'Hi,' he said.

'Hi,' Anita replied, eyeing him with a 'can I help you?' kind of look.

'I was just wondering if you'd given any more thought to my invitation?'

'Oh, was that what it was?' she asked, feigning surprise. 'You see, I was under the impression that it was more of a command than an invitation.'

Marcus looked back at her, a disorientated look morphing into a playful one. 'I see. Well for that I must apologise, Anita, I should clearly make an effort to clarify. Anita, Champion of the Chase, would you do me the exceptional honour of attending the ball with me?' he asked, in a flamboyant, dramatic way.

'I'm not sure that invitation was afforded the level of gravity I would expect for something so important. How am I to know your invitation is earnest?' she flirted back.

'You're concern is the sincerity of my proposal?' Marcus responded, although Anita wasn't quite sure if he was jesting or not.

'There is a certain delicious frivolity to it,' she replied, not meaning to take the flirting to quite this level in such a public place, 'but I suspect your invitation is genuine.'

'Well in which case...' he said, looking expectantly at Anita.

Anita paused, considering how to respond. Should she say yes? Cleo would certainly be happy. She tilted her head up towards his, looked searchingly into his eyes. It strongly reminded her of their encounter by the river, and she could see in his eyes that it had brought it back for him as well. Luckily, at that moment, Austin's voice came booming across their thoughts.

'Marcus. There you are,' he said, seeing Anita as he reached where they stood. 'Ah, the champion. How are you, Anita?'

'Very well thank you Austin, and you?'

'Yes, yes, very well,' he replied affectedly, before casting her aside. 'Come on Marcus, we have a lunch to get to.' And without another word, Austin dragged Marcus after him, Marcus briefly looking back at Anita, who mouthed the word 'maybe' at him as he departed.

Anita felt elated as she spotted Alistair, Bas and Cordelia and made her way over to them. She had managed to put off giving Marcus an answer for a bit longer and had got the last word. 'Where have you been?' Cordelia questioned suspiciously as Anita joined them.

'I just spotted a friend and said hello,' she answered defensively, which wasn't entirely untrue.

'We're heading up to Alistair's for lunch,' said Cordelia, 'I take it you don't have any other plans?'

Bas looked at Anita; he clearly wanted her to join them. 'No, I'm free as a bird,' sighed Anita. 'Lead the way.'

*****

After lunch, Anita took her wine out onto the balcony. She loved the view from here, at the top of the hill, looking out over the wild countryside and river below. She would love to live up here; the house was spectacular, set just outside of Empire. It was prominent and modern yet not overpowering, with clean, angular lines. If only she were in love with Bas in the way he was in love with her; life would be divine. Bas slid the door closed behind him as he joined her on the balcony and came to stand next to her, leaning on the wooden railing, their arms touching.

'You're one lucky guy Bas,' she said.

'How so?' he asked, bemused.

'You can wake up and look at this wild, beautiful view every morning, then go to the Observatory and stare out over Empire to your heart's content.'

He laughed. 'Yep, I've got to admit it, I'm exceptionally lucky when it comes to good views. I can't argue with you there.' They stared out in silence, taking in the view for a few moments, before Bas said awkwardly, 'the ball.'

Anita looked at Bas, anxiety screwing up inside her. Don't do it, Bas, she silently pleaded. 'Yep,' she replied, as calmly as she could.

'I know you said you weren't going before, because it wasn't your thing, but now that you have to go…well, I've asked this girl called Missy, but only because her father is a friend of Dad's and I said I'd do it as a favour…' he paused, taking what looked like a difficult breath, '…but if you would want to go with me, I'll tell her there was a misunderstanding or something,' he rushed the words out, presumably in case he bottled out at the last minute. 'I'd hate for you to have to do the first dance on your own,' he joked, shoving her arm playfully.

Anita took a long inward breath. 'Bas,' Anita turned to look at him, barely bringing herself to hold his gaze when she saw the hopeful look in his eyes. 'Any girl in this town would jump at the chance of going to the ball with you. You know that. And I'm sure Missy is really looking forward to going with you…'

'…yes, but…' Bas tried to interrupt, and Anita put a hand on his arm to silence him.

'You know I love you Bas, but I love you like a brother. I wish I loved you as you love me, it would make it so simple…but I'm sorry, I just don't see you that way.' She paused, racked with guilt at Bas' crestfallen face. 'You should go to the ball with Missy. I'm sure she's great.'

Bas turned back to look down at the river below. He sighed and eventually nodded, looking deeply hurt but resigned to accept what Anita had said. 'So, who are you going to the ball with then?'

'That's not yet confirmed,' she said, moving towards the door, 'we'll both just have to wait and see.' Bas thought about pursuing it, and ordinarily probably would have, but given the circumstances, he decided it might be best to just let it go. Silently he turned and followed Anita back inside, feeling like a shining light inside of him had been brutally extinguished.

*****

The following day, Anita woke up feeling like a weight had been lifted. She hadn't wanted to hurt Bas but was glad that he finally knew how she felt. She had also just about survived her grandmother's questioning about Marcus on the way home, turning the conversation to Bas and how she'd told him that she didn't want to go to the ball with him instead. Cordelia had been pretty indignant about the whole thing. She thought Anita and Bas were perfect for each other and couldn't imagine why Anita couldn't recognise when she was on to a good thing, but she was glad to hear at least some of the details of Anita's life, which placated her for the moment.

Anita decided today was a good day for a ride, and given her good spirits, for jumping in the woods. She galloped across the open field in the direction of the woods, feeling like she was flying as they easily cleared the ditch in the middle and hurtled towards the trees at breakneck speed. As she was approaching the woods, she felt extraordinary energy coming towards her through the trees. She slowed to a canter just as a colossal black stallion sailed over one of the enormous jumps out of the woods, circled wide into the field and headed back over the next jump, returning to the woods. Given the power of the energy that had come off the rider, along with their dishevelled hair, Anita knew it was Alexander. This was confirmed moments later when a bay stallion, also bearing a rider with powerful energy, but this one with neat, short hair, soared over the fence into view and completed the same wide circle before hurrying back into the woods after Alexander. Without thinking, Anita spurred her grey mare back to a gallop, heading for the corner of the woods, where she hoped she would be able to catch them up and join in with what was obviously a race.

Anita easily cleared the fence into the woods. As she landed, she heard hooves thundering just in front of her and to her right. She manoeuvred her mare, Iona, through the trees and came out just behind Alexander's black stallion, who was preparing to launch them over the next jump. Anita hurriedly collected her mount and followed Alexander over, urging Iona up beside the stallion when they landed easily the other side. Alexander looked over at her as she came level with him. 'What are you doing here?' he shouted angrily.

'I was out for a ride and saw the fun, so thought I'd join in,' she replied impishly, flashing him a disarming smile and ducking to avoid a branch.

'Has spectating ever occurred to you?'

'Ha,' she laughed, 'don't be ridiculous.'

Alexander pulled in front to clear the next jump, this one taking them back out of the woods into the field. The other side he hurtled towards the hedge between this field and the next and easily cleared it, Anita once again following him over without hesitation. Marcus had followed them out of the woods and was gaining ground, his stallion fast across the flat open field. He recognised Anita on the grey mare and urged his stallion faster still, catching Anita, who had dropped slightly behind Alexander before they reached the woods again.

'Fancy seeing you here,' Marcus shouted over to her.

'Is that the only line you know?' she quipped back.

'If you ever agree to spend some time with me, maybe you'll find out,' he replied, as Alexander cleared another mammoth fence back into the woods. Anita followed him over, but Marcus clipped the fence as he jumped. His stallion lurched forward as they landed, Marcus thrown clear into the undergrowth, his horse bolting. Alexander and Anita, hearing Marcus' expletives as he thudded to the ground, reigned in their mounts and turned back to see if he was alright, his stallion galloping past.

Anita leapt off Iona and ran to where Marcus had landed. He was trying to sit up as she got there and smiled when he saw it was her. 'We meet again, Anita,' he flirted. He can't be too badly injured then, Anita thought, as she considered how to reply. However, before she could come up with something good, another voice piped up.

'How careless of you to lose your steed, Marcus,' Alexander goaded, as he walked towards them. 'I do believe that means you owe me your next shipment of chocolate,' he jeered triumphantly.

Anita felt Marcus' energy turn. He was exceptionally angry. Alexander's energy on the other hand brightened as soon as he felt Marcus' rage. He was enjoying himself, but Anita couldn't see why. Marcus had lost, Alexander hadn't won. 'And to lose in front of your girlfriend, well, I suppose more have to withdraw technically, how embarrassing for you.' Anita had never felt energy as hostile as Marcus' was now.

'She's not my girlfriend,' he spat, through gritted teeth.

'I see,' said Alexander, lifting an eyebrow, 'you can't even get someone like *her* to go out with you. Interesting.'

Anita reacted badly to this. It was one thing to goad Marcus for loosing, even if he was taking it a bit too far, but it was quite another to insult her to her face like that. Anita's energy turned hostile towards Alexander with a force that surprised him. 'I may not be his girlfriend,' she said easily, 'but we are going to the ball together.' She almost laughed when she saw the look on Marcus' face. 'It's funny, I would have thought somebody as high and mighty as you wouldn't have the time to gloat for so long about winning some poxy jumping game. Shouldn't you be going?'

Alexander sniggered as he turned and galloped away. He forced his energy to remain light hearted until he was out of range for Anita to be able to read him, then allowed his true feelings to surface. He had been surprised by the venom that Anita had shown towards him, but what was even more surprising was that he felt hurt by it. His plan had sort of worked; he had wanted Anita to be under Marcus' protection. It was unlikely that Austin would harm Anita whilst Marcus had feelings for her, although he hadn't quite planned for it to happen like this. He hadn't wanted to make her hate him in the process; he wanted to help her. He easily cleared the fence out of the woods and galloped towards home, trying to convince himself that he could rectify the situation, he just wasn't sure how.

Marcus sat gobsmacked, staring up at Anita. 'You're coming to the ball with me?' he asked.

'It would appear so,' she said, as surprised as Marcus and feeling the need to escape, to consider what she had just done. 'Well I hope you have a good walk home,' she said, mounting her mare.

'What? You're just going to leave me here?' asked Marcus, his indignant, disbelieving tone comical. 'You tell me you'll go to the ball with me and then you just leave?'

'Uh, yes. It would seem so.'

'But I'll see you before the ball?'

'I'll probably be at the Crownings, so you might see me there.'

'But where should I pick you up?'

Anita thought briefly about this. 'At my grandmother's. Where you dropped me off the other day.'

'Right, well I'll let you know what time?' Marcus stammered.

'Great. I'll look forward to it,' she replied, in an entirely sterile way.

'Me too,' said Marcus hesitantly, not really sure what to say as Anita turned and cantered away, feeling a lot like he had just been flattened by an energy train.

*****

Anita and Cleo sat by the river; Anita had been to work at the Observatory, but Bas had been so down in the dumps that she'd left early. She wasn't sure if it was the conversation she'd had with him, the energy, or both, but she couldn't bear to be around him when he was so depressed.

'So I told Bas it wasn't going to happen,' Anita said absentmindedly, looking down at the river.

'You did?' Cleo turned to look at her, amazed. 'I didn't think you'd ever get round to finally doing that. At least that explains why he's been in such a bad mood over the last few days.'

'I hope that's not the only reason.'

'Why else?'

'The energy,' Anita responded simply. Neither Anita nor Cleo knew in any exact way what that meant, but they knew whatever effects the recent energy downturn would have, they would almost certainly not be good. 'And I'm going to need your help.'

That comment practically put Cleo into shock. Anita rarely needed help from anyone, or she didn't admitted that she did anyway. 'Go on.'

'Getting ready for the ball.'

Cleo's reaction was immediate and as Anita expected, totally disproportionate. 'Oh my Gods. No. Really? With Marcus?!' Anita nodded, throwing Cleo an indulgent look. Cleo grabbed her and hugged her excitedly. 'This is too exciting,' she squealed. 'So we need to get you a dress, and work out what you're going to do with your hair, and your make-up, have you thought about make-up? And jewellery, and what about shoes? How high can you go? How much taller is Marcus than you?'

'Um, well, he's definitely taller than me,' she said, reliving a flashback to the encounter by the river; she had had to look up at him to meet his eyes. 'I'm, what, 5 foot 10? So he must be at least 6 foot 2?' Anita supposed.

'Yep, that sounds about right,' said Cleo. 'All the Descendants are tall, apart from bitch-face obviously, the good genes clearly skipped her generation. So, ridiculous heels it is then and I'm taking you shopping. You need something spectacular to wear, and I'll get my hairdresser to do your hair. We need all the help we can get in that department,' said Cleo, eyeing Anita's almost shoulder length dark hair suspiciously. It would definitely pose more of a challenge than Cleo's long, silky, black tresses, but some kind of up-do would work. 'So, sky high shoes, hair up, subtle makeup I think, floor length dress…'

'…everyone will be in floor length dresses,' Anita laughed.

'Just clarifying, in case you get some crazy idea in your head and go shopping without me.'

'I see,' said Anita. 'Well I'll leave it to you, my style guru. Just don't tell anyone who I'm going with, okay?'

Cleo was going to ask why, but realised she knew perfectly well, so left it. 'Okay, deal. We can go shopping tomorrow. This is too exciting for words,' she said again, giving Anita another quick squeeze.

*****

The following day Anita and Cleo went shopping. Quite a successful shopping trip by Anita's standards. As Cleo had been in charge, they'd gone to Temple Mews, the most expensive area in Empire, obviously. Temple Mews was a beautiful cobbled street, lined with shops selling the kind of things that made you feel you were living in a surrealist painting. There were florists with displays that took you to a secret garden, tea rooms selling cakes so tall that they seemed to defy gravity and so light and fluffy that you felt like you were eating a cloud. The perfumers' shops smelt like heaven with scents of bay, lavender, rose, rosemary and grapefruit wafting from their doors. The coffee and chocolate shops evoked daydreams of sailing off into the Wild Lands to explore, and the outfitters had displays that made you wonder if you had accidently walked into the land of the Gods, the beautiful swathes of silk hanging in ways that could only have been designed for a Goddess.

Anita and Cleo found what they were looking for in the third outfitter they entered. Cleo had already bought her dress, so the trip had been entirely for Anita. It was the seventh dress she'd tried on and it was perfect, even Anita had to admit. It was a rich blood red silk, cut straight across the front with a deep, seductive v that showed off her perfectly toned back. It had a band around the front that fitted Anita's athletic waist as though it had been made especially for her and dropped straight to the floor, kicking out at the bottom so it swished beautifully as she walked. They had both stood and stared for what must have been a full minute before either of them said anything.

'Well I think this is the one,' Cleo eventually piped up, in a mock business like declaration. 'Seductive yet sophisticated. Exceptionally elegant, and it will match lover boy's cloak like a charm.'

'Shut up,' Anita hissed, 'someone will hear. And he is not my lover boy,' she rushed the words as though they were painful. Anita bought the dress along with some gorgeous, sky high, black stiletto sandals with silk satin tie straps, and then dragged Cleo out of the shop and back to her grandmother's before she was responsible for any more damage to Anita's bank vault. Thank the Gods her mother had left her some money when she'd died, as shopping in Temple Mews would not have been possible on her salary from the Observatory alone.

*****

'So, is Marcus any good at dancing?' Cleo asked, as she helped herself to a piece of Cordelia's pumpkin and walnut cake.

'How should I know?' replied Anita. 'But I would imagine so, given that the Descendants seem to be trained for every possible eventuality.'

'You know Cordelia is a genius,' Cleo garbled, through a mouthful of cake. 'She really is.'

'Thank you Cleopatra,' came a voice from the corner. Anita whipped round to see Cordelia looking smug. How had she come in without them hearing? Great, now Cordelia knew, she was never going to live this down. 'So you're going to the ball with Marcus?' Cordelia asked, clearly amused.

Anita glared at Cleo, who shrugged apologetically. 'She was going to find out eventually.'

'Yes,' sighed a resigned Anita, 'I'm going to the ball with Marcus.'

'I knew you were up to something,' said Cordelia, settling into an armchair. 'Come on, tell me.'

Anita recounted the story about the run by the river (leaving out the kiss), the encounter after Christiana's funeral, and the ride in the woods, Cordelia listening intently, fascinated. 'We need to get you a dress,' said Cordelia, frivolously, when Anita had finished. 'Something show-stopping, and shoes, and what are you going to do with your hair?' Cleo jumped in before Anita could utter a word, but she just went with it. She showed Cordelia her dress and shoes and listened to how she would have her hair and makeup, and observed Cordelia and Cleo's childish excitement as they conspiratorially speculated about the first dance. After what seemed like an eternity, Cleo got up to leave.

'See you tomorrow at the Crowning,' she said, making her way to the door. 'Don't forget to get your beauty sleep. Tomorrow is a big day.'

'Yes ma'am,' said Anita, half saluting, half waving as Cleo left the room. As she left, Cordelia turned to face Anita square on. 'I know, I'm sorry…' she started.

'…sorry for what?' Cordelia cut her short. 'I'm thrilled for you and you two are going to look fabulous leading the first dance; you always were a wonderful dancer. Wait here, I've got something for you.' Cordelia disappeared out of the room and came back a minute later carrying a large wooden box. She opened the lid and fumbled around inside before lifting out a beautiful gold and diamond tiara. It was made in a swirling, almost Celtic pattern with upward points designed to sit low on the wearer's head. Anita sat and stared, totally speechless. 'It was your mother's,' said Cordelia softly. 'She would have wanted you to have it and it will go perfectly with that dress.'

Cordelia very rarely mentioned Anita's mother, Clarissa. She presumed that was because she didn't know that much about her. Cordelia was Anita's paternal grandmother, not that she ever really spoke about her son, Jeffrey, either. 'It's beautiful,' said Anita.

'It will look beautiful on you,' she said finally, closing the wooden box, and Anita knew the conversation was over. She'd tried in the past to probe about her parents, but Cordelia simply would not open up. Anita presumed that it was just too painful for her. She had rummaged around the cottage enough to know that Cordelia kept nothing that would give Anita any clues. She had been to the Archives but they had been useless; nothing but birth and death records for each of them and nothing significant in any of the newspapers. Her only hope was that one day Cordelia would decide it was time to tell her more.

CHAPTER 7

The following day, Anita woke up early, as she always did, and completed her usual yoga session in the garden, surrounded by her grandmother's spectacular flowers and listening to the stream at the bottom of the garden gurgle by. As she lay on the ground afterwards, her arms outstretched, she couldn't stop her mind from speculating about how that night would play out. She wasn't worried about leading the first dance, that would be a walk in the park, but what did worry her was how everyone would react to her turning up with Marcus, not to mention what was going on with schizophrenic Alexander. One minute he wanted to 'help' her (although she was still far from clear on what this meant) and the next he was insulting her. She lay there, eyes open, staring blankly up at the puffy white clouds sliding seamlessly across the powder blue sky, her thoughts racing, when she suddenly became aware of powerful energy very close by. She held her breath, adrenaline spiking through her veins, poised to take defensive action at any moment as she waited for movement.

'Fancy seeing you here,' drawled a voice from near the house, and Anita immediately relaxed.

'Still a master of originality I see,' Anita smiled sarcastically, staying where she was on the ground, looking up at the sky. Marcus walked towards her, Anita feeling his energy intensify as he came closer and hers responded in the same way. Thank the Gods he wasn't a reader, she thought again. 'Did you come for any particular reason, or just to watch me doing yoga?' she flirted, turning her head to watch as he approached.

Marcus said nothing, but kept coming steadily towards her until he was standing right over her. He crouched down beside her and she half sat up as he took hold of her hand, seductively kissing the back of it. 'Are you always so feisty?' he mused.

'As a general rule,' she answered sulkily, pouting a little.

'I just came by to tell you that I will pick you up at seven o'clock, if that's to your satisfaction?'

'Seven o'clock it is,' she said, flashing him her sweetest 'see, I'm not feisty when I don't want to be' smile.

'In which case, I will look forward to seeing you then,' he said, with a matching 'now that wasn't so hard was it' face, as he stood up, gently released her hand and disappeared back the way he'd come.

Anita slumped heavily back to the ground and took a long, deep breath, relishing the excited anticipation she felt bunched in her stomach, butterflies fluttering endlessly around, their wings brushing her nerves, sending tingles to her brain. Eventually she got up and headed back inside; she would be late for the Crownings if she didn't get a move on. As she approached the back door, she stopped in her tracks, spotting an enormous bouquet of dusky pink peonies sitting against the wall. She opened the attached card, reading the words 'until later…' that had been scrawled across it, in perfect, old fashioned script, and rolled her eyes; trust him to have perfect handwriting.

Anita showered and got dressed, paying quite a bit more attention to her appearance than she normally would. She told Cordelia this was just in case Marcus had mentioned to anyone he was going to the ball with her and she attracted any resultant attention. Cordelia knew full well it was really just in case Marcus clapped eyes on her; she had never cared about looking good when drawing attention before. Anita walked with Cordelia to the Temples, just about managing to supress an enormous grin, but unable to curb it completely, so a faint smile played across her lips all the way.

As it was a double Crowning, both the Temple of the Body and the Temple of the Spirit would be used. Most of the ceremony would take place in the Temple of the Body, but Alexander's actual Crowning would take place in the Temple of the Spirit. This would take place after the Descendants had gone to whatever it was beneath the Temples, to do whatever it was they had to do. Anita and Cordelia once again sat at the back of the Temple of the Body and luckily, this time, Marcus was already at the front, so no opportunity for embarrassing looks as he walked past, Anita was relieved to discover.

Once again music flooded the Temple, however, whereas at Christiana's funeral it had been haunting, today, the hidden organ boomed out a theatrical, moody, full-bodied piece as the procession began. First came the Spirit and Body Councillors, all in full length cloaks with hoods up, so no-one could see their faces. Nobody was quite sure why they did this, other than to make sure the main focus was on those being crowned, but it invoked powerful visions of cult members on their way to make a sacrifice to the Gods and therefore looked utterly terrifying.

After the Councillors came Peter, looking easily the best he ever had. But despite his cloak, he still didn't quite feel like a Descendant. He was tall and reasonably good looking, but had a sort of scrawny, wispy look about him, his wavy dark hair tinged with grey, making him look tired, robbing him of the gravitas of the others. Next was Alexander, looking frankly like a God, his cloak billowing around him, his hair cut slightly shorter for the occasion, and Anita could feel her energy rise as he ascended the steps into the Temple. Alexander felt it, but kept his head facing forward down the aisle, 'she has got to learn to control that,' he said again to himself as he strode after Peter, every female pair of eyes making no attempt to hide that they were following him, transfixed.

Last and most melodramatic of all was Austin. He had his floor length, red cloak on, but also had a hood over his head, so nobody could see his face. He moved down the aisle as theatrically as he could, relishing his time in the spotlight. He's not going to like sharing that with the other two, thought Anita, as he made his way to the front of the Temple. She got the impression that Peter would go along with whatever Austin wanted, but she wasn't sure Alexander would be so easy to control.

By the time Austin had reached the front, the Councillors had taken their seats and Peter and Alexander had sat down in the elaborate gold thrones that had been placed in front of the altar for them. Austin stopped a couple of metres in front of them and turned to face the congregation, throwing back his hood, revealing his face with a flourish.

He paused, surveying the scene before addressing the crowds. 'Descendants, Councillors, children of the Temples of the Mind, Body and Spirit. We are here today to observe a momentous occasion in our history; the Crowning of two Descendants, Alexander, son of Anthony, and Peter, son of Christiana. As ever, a Crowning evokes mixed feelings; a sense of loss for those who have moved on from this world, yet joy for the instatement of two new Descendants, about to begin their reign. As the ceremony is being held here in Empire, rather than in Kingdom by the relic, some of the ceremony will take place privately, below the Temples. However, this will only form a small part of today's proceedings. Peter's Crowning will take place here in the Temple of the Body, and Alexander's will take place in the Temple of the Spirit, however, the main part of the ceremony will take place here. I would like to take this opportunity to say how proud I am of both Peter and Alexander for the way they have handled this difficult time, and I look forward to having them join me as reigning Descendants.'

Patronising bastard, though Anita, 'how proud' he is of them? Please. As Austin moved to his front row seat, a Body Councillor stood gracefully, then moved slowly and purposefully to the centre of the altar, behind Alexander and Peter. She still had her hood up, her cloak falling elegantly from her shoulders, but despite this, it was clear she had an athletic build and was still fit and toned at the age of 55. Anita knew her well; her name was Helena. She was the cousin of Celia, Alexander's mother and she resided in Empire. Helena had been a great source of counsel and guidance to Anita growing up. When Anita was thirteen and displaying considerable Body abilities, Helena had helped her harness and use her skills. She'd been there when Anita had been teased about being different and when people were scared to be friends with her, because, with her abilities, the other children imagined that she must have been sent from the Gods.

Despite her help, Helena had never been a motherly figure and had always kept Anita slightly at arm's length. She was not warm and cuddly, far from it, she was the most formidable person Anita knew; she made even Austin look like a pussy cat. But she had always been there to guide her, and there had been a curious connection between them that Anita found both strange, yet oddly comforting.

Anita had hardly seen Helena for the last few years. She was now the most senior Body Councillor, hence why she was performing today's ceremony, and spent a great deal of time with the academics, studying and teaching Body skills to those, like Anita, who displayed potential. Helena had invited Anita to join the academics a couple of years back, but she'd turned her down. Cordelia hadn't been keen on it; she'd never really liked Helena, and anyway, Anita had been far more interested in continuing to study the energy. Luckily, Alistair had offered her a job at the Observatory a few weeks later, so it had ended up being the right decision, but Helena and Anita had barely been in touch since.

Helena bowed her head when she reached the centre, facing the audience but not looking at them directly. She paused there for several moments before lifting her head to reveal her deep green eyes. She raised her arms out and upwards, her cloak fanning out with her arms, making her a striking figure at the front of the Temple. The congregation held their breath. You could hear a pin drop, the anticipation almost palpable.

In a low, controlled, powerful, rich voice that instantly commanded the attention of everyone who heard it, she began. 'In the beginning, there were three Gods, Theseus of the Mind, Tatiana of the Body, and Jeremiah of the Spirit. The three Gods created three worlds, each with a mix of the three God's unique skills. In each world they created people who lived to serve the Gods, and in return, the Gods would keep the energy stable, so resources would be plentiful. The people built Temples to thank the Gods for their generosity and worshipped the God to whom they belonged. For hundreds of years, the people of this world lived like this in harmony, serving the Gods and living with all the food and wealth they required, until, in the year 769, the Gods decided it was time to make a change. In that year, they sent three people to the world to rule for them; Janus for Theseus, God of the Mind, Georgiana for Tatiana, Goddess of the Body and Julius for Jeremiah, God of the Spirit. Each was known as a Descendant of the God that had sent them, and each would pass their Descendancy down to their children, Janus and Julius through male heirs and Georgiana through her female ones. It was the job of the Descendants to rule the world for the Gods, ensuring energy harmony and plentiful resources. The people showed great respect for those who had been sent to lead them and there was harmony for over two hundred years, until at the turn of the century, the Gods decided to make another change; they sent the relic. With the relic came a prophecy, that one day the Descendants would send the relic back, and this act would free the world. The energy would be stable, and the people could rule as they pleased, free to choose their own leaders. The relic brought great hope, yet great disruption. The world's energy has been volatile ever since, and we live in hope with each generation of Descendants that they will be the ones to free the world.'

Helena was joined at the altar by another Councillor, this time one that Anita did not recognise, from the Temple of the Spirit. He was a short, portly man who had the look about him of someone who had enjoyed one too many long lunches and a great deal too many cigars. He too faced the congregation, standing directly behind Alexander, Helena moving to stand behind Peter. 'Children of the Temples,' he started, in a voice that conveyed far more authority than his stature suggested, 'we have heard the history and the prophecy, and it is now time for our Descendants to begin their journey to rule.' He paused and raised his arms as Helena had done earlier. 'Alexander, son of Anthony, of the Temple of the Spirit, do you promise to uphold the quest for energy balance, to seek, before anything else, to fulfil the prophecy, and to rule according to the wishes of Jeremiah, God of the Spirit?'

'I promise,' Alexander's unwaveringly steady reply floated through the Temple. Anita's energy rose at the sound of his voice, but she didn't even notice, she was too busy gazing at Alexander's god-like form. He looked every inch the confident ruler, a tad dishevelled perhaps, but only in a way that seemed to enhance his right to reign. By the time Anita wrestled her attention back to the proceedings, Helena had started talking.

'Peter, son of Christiana, of the Temple of the Body, do you promise to uphold the quest for energy balance, to seek, before anything else, to fulfil the prophecy, and to rule according to the wishes of Tatiana, Goddess of the Body?'

'I promise,' answered Peter, in a confident, clear enough voice, but that somehow hinted at nerves. Whereas Alexander had conveyed a sense that he was meant to be exactly where he was, it was almost as if Peter wasn't quite sure. Then again, he may be the one to break the prophecy entirely, so he's probably at least a little bit worried about being mobbed on his way out, let alone about ruling, Anita chuckled inwardly.

'The Descendants will now privately perform the next stage of the ceremony in the sacred place below the Temples,' the male Councillor's voice rang out, 'they will return shortly.' Alexander, Peter, Gwyn, Marcus and Austin all got up and approached the circle in the floor in the centre of the Temple. Anita didn't know where to look; both Marcus and Alexander were walking directly towards her, and both seemed to be looking directly at her. Her energy was sky high again, so she concentrated on trying to get that under control, trying desperately to tear her eyes away from them. She failed on both counts, obviously, succeeding only in making herself look awkward. As they descended the steps, through what was now a hole in the floor, both Alexander and Marcus smiled. Marcus, presumably, because he thought he alone was having this effect on her, she made a mental note to put him firmly back in his place later, but a great deal more embarrassingly, Alexander, whose smirk was doubtless because he could feel her ridiculous energy. Both reactions made Anita cross, which meant that Cordelia had a rough fifteen minutes trying to make conversation whilst they waited for the Descendants to return. Cordelia gave up after a few attempts and resigned herself to listen to the music that was once again filling the Temple.

Almost exactly fifteen minutes later, the party of Descendants returned. Austin looked a bit put out, but the rest of them seemed to be in high spirits as they made their way back to the altar. This time, instead of sitting in front of the altar, Alexander sat in the front row with the other Descendants. His throne had been moved out of the way so that Peter's actual Crowning could take place and Helena was once again directing proceedings. Peter was now sitting alone, all eyes on him.

'Peter, son of Christiana, I summon you to the altar of your Goddess to make public your allegiance to your ruler.'

Peter stood up a little too quickly and made his way to the altar where he knelt, arms open, looking up towards the ceiling. 'I, Peter, son of Christiana, of the Temple of the Body, declare myself at the disposal of my ruler, the Goddess Tatiana.'

Helena, who seemed to have conjured a crown from nowhere, stepped in front of Peter and held the simple gold band above his head. 'I, Helena, Councillor of the Temple of the Body, and servant of the Goddess Tatiana, crown you, Peter, son of Christiana, of the Temple of the Body. May you be always guided by the Gods, as you seek to free the world.' Helena slowly lowered the crown onto Peter's head. Remarkably, it fit, which seemed strange given that it was a crown made for a female head. They can't possibly have resized it, thought Anita, that must surely be against the rules. Helena removed her hands from Peter's head and backed away a couple of steps as a fanfare flooded the Temple. Peter stood up, looked at Helena, who gave him an uncharacteristically reassuring nod, and stiffly turned around to face back down the Temple. As he did so, the congregation begrudgingly bowed to him. Peter paused, seemingly unsure about what to do next, when Austin rose from where he was sitting and made towards the aisle. This seemed to galvanise him, and he hastily started the procession back out of the Temple and into the sunlight beyond. He was followed by the rest of the Descendants, along with the Body and Spirit Councillors that had processed in earlier. Anita was very pleased with herself for this time managing to avoid looking at either Alexander or Marcus.

The procession immediately turned to head towards the Spirit Temple where the same ceremony would take place for Alexander. Unfortunately, the Spirit Temple was full of Spirits, which meant that Anita and Cordelia had to stand outside at the back. Anita managed to scale one of the pillars, which gave her a pretty good vantage point from which to view Alexander's majestic performance at the altar. When he turned to make his way back down the aisle, there was no hesitation; he confidently strode out of the Temple and through the cheering crowd. He shot Anita a quick glance as he approached her perch, internally remarking at how she had managed to get up there at all. This time, it was Anita's turn to feel Alexander's energy rise at seeing her, which improved her mood significantly. She was really quite jovial by the time she dropped back down to where Cordelia was waiting for her.

*****

By the time Anita and Cordelia got home, Cleo had set up shop in the sitting room. She had brought with her a chest that seemed to be full of some kind of ancient torture devices and immediately set about using them on Anita. It was 4 o'clock by the time Anita was allowed a break, and only then because Cordelia appeared with some sandwiches and a carrot and ginger cake. At 4.30pm, the hairdresser and make-up artist arrived and set to work on Cleo. Harry was picking her up at 6.30pm, as everyone who wasn't going with a Descendant had to be in place and ready by 7.00pm for the Descendants' procession at 7.30pm. Seeing as Cleo was going with a Councillor's son, she didn't feel this was an occasion to be late.

Once they'd finished with Cleo, she looked extraordinary. Her hair was in a loose up do; several delicate plaits interwoven with her normal silky locks in a way that accentuated her spectacular cheekbones, her eyelids a shimmering palette of bronze and gold.

'Wow, Cleo, you look amazing,' said Anita. 'I mean you always look great, obviously, but you've somehow reached a whole new level.'

'Thanks,' Cleo laughed, 'but just wait until you see the dress!' she said animatedly, practically running upstairs to get changed.

Whilst Cleo dressed herself, the hairdresser and makeup artist began on Anita, building her up do around her mother's gold and diamond tiara. The results, even Anita had to admit, were pretty good. They'd somehow managed to make her look imperial, yet soft and approachable, and her makeup was understated, yet somehow striking. Anita was admiring their handy work in the mirror when Cleo re-entered the room. 'Bloody hell Cleopatra,' Anita blurted. Cleo was a vision in a floor-length, golden, shimmering, figure accentuating, sleeveless, refined dress, with a low v at the front. It fitted her magnificently and gave her a flirty yet sophisticated air. She had simple, sky-high gold sandals on her feet, which, of course, she moved in effortlessly.

'Stop staring and go and put on your dress,' chastised Cleo, clearly pleased at Anita's reaction.

Anita went up the narrow stairway to her cramped room, where she slipped on her flowing red dress. She grinned as she zipped herself up and did a quick twirl to feel the fabric pouring around her legs. Maybe this wouldn't be so bad after all. She slipped on her ridiculous black sandals before returning downstairs. As she entered the room, she got a gaggle of approving comments and her face cracked into a broad smile. She and Cleo thanked the hairdresser and makeup artist profusely as they left. 'Can you believe I'm actually looking forward to this?' Anita laughed when they'd gone.

'By the Gods, if we can get you to look forward to a ball, then there's nothing we can't do!' giggled Cleo. Cordelia, who had just got back from walking Thorn, entered the room.

'Ha! Did she just say she was looking forward to this? It's amazing what a bit of makeup and a pretty dress can do! You both look beautiful by the way,' she said, as there was a knock on the front door.

'Thanks,' they said together, giving independent twirls and laughing as they did it, feeling a lot like little girls playing dress-up.

'That will be for me,' Cleo squealed, giving Anita an excited half hug and rushing to the door, pausing for a moment to regain her composure before swinging it open. 'See you later!' she called over her shoulder, gliding through the door and saying, 'hello Henry,' in her most sassy voice.

Anita and Cordelia could just about make out Henry's stuttering, 'hello,' as Cleo closed the door behind her.

'Poor thing has no idea what he's got himself into,' Anita joked.

'Indeed,' Cordelia laughed back. 'She always was determined that one.'

'That's an understatement,' sniggered Anita, 'but if he can't even manage to say hello, I'm not convinced he'll last the night!'

Five minutes later, Cordelia tactfully removed herself so she wouldn't be lingering when Marcus arrived, saying, 'I'm off to sit by the stream for a while. You look lovely Anita, and I hope you have a wonderful time.' Cordelia gave Anita a brief hug before heading to the back door. She had never been especially sentimental, nor was she very good at expressing how she felt, so this was pretty touching.

Anita looked at the clock. 6.40pm. Plenty of time to contemplate both how to handle Marcus this evening and what to do about the Alexander problem. She perched on the arm of a sofa thinking the situation through, when she heard the gate squeak open outside. She jumped up and looked through the window to see an energy town car parked the other side of the gate and Marcus striding up the path towards the front door. Anita retreated from the window and took a couple of deep breaths. 'Well, guess I'll just have to wing it,' she muttered, taking a deep breath as Marcus rapped forcefully on the door. Anita waited a few moments before making her way slowly to the door. She wanted to let him sweat a bit; he had, after all, turned up twenty minutes early; a most ungentlemanly thing to do. In fact, maybe that should be her opening line. Or is that taking it a bit too far, she wondered, as she reached the door and pulled it open.

The door swung aside, revealing each to the other, and they stood in silence for a moment as they took in the other's form. Anita could feel Marcus' energy make a sharp, upward turn, and heard his breath catch in his throat. She felt her own energy soar as she surveyed the impeccably dressed, dazzlingly handsome specimen in front of her. They half-smiled at each other, relishing the magnificent anticipation of what would happen next, before Marcus took glorious control. He stepped towards Anita and kissed her slowly and seductively on each cheek, Anita's energy tingling delightfully as he did so.

'Good evening Anita,' he said in her ear.

'Good evening Marcus,' she replied slowly, enticingly, as he took a step back. 'I think you'll find you're early,' she teased.

'Well I couldn't wait a moment longer,' he flirted, although there was a hint of sincerity in his tone, 'and there's somewhere I want to take you before we surround ourselves with people.' Anita stepped forward, raising an eyebrow, Marcus closing the front door behind her. He turned and offered her his arm. 'You are exceptionally beautiful,' he said softly, as she took it, leaning in towards her. Anita tilted her head and smiled modestly, almost shyly before he guided her down the path and through the gate.

By the time they reached it, Marcus' chauffeur was holding the door to the very spacious town car open, and Marcus helped Anita inside. He waited until she was settled before climbing in after her.

'So, what is it you want to show me?' probed Anita, intrigued after a couple of minutes of driving. The ball was taking place on Austin's estate just outside of Empire, which was where they seemed to be heading, so Anita was keen to know what lay in store.

'It's a surprise,' he shrugged back, boyishly, as though it was something he couldn't tell her even if he wanted to. She shot him a simmering look before bowing her head a little and smiling in submission. They travelled in silence, Anita watching the scenery go by, Marcus watching Anita, both feeling a little pacified by the mellow music playing from the front. They were up in the woods above the river now and still climbing. Anita suspected that Austin's estate would be at the top of the hill, naturally with a spectacular view. That would be where she would choose to live if she were in his position. They passed a pair of imposing gates, enormous, protective lions on pillars either side. Anita threw Marcus a curious look as they passed.

'We're going in a different entrance,' he said, by way of explanation, confirming Anita's suspicions that this was it. About a mile further through the woods, the chauffeur turned the car through a pair of much smaller, far less intimidating gates, the car soon popping out into open heathland. This ran to the edge of a cliff, which had spectacular views of the surrounding landscape, including both Empire and the Observatory.

The Chauffeur pulled up near the edge of the cliff and came round to open the door. Marcus stepped out and helped Anita do the same. She walked to the edge and looked down the vertical drop to the river, a long way below. It was incredible, she thought, as she turned to look back at Marcus, but as she did so, she caught sight of something behind him that was altogether more unexpected; an enormous, imposing castle, complete with fairytale battlements and turrets. Bloody hell, she thought, but successfully fought to keep her reaction hidden. The chauffeur unloaded a picnic basket and blanket before nodding to Marcus and striding off into the woods to give them some privacy.

'Where's he going?' asked Anita, shocked. 'You're not going to make him hang out in the woods?!'

Marcus laughed. 'No, even the evil Descendants aren't that mean. There's a summer house in the woods; he's gone to make himself a cup of tea and put his feet up until I call him back. Come on, we don't have very long until we have to put on a show,' he said, taking her hand and leading her to the blanket. They sat, Anita as elegantly as she could, given the restrictive dress, thanking the Gods that she wasn't wearing the figure hugging number Cleo had on.

Marcus opened the wicker basket and produced two beakers and a bottle of Ginger Champagne. 'Sorry,' he said, expertly popping the cork and pouring generous quantities into each beaker. 'I couldn't find any champagne flutes that dad wouldn't have killed me for bringing out here, and the caterers for the ball were watching theirs like hawks,' he said, as though this were dreadfully unjust of them. He handed Anita a beaker and she giggled.

'Thanks.' Hearing Marcus call Austin 'dad' made Austin seem almost human. Anita had visions of Marcus as a small boy being chastised by his father and she found it quite endearing. 'It's quite some view you've got here,' she said, turning to look at the landscape and taking a sip of the delicious wine, bubbles gently fizzing on her tongue.

'I thought you'd like it,' he replied. 'I come out here quite a lot. My mother often comes with me too.'

The mention of Marcus' mother shocked Anita. She'd never heard anyone talk about her, and she hadn't been at any of the events over the last couple of weeks, had she?

'I'll look forward to being introduced to your mother,' said Anita, hoping he would offer up more information.

'Well you might have to wait a while for that,' Marcus breathed heavily. He saw Anita's inquisitive expression, so went on tentatively. 'My father and mother don't exactly see eye to eye anymore, on pretty much anything, so they try to lead separate lives. My mother comes out here when dad's in Kingdom, and she goes back to Kingdom when he comes out here. I go between the two, although I spend far more time with dad now, obviously.'

'That must be hard,' Anita mused.

'Not especially,' he shrugged, indifferent. 'You're used to what you're used to I suppose. Like I imagine you're used to living with your grandmother and not seeing your parents.'

'Well it would be tricky to see my parents given that they're both dead,' she said, evenly.

Marcus' eyes flew open. 'Anita, I'm so sorry, I had no idea.'

She laughed. 'Why would you? It's fine. I don't even remember my parents, so I've never known anything else. As you say, you're used to what you're used to, so living with my grandmother seems normal to me. Anything else would feel a bit odd.'

Marcus topped up her beaker. 'So, ready for the first dance?' he asked, the mood regaining its flirtatious edge.

'It's not the first dance I'm worried about,' she smirked, 'I'm more concerned about how everyone will react to me turning up with you. I can almost hear the ripple of whispers we're going to cause when we go in.'

'Ah yes, the gossip mill. It's surprising that Cleo's managed to keep our secret, and even dad hasn't found out about you, which is pretty much a first for him.' Anita's guts tightened at this news. It was one thing dealing with the gossip mill, it was quite another, she suspected, to have to deal with Austin as well. Marcus got up and walked over to the car. 'Anyway, I wasn't talking about the first dance in there,' he nodded towards the castle, 'I meant the first dance we are about to have out here,' he said, turning on the car radio, so a vibrant, sassy, melody rippled out of the speakers. He sauntered back to Anita and roguishly held out his hand. She took it and got delicately to her feet.

'I do hope you know how to lead,' she played.

'I'm more concerned that you might not know how to follow,' he quipped back.

Anita smiled. 'Touché,' she said, raising one eyebrow. 'I suppose we'll just have to find out then, won't we.'

Marcus pulled her firmly towards him, placing his free hand on her waist. He took control, and Anita let him. They danced for what seemed like forever, silently flirting, testing each other. Marcus occasionally spun Anita out before guiding her back into his hold. Not bad, thought Anita, as she started to enjoy herself. Not quite as good as Bas, but the first dance would be a long way from embarrassing. As the song came to an end, Marcus bent Anita gently backwards, holding her there as the last remnants of the song floated away into the twilight. Stillness filled the air and Marcus gently pulled her back to him, so their faces were inches apart. They paused there, pulses racing, before Marcus leant in, his intention plain. Anita pulled away.

'You'll smudge my lipstick,' she breathed seductively, her eyes throwing him a challenge. Marcus grabbed her hand as she moved away and pressed it lightly to his lips, meeting both her eyes and her challenge.

'As you wish…,' he purred.

*****

'Anything new?' Austin snapped at the man dressed head to toe in black in front of him; a guard from his security team sent to give him an update. Austin had no idea who he was and didn't really care. He was annoyed that Amber hadn't deigned to come herself and this man seemed as good a person as any to take that out on.

'We know who Marcus has asked to accompany him to the ball this evening,' the man started. He spoke with care, taking time over every word in a way that Austin found patronising and therefore intensely irritating.

'Oh?' replied Austin, his interest piqued, though he didn't show it, making a mental note to get Amber to sack this dithering imbecilic later.

'Anita. The girl who won the Chase. By all accounts she's an excellent dancer, so the first dance should be quite a spectacle,' he prattled, when he really should have stopped the moment he'd uttered Anita's name. Austin's face was dark as night.

'You mean to tell me that my son is bringing to a Crowning Ball some girl he has met only twice? Some low life, unorthodox girl that everyone thinks is peculiar?' He said it in a chillingly quiet voice, but the imbecile continued confidently, seemingly oblivious to Austin's alarming reaction to his words.

'She seems exceptionally skilled sir,' he said, in an enthusiastic tone.

'I know that you simpleton, that's why I have a security detail on her. Why else do you think you currently find yourself in my employment?' Austin's voice was louder now, as he snarled out his wolfish response.

The man tried to stutter a reply, but a cool, enticing female voice put him out of his misery before he could dig himself into any further danger. 'Thank you, Thompson, you can go.' The woman was around 5 foot 7, lithe, with heavy auburn hair that she wore cut short in a bob. Her skin was porcelain white and flawless, her eyes cat-like and treacherous. Thompson didn't need to be told twice and made his way swiftly past the stiff, heavy, leather, drawing room furniture, past where Amber was standing seductively by the colossal, crackling fire, towards the ancient oak door. She waited for him to leave before meandering her way bewitchingly towards Austin, his face still alive with his fury. She pouted provocatively as she approached him. 'Austin,' she said sulkily, putting one hand on each lapel of his dinner jacket and kissing him lightly on the lips, 'aren't you going to tell me how enchanting I look?' She spoke slowly, lingering over the word enchanting, stepping back and completing a slow turn as she said the words.

'Amber, you look captivating, as you always do. But your feminine charms are not going to get you out of this one,' he growled, perhaps not quite as aggressively as he could have done. 'Why didn't you know that Marcus was bringing our number one suspect to the ball?'

'I had my suspicions,' she started, stepping forward and playing with his bow tie as though their conversation was trivial to her, 'but didn't want to tell you until I was sure. And now I'm sure, so here we are. It would appear that they may have met more than twice, as we previously thought, but they have only ever met briefly. It makes perfect sense. She's powerful, and Marcus has always been attracted to powerful people. You can hardly blame the boy; I can only imagine how dull it is to have to spend time with all the vacuous girls he normally hangs around with, and at least Anita seems to have a bit of fight in her. I would quite like her,' she paused, pretending to consider what she'd just said, before looking up through her lashes at Austin, 'if of course, she wasn't number one on my hit list,' she smiled, a vindictive, dangerous smile.

Amber was head of Austin's private security and research team. They had been on constant look out for powerful girls of about Anita's age, especially powerful people from the Body Temple, ever since Christiana had told Austin they were going to Empire to look for the girl.

'Speaking of your hit list, have you made any progress?' Austin inquired, seeming to have taken Amber's bait, his thunderous mood abating a little, now absently caressing her lower back. Amber took this to be a good sign, so she arched her back to press her body forwards against his. He did always love to discuss the hit list.

'We have one or two more to add to the list, both from the Institution, but Anita still outstrips everyone else we have,' she said, matter of factly. 'Let's face it; Marcus might be doing us a favour. It may mean we have the perfect opportunity to study her more closely.'

'Which is great, until he falls in love with her, and she does turn out to be the one,' he sneered.

She smiled a slow, ruthless smile. 'Marcus is far too much like you to do something as stupid as fall in love. It's lust and infatuation, nothing more,' she said, pulling back from him.

Austin smirked and used the hand at the base of her spine to pull her roughly back against him, their noses almost touching, 'is that what it is?' he mocked. She bit his lip so it was almost painful, Austin forcefully pushing her away in retaliation. 'My adoring public awaits,' he announced, as he made his way to the door. Amber had placated him for now, but she couldn't help wondering for how long.

*****

Austin came out of the drawing room just as Marcus and Anita were climbing the steps through the front door and into the imposing entrance hall. They were a breath-taking couple, even Austin had to admit it. They looked positively regal as they gracefully ascended the stairs, Anita's arm laced through Marcus'. Marcus, oblivious to Austin's presence, turned his head to look down at Anita in a way that was half predator, half puppy dog. Anita looked up at him and rolled her eyes, shaking her head in mock contempt. Austin could feel his mood blacken once more; that had better be what lust looked like, he thought, or Amber would not get off lightly this time. Anita felt a sudden shift in energy ahead and looked up to see who it belonged to. Spotting Austin, she tried to pull away from Marcus, but Marcus, who had now also spotted Austin, held her resolutely in place.

'You're late,' snapped Austin, sharply.

'Father, you remember Anita?' Marcus replied brightly, ignoring Austin's terrible mood, 'our guest of honour this evening?'

'Anita,' Austin nodded curtly, before whirling around and striding towards the great hall, his cloak billowing out behind him.

Marcus turned to Anita and gave her an apologetic look. 'That went well,' Anita said sarcastically as they made their way after Austin towards the great hall.

'Ignore him. He was obviously in a bad mood already,' he whispered conspiratorially.

They approached the huge, studded oak doors that led into the great hall and joined Peter, Gwyn, Alexander and Austin, who were already there. Anita shot Marcus a hostile look, given the lack of dates present for the other Descendants. 'We don't normally process with non-Descendants,' he murmured in her ear, 'but seeing as you are the guest of honour, we will process in last.'

Great, thought Anita. One more thing to make her stand out, as if there wasn't enough already, but at least Marcus and Alexander looking as dashing as ever would draw some of the female attention away from her, and she definitely looked better than Gwyn, she thought cattily. Gwyn had a very impressive emerald and diamond necklace on, but the dress she was wearing seemed to somehow wear her, rather than the other way round. Her black, low cut, velvet dress, complete with a very high slit up the side, was beautiful, but she just couldn't quite pull it off. Hopefully that would attract the attention of the bitchy girls, so she might get off quite lightly.

The hum of chattering that been audible through the doors faded abruptly into silence, hauling Anita hastily back from her thoughts. The Descendants lined up ready to process, first Gwyn, then Peter, then Alexander, then Austin and then Marcus and Anita. Marcus offered Anita his arm and she begrudgingly took it; it would, she reasoned, look a bit odd if she didn't.

They could hear the muffled sound of a Councillor instructing everyone to stand for the procession and the scrape of chairs as everyone obliged, followed by the announcement of their arrival. As soon as the Councillor had finished, the thick doors swung easily open, and Gwyn immediately and confidently led the way through them. There was absolute silence for a few moments as all eyes tracked the procession, before, just as Anita and Marcus reached the entrance, the band started to play. Anita could not have been more appreciative of the music and from the moment it began, the whole experience felt abstract, almost dream-like. She felt she was floating through the hall, in her own little bubble of a world, making it surprisingly easy to block out the indelicate eyes that followed her.

The hall had three enormous banqueting tables set up, one down each side and a third across the top to form a horseshoe. They were heading for the top table, where the dates of the other Descendants, along with some of the most senior Councillors, were waiting. They processed past the rest of the guests, who were already at their seats in front of an impressive array of silver and glassware, all eyes fixed intently on the small group before them. They passed underneath many spectacular crystal chandeliers and Anita noticed several mesmerising works of art hanging on the walls behind the banquet tables. They were modern pieces, depicting energy waves in abstract ways, yet oddly were somehow perfect for the grand, old environment and gave it a contemporary feel, devoid of any of the stuffiness that you might expect. As they were nearing the top table, Anita noticed Cleo, already looking bored, next to Henry, who was positively beaming. That's going as expected then, thought Anita, spotting Bas sitting next to a girl she could only assume was Missy. She looked quite nice, although very plain, and she needed someone like Cleo to take her shopping, as her dress was extremely conservative. Anita felt Bas' energy pick up as she went past and she shot him a warm smile. Alistair was sitting the other side of Missy, but looked preoccupied with something; he seemed to barely notice the procession. Anita wondered what it could be, realising just in time that they had reached the top table, where they had to split from the others to get to the far side. Anita, Marcus and Alexander went to the right and Austin, Peter and Gwyn went to the left.

Austin sat in the middle of the top table, which Anita thought was reasonable, it was his castle after all, with Anita to his left as the guest of honour, and Gwyn to his right. Marcus was on Anita's other side, and he had some Councillor's daughter, then Alexander, and then Helena to his left. Gwyn was sitting next to her date, someone else Anita didn't recognise, but who was presumably from a Council family, then Peter, then several other Councillors to her right. Peter's wife and Gwyn's mother, Olivia, Anita had learned from Marcus, had died during childbirth and Peter had never had another relationship. She hadn't yet spoken to Peter, but he seemed to keep himself to himself and she imagined him to be quite shy. Anita resolved to speak with him later to see what he was like.

Everyone sat down except Austin, who remained standing to make the opening speech, his voice creamy as ever. 'Descendants, Councillors, Children of the Temples of the Mind, Body and Spirit. I welcome you to my home for the celebration of a truly significant moment in our history; the Crowning of not one, but two Descendants. Tonight we bring to a close the Crowning traditions, having had a fantastic Chase and a poignant Crowning ceremony, both with record turnouts. We shall, of course, look forward to seeing our Chase Champion and tonight's guest of honour, Anita, lead this evening's dancing after dinner, but first, let us toast our new Descendants, Peter, son of Christiana and Alexander, son of Anthony.' Austin picked up his Ginger Champagne, saying, 'to Peter and Alexander,' as he lifted his glass in the air.

The rest of the hall mirrored his actions, standing up and lifting their champagne, echoing, 'to Peter and Alexander,' enthusiastically as one.

Austin finished his uncharacteristically short speech with, 'I look forward to seeing you all dancing after dinner, bon appetit.' Austin sat down and the gaggle of gossip started, with many very obviously looking and pointing at the top table.

'Just as I thought,' Anita said to Marcus, incisively, as a mountain of food was placed in the middle of the table in front of them.

Anita managed to make it through dinner without enraging Austin. He asked her a series of probing question, such as how Alexander had managed to run so fast at the Chase when he had never previously displayed Body skills quite like it. Anita's reply had been that maybe it was just that she had had to slow down to Alexander's speed as her energy metre was broken, although this was definitely a lie. He asked about Anita's family life and her parents in a way that made Anita suspect he already knew the answers. He asked why Marcus had kept it a secret that he was bringing Anita, to which she replied that she didn't know. But most oddly, he seemed very interested in her relationship with Helena, and why, given her considerable Body skills, Anita had chosen not to become an academic. Anita told him the truth; that she had wanted to study the energy and Alistair had given her a job at the Observatory around the same time, but he didn't seem satisfied with her answer. Luckily, at that point, Gwyn interrupted with some inane comment, shooting Anita a deathly glare and drawing Austin into conversation with her. Anita couldn't have been more pleased and turned towards Marcus, to make sure that by the time Austin turned back to her, she would be engaged in another conversation.

As she turned, she spotted Cleo speaking animatedly with the man to her right and Henry trying desperately to get involved. Anita laughed inwardly. She also glanced in Bas' direction, who was, ever the gentleman, doing his best to chat to Missy, although this appeared to be a struggle. Alistair, she noticed, still seemed like he wasn't really in the mood for a party. Marcus was discussing the Chase with the girl to his left, and on the other side of her, Alexander was talking in low tones with Helena. Anita sat for a moment, looking down at her food, following the ebb and flow of Alexander's energy as he conversed with Helena. Surprisingly, she found this comforting.

Alexander became aware that he was being observed and turned a little to see who it was. The last thing he needed was Austin watching him when he was speaking intently with Helena. He relaxed when he saw both Austin and Marcus deep in conversation and his energy picked up a bit when he realised it must be Anita. He didn't bother to hide his reaction, so she felt it, but she didn't let on. He focused on Anita and she felt a warm pressure at the edge of her energy field. She had never felt anything like it before and looked up cautiously to see what was happening, but Alexander had turned swiftly back to his conversation with Helena.

After three, enormous courses and a significant quantity of various types of wine, Anita decided it was time to open the dancing. In line with tradition, there would be no announcement, but Anita and Marcus would take to the floor at a time of their choosing, throwing a signal to the band and surprising the audience by launching into their dance.

Anita reached over and took Marcus' hand under the table. She inclined her head in the direction of the open space between the banquet tables and he smiled in agreement. He led Anita around the top table, waving to the band as they passed. The band immediately sprang into life, striking up a jaunty number and the room quietened in expectant anticipation. Anita could hardly contain her excitement. She loved to dance and leaving Marcus by the edge of the tables, she spun her way to the middle of the floor. Marcus ran after her and caught her just as she stopped spinning, leant her backwards seductively, then restored her to an upright position in a slow, fluid, silky movement. They smiled at each other as they came back face to face, each reminded of their dance on the cliff, before Marcus almost violently spun Anita out and back in again. They tangoed around the floor, paying no attention to their audience, who watched open-mouthed at the display. They had all expected a polite waltz to start proceedings, and certainly no one had expected this.

After a couple of minutes of the borderline inappropriate spectacle, complete with too much body contact, a number of improper looks and all topped off by the suggestive backing track, the others eligible to join the first dance got up and made their way to the floor. All expect Austin, whose face was like thunder as he watched his son's embarrassing exhibition with the girl he was beginning to hate. Marcus and Anita finished their opener with a flourish, Marcus spinning Anita around so they were back to back before lifting her high on his shoulders, her arms outstretched. He spun several times before letting her slide back to the floor, having masterfully positioned them to join the set laid out by the others in preparation for the formal dancing, kissing her hand racily and throwing her one last risqué look as they took their places.

This part was a group dance, where two couples danced a set routine together before moving round to dance with another pair. The band changed the tone significantly, launching into what was almost a jig. Marcus and Anita started with Alexander and his date; Anita still had no idea what she was called. First Anita and Marcus, and Alexander and his date danced a few steps with each other, then they all danced a few steps together, before they swapped partners for a couple of twirls. Anita took Alexander's proffered hand when it came to the partner swap and immediately felt a tingle of energy run through her. If he felt it too he didn't let on, looking her indifferently in the eyes for the whole time they danced together, Anita frustrated that she had no idea at all what he was thinking.

The music went on and Anita and Marcus cycled through many more couples, including Gwyn and her date (which Gwyn made sure was uncomfortable), Cleo and Henry, where Cleo threw Anita so many 'meaningful' looks, she presumed both about Henry, and Anita and Marcus' dance, that Anita almost burst out laughing, and Bas and Missy. Not only did Missy look boring, she was also an uninspiring dancer and she moved in a stiff, uncomfortable way. Bas, on the other hand, danced easily and gracefully, and lifted and twirled Anita when they came to dance together, embellishing the set routine and looking dashing whilst he did it. Anita beamed at him as they moved on.

The dance came to a close when Anita and Marcus met up with Alexander and his date again. The band finished their jig with a flourish and the couples bowed and curtsied to each other. Alexander immediately led his date away and Marcus took hold of Anita's elbow and steered her as far away from Austin as it was possible to be; Austin's expression had not gone unnoticed, especially not by Marcus. He led Anita out through the doors of the great hall, across the lobby and into another very large room, with a bar that, during the day, had views over where Anita and Marcus had danced by the cliff edge. Marcus grabbed two glasses of Ginger Champagne from the barman, handed one to Anita and headed for the open door out onto the balcony.

'You do like to ruffle feathers, don't you,' said Marcus, with mock disapproval, his eyes telling another story.

'Me?' Anita shot back flirtily. 'I think you'll find you were leading.'

'Well, we'll just have to agree to blame the band then, who, for some reason, selected a raunchy number for the first dance.' He said it innocently, over-emphasising the shrugging of his shoulders and the perplexed look across his face.

Anita's eyes flew open, 'that was you?' she accused, punching his arm not quite hard enough to cause any harm.

'I don't know what you're talking about,' he protested, raising his arms in surrender, confirming that he knew exactly what she was talking about. Luckily for Marcus, before Anita could launch a proper attack, a squeal invaded the air and Cleo bounded over to Anita and wrapped her arms around her.

'You. Looked. A-MAZING,' she sang. 'You should have seen everyone watching you. I cannot believe you just did that. But the way your dress kicked out…definitely a great choice, and he isn't a half bad dancer either,' she gushed, nodding her head in Marcus' direction and squeezing his arm.

'Thanks,' replied Marcus, rolling his eyes and telling himself to be patient during the lengthy debrief of the night so far that he knew was about to follow.

*****

Alexander had finally managed to ditch his date. She'd proven a great deal more clingy than he'd expected, so it had taken a bit of work, but luckily, Cleo seemed to have done the same thing to Henry, so Alexander had left her with him. He made his way into the library, where thankfully, no one else had ventured, and helped himself to a shimmering crystal glass full of Austin's brandy. He sat down heavily in a chair by the open doors onto the balcony and contemplated the night's events so far.

Firstly there was the conversation he'd overheard two of Austin's security guards having just before the procession. They'd been talking about Austin's hit list, and it was clear from what he'd overheard that Anita was at the top of it. Austin was always scouring for powerful people, to either recruit or get rid of, but this search seemed to be more frenzied than ever before. Alexander assumed it must have something to do with the bloodline; was Anita the girl Christiana had wanted to find? Austin obviously knew more

84

about why Christiana had wanted to come to Empire than Alexander did, but Alexander couldn't think of a way to tap him for information. His trip to the Archives had left him with nothing to work with, so he'd had to put his investigation on hold until he could come up with another place to look.

Then there was his conversation at dinner with Helena. She'd pretty much tried to recruit him into the Institution; a bold move under any circumstances, but downright dangerous under Austin's roof and right under his nose. Austin hated the Institution and would no doubt hate them even more at the moment, with the controversy around the prophecy. And then there was Anita. Her energy was extraordinary, like nothing he had ever felt before. It had such a strong mix of Body and Spirit that it would be strange for her to be a Body Descendant, not that there was any guarantee that was who Christiana had been looking for. He recalled the tingle he'd felt when they'd touched, something he had never personally felt before; it was extremely rare. He'd heard others talk about a tingling sensation, or a jolt, but had never known anyone that had experienced them and no one knew what caused them.

Anita fascinated him, and although he was trying to keep it firmly hidden, he found himself drawn to her. She was reckless. The way she'd won the Chase, exposing her reader abilities to everyone, and the way she'd danced around the floor earlier, were both incredible, but would only serve to enrage Austin, and she was already in an extremely dangerous position. Alexander was relying on Marcus to keep her out of harm's way, but with stunts like this evening, that would be increasingly difficult. Austin hadn't even tried to hide his fury.

Alexander's thoughts were interrupted by voices on the balcony moving in his direction. 'I'm looking for Alexander, have you seen him?' came a whiny female voice that Alexander recognised as his date's. In one swift movement, Alexander got up from the worn leather chair and silently made his way to the library's side door. He ducked through just as the voices reached the window, and headed for the stairs. Only Descendants and a handful of the senior Councillors would dare to go upstairs in Austin's castle without permission, so he reasoned he should be safe up there. Alexander took the steps two at a time and turned left when he reached the top. He headed out onto a large internal balcony that wrapped its way around the four sides of a courtyard below.

This was his favourite part of Austin's castle. The courtyard was exposed to the night sky, however the balcony was covered, with pillars all the way around holding up the roof. The pillars had climbing plants crawling all over them, with wispy braches covered in flowers falling down onto the stone benches below. This was the creation of Marcus' mother, Amelia, and in Alexander's opinion was a perfect demonstration of why Austin and Amelia now lived separate lives. Whereas Austin was transactional and controlling, Amelia was kind with far-reaching openness, just like the plants she grew. Alexander walked round to the far side of the balcony and lay down on one of the stone benches there, placing the brandy glass, that he had luckily had the foresight to pick up during his escape, on the floor. Hopefully nobody would find him up here. He found it wearing being around other people for too long, with all their energy waves bouncing around. It was a relief to be on his own, where he could think without the interruption of the energy of others.

However, he'd been lying there for only a few minutes, listening to the silence, with the occasional muffled screech from downstairs, when he heard the courtyard door below creek open, and what sounded like two sets of cautious footsteps make their way though. Alexander easily picked up their energy, one anxious and the other angry.

'What is it?' questioned a fierce voice, that Alexander recognised as Alistair's. 'I thought we agreed never to talk about this again.'

The anxious person didn't immediately reply, pacing around the courtyard to make sure there was no one else there. They couldn't see Alexander from the courtyard and as there didn't appear to be anyone else present, the second person replied. 'That was before Austin went on his most recent vendetta.' Alexander was surprised to hear Peter's thin voice and his interest piqued. What could shy, pathetic, Peter possibly be wrapped up in?

'What is that supposed to mean?' asked Alistair edgily, surprise clear in his voice.

'It means that Austin has put together a hit list of powerful girls of between about twenty-three and twenty-seven years of age. He's trying to track her down to finish off the prophecy for good.' Alexander could not believe his ears. What could Peter possibly know about what Austin was looking for? Had Christiana told him? But at least it confirmed their being here did have something to do with the prophecy and therefore the bloodline.

'But how does he know?' Alistair spat.

'Well he obviously knew she got away, but he always assumed she would never resurface. When Christiana told him why she wanted to come to Empire, Austin went crazy. He ordered Amber to double her 'researchers' and gave her until we leave Empire to track the missing girl down.'

'And?' said Alistair. 'He doesn't know?' The concern in his voice palpable.

'No. Not for sure, but she's at the top of his hit list. Just her winning the Chase would have been enough to keep her there, but her reader stunt has wound him into a frenzy, and he wasn't exactly hiding his feelings about the display earlier. She's signing her own death warrant. You've got to do something.'

Alexander could not believe his ears. How did Alistair and Peter know anything about this? And more importantly, why was it Alistair's responsibility to do something about it?

'And what exactly do you suggest I do?'

'Take her into the Wild Lands and keep her there.'

Alistair laughed. 'Aside from the obvious difficulty of kidnapping someone as adept as Anita, how do you suggest I keep here there? Lock her up? Stay there and supervise her myself?'

'Persuade her to go with you. Say you're going on a trip to record the energy or something.'

'That would never fool her, or my son. And even if it did work, there's the obvious problem that Marcus seems totally besotted with her. You think he would just let her go? Never forget that he is Austin's son, regardless of how much of Amelia he has in him. He'll turn out to be just as ruthless and just as possessive. You can see that just in the way he looks at her.'

'Well, you have got to do something, otherwise, she's going to wind up dead.'

Alistair turned angry. 'We should never have got involved in the first place, and anything we do now to try and save her will be the final nail in her coffin, exposing us along with her. Listen to me very carefully Peter. Do nothing. Absolutely nothing, you hear me? Do not so much as mention her name to anyone. Do not try and contact anyone who knows about this. And never, I repeat, never, talk to me about this ever again, unless you want to wind up dead as well.' A silent chill filled the courtyard as the enormity of Alistair's words sunk in. Alistair turned sharply and left, furious. Peter, now beside himself with worry, hung around for a few minutes pacing up and down, getting his emotions under control before following him out. Alexander lay there in shock; he couldn't quite believe what he'd just heard. Anita was a Descendant? That was the only thing they could have meant, unless there was some other way to fulfil the prophecy, and everyone knew there was only one way; the Descendants had to send back the relic. Either way, Anita was in serious trouble.

*****

Marcus endured a few more minutes of Cleo's overexcited squealing before cutting past her, placing his hand firmly on Anita's waist and drawing her away. 'If you will excuse us Cleo, there's something I promised to show Anita.'

Cleo raised an eyebrow at Anita, her embarrassment causing her face to flush a soft shade of red, as she was guided back inside, past the bar and up the stairs. 'You promised to show me something?' Anita scorned. 'Was that the best you could come up with?'

'Does that girl ever get tired of talking?' he asked, ignoring Anita's comeback.

'Not that I've ever witnessed,' Anita smiled.

'And anyway, there is something I want to show you.'

'Oh?' Anita looked at him warily.

'This way,' he said, when they reached the top of the imposing staircase, his hand refusing to leave her waist as he opened a vast door and ushered Anita through in front of him. They were in a large sitting room, with floor to ceiling windows and light curtains that wafted softly in the breeze, seeming to invite them out onto the balcony beyond. The balcony was directly above the one they'd been standing on outside the bar. Anita looked at Marcus, her eyebrows raised expectantly. 'This is my suite,' he said, by way of explanation. 'I wanted you to have a good view.'

'Of what?' she asked, exasperated.

He led her out onto the balcony just as the night sky lit up with an explosion of twinkling lights. 'Of that,' he smiled.

Anita walked open-mouthed to the stone railing and leant against it as the next release of energy hit the sky. It was beautiful. Anita had never seen anything like it, and not only could she see the smoky, shimmering lights, she could feel them as well. It was extraordinary, a series of small bursts that felt like popping candy on her skin.

Marcus couldn't take his eyes off her; a light seemed to radiate from her as she watched the display. He walked up behind her, placing his hands either side of her waist. 'I thought you'd like it,' he murmured, as he bent his lips to the base of her neck and gently brushed them against her delicate skin. The movement sent delicious shivers of energy down Anita's spine, all the way to her toes, then back up to rest where Marcus' fingers lay on her waist. Could he feel that too? Not that she currently cared; she was too preoccupied with the energy display to bring it up. Marcus slipped his hands around Anita's waist and pulled her back towards him. She didn't fight him, leaning her head back against his shoulder, resting her hands on his arms. They watched the rest of the display in silence, Anita's skin greedily drinking in this new sensory excitement.

It ended, and Marcus drew her back inside, her skin still tingling, both from the, now phantom, energy bursts, and the continued contact between Marcus' skin and hers. 'We had better go back downstairs,' he said softly, 'unless we want to give the gossip mill something else to talk about.'

Anita smiled in agreement, hiding her disappointment. 'I suppose you have a point. I'm just going to use your bathroom, and I'll join you down there. I'm assuming you have a bathroom up here?'

'Through the bedroom,' he said, pointing to the right. 'You might want to wait a while before coming to find me. I'm going to go and find dad to apologise. It's definitely better to do it when the castle is full of people, and hopefully he'll be full of Ginger Champagne or something stronger by now.'

Anita laughed. 'Good luck,' she said, heading for the bedroom. Marcus watched her go before making his way back downstairs.

To her surprise, Marcus' bedroom had windows on both sides. One side looking out onto the balcony where they'd just been standing and the other leading to who knew where. Other than that, the bedroom was pretty much exactly what Anita had expected. There was an enormous four-poster bed, covered with the most comfortable looking duvet and pillows Anita had ever seen. The bed had been turned down and there was a sprig of lavender on the pillow. Of course, thought Anita, they have people to turn down their beds! The rest of the room was relatively simple. There was a large wooden chest at the end of the bed, a simple mahogany dressing table in front of the balcony window, and a round table with a chessboard inlaid, with beautiful, simple, gold and silver chess pieces on top. The pieces had been left in the middle of a game and Anita found herself wondering who Marcus brought in here to play with him.

Once she'd freshened up in the bathroom, which was also exactly what she had expected, complete with spectacular roll top bath, Anita headed back into the bedroom. She couldn't resist seeing what was on the other side of the mystery windows, so walked over to have a look. As she approached what she could now see were, in fact, doors, she felt powerful energy coming from the other side. Peeking through the curtains, Anita found Alexander's familiar, delectable form lying on a stone bench on a balcony, and without hesitation, she opened the door and stepped through. Alexander had felt her energy before she'd opened the door and sat up as she appeared.

'Anita,' Alexander blurted, both his tone and his body language communicating his surprise. He obviously thought Marcus was about to emerge, she thought to herself.

'Hi,' she said hesitantly, for once managing to keep her energy under control. Probably something to do with her curiosity as to why he was out here, not to mention all the alcohol she'd consumed. 'What are you doing here?' she asked quietly.

'Getting away from everyone downstairs,' he answered truthfully. 'Sometimes all the energy waves get a bit much.'

'I know that feeling,' she smiled back warmly. 'Where's your date?' she asked, relishing the opportunity to fish for more information about this mysterious man. 'What was she called again?'

'Patricia.' Alexander's face cracked into a clandestine smile. 'She's probably got a search party out looking for me by now. Excruciatingly boring and wildly stuck up,' he exclaimed. 'I only agreed to come with her as a favour to her father, and now I can't get rid of her!'

'I see,' she said, raising her eyebrows, surprised by this sudden rush of information.

'Anyway, what are you doing up here? I'm surprised Marcus let you out of his sight after your show earlier.' Alexander was as brisk as he could manage, but he too wanted to find out more about his unexpected companion, the girl who was supposedly the rightful Body Descendant.

Alexander's upfront appraisal took her by surprise. It was one thing to think things like that, but quite another to just come out with them. She paused, taking the time to carefully sit down next to him, just far enough away to mean there was no actual skin contact, but close enough for them both to be agonisingly aware of the other's proximity on the cold stone bench. 'He's gone to find Austin to apologise for our dance,' she said honestly. 'Judging by the way Austin was glaring at us, I can't image it's going to go especially well.'

'No, I wouldn't have thought so,' Alexander said slowly, studying her quizzically. 'Austin is a dangerous man to cross you know, and you've done it several times now.'

Anita smirked offhandedly. 'Why does it matter? You'll all go back to Kingdom in a couple of days and Austin will forget he ever knew I existed,' as will the rest of you, she finished dejectedly in her mind.

'Is that really how you think this will play out?' he asked, clearly shocked at her brazen response.

'Yes,' she said firmly.

Alexander propelled himself to his feet and turned to face Anita. 'Anita, Austin doesn't just forget about people like you. You're powerful. Very powerful, and as I've told you before, you'd be a valuable asset for someone like him. Austin isn't the only one who's interested in you, especially after your display at the Chase, and after tonight's performance, you'll take some forgetting. Austin will view what you did as a public humiliation. Not only did you have the audacity to turn up here tonight with his son, you proceeded to make a spectacle of the first dance. People will be talking about that for years, and Austin will take a very long time to forget you, that's if he ever forgets you.' Alexander's tone had turned and the mood between them had shifted from open and light-hearted to separated and a little fierce.

'So what?' He was lecturing her, and she didn't like it. 'Even if he doesn't forget me, what's he going to do? And what do you mean I could be a valuable asset? And who else is interested in me? I have no idea what your riddles mean,' she said crossly, mainly at herself, because she hated it when she couldn't quite keep up.

Alexander took a frustrated step away from her, running his hands through his dishevelled hair. How could she be so blind? 'Did you see the woman downstairs with ginger hair?' he snapped, turning round with a sharp purpose that Anita found distractingly attractive. 'The one that always seems to be hanging around not too far from Austin?' Anita nodded dumbly; now she thought about it,there did always seem to be a woman fitting that description hanging around. 'That's Amber, and she's head of Austin's private security and research team.'

'His what?! What does Austin research?' Anita laughed emptily, still unable to connect the dots.

Alexander threw Anita a menacing look, wiping the smile from her lips. 'He researches people like you, Anita, powerful people who he wants to either use or get rid of.'

The words landed and Anita went pale. 'What do you mean 'get rid of'?' she asked quietly, the wind snatched from her sails.

'I mean kill, Anita.' Alexander rounded on her to bang the point home, only just managing to resist shaking her, wanting to physically knock the naivety out of her.

Anita looked up at him confused. 'Kill?' the word hung in the air like a threat. 'And Marcus? Does he want to use me or kill me too?!'

'No,' he said quickly, almost reassuringly, a shadow flashing behind his eyes that Anita had neither the ability nor the inclination to process in the current circumstances. 'Marcus doesn't know the full extent of Austin's activities. Either that or he ignores them. Your best bet is to stay as close to Marcus as you possibly can. Austin won't risk losing Marcus, not in the current climate anyway.'

'Won't risk losing him?' she asked, as she would have if he'd just told her that aliens had landed in Empire; a mix of disbelief and misunderstanding.

Alexander couldn't quite believe he had to spell this out for her. 'If Marcus falls in love with you, which he seems well on his way to doing by the way, and he finds out that Austin is a threat to you, there's a risk that Marcus will choose you over Austin, which could drive a split through the Mind line. Austin can't afford for that to happen in the current climate. He needs all the support he can get, and he'd rapidly lose supporters if there were another internal rift in his family. He suffered too many defectors when he and Amelia separated; Austin won't risk what might happen if he were to lose Marcus too.' He said the words quickly, as though this were the most obvious thing in the world, something one just had to quickly recap to clarify.

'What do you mean defectors?' she demanded. He was making her feel obtuse, and she was nothing of the sort.

'You really know nothing do you?'

'It would appear not,' Anita sparked, standing up too, turning her back on Alexander and walking over to lean against the railing, now pretty pissed off.

Alexander softened a little; he supposed it wasn't entirely her fault that she was so oblivious to what made the world go round.

92

He took a deep breath. 'The Descendants rule by right; that much is true. But that doesn't mean we don't have politics. We're not the only influential players. The Academics and the Councillors are both formidable groups in their own right. They have powerful individuals, those with significant energy, and they know secrets about various Descendants; secrets we wouldn't want to get out. Amelia was a senior Mind academic when she and Austin married, which brought Austin some significant supporters. Those supporters defected when they split. Marcus didn't bring supporters with him when he was born obviously, but another rift may cause Austin to lose more support; something that he would clearly like to avoid.'

'But what if Austin lost all his supporters? What difference would it make?'

'Worst case scenario? It could lead to a total loss of confidence in the current system, especially if it coincided with a large drop in the energy. Ring any bells? Ultimately, it could lead to an uprising and the Descendants being overthrown.'

Anita gave him an amazed look; was he mad? 'But that would never happen. It would mean we'd never have a chance to be free of the Gods.'

'The prophecy may already be broken, and some may think it's better to take an eternity with the Gods than a lifetime with the Descendants. The balance is fragile, far more fragile than most people realise. Austin, on the other hand, is only too aware of its fragility, so the safest place for you is next to Marcus.'

'And if I don't want to be next to Marcus?' she challenged fiercely, spinning round to look at him.

'You do,' he replied simply. 'I can read your energy, remember?'

'Don't worry, I remember,' she said, searching his eyes intensely, looking for some indication that he reacted the same way to her as she normally did to him, before dramatically changing the subject. 'How do you hide your energy?'

Alexander looked taken aback. 'What do you mean?'

'Do I have to spell it out for you?' she said, trying to recover some of the upper hand. Alexander was surprised at her choice of words. He didn't say anything but held her gaze until she continued. 'You have extremely powerful energy, but I've only felt glimpses of your true power. Most of the time you hide it, or suppress it, or something. You've told me I need to get my energy under control, so I'm asking how.'

'It's not quite as simple as that,' he replied. 'It takes practise, and I'd have to show you; it's not something I can just tell you.'

'Then show me,' she said insistently.

'Now is not the time, and I'm pretty sure Marcus wouldn't be too pleased about me showing you.'

'Why not?' she asked, surprised.

'He's like a child with a toy. He doesn't like to share. Now, if you will excuse me, I should probably go and find my date and offer to take her home.' Alexander headed back inside, but paused and turned back to Anita just before he reached the door. 'Do not tell anyone about this conversation, especially not Marcus. Do not let on you have any idea about any kind of politics. Do not try to find out more about any of this. Stay as close to Marcus as you possibly can; make him fall in love with you, and above all, avoid Amber and her henchmen at all costs.' With that, he disappeared through the door, leaving Anita feeling infuriated, confused, deflated, excited, full of questions, and above all, intrigued. She had to get him to show her how to hide her energy, if for no other reason than so she could spend more time with him.

Anita was still preoccupied when she reached the top of the stairs and almost bumped into Marcus who had just ascended them. He reached out and grabbed her waist to stop them from colliding. 'I was going to send out a search party,' he teased, leaning his head flirtily down towards her, the woody smell of cigars on his breath.

'Sorry,' she breathed, trying to pull herself together, 'I was just admiring your suite and enjoying the time away from prying eyes. How did it go with Austin?'

'It could have been worse,' he shrugged flippantly, quickly changing the subject. 'I think we should get you a drink,' he said, leading her back downstairs and into the bar. Marcus handed Anita a glass of Ginger Champagne before they joined Bas, Cleo, Missy, Henry and to Anita's surprise, Gwyn, on a group of sofas around a low table in front of the fire. Cleo was leaning against Henry; she's changed her tune since earlier, thought Anita, and Bas, Missy and Gwyn were sitting awkwardly on the opposite sofa, Bas clearly not quite sure what to do with his arms, wedged between the two girls. Marcus and Anita sat down next to each other on a third sofa, their legs touching. Marcus stretched out an arm on the back of the sofa behind them, and Anita leaned in a little to get comfortable. They sat there chatting and laughing for hours; Henry throwing in pompous comments every now and again, Bas tutting about how much energy was wasted on the display, Missy barely saying a word,

Gwyn paying Bas a little more attention than was strictly necessary, and Cleo shoehorning in as many provocative comments as she could. Marcus and Anita laughed easily along with the rest of them, but Anita couldn't shake the feeling they were being observed the whole time. Amber was nowhere to be seen, but Alexander's earlier warning had made her uneasy.

Eventually, Bas got up and indicated it was time to leave. He was taking Missy, Cleo and Henry back to Empire and offered to take Anita too. Anita nodded. 'That would be great, thanks Bas.' Marcus looked crestfallen as he walked them to the front door, where Bas' car was waiting. The others climbed in, but Marcus pulled Anita back towards him. A look of panic swept across her face, concerned that Marcus would try to kiss her here in front of everyone, including Amber, who had just appeared at the door. But instead, he drew her hand to his lips. He bowed his head then looked brazenly up at her. 'Good night Anita,' he whispered playfully, before closing his eyes and brushing her knuckles with his lips.

'Good night Marcus,' Anita murmured imprudently, before climbing into the car with the others, to be whisked away down the magnificent drive and back to Empire.

*****

Anita was the first to be dropped off; they let her out at the end of Cordelia's road so they wouldn't have to make the tight turn outside the cottage. Anita climbed out of the car and called her goodbyes to its drunken occupants, picking her way along the short distance back to the gate. She had given up on her shoes and was carrying them in one hand, holding up her dress, which was now too long, with the other. She was a little dishevelled, wisps of hair, having escaped their pins, falling around her face, and her mind was foggy from all the wine. It was misty and the only light came from the moon, Anita glad she knew the road like the back of her hand; she could have made it blindfolded. As she approached the cottage, she felt powerful energy up ahead and immediately tensed, on guard. She kept moving cautiously towards the house, trying to make as little noise as possible, until, out of the mist, emerged a familiar, lean figure leaning against the garden wall. The figure was clad in a dinner jacket with his bow tie and top button undone, and Anita stopped dead when she saw him.

'Marcus?' she asked, a little confused.

95

'Hi,' he said, smiling secretly when he saw her, pushing himself easily off the wall and walking tantalisingly towards her.

'What are you doing here?' she asked, laughing lightly, her eyes flirtatious.

He stopped just in front of her and sent her a soft, teasing smile. 'You forgot something,' he said scathingly, his energy building, an electric tension filling the air between them, seeming to draw them together.

She didn't say a thing, looking provocatively into his chocolate brown eyes as he brushed a stray strand of hair seductively behind her ear. He dropped his fingers casually to her neck, caressing the soft skin below her ear, a dangerous smile dancing across his enticing lips before pulling her slowly towards him, bowing his head to meet her waiting mouth. She felt shivers of energy pass between them as they kissed. He tasted of cigars and ginger, his other hand reaching for her cheek, pulling her voraciously to him, his tongue probing impatiently against hers. Anita was lost; the ground seemed to disappear, her head began to spin, her senses useless as she responded to his touch. She regained her composure as Marcus pulled back, both hands now on her cheeks, his face an inch from hers, hungry eyes bearing down on her, full of unsated desire. She dropped her gaze and raised her hands to his waist, running them alluringly up his toned torso to his chest, where they pushed him sensuously backwards. She left her hands on him as she looked up heatedly, her eyes on fire, her silent rejecting yet enticing challenge plain. He held her gaze, a carnal smile accepting, as she leaned back in for a short, final, calculated kiss. 'Goodnight Marcus,' she whispered, in a slow, sultry voice, before brushing past him.

'Good night,' he replied elated, matching her tone as she veered off the path and around the back of the cottage. There was nothing Marcus loved more than the thrill of the chase.

CHAPTER 8

Anderson climbed back down the pole they'd erected just outside one of the trading posts in the Wild Lands and scooped Arabella up into a bear hug when he got to the bottom. He planted a kiss squarely on her lips before she pushed him away in mock exasperation.

'You're in a good mood,' she said. 'Only the Gods know what you'll be like if we ever actually find anything.' She raised her eyes and looked hopefully at the receiver dish on top of the pole. 'Chances we'll find anything here?' she asked, knowing full well what Anderson's answer would be. He was eternally optimistic and never seemed deterred when a site left them empty handed.

'As good as our chances anywhere,' he beamed at her.

Both Arabella and Anderson were around thirty years old, but where Arabella was short, carrying a little more weight then she would have liked, with long, dark hair, Anderson was a tall, skinny man with an unkempt ginger mop. He was a relic specialist. In fact, he was now the only remaining relic specialist and nobody really knew how he got away with it. Austin had put a stop to any relic research several years back, and Philip and Christiana hadn't put up much of a fight to try and stop him. Anderson had devoted his entire life to studying the relic, trying to work out how to send it back and free the world. It wasn't that he wanted to be a hero, quite the opposite, he never coveted attention for his research, and there were very few people who even knew he existed, which was probably one of the reasons Austin left him alone. Anderson had just always been fascinated by the mystery of the relic and wanted to solve its puzzle. Anyway, he'd never found anything better to do with his life and it meant he was able to travel the world with Arabella, so he wouldn't change one thing about what he did, even if they very rarely took any steps forward in their research.

They were currently at the spot on exactly the other side of the world from where the relic lay, to see if the energy there was any different to anywhere else. They'd put the receiver up at a number of spots along the way, finding nothing significant at all. His expectation that they would find something here was pretty low, but they had to try.

*****

Anita woke up to the delicious smell of bacon cooking downstairs. She got out of bed and decided to skip her usual early morning yoga session, given that she was feeling a little delicate after all the ginger wine, and headed straight to the kitchen. Cordelia was standing over the stove singing to herself and turned when she heard Anita come in.

'Morning,' she said cheerily.

'Morning,' replied Anita. 'What's got into you?' Cordelia was not a morning person, in that it was usually difficult to get her to be cheerful about anything before about eleven o'clock and at least three cups of tea, but today she seemed positively sparkling.

'You got home late last night,' Cordelia chirped, ignoring Anita's remark.

'That's why you're happy? Because I got home late last night?!'

'So, tell me all about it,' she said, putting an enormous plate of sausages, bacon and eggs down in front of Anita.

'There's not much to tell really,' she shrugged. 'We ate, we danced, we drank and then I came home.'

'Really. You expect me to believe that's all? You can't think of anything else you might like to tell me?'

Anita shot Cordelia a curious look. 'What else do you think happened exactly?'

Cordelia changed tack. Mildly subtle wasn't working, so she may as well go for the obvious approach. 'And Marcus? Any news there?'

'Any news? You're going to have to be a little more specific.'

Cordelia huffed; why did she have to be so damned difficult? 'Do you think you will see him again?'

Cordelia didn't need to wait long to get her answer, as at that moment, there was a knock on the back door, followed by Marcus' polished voice saying, 'hello?'.

Anita jumped up and ran out of the kitchen, throwing Cordelia a look which clearly said 'don't you dare follow me'. She approached the open back door saying, 'hi! What are you doing here?' as casually as she could.

Marcus leaned in and gave Anita a deep, enthusiastic kiss. 'It's lovely to see you too,' he said, as he pulled away. 'Can I smell breakfast?' he asked, grabbing Anita's hand as he pushed past her, dragging her behind him towards the kitchen.

Cordelia couldn't contain her excitement when she saw them enter. 'Marcus, how lovely to meet you. I'm Cordelia, Anita's grandmother. She's told me all about you,' she lied convincingly.

Marcus flashed a charming smile, replying, 'it's an absolute pleasure to meet you too,' whilst shaking her hand.

Anita gave Cordelia a stern look from where she was standing behind Marcus, before saying, 'Cordelia was just leaving, weren't you Cordelia?' Anita placed her hand on Marcus' arm to draw his attention away from her grandmother. 'She was just about to take Thorn for a walk. You remember Thorn?' she said with relish, denying Cordelia the chance to dispute her story.

'Yes, I certainly do,' said Marcus, shooting Anita a devilish smile.

Cordelia, who Anita had to admit, did at least know how to take a hint, rolled her eyes heavily as she placed a second plate of food down on the table. 'There you go, Marcus. Come on Thorn. See you later Anita,' she said, barely trying to hide her disappointment as she set off out of the back door with her dog, more than a little put out.

Anita and Marcus finished breakfast, then Marcus waited downstairs while Anita got dressed. She had lessons today, so he said he would walk her to the Temples as he had to go there anyway.

'How did you get here so quickly last night?' Anita asked, as they left the house. 'We came straight here, but you got here first.'

Marcus smiled and looked pleased with himself. 'There's a back way that cuts across our estate, so nobody uses it. It's much more direct,' he said smugly.

But of course, thought Anita. They walked on in silence for a few minutes before she said, 'so, what did Austin say last night?'

Marcus didn't reply for several paces, seeming to contemplate what to tell her. 'He wasn't exactly happy. He thought the dance was totally inappropriate and made a mockery of the occasion, and he blamed you for leading me astray.' Marcus smiled at Anita as he said the last bit and Anita raised an eyebrow, both of them acknowledging the absurdity of his assumption. 'Amber, dad's Chief of Security and Research, was there too; he's always worse when she's around. She really brings out his unpleasant side. Anyway, long and short of it, dad doesn't like you. He thinks you're a bad influence and not the sort of person that a future Descendant should be hanging around with, let alone going out with.'

Anita ignored the 'going out with' bit; they could deal with that later. 'So he must be annoyed that you came here last night and again this morning?' she probed.

'He doesn't know,' he said honestly, 'but even if he did, he can't stop me from seeing you, or anyone else I want to see for that matter. Sooner or later he's got to realise I'm not twelve years old any longer and he can't dictate what I do and who I see.'

'I'm not sure he wants to realise that.'

'He doesn't have a choice.'

'So, how come the Descendants get to skip weekend classes when the rest of us have to suffer?' Anita firmly changed the subject, trying to brighten the mood.

'Because they make us study three times as hard as everyone else when we're children. When you lot were all running around playing after school, we were still in lessons learning how to be Descendants. We're not born with all the skills we have; a lot of them are taught. I mean, obviously, something like Alexander's ability to read energy you're either born with or without a tendency towards, but pretty much everything can be learned, if you work hard enough. Descendants have to be adept in all disciplines, which means we have to work hard when we're growing up to get there. It was bad back when I was eight, but it does have its advantages now, like, for example, not having to go to school at the weekend.'

'So that's why you were all at the front of the Chase?' she asked happily, the pieces all falling into place.

'Yep.'

'So even though I'm appallingly bad at Mind disciplines, there could be hope for me yet?' Anita joked.

'Yep, maybe even for you,' he said, smirking, shoving her playfully.

'Have you ever seen anyone move anything using just their mind?'

'Of course I have. I've done it myself once or twice.'

'Really?' said Anita, her voice heavy with scepticism.

'Really,' he replied, looking absolutely serious.

'Could you teach me?'

'It's not something you can learn to do overnight, Anita. You need to be really good at the basics first and build up to it. I've been dedicated to Mind disciplines my whole life, and I've only managed it a couple of times.'

'But we could try?' Anita wasn't sure why she even wanted to. She'd never liked Mind disciplines, but somehow private tuition with Marcus made it sound much more appealing. Besides, it was a challenge now she knew moving objects with one's mind was actually possible, although she wouldn't one hundred per cent believe it until she saw it herself.

Marcus looked at Anita. 'Would you take no for an answer?'

Anita didn't say anything. She smiled at the ground before looking Marcus defiantly in the eye.

'As I suspected,' he said, rolling his eyes. 'Yes, Anita, I suppose we could try,' he said, draping his arm around her shoulders and playfully kissing her hair.

They arrived at the Temples; Anita relieved that Marcus had removed his arm from around her shoulders by the time they got there. They ran into Cleo and Bas outside the Mind Temple, which was good, Anita thought, as it would give everyone less to talk about than if she and Marcus had walked in on their own together.

They entered the Temple, and Marcus said he would come and find Anita later, when he'd finished what he needed to do. He left them and headed for the hole in the floor, which he descended through effortlessly. Bas, Cleo and Anita sat down in seats as close to the back as they could. Anita's hangover was abating, but the other two, along with the rest of the class, didn't look in such great shape, so the lesson was pretty subdued.

The Spirit lesson was also a total waste of time, with most people requiring concentration just to stay awake, let alone do something that required as much focus as meditating.

As usual, Anita didn't attend the Body lesson, telling the others she was going for a run instead. However, as she went back passed the Spirit Temple, she thought about what Marcus had said. If someone like Gwyn could master the art of meditating, or the Mind disciplines, through nothing more than practice, then Anita was pretty sure she could too. Then there was the added benefit that if she hung around the Spirit Temple enough, she would have to bump into Alexander eventually, so she entered the Temple and picked an open space on a large rectangular mat near the back, and sat down to meditate. She closed her eyes and cleared her mind, trying to push away thoughts of kissing good looking men in the middle of the night. After about five minutes of sitting with blankness in her mind, the image of an eagle soaring high above the world glided into her thoughts. The eagle started to descend towards the ground, and Anita could see only Wild Land all around. There were no houses and no people, just heather and trees and rocks, but as the eagle swooped further downwards, she could make out a large, earth coloured yurt in a clearing. The eagle flapped its wings and Anita suddenly felt herself falling, before landing like a cat on the ground next to the yurt's entrance. It felt safe and familiar here, so she stood up and walked towards the tent, pushing aside the canvas covering the door and making her way through to the other side.

She emerged in a place that looked exactly like you would imagine the inside of a yurt to look, although oddly it was filled with light. There was a low bed covered with animal hides, several small tables and chairs made out of bits of wood lashed haphazardly together, and a rack of drying herbs. However, in the centre of the yurt, sat on top of a waist high pillar, was a brass cylinder. This looked alien, like it wasn't supposed to be there, and Anita felt suddenly uneasy. She made her way towards the cylinder, about to pick it up to see what was inside, when she felt an overwhelming urge to leave it and turn around. She turned, and to her surprise, saw Alexander sitting on the bed, hair unkempt, shirtless, revealing a glorious honed torso and wearing a pair of battered old cotton trousers. He looked amazing and it was all Anita could do to keep herself from running to the bed and jumping on top of him right there and then.

Anita's energy was at an all-time high and Alexander smiled knowingly at her. 'Anita, you need to leave the cylinder alone. You need to make it disappear. Reject it from your mind and it will go.'

He spoke to her, and she could hear him, but his lips didn't seem to move.

'Why do I need to leave it alone? What is it? Why's it here?'

'I can't explain now; we need to be careful, but trust me, you need to reject it.'

'How?'

Alexander got up and moved towards Anita. He stood in front of her so he could see the cylinder behind her back and looked into her eyes. 'Do exactly what I tell you.' Anita nodded, no idea what was going on. 'Imagine the cylinder lifting off the pillar,' he said. 'It will be difficult and heavy, but lift it up. You're strong; use your strength to raise it.' Anita concentrated. She did everything she could to lift the cylinder, but it wouldn't budge. 'Try harder Anita,' came Alexander's gentle yet firm command. She tried, but nothing she did would lift it. She could feel her energy draining and she dropped her eyes to the floor. 'Anita, look at me. I'm going to help you, but it's very important you stay focused on the cylinder, okay?' Anita nodded. Alexander reached forward and touched Anita's index finger very lightly with his, and the cylinder felt immediately light as air. She could easily lift it now and made it fly into the air behind them. 'Very good Anita. Now I need you to imagine the cylinder falling to the floor, but before it gets there, it vanishes, okay?' Anita nodded again, Alexander's finger still touching hers. She was concentrating on the cylinder falling when the mood shifted. She felt both another presence and Alexander's finger leave hers. The cylinder fell, but bounced when it hit the floor and rolled through the door out of the tent.

Alexander had disappeared, and a furious voice suddenly invaded her mind. 'What the hell do you think you're playing at?'

Anita was jolted back to the Temple and almost fainted when she got there. She looked up to see Marcus and Alexander standing over her, Marcus looking livid. 'I was teaching her a thing or two about the arts of the Spirit,' Alexander replied easily. 'Maybe you should think about doing the same with the Mind disciplines, so she's not so vulnerable to attack.'

'What?' said Anita and Marcus together.

'You attacked her?' spat Marcus, squaring up to Alexander. Anita had to suppress a smile despite the situation, as the idea that Marcus could beat Alexander in a fight was pretty funny.

'Don't be ridiculous; I didn't attack her. But given what I just saw, it wouldn't take much for someone else to try and almost certainly succeed.'

'Who would want to attack me?' asked a confused Anita. Alexander rolled his eyes, giving her a 'do we really have to recap already' look, but Marcus answered.

'It's just a good idea for you to know how to defend yourself,' he said. 'It's basic training for Descendants, and I'm not sure why it's not taught to everyone. It just means that if some crazy person tries to get into your mind, you'll know about it and will be able to defend yourself. Much as it pains me to admit it, he does have a point. I'll have to teach you.'

Alexander laughed openly. 'You think you'll be able to teach her? You can barely defend yourself, let alone teach someone else how to do it. Don't you think you should leave that to an expert?'

Marcus was livid now, both Alexander and Anita could tell from the energy steaming off him, but neither said anything, each holding their breath, waiting tensely for his answer.

'Well, I suppose, seeing as I've already agreed to teach you about the Mind disciplines, it would be a bit intense for me to teach you about the Spirit ones as well. And I'm not too proud to admit that, although I am far from a beginner, I'm not a Spirit expert. Alexander would be a more suitable candidate. But if you lay so much as one finger on her, you'll regret it.'

'Marcus, I'm not in the least bit interested in your little girlfriend here. But I am interested in someone close to you being vulnerable to attack. As you know, I would feel the same way if any other Descendant were in this position.'

'I suppose you have a point. We don't want someone getting at me via Anita.' Marcus sounded cringingly pompous, reminding Anita strongly of Austin, but she didn't say anything given how close she was to being able to spend a great deal more time with Alexander.

'Although I'll obviously be laying a finger on her in a plutonic way. As you know, some of the meditations require it.'

'There is no requirement for you to show her those poses.'

Alexander looked at Marcus as though he were a petulant child. 'Marcus, you know I need to show her every pose if she's to be properly protected.' Anita was intrigued, wondering what the offending poses were, but again thought it best to keep her thoughts to herself for the moment.

'Fine,' spat Marcus, 'but not until she is ready.'

Alexander gave Marcus a terse look and walked away. 'Meet me here tomorrow evening at seven, Anita. Marcus, don't even think about coming too.'

Marcus helped Anita up, his face like thunder. Alexander was right, he was possessive, and half of her loved it while the other half couldn't stand it. On the one hand, she wanted to spend more time with both of them, and that was what it looked like she'd be doing, and she quite liked having men fight over her, but on the other hand, she'd had no say in the matter, something she was really quite irked about. However, this didn't seem like the right moment to bring it up, so she tried to lighten the mood instead. 'So,' she said flirtatiously, 'when do we get started on my Mind lessons?' Marcus visibly perked up.

'Tomorrow morning at mine?' he replied, and she nodded, kissed him playfully on the lips, flashed him a flirty, disarming smile and sauntered out of the Temple.

*****

Anita didn't wait for the others; she hadn't been for a run and that would inevitably lead to difficult questions. Instead, she decided to run to the river to climb one of the cliffs. She hoped that would help clear her head; she'd been feeling a bit fuzzy since the meditation.

She arrived at the river lost in her thoughts, so was startled when a voice called her name.

She turned around to see Helena jogging into view. 'Helena. Hi,' she said, bemused. 'What are you doing here?'

'I thought it was a good day for a spot of climbing,' she said, descending the steep grassy slope down to the river bank where Anita stood.

'Great minds and all that,' Anita replied warmly. 'In fact, it's probably a good thing you bumped into me,' she smirked, 'at your age, it's a wonder you can still make it out here.'

'Alright, enough of that thank you,' Helena scolded. 'I'll still beat your sorry little ass up the cliff.' They smiled at each other; it was just like it used to be.

They were free climbing obviously. Body types had a healthy scorn for ropes and were half way up the cliff, just reaching a tricky overhang, when Helena casually dropped in, 'so I see you and Marcus are getting along well.'

'For the love of the Gods, not you too?'

'What do you mean, not me too?'

'I didn't have you down for a gossip.'

Helena laughed. 'No, I'm not generally, and I'm not very good at it either. I was wondering more about how Austin feels about your relations with his son? You should be careful of him you know,' she said, offhandedly, launching herself upwards to grab a hold that had been just out of reach.

'So you fall into the 'save Anita from Austin' camp,' Anita replied evenly, placing her foot and all her weight on an impossibly small crease by her waist to reach her next hold.

'There's a whole camp of us?' she said sarcastically.

'It's growing.'

'Well, I just think you should know that Austin's dangerous, and that woman Amber comes in a close second. She's very adept at getting into peoples' minds. You should stay away from her.'

'What do you mean 'getting into peoples' minds'?'

Helena looked over at Anita, glad she'd finally caught her full attention. 'I mean that, in the same way as we have Body skills not taught at a school level, there are also Mind and Spirit skills that most people don't know much about. Amber is extremely adept at a couple of particularly manipulative ones, and crucially, is exceptionally good at getting into peoples' heads. Sometimes she simply uses the power of suggestion, planting things into conversations, repeating words or phrases a number of times so people remember them unwittingly. But when she feels the situation calls for it, she's been known to launch a full-scale attack, which involves finding a way into a person's mind, such as when they're meditating, or praying to the Gods, or concentrating extremely hard on something, and planting something in there. Most people who've had this done to them will never even know about it. The only way to tell is to meditate to one's Centre and recognise something that's slightly out of place.' Helena paused while they lifted themselves over the top and sat dangling their legs over the edge, admiring the view down the river. Helena noticed Anita had gone both very quiet and a dangerous shade of grey.

'Are you alright,' she asked, concerned.

Anita paused, considering her answer. Given her meditation earlier, she wasn't entirely sure. 'And what's the purpose of planting something?' she asked.

'Well, it depends. It can be a very effective way to kill a person and make it look like they just dropped down dead, but generally, people like Austin don't care about how deaths look, given there's nobody he has to answer to. Or it can be a way of gathering information, but the tricky thing there is working out a way to extract the information, as you'd need someone with expert Mind skills to plant the idea and a skilful Spirit to extract it through meditation. Or it can be a way to store or pass information secretly between people without there being any physical evidence or conversation. For example, people used to widely use brass cylinders as a way of passing messages or storing information and then when people found them whilst meditating, they would know what they'd found. The only problem with that, of course, is that people then started to plant hostile brass cylinders as a form of attack, which were extremely effective because people thought they were safe, so would open them and immediately drop down dead. Only a handful of people practice planting and extracting any longer; the world is a much safer place now than it used to be, but most academics will know about and often practice them to keep the arts alive.'

Anita sat and contemplated what she'd just heard. After the first mention of death, she'd been on the verge of telling Helena about her experience in the Temple, but now that she'd brought up brass cylinders, Anita didn't know if this was such a great idea. 'Can you find out when something was planted? That way you could agree certain times to plant so you would know it was safe?' she eventually asked.

'No. Not unless you actually caught the person in the act. But that's very difficult to do, as you'd be concentrating extremely hard on something else whilst the plant is taking place. The only thing you can do is learn to protect your mind from attack, which means there are barriers that an attacker has to get through to plant something. And seeing as getting through barriers takes time and energy, it takes someone more skilled to do this, and obviously makes it more risky to try. You can give friendly planters clues as to how to get through the barriers, making it easier for them to plant. The Descendants are all trained to protect themselves in every way possible as they're obvious targets for attacks. However, Austin has taken this one step further and takes Amber with him everywhere he goes, just in case he feels the need to be hostile himself, which he often does.'

'So why do I need to be careful of Austin? Why would he be hostile towards me?'

'You're powerful, and it's common knowledge that Austin doesn't like having powerful people around. It makes him feel threatened, vulnerable, so he does all he can to identify and either use or rid the world of those he sees as a threat.'

'And when you say 'use'?'

'He employs them for their skills. In the same way he uses Amber's planting skills, he might want a powerful Spirit as an extractor, or a powerful Body to seduce somebody or beat someone up.'

'Seduce somebody? I would have thought that would be a Mind trick too.'

'There's a lot of cross over. Yes, Minds tend to be proficient in seduction and manipulation, but a Body can be good at seduction too. Instead of using their mind and manipulation to seduce, they simply use their bodies. In reality, people tend to have a mixture of the three Gods in them, so it's never as cut and dried as attributing certain skills only to Minds, Bodies or Spirits. You might be a strong Body but have very little Mind at all, meaning you may find seduction hard, or you may be a strong Spirit but have a lot of Mind, meaning you may be able to master both planting and extraction, or you may have a little of all three and be passable at everything but excel at not very much. There's no set formula. There are a handful of academics who research skills inheritance, but they haven't found much to go on yet. I think the most interesting research is being carried out by a very small group, who are looking at people who can give energy jolts and shivers, but they've made virtually no headway at all given how rare those abilities are, and they don't seem to follow any obvious inheritance rules.'

Anita thought about telling Helena what she'd felt when she'd kissed Marcus and touched Alexander, and ask whether that meant they had the power or that she did, but given that would mean having to tell her about the kissing, she decided to keep it to herself. Maybe she'd do a little independent research on the matter.

'Anyway, the point is that you would be wise to steer clear of Austin and Amber, which also means giving Marcus a wide berth, especially after your display the other night, spectacular as it was.'

'Thanks,' she half laughed, 'I think. And what if I decide I don't want to give Marcus a wide berth?'

'Then you're taking a tremendous risk. Marcus is Austin's son,' she turned serious, 'remember that. He's becoming more and more like him, and I wouldn't want you to get caught in the middle of that transformation.'

'It's not a foregone conclusion that he'll turn into his father,' Anita said, prickling. 'And anyway, Alexander, your fellow 'protect Anita club' member, seems to think the safest place for me is with

Marcus. You two should have some kind of 'protect Anita' convention and get your advice together.'

Helena ignored her outburst, saying cautiously, 'just how close are you and Marcus?'

'Not that close,' she replied uncomfortably, 'not that it's any of your business.' This was new territory for Anita, and she didn't like Helena prying. She'd never had to explain any of her previous relationships, probably something to do with a lack of nosey parents and living with a grandmother who protected her own privacy and therefore respected the privacy of others.

'Anita, if Alexander thinks you're safest with Marcus, then it's probably gone too far already. Marcus has always been possessive, just like Austin, which will work both in your favour and against you. It does mean that Austin's unlikely to harm you and less likely to try and recruit you, but it also means if you ever want to walk away, you could have serious problems. Marcus might not want to let you go.'

'This gets more and more crazy,' said Anita, exasperated. 'If Marcus and I have any kind of relationship, it's not like I'll suddenly belong to him.'

'That's what Amelia thought too and look at her now.'

'Marcus is not Austin.'

'And you are not Amelia.'

Anita didn't know what she meant by that, but it clearly wasn't anything good, so she didn't ask. Unfortunately, Helena seemed to think it was something Anita needed to know, so she carried on anyway.

'Amelia was, and indeed still is, an extremely adept Mind academic. When she fell in love with and married Austin, she brought a lot of influential supporters with her. When they separated, which had a lot to do with Austin turning into a carbon copy of his father, Tobias, by the way, Austin lost a lot of those supporters, but he couldn't harm Amelia, or he would risk a faction forming within the Temple of the Mind. Obviously, given how fragile the balance is at the moment, Austin should leave you alone whilst Marcus wants you, but if Marcus changes his mind, or you want to leave him, you'll be in a great deal of danger, and you don't have powerful supporters to protect you.'

'The fragility of the system seems to be the topic of the moment,' said Anita dismissively.

'Anita, the possibility of a revolution is not something to be flippant about. It could happen. The Institution is growing, and given the current bloodline situation and energy crisis, now seems like a likely time, don't you think?'

Anita looked blankly at Helena. 'The Institution?' she questioned.

Helena rolled her eyes. 'It always amazes me how little your generation knows. You lack any kind of political zeal; so unlike your parents.'

Anita wasn't sure whether Helena meant her parents specifically, or just her generation's parents in general, but she made a mental note to drop them into conversation later to find out.

Helena continued. 'The Institution is a group of powerful individuals, mostly academics, Councillors and a few traders, whose purpose is to ensure the energy stays steady.'

'I thought that was the job of the Descendants?'

Helena searched for how to answer. 'Theoretically yes, but the Descendants have never really been interested in ruling for the good of all. Historically, they've been more preoccupied with personal gain and adoration, and in reality, they have no interest in sending the relic back to the Gods, given that to do so runs counter to their personal interests, regardless of what they swear at their Crownings.'

'Hmm.'

'So the Institution was formed centuries ago to ensure the energy remained stable and has dedicated itself to freeing the world ever since.'

'But only the Descendants can free the world.'

'Only if the only freedom you consider is from the Gods. What if freedom was from the rule of the Descendants?'

'So why wait until now? Why hasn't the Institution acted already?'

'The Descendants hold some information they'd use to discredit the Institution if we tried to act, which means we've been at a stalemate since they stole it. If we overthrow them, they'll discredit us, the world would descend into chaos, and the energy would plummet. It would mean destruction of the world as we know it and the Institution would have failed in its purpose.'

'So when you say 'we', I take it that means you're part of the Institution?' Anita asked. 'Why are you telling me all this?'

'Because we need powerful people like you to join us,' she replied simply.

'But what's the point of growing if you can't act?'

'Because, as you know better than most, the energy is failing. If we don't act now, then it may be too late.'

'And how are you going to deal with the 'information' issue?'

'We're going to get it back.'

'What is 'it' and how do you plan to get it back? Information's not something you can just steal!'

'I can't tell you that Anita, unless of course you agree to join us.' Anita almost laughed, but saw the look on Helena's face, so thought better of it.

'Join you? Given the earlier warning about Marcus and Austin, do you think that's such a great idea?'

'I'm not saying it wouldn't be dangerous, but having you with us may be the key to getting the information back.'

Anita looked shocked. 'How did you work that out?'

'Think about it. If your relationship with Marcus develops, you'll be in a position to probe for information about the whereabouts of the information, find out how heavily it's guarded, and you may even be able to recover it for us.'

'What? You want me to play the spy right under Austin and Amber's noses? What if they were to find out?'

'As I said, I'm not saying it wouldn't be dangerous, but you'd be helping to protect us all.'

Anita looked away; it all seemed so absurd. 'Helena, I'm going to have to think about it. Until about five minutes ago I had no idea the Institution even existed, and now you're asking me to make sure my relationship with Marcus develops so I can spy for you and steal back some kind of 'information'? It's a bit full-on don't you think?'

'I know it is, but that's the world we now live in. The energy's plummeting and the Descendants are doing nothing. You have some of the strongest energy I've ever known, and I wouldn't have told you about the Institution or what we are trying to do if I didn't trust you, or think you could do it. You don't know it, but you've been wrapped up in this for a very long time.'

'What's that supposed to mean?'

'I can't tell you that until you join us and prove you're committed. If you get the information, I'll tell you everything.' She paused for a moment before adding, 'including all about your parents, who I knew very well.'

'You were friends with my parents and you never told me? Through all the time we spent together, you never thought once to mention it?' Anita was partly furious, partly hurt and partly captivated. Helena could answer all the questions she'd never been able to ask Cordelia, or anyone else for that matter. She desperately wanted to know about her parents, and if they had been wrapped up in the Institution, could it really be that bad? But what if her parents had been bad people? She'd never known them; maybe she should stay as far away from the Institution as possible, after all, this could be the reason they'd ended up dead. She was totally confused. Half of her wanted to agree to anything Helena asked of her, but the other half knew she should be cautious. Helena admitting something was dangerous meant it was really dangerous and that wasn't something to be taken lightly.

'Anita, I couldn't mention it. The Descendants don't know I'm a member of the Institution. They may suspect, but they don't know for sure. If I'd told you about your parents when you were younger, it would've put both of us, and many others, in serious danger.' Anita was really intrigued now. 'By all means, take some time to think about it, but please don't tell anyone about this conversation. No one at all. It would be dangerous for you and could get me killed.'

Anita felt suddenly cold and a little bit sick. She'd never had to consider that someone might want to harm or even kill her for something as simple as a conversation. Sure, she had used an energy gun before, and a bow and arrow, and had trained to fight with knives, and just her hands, but that had all been a game, or for practice. She'd never considered she may actually have to use the training someday, or that someone else may try to use their training on her.

'I won't tell anyone,' she promised. There was no one she could tell something like this anyway.

'Thank you. I'll come and find you in a few days to hear your decision, but you're the most skilled Body I have ever known, and you learn quickly; if anyone can help us, it's you.'

Helena squeezed Anita's arm warmly as she got up and jogged away, calling, 'I'll see you in a couple of days,' back over her shoulder.

Anita couldn't quite believe what had just happened. She'd had lessons with Helena every day for years and she'd never mentioned anything about any of this. Helena hadn't even tried that hard to recruit her to be an academic, and now this? Anita was astute enough to know that Helena hadn't really been warning her off Marcus, nor had she accidently bumped into Anita at the river. Helena had obviously known about the direction Anita's relationship with Marcus was going, so saw the opportunity and went for it. But that didn't help Anita decide what she should do next.

She was also a little worried by the brass cylinder in her head and the notion that it could be something hostile that was waiting to kill her. She didn't think that Amber had had an opportunity to plant something, but then Anita didn't know what to look for and she had no idea how long it had been there, so it could've been anybody, for any reason, over the course of her life. It could have been Helena for all she knew.

*****

The following day, Anita was still pondering what she should do as she ran to the castle for her first Mind lesson. She arrived and almost ran headlong into Austin and Amber descending the steps, and was instantly on guard.

'What are you doing here?' Austin sniped, shooting a questioning sideways glance at Amber, while Amber ignored him and stared intently at Anita. Anita stood her ground, wondering again if the cylinder in her head was hostile and had been put there by her.

'I'm here to see Marcus,' she replied cheerily, pretending she hadn't noticed their hostility.

'I see. What for?' he fired back in crisp rounds, not happy about the prospect of Anita spending more time with his precious son.

Luckily, as Anita was contemplating her answer, Marcus came striding out of the entrance towards them. 'Anita, hi,' he called openly.

'Hi,' she said, visibly relieved, the tension going out of her.

As Marcus reached her, he put an arm around her shoulders in a plutonic, brotherly way and shepherded her into the castle. 'See you later dad,' he called calmly over his shoulder. Marcus didn't say a thing until they were safely up the stairs and in his suite. He closed the door firmly behind them and took a deep breath. 'That was almost very interesting,' he said frivolously. He took a cavalier step towards her, and she casually moved away. The energy changed, charged at the realisation they were now alone in Marcus' suite, no prying eyes, and Marcus changed too, his movements becoming calculated, reminding Anita of a big cat stalking its prey. 'Nothing like a dangerous encounter to liven up a morning,' he purred, his predator's eyes fixed on her.

'Something like that,' she countered defensively, moving cautiously away from him, over to one of the enormous light grey sofas, and sitting down informally, legs tucked underneath her. She pulled a large, patterned, cushion protectively in front of her, trying to ignore the delicious reaction she was having to Marcus' honed form stalking her every move. 'So, tell me, what am I learning today?' she said, as strongly as she could, averting her gaze. She wanted to keep him focused on the matter in hand, something it was difficult enough to keep her own mind on, let alone his.

Marcus smiled as he sat lithely down next to her, a knowing, victorious smile, casting aside her weak attempts to divert him. She felt his energy lift as he leaned in towards her, and despite herself, felt hers respond, her skin prickling as the heady smell of vanilla invaded her lungs, eroding her resolve. Impulsively, she moved towards him, meeting his lips with hers. They kissed with urgency, Anita feeling tingles shoot all over her body as Marcus put his hands on her waist and pulled her astride him. She grabbed handfuls of his hair and kissed him more deeply while his fingers explored her, finding the chink between the back of her running tights and her vest, pushing their way under to caress her back. But Anita stiffened as he did it, pulled her lips away, placed her hands either side of his face and rested her forehead on his, closing her eyes. Marcus removed his hands, alarmed, pushing her backwards so he could see her face. She dropped her hands from him and in one supple movement removed herself from his lap, curling herself up against the arm of the sofa.

'What's wrong?' he asked, reaching for her hand, a look of concern on his face, but she didn't let him take it.

She briefly met his worried eyes. 'Marcus,' she paused, trying to work out what to say next. 'Why did you invite me to the ball?'

He looked confused, his eyes wide as he considered the question. 'I was intrigued by you. You're different. I find you exciting.'

'And so far this has all been a game,' she said cryptically.

'I don't understand,' he said, although Anita could tell in his eyes he knew what she meant.

'Yes you do. I didn't react to you like the other girls normally would, so your instincts were aroused and you chased me. And because I knew that, I pushed you away, which made you chase me more. But now we're here, in your bedroom, and we're in too dangerous a position to play games.'

'I suppose that's one way of looking at it,' he said sceptically.

'It's the only way to look at it,' she snapped. 'You know Austin doesn't approve of me and we live in an increasingly dangerous world. I need to know you're not playing a game now.'

'Anita, I'm not. I like you. I genuinely like you; you're confident and clever, and ballsy and you don't cower at the sight of my father, and you're reckless and sexy, and most importantly, I can talk to you. I've never spoken about my mother to anyone, but with you it seemed like the most natural thing in the world.' His voice had taken on a pleading edge, worried he was about to lose her.

Anita tempered, her defences falling away. She wasn't totally sure he was telling the truth, but she found herself wanting to believe him. She took his hand and kissed it gently, signalling that she believed him, at least for the moment, before saying softly, 'what am I learning today?'

He smiled, leaned forward, and placed a gentle kiss on her lips, before leading her by the hand into his bedroom. 'Today you're going to learn the arts of suggestion and persuasion,' he said brightly as they went.

'You mean manipulation,' she said bluntly.

'Call them what you will, they're very powerful skills.'

They spent the next two hours playing chess, with Marcus teaching Anita about the nuances of suggestion and idea planting to influence the thoughts and actions of others. The idea was that she would distract him with the chess, then casually plant an idea into the conversation that he was supposed to pick up and think was his, but by the end, she hadn't got very far. Marcus assured her the main problem was that he knew what she was trying to do, so he told her she should practice on other people. He explained that it was best to start with people who trusted her implicitly, or who were naturally inclined to believe her, and after a brief internal moral debate, she decided Bas was the best person for the job. She just had to work out what she wanted to plant.

Anita left the castle frustrated. She didn't like it when she couldn't do things, and she was cross about Marcus' comment before he had kissed her goodbye; 'be careful with Alexander'. She would do what she damn well wanted, and judging by what everyone kept telling her, it wasn't Alexander she needed to be careful with.

*****

115

Anita had just about managed to throw off her bad mood by the time she arrived at the Temple of the Spirit to meet Alexander, but she suspected that may have had something to do with the prospect of spending an evening meditating with him. Her stomach flipped as she thought about his piercing blue eyes, and she fought to get her energy back under control as she climbed the steps into the Temple. As she entered on the dot of seven, she saw Alexander striding towards her, his cloak billowing out behind him and his hair looking wild, as though he had run his hands through it in despair many a time that day. Even slightly worn as he looked now, he was exceptionally attractive. She felt her energy respond mischievously to her thoughts and Alexander looked up when he felt it, no hint of a smile on his face.

'We'll start here at the back, where you were meditating yesterday,' he snapped.

Anita's energy deflated at the curt greeting. Obviously he wasn't as pleased to see her as she was to see him, unless, of course, it was just that he was hiding his energy; I need to learn to do that, she thought.

'How do you hide your energy?' Anita asked again.

Alexander, whose back was facing her, paused, a flash of surprise showing on his face before he turned to look at her. He glared at her, slightly more fiercely than he'd intended, but it was taking every fiber of his control to keep his energy in check at such close proximity. 'I think maybe we should master the basics first. Seeing as you seem to have particular trouble keeping your energy under control, that may never be something you manage to grasp.' The words were quiet and menacing. Anita looked hurt; she was embarrassed and confused and Alexander felt a tug on his heartstrings. He didn't want to be nasty to her, but he had to keep his distance, she was in enough danger as it was.

'Sit down,' he said, pointing to the place on the mat where she'd been sitting yesterday. Anita sat down and said nothing. Her energy had plummeted; she was empty and deflated. She wasn't angry, her usual reaction, but instead felt drained.

Alexander sat down in front of her, the knees of his crossed legs so close to hers that she swore she could feel a tension in the air between their skin. Alexander looked Anita in the eye and it was all she could do to hold his gaze, searching his lovely blue eyes while he struggled to keep them from showing any warmth.

'Close your eyes, clear your mind and breathe deeply,' he softly commanded, and she did as he said. She relinquished control, following his instructions to the letter, feeling strangely tired. As she closed her eyes, Anita was almost instantly transported to the sky above the clearing with the yurt, then felt herself falling, and landed in front of the door. Again, Anita pushed the curtain aside and entered the unexpectedly light space inside; it was exactly as it had been last time, apart from the brass cylinder, which had disappeared. She looked over to the bed to find Alexander where he'd been last time too, still topless and disheveled, and she made her way towards him. As she neared him, she felt a warm nudge at the edge of her energy, similar to the nudge she'd felt at dinner at the ball, and she smiled.

'So that was you,' she said, encouraged, although weirdly her lips didn't seem to move as she spoke.

'You can feel that?' Alexander shot back, the surprise clear on his face.

'Of course,' she said, sitting down next to him and bringing her legs up so she could sit cross-legged on the bed.

Alexander was amazed. He'd never met anyone else who could feel nudges; it was a rare skill. He was tempted to touch her to see if she felt tingles in her fingers, as he had when they'd danced, but to test that would require touching her outside of the meditation, and it wouldn't surprise him if Marcus was watching, to make sure Alexander wasn't trying anything untoward. He knew there would be another opportunity.

'So how did it feel when you got rid of that brass cylinder?' he asked instead.

'I don't know, as I didn't manage to get rid of it.'

'What?' Alexander replied, alarmed, 'where is it then?'

'It hit the floor and rolled out of the door, but it wasn't in the clearing outside when I came in a second ago.'

'Great.'

'What does that mean?'

'It means you have a brass cylinder roaming around in your head somewhere and we have no idea where. Have you ever meditated to anywhere else?'

'Ha,' Anita laughed. 'Not really. I didn't even believe this was possible until a couple of months ago, when Cleo and I meditated to a boat on the sea, only I didn't actually see her there, so I only had conclusive proof it's not total rubbish when I meditated here yesterday and saw you.'

'Gods, they really do teach you nothing.'

117

'It's looking more and more that way,' she replied sardonically, clearly conveying this was not a helpful comment. 'So where are we now?'

Alexander looked at her as though she'd just landed from another planet. 'You're kidding?' Anita shook her head and frowned impatiently. 'You have no idea where you are?'

'Nope, none whatsoever,' she said irritably.

'Anita, this is your Centre,' he said gently.

'My what?'

'You're Centre. The place that comes together when you're thirty, remember?'

'Well yes, obviously I've heard of my Centre, but I've always thought it was just some rubbish made up to keep people in lessons after school. You're telling me this is the place that will 'come together' when I'm thirty? What does that mean anyway?'

'It means that this place reflects your most prominent skills, the ones you're most comfortable with and that come most easily to you. So for you it's a mixture of Body and Spirit with very little Mind at all, but there are also other places inside your head that represent different combinations of skills, and any of those places can be developed. When your Centre comes together, all the different places in your mind merge or 'come together' into one new Centre that you will have for the rest of your life. Why that happens at thirty, no one knows, but from the time when your Centre comes together it becomes much more difficult, if not impossible, to truly develop new skills. The reason you're feeling so tired now,' she gave him a questioning look, 'and I know because I can read your energy remember?' she nodded yieldingly. Of course he could. 'Is because this morning you had a session with Marcus to try and develop your Mind skills. That doesn't come easily to you, so it takes a great deal of effort to build up your abilities. Just like when someone practices Body skills and they feel tired and stiff while their muscles recover, your mind is currently doing the same thing, and you'll feel empty and drained until it has time to recover. Hopefully, as you already have a lot of Spirit in you, you won't find these sessions take too much of a toll. You may feel a bit tired afterwards, but that should wear off after a couple of sessions. The Mind sessions on the other hand, you are likely to find very draining, so you're going to need to be careful that Austin or Amber don't try to take advantage of you in the next few weeks, as you'll be especially vulnerable to attack.'

118

Normally Anita would have said Alexander was being ridiculous and that of course no one would attack her, but she was beginning to believe that maybe he and Helena might be right, especially after the way Austin and Amber had looked at her this morning.

'In fact,' he continued, 'it wouldn't surprise me if Marcus is watching us right now, and he probably will for the first few sessions, until he trusts that I'll behave myself.' Anita remembered the look on Marcus' face when he'd said goodbye earlier and she knew he was right. It was highly likely that he was watching them from the outside, but she wasn't sure she wanted Alexander to behave himself.

'Well at least he can't tell what's going on in here,' she said.

'No, he can't exactly, but there are a few tells on the outside that give clues as to what's going on inside the meditation, so we need to be careful not to give anything away about that cylinder of yours. But we do need to find it.'

'Or it might explode in my head and kill me?!' Anita laughed.

Alexander gave her another stern look. 'Yes, and you can find that funny if you want to, but if you die while I'm in here, I could very well die too, so I'd rather we take this seriously if you don't mind.'

Anita went pale. 'You think someone may actually have put it in my head to try and kill me?'

'Who knows, but what I do know is that it's best to find it and get rid of it before we get a chance to find out.'

'But what if it contains something really important from a friend?'

'Do you have any friends who need to pass important messages to you through cylinders in your mind?'

'Not that I know of, but you never know.'

'And what if it's been put here by Austin or Amber to try and kill you?'

'I know they don't like me seeing Marcus, but really, you think they would resort to trying to kill me? You said yourself they wouldn't try that if I was close to Marcus, if they would even try it at all.'

'Believe me, they would try it if it suited them, and they can use it at any time they like, which means they could have planted it just in case you and Marcus don't work out, so they have a convenient way to kill you.'

'I still find it hard to believe that Austin wants to kill me just because I have strong energy.'

'He's killed for much less. He thinks he can do whatever he wants and get away with it, and to be honest, there aren't many people queuing up to try and stop him.'

'Are you trying to stop him?'

Alexander ignored the question. 'So we need to find and get rid of the cylinder in your head. I need to teach you how to hide your energy, along with all the meditation poses, and then we may get on to visiting the Centre of others and extraction, depending on how quickly you learn.'

'Hopefully I'll pick this up quicker than I seem to be doing with the Mind skills. I'm abysmal at those,' she said, considering Alexander's comment about visiting the Centre of others. Would she get to visit his Centre? Just the very prospect sent shivers up and down her spine. 'So, where do we start?'

Alexander and Anita spent the next hour trying to locate other places in Anita's mind, where the cylinder may have hidden itself. Alexander didn't tell Anita this, but he was surprised the cylinder had run away. It meant that someone very powerful, more powerful than Austin or Amber and with a mix of Mind and Spirit had planted it, and it would be difficult to get rid of, but they could cross that bridge, if and when they got there. They located two other places in Anita's mind; one by the river in Empire and another on top of a beautiful cliff looking out over the sea. Alexander knew this place well, the cliffs overlooking Kingdom, but neither showed signs of the cylinder. Both places were steeped in Spirit and Body, hence why they were the first and easiest places to find. Alexander found himself wondering what Anita's Centre would look like when it came together; it would be an interesting one, of that he was sure.

When Alexander felt Anita's energy dip even further, he decided it was time to call it a day. 'I think we're done here for the moment,' he said, taking one last look out to sea from the cliff that was so familiar to him. Anita nodded, feeling very much like she wanted to go to sleep and followed Alexander's instructions to lift herself out of the meditation and back to the Temple. When she woke up, her vision was filled with Alexander's concerned features and she smiled to see a softness there that he had hidden before.

'That was interesting,' she said, 'and very educational. Who knew there was all that stuff in my head.'

'Well, if I were you, I wouldn't go into too much detail about it with Marcus when he takes you home,' said Alexander, in a low voice, helping Anita to her feet, feeling a slight tingle as their fingers touched. He would have asked her if she could feel it too, but seeing Alexander actually touch Anita was too much for Marcus, so he broke cover and hurried over to them, slipping his arm around her and pulling her towards him.

Anita leaned in to him; all she wanted now was to go to sleep. Alexander turned to leave, saying, 'same time tomorrow,' nonchalantly as he strode away.

'Hey,' Marcus whispered into Anita's ear as he gently pulled her into a hug, kissing her hair as she wrapped her arms around him.

'Hi,' she said weakly, feeling as though she might fall asleep right then and there.

Marcus pushed Anita away a little as he bent slightly to put one arm behind her knees and scooped her up into his arms, carrying her out of the Temple to his waiting car. Anita couldn't have been happier to let him and she fell asleep in his lap as soon as they were in.

They reached Cordelia's and Marcus lifted Anita out of the car without her so much as stirring. He carried her to the back door and straight up the stairs, pausing for a moment to work out which was Anita's bedroom. He went for the smaller of the two, as it had the dress Anita had worn to the ball hanging on the outside of the wardrobe, and gently placed her on the bed. Anita woke up as he put her down and smiled a groggy half smile up at him. He crouched down beside the small double bed and lightly pushed a stray lock of hair back behind her ear. Anita reached out and fumbled for his neck, pulling his lips towards hers and kissing him sleepily.

'Thank you for bringing me home,' she mumbled into his mouth.

'My pleasure,' he smiled, before leaning in to kiss her forehead then getting up to leave.

'Don't go yet,' Anita murmured. She rolled to the other side of the bed, indicating he should lie down too. Marcus hesitated for only a split second before slowly lowering himself down next to Anita's warm, toned form. They lay there, face to face, Anita struggling to keep her eyes open, each feeling the warm breath of the other landing on their lips. When Anita couldn't fight sleep any longer, her eyelids fluttered closed, and Marcus kissed her lightly. He placed his masculine hand over the feminine one on his neck and gently played with each finger in turn, mesmerised by the rise and fall of Anita's sleeping body, before carefully turning his head and lifting her palm to his mouth. He kissed it softly before placing it delicately next to her head on the pillow, then used every ounce of his resolve to tear himself away.

CHAPTER 9

As usual, Anita woke up early the following morning, but whereas she normally felt energised and refreshed, this morning she felt drained and groggy. She hadn't felt like this for years, not since she'd first started training with Helena when she was thirteen years old. Well at least it shows I'm doing something, even if I'm not yet doing the right thing, she thought, as she prised herself out of bed and went downstairs to do some yoga.

After her workout, she showered, ate breakfast and headed to the Observatory. She felt a bit better, but yoga had been harder work than usual. She wasn't having a Mind session with Marcus today, as she was supposed to practice what she'd learned yesterday instead. She was going to try and plant an idea in Bas' head, but she still hadn't quite decided what it should be. She pondered as she strolled along, walking at a much more sedate pace than her usual march, as she considered her options. She could plant the idea that Bas should invite Anita to sing in his band, but if he took her up on the offer, he might try and make her sing a love song with him, and that would be horrible. She could try to make him suggest they play a game of chess together, but that was probably a bit advanced for her current level of skill; Bas hated chess with a passion, and it wasn't exactly like Anita was keen on it either. Eventually she settled on trying to get Bas to suggest they go for a swim in the river. It was getting cold now as they were heading for the end of the year, which meant this wouldn't be something he would suggest naturally, so if he did suggest it, she could claim the plant a triumph.

Anita climbed the Observatory's spiral staircase and entered the room at the top. Bas and Patrick were having what seemed to be quite a heated debate, presumably about the current energy predicament.

'Hi,' she said loudly, so they would notice she was there. 'Just came from the river, it's lovely down there at the moment.'

They looked up, bewildered, to check it was Anita, and when they confirmed it was, looked at her like she must have had a nasty fall and hit her head. Anita wasn't usually a fan of volunteering information, especially when there was an energy conversation to get involved with. 'If you say so,' said Patrick, looking at her suspiciously. 'We're just discussing that we're already seeing adverse effects on crop yields as a result of the energy drop.'

'Really?' she said. 'Are we seeing effects anywhere else, for example in the river?'

'Um, no, not yet,' Bas said slowly, giving Anita an 'are you alright' kind of look. 'Just the autumn crop yields are down a bit on last year. Austin's harping on about it being a coincidence and is convinced that it's all down to the weather. Total idiot.'

'There's a surprise,' said Anita, sitting down at one of the dashboards. 'How can someone so well educated, who has access to so much information indicating that the energy balance is crucial to our survival, be such a total prat?'

'I don't know,' said Patrick, 'but he'll have to pay attention eventually, unless he has a way of producing food out of thin air. I'd like to see how he deals with the situation when people don't have enough to eat.'

'Mmm, that wouldn't be pretty.'

They got to work and there was silence for a few minutes, until Anita chirped, 'Thorn jumped in the water this morning. It looked so refreshing.'

Bas and Patrick looked at each other, perplexed. 'Is everything alright Anita?' Bas ventured.

'Of course. Why do you ask?'

'Because for the entire time I've known you, which is quite a long time, you've never once volunteered any information that you felt you didn't have to, and you've done it twice now in one morning.'

Anita went red. Damn, she thought. She really was hideous at this Mind stuff. 'Sorry for being chatty,' she retorted defensively, furious at herself for failing to plant the idea. 'I'll keep my thoughts to myself in future.'

'And she's back,' said Patrick, giving Anita an infuriating wink.

Anita sat in silence for the remainder of the day, angry at herself, and plotting who to try next. After work, Anita tried first Cleo over drinks at The Island, then Alistair, who she bumped into on her way home, and then Cordelia when she got there, and everyone just thought she was being weird. Cleo was the only one who'd seen right through what she was doing, she'd come straight out with it saying, 'Anita, are you trying to plant an idea in my head?'

You idiot, she chastised herself, Cleo wasn't exactly the best person to try and plant an idea on. Cleo was, after all, a Mind, and manipulation was one of her strongest suits, so of course she'd be able to see through what Anita was doing. 'Yeah, sorry. I'm getting Marcus to give me Mind lessons and he told me to practice planting ideas. But as you can see, I'm rubbish at it.'

'Well, my advice, for what it's worth, is that you've got to play to your strengths. When you try to plant an idea, don't try and simply impersonate what a Mind would do. Use your Body and Spirit skills to help you. You can't be someone you're not, so put to use the skills you have.'

Anita nodded and quickly changed the subject. She had no idea how to implement what Cleo was saying, but was both embarrassed and cross with herself for being so easily caught out, so she didn't want to dwell.

*****

The following weeks entailed classes with both Marcus at the castle and Alexander at the Temple (with Marcus always managing to find some reason to be in the Spirit Temple at the same time).

The lessons couldn't have been more different. Marcus was prescriptive and controlling, trying to force Anita to imitate the way he did things, whereas Alexander let Anita find her own way, there only to guide her if she needed him. Anita left Marcus' lessons feeling frustrated and exhausted, and usually wanting to hit him. On the other hand, she left Alexander's lessons feeling drained, but somehow liberated and content. They found several more places in her mind during their lessons, including the boat she had visited with Cleo, which Alexander said was a place that contained a good mix of Mind, Body and Spirit, so it made sense that Cleo and Anita would have ended up there. They also found a waterfall that Alexander said was full of Spirit, as well as a stable with a beautiful chestnut mare that was a mixture of Body and Spirit, but Alexander was convinced Anita had a Mind dominated place somewhere in her head, and it was only a matter of time before they found it. There had been no sign of the cylinder in any of the places they'd found so far, and secretly, Alexander suspected the cylinder was hiding in a Mind place; it would be the most difficult place to banish it from. He thought again how skilled the person who'd planted it must have been.

Of course, Anita didn't tell Marcus about her success in the Spirit sessions; her Mind sessions were going so badly, and Marcus was always very glad to hear that Alexander's lessons had not gone well either. 'Maybe there's a reason only the Descendants are taught all the skills to such a high level after all,' he said pompously, after another Mind lesson had gone disastrously.

'Yes, maybe,' Anita had agreed sincerely, inwardly smirking.

As the weeks went on, two things became clear. Firstly, that Marcus and Anita were not going to get anywhere with their Mind lessons, and if they wanted to continue their relationship, it would be a good idea to stop trying, and secondly, that the Mind place in Anita's head was exceedingly elusive, so Alexander decided to stop trying to find it for a while and move on to work on other skills, specifically, how to hide energy.

The conversation with Marcus had not gone well. At first he took it as an affront to his teaching skills, then switched tack to blame her lack of progress on all the time Anita was spending with Alexander. She eventually managed to bring Marcus round, by reassuring him it was nothing to do with his teaching skills. She'd said she was naturally pre-disposed towards Spirit and Body skills, and was useless at Mind, and it was always good to know when to stop flogging a dead horse. Anita had sealed the deal though, when she'd said that the main reason she wanted to stop lessons with Marcus was so that they could spend more time together as a couple, and not as teacher and pupil. Maybe she was better at Mind skills than she let on, she'd thought, as he had softened.

Marcus had liked this very much, and as he was getting bored of teaching Anita anyway, especially as she never seemed to get any better, he finally relented. However, it was a much harder sell to convince Marcus that he should not be present for her future meditations with Alexander. It had shocked Anita a bit to see him act so much like a spoilt child as she'd told him. She hadn't quite believed the warnings about Marcus' possessiveness, but when she saw it with her own eyes, she began to wonder what she'd got herself into. She had, again, managed to avoid a serious argument with a bit of flattery and a good measure of flirting.

'It's not that I don't want you there,' she had said, sitting on his lap and wrapping her arms around his neck, 'it's that we're working on hiding energy next, and when I know you're around, my energy soars. It's impossible to control,' she'd said, before playfully biting his ear lobe. It may not have placated Marcus entirely, but it had certainly distracted him. He had thrown her back onto the bed in retaliation, climbed on top of her and pinned her arms above her head.

'Fine,' he'd said sulkily, 'I won't come to your lessons.'

'You promise?' she matched his tone, looking up at him through her lashes.

'I suppose so,' he said, before leaning down, running the tip of his nose down the length of hers and roguishly kissing her lips.

*****

Anita was very happy with where she and Marcus were now, and even more happy that she'd managed to use a bit of seduction and manipulation in the process. She soothed her conscience by thinking that some of what Marcus had tried to teach her must have rubbed off, and was very much looking forward to the Spirit lesson she was heading to, away from Marcus' prying eyes. Today they were meditating down by the river. Alexander thought they could do with a change of scenery, and wanted to teach her about controlling her energy somewhere more private than the Temple; it could be an emotional skill to learn.

'Hey,' said Anita, when she got to the large flat rock that Alexander was already sitting on, cross legged, above the angry water below.

'Hi. No chaperone today?' Alexander mocked.

'No,' she smiled triumphantly. 'Marcus has agreed to give me some space during these lessons.'

'I see,' said Alexander, a little surprised. He had no idea how she'd got Marcus to agree to that, but he felt his energy rise a bit at the thought. He quickly suppressed it and motioned for Anita to sit down. 'Learning to suppress your energy is a bit different to finding places inside your mind,' he started. 'It requires you to appreciate how you react to situations and to others around you; you need to anticipate your reaction and divert the energy. You can't get rid of it, but you can channel it elsewhere.'

'And how do I do that?'

Alexander smiled. 'You push it through your feet.'

'Right. What the hell does that mean?'

'It means exactly that. You push all the energy towards your feet, so it's utilised elsewhere, and nobody can read your reaction.'

'How does the energy get used up?'

'By propelling your body upwards.'

Anita laughed. 'What?' This was ridiculous.

Alexander had hoped for something along the lines of wonderment at this revelation, not humour. 'It's the same principle as energy cars and trains,' he said, looking a little put out. 'You pushing your energy downwards propels you upwards. Most people aren't powerful enough to actually walk on air, but it can make you look weightless, almost like you're floating as you walk. But, of course, you learn to hide that too, so only those who really know what to look for can tell what you're doing.'

Anita wasn't sure if he was joking or not; it sounded totally ridiculous, but then she supposed it made sense when you thought about how energy cars worked. 'Alright, so how do I do this...pushing downwards?'

'First we need to make your energy rise,' he said coyly, cocking an eyebrow.

Anita blushed. 'And how are we going to do that?' Anita thought about how her energy used to react at the mere sight of either Marcus or Alexander, but that had subsided now she'd spent so much time with both of them.

Alexander took a meaningful step towards her. 'I can either challenge you or seduce you,' he said recklessly, the atmosphere shifting wildly as his piercing eyes bored into hers.

Anita's energy reacted immediately, full of shock and delightful anticipation at the prospect of either. Feeling smug at her instant reaction, Alexander reached out and took her hands. She felt like she might burst, tingles shooting all over her body as their skin touched for the first time in weeks. 'Good,' he said gently. 'Now, think the energy downwards and imagine yourself being propelled upwards.' Anita did as she was told, and surprisingly, felt some weight leave her body. 'Good,' said Alexander again as he felt it, doing nothing to try and hide his own energy's rapidly rising tide. 'Now, push down on my hands and imagine someone is tugging on your hair and pulling you upwards.' Again, Anita did as she was told, and felt her weight completely leave the ground. As she felt it, she panicked, and the weight immediately returned, her feet reconnecting unsteadily with the ground, Alexander catching her as she stumbled into him, preventing her from tumbling to the ground.

'By the Gods, Anita. I've never seen anyone levitate on their first attempt,' he said, full of adoration. 'How did it feel?'

'Great,' she beamed, probably more because he hadn't taken his hands off her than as a result of the levitation. This is so much more fun than Mind lessons, she thought, her energy once more rising as she looked up at Alexander, her hands enjoying the muscular contours of his chest. 'Let's try again,' she said eagerly, looking like an overexcited small child on her birthday.

'Ok,' he breathed indulgently, his energy still singing as he stepped back and held her hands, relishing the tingle of energy he too felt when they touched. Surprisingly, the tingles were more intense with Alexander than with Marcus, but Anita was more interested in levitating at the moment, so ignored it.

Anita managed to levitate a second time and even took a few steps in the air, with Alexander's support, before she lost concentration and came crashing back down again. She was drained and Alexander felt it. 'I think that's enough for today. I don't want to wear you out completely or Marcus will be after me.' He said it sternly, but Anita detected an ironic edge. 'Tomorrow we can work on not sending all the energy downwards, only some of it, so you still stay connected to the ground. If you levitate in public, it pretty much defeats the point of trying to hide your energy!'

'Ok,' said Anita, attempting to hide her disappointment. 'Are you walking back to Empire?'

'I will do in a bit, but it's best that Marcus doesn't see us walking back together. He may have agreed to give you some space for the lessons themselves, but I shouldn't have thought he's too far away, and I doubt he'll be keen on us walking back to town together.'

Anita nodded, annoyed by how Alexander spoke about her boyfriend; she supposed he was her boyfriend. What he said may be true, but it was still annoying. 'See you here at the same time tomorrow?'

'Sure,' he said, sounding a little disinterested. 'Same time tomorrow.'

Anita walked away feeling confused. She had felt his energy rise when they touched, and he'd seemed the most warm he'd ever been today, probably because Marcus wasn't watching, but now he was acting all aloof again. Did he see them as friends? Did he want more than that? Could he care less? Was he doing all this just to make sure the Descendants were protected from attackers? What was most strange, was that they'd spent so much time together, yet had barely had a conversation. It took so much concentration to meditate, there was no room to chat. She knew nothing about him; she had no idea at all who he was. Before she stopped to think, Anita turned around and called back to Alexander, 'Marcus, Cleo, Bas and I are going to The Island for drinks later. You should come too.'

'Do you think that's a good idea?' he said dryly, raising an eyebrow at her.

'Of course it's a good idea. Why wouldn't it be?' Obviously she knew full well why it wouldn't be, but if they all spent some time together socially, she was sure Marcus would relax a bit about the lessons.

Alexander half laughed and shrugged compliantly. 'Alright. See you there.'

'Great,' she said triumphantly, thinking that more Mind skills must have rubbed off on her than she'd originally realized. 'See you there at eight.' She turned and walked away, feeling quite smug. Alexander took a deep breath and hung his head, shaking it slightly. What are you doing, he silently questioned.

CHAPTER 10

'Don't you always know how to brighten up my day,' Amber teased, kissing Austin finally, before climbing off him, buttoning her shirt and pulling down her pencil skirt.

'I aim to please,' he smirked, as he stood up from his office chair, did up his fly and walked over to his drinks cabinet. 'Brandy?'

'Why not?' she said, sinking into one of the chesterfields and curling her legs up under her. She took the glass Austin offered. He did always provide quality booze, she thought, as she savoured the first mouthful. Austin sat down next to her, and thinking this was probably about as good an opportunity as she was going to get, she launched her assault.

'I think we should talk about Anita.'

Austin stiffened, took a slow, deep sip, then said, 'go on.'

'I think it may be turning into more of a problem than we originally anticipated. Marcus seems to be increasingly interested in her; he's become possessive and he's spending a great deal of time following her around.'

Austin's face told Amber everything she needed to know. He was furious. 'What happened to infatuation and lust?' He hissed the words.

'It would seem that the lust hasn't been sated and infatuation is turning to something more. I think it might be time for you to have a gentle word with him. Talk some sense into him.'

'I told you we should've put a stop to this at the start,' he snarled. 'Now who knows what damage has been done.'

'Austin, there's still time to solve this. We just need to focus his attention elsewhere; get him more involved in your business activities, make him feel more important, give him something to concentrate on other than her.'

'Can't we just get rid of her?'

'Not yet,' she laughed. 'You know we can't. If he starts to move away from her, we can take action, but we can't take her away from him; the consequences would be dire. He's extremely protective of her and he won't appreciate being told what to do by you, me, or anyone else.'

Austin's mood was deteriorating and Amber knew it was time for her to make an exit. 'Just think about it,' she said, getting up and slipping on her stilettos. She leaned back over him and ran her hands placating through his hair. 'If anyone can make him see sense, it's you,' she said adoringly, before giving him a short kiss on the lips and leaving. By the Gods, I hope this all works out, she thought, as she closed the door behind her, resting her head back on the wood. She wouldn't like what would become of her if it didn't.

*****

Austin heard Marcus return from wherever he'd been, his footsteps indicating he was heading in the direction of the kitchen. There's no time like the present, he thought, as he left his office and headed after him. He reached the kitchen and did a quick sweep around with his eyes. Luckily, they were the only ones there, and Austin moved over to the enormous range cooker to put the kettle on to boil. 'Cup of tea?' he asked, as Marcus pulled out a tin of shortbread.

'Sure,' he replied, a little suspicious. It was always ominous when his dad was overtly nice.

'Had a good day?' asked Austin, conversationally.

'Yep, fine thanks. You?' It was a lie. Marcus had been in a dreadful mood since Anita had gone for her lesson with Alexander, and it was killing him that he had no real idea what had happened. He'd felt slightly better when she'd told him it had been another difficult session, but still, he was uncomfortable with the whole arrangement.

'Yes, fine thanks; all very mundane today, nothing exciting going on. What have you been up to?'

Marcus was really suspicious now. His dad being chatty was an extreme rarity, but he thought it best to play along. 'I just went to Empire. I had a few things to do at the Temple.'

'Good good. Been seeing much of that Anita girl since the ball?'

Knew it, Marcus thought. He had got to the point just as the kettle was boiling. 'Yep, been seeing her a bit.'

There was silence as Austin made them tea, and Marcus picked up a large piece of shortbread and took a bite. 'I just think you should be a bit careful Marcus. I wouldn't want you to get hurt.'

'Oh?' asked Marcus innocently.

'I'm not sure I trust Anita, that's all.'

'Any particular reason why?'

'Because she's very powerful, and I think it's suspicious how she's latched onto you since the ball.'

'I'm not sure she's *latched* onto me. She's nice. We have a lot in common, so we spend time together. I don't see much harm in that.'

'Marcus, don't you think you should find someone more appropriate? Someone from a better background…'

'…what's wrong with Anita's background?' he interrupted defensively. Marcus knew this was a pivotal moment and from it he would be able to tell how strong Austin's feelings were about Anita. If he admitted that he'd looked into Anita's background, it was bad. If he made a comment about her not being from a Council family or something similar, it wasn't quite so dire. Luckily he did the latter.

'I just think you'd be much better off with someone more like us. What about one of the Councillors' daughters? There are lots of very nice, well connected girls who are far more suitable for a Descendant.'

'Well I'm afraid I'm going to have to disappoint you. I like Anita, she's so much more interesting than the other girls I know, so thanks for your concern, but I'm confident I can judge who I should spend time with and who's best to avoid.' With that, he picked up his tea, along with another piece of shortbread, and headed up to his suite, a little baffled. It was so unlike Austin to pussyfoot around the edge of a topic. He was usually more comfortable taking the direct approach and Marcus was surprised he didn't simply try to ban him from seeing Anita again. It wouldn't have worked, obviously, but it would have been more in character. Something was going on, and he had to find out what.

*****

Marcus made his way to The Island later that evening, still confused by his father's earlier words. He knew Austin didn't like powerful people, but Anita was hardly a threat. He arrived, very pleased at the prospect of spending an evening with Anita, even more so now he knew how much his father disapproved.

He walked in and scanned the room, smiling as he spotted Anita, Bas and Cleo, before recognising Alexander's unwelcome form, his leg dangerously close to Anita's as he sat smugly with the others at Cleo's favourite table. In the name of the Gods, what is he doing here, Marcus silently cursed as he saw Anita smile at something Alexander had just said. His mood blackened as he made his way towards the table, greeting everyone, except Alexander, warmly when he got there. He sat down next to Anita, then leaned in to kiss her briefly and purposefully on the lips. Anita felt an energy reaction from everyone as he did it, not least from herself, as she felt a mix of embarrassment and excitement rise in her. Marcus carried on as though what he'd just done was totally normal and ordered a bottle of Ginger Champagne, feeling especially pleased with himself, to celebrate.

Anita was now sandwiched in a booth between Marcus and Alexander, with Bas directly opposite, and she felt intensely uncomfortable. It was very pleasant to be in the company of either Marcus or Alexander when they were on their own, however, both together like this was not something she would want to repeat in a hurry. Marcus' hand made its way to her leg and Alexander's knee was so close that the fabric of their clothes made it difficult to determine whether there was actual contact or not. Why had she invited Alexander, she asked herself.

Cleo, obviously enjoying Anita's current predicament, and wishing to stir the situation further, broke the awkward silence. 'Marcus, we were just discussing a trip to Kingdom this weekend. Can you believe Anita has never been?'

'Really?' Marcus looked at Anita, and she shook her head in confirmation. 'Well I'll come too to show you around then.'

Cleo smirked and looked at Anita. 'I thought you had to see your mother this weekend?' she said tentatively, trying to suppress a worried look.

'Damn, yeah, you're right. Well go without me then and I'll give you a list of things to do. I also have a brilliant driver there, who you can, of course, use, and you must stay in the house.'

Anita was devising a tactical way to break it to Marcus, when Cleo, true to form, jumped in again. 'That's so kind Marcus, but Anita, Bas and I are going with Alexander, so we're planning to stay with him.'

Marcus' face was a picture and everyone held their breath to see what would come next, Anita noting that Alexander's energy was steady as a rock. 'You're staying with Alexander?' Marcus asked, directing the question at Anita.

'Yes,' interjected Alexander. 'It will be more comfortable for everyone than staying in a hotel, not to mention safer,' he shot a meaningful look at Marcus, 'and besides, I'm not sure Austin would welcome a house full of guests when he's in Kingdom this weekend.'

Anita felt Marcus' negative energy rising towards Alexander and knew she had to defuse the situation. 'I'm sure your mother's really looking forward to seeing you after all the excitement of the last few weeks,' she said quickly, placing a reassuring hand on Marcus' thigh. The distraction worked and Anita felt Marcus mellow a little, but it wasn't enough to make him let it go. 'And it's only for the weekend,' she said innocently, leaning in to him. 'We'll be back before you know it.' She smiled sweetly, trying to look something like a lost puppy that might cry if he tried to stop her. It worked; his energy returned to more normal levels.

'Ok, fine,' he said, relenting, leaning in and giving her another, much longer kiss. Under normal circumstances, Anita would have gone a shade of purple and everyone would have taken the piss out of them, but everyone, perhaps apart from Bas, who looked pretty uncomfortable, realised that Anita had just adverted a crisis, so didn't say a thing.

'So, why are you going to Kingdom?' asked Marcus, his tone a little edgy.

Cleo jumped in again, which Anita was this time grateful for, as it shifted everyone's focus away from her and Marcus. 'Well Alexander has some business stuff to do, Bas is going to see someone to talk about energy, and I'm going to see my dad. Dad's a trader you see, so he's been out in the Wild Lands for ages and I can't wait to see him. He's very fond of Anita, so she's coming along for the ride.' This wasn't entirely true. The way it had really happened was that Cleo had told them she was going to Kingdom this weekend to see her dad and Alexander had said he was going too. He had suggested that Bas come along to meet with some guy that had an interest in the energy. Bas had agreed immediately and Cleo had then suggested that Anita might like to come along too. Cleo's motives had nothing to do with her dad, but Marcus didn't need to know that.

Marcus lost interest as Cleo started rabbiting on about the commodities her father traded and how he was hardly ever in Empire any longer, so he put his arm around Anita and pulled her closer towards him. She was his and Alexander had better not forget it.

CHAPTER 11

By the time Friday rolled around, Anita was glad at the prospect of a break from Marcus. He had monopolised her time since he'd learned she'd be going to Kingdom with Alexander. He had come to meet her every morning to walk her to the Observatory, had spent time in the Observatory asking questions about what exactly it was she did, had walked her home every day, and had insisted she spend every evening with him, meaning she'd had to cancel her lessons with Alexander. Anita loved spending time with Marcus, but it was starting to feel claustrophobic, so was looking forward to the weekend away. Friday afternoon eventually arrived and she got in an energy car with Bas, Alexander and Cleo (with Marcus there to wave them off, of course), full of excitement as they headed to Kingdom. The car had some seats facing forwards and some facing backwards, so they chatted easily all the way to Kingdom.

After several hours, the tension of his proximity to Anita now almost unbearable, Alexander cut across the conversation, having glimpsed the first outline of Kingdom. He always felt awed when he laid eyes on the city's distant silhouette, as despite the distance, it still conveyed a magnificent power that made the blood race around his veins. Kingdom sat just above the sea, a cluster of soaring spires and elegant outlines, with a wall around the city that seemed to hug it to the coast. In its centre were three imposing spires that rose above to dominate the rest. They belonged to the Temples, their sheer, dominant size masked from this far out. Whereas Empire had a stately, romantic feel, Kingdom had none of this charm; it was majestic yet harsh, radiating a feeling that untold opportunity lay within its walls, but that opportunity came with a risk, that you would never be totally safe there, regardless who you were.

'There it is,' he said, looking across at Anita and gesturing out of the window towards the capitol. He watched Anita's face as she saw it for the first time, feeling her energy soar as her face lit up. This was Anita's kind of place, where a challenge waited at every corner, and those who fought the hardest won the day.

They raced towards, then through, the gates, flying across the city, along ancient streets and past the colossal Temples in the middle. Anita strained to spot the relic, but, frustrated at their speed, couldn't quite catch a glimpse. 'Don't worry,' laughed Alexander, 'we can go and see it tomorrow.' They carried on through Kingdom, past a wide array of spectacular looking shops, restaurants and houses, until they passed out through the gate the other side.

Anita looked at Alexander, confused. 'We're not staying in Kingdom?'

'Afraid not. My family tend to rank privacy over convenience, so our residence is just outside. We'll be spending most of our time in the city though.'

Anita was disappointed to be leaving the city before she'd had a chance to explore, however she was excited to see Alexander's house. A couple of miles outside Kingdom, the car pulled through some understated gates onto a large, sweeping drive, which swung in a wide arch to dramatically reveal a spectacular house, large but not vast, covered in magnificent purple flowers and with wonderful lawns that rolled out to the top of a cliff, the sea crashing into the rocks below. Anita's energy soared when she saw the house and Alexander's responded when he felt her reaction; he'd been worried that she wouldn't like it.

She turned to face him when she felt his energy rise and beamed at him, Cleo and Bas making appreciative noises. 'It's beautiful,' she breathed, before spotting the breath-taking view out of the other window. She froze and all the colour drained from her face. 'Alexander...' she started, feeling sick, then stopped, lost for words.

His face froze, his energy seemed to too, but before he could respond, Cleo broke the spell. 'In the name of the Gods, Alexander. That is bloody glorious,' she said, looking in the same direction as Anita, out over the sea. However, although the sea itself provided a theatrical backdrop, what had caught her attention was the view back across the bay; a view that contained the other side of Kingdom. It was breath-taking; Kingdom looked like it belonged in a snow dome, a perfect city contained within a neat, protective wall.

However, Anita's surprise was quite different to Cleo's. Apart from the city, which didn't feature, this was identical to the cliff in her mind. To her surprise, she felt afraid. She had never been here before, so how was this place in her head, and why without Kingdom? Alexander smiled sheepishly and sent a nudge to the edge of her energy field, but it had no impact, and Anita's mind started to race. Was it someone from Alexander's family who'd put the cylinder in her head? Was that how the cliff had got there? Did Alexander know something? Had he brought her to Kingdom under false pretences?

Alexander felt Anita's energy turn wary, and wished they were alone so he could reassure her. He'd wanted to warn her before the trip, but he hadn't been able to get anywhere near her since drinks at The Island; Marcus had practically been her shadow for the last few days.

They pulled up to the front door, Cleo talking at a hundred miles an hour about how wonderful the house was, and how lucky Alexander was to have such a spectacular view, but nobody was really listening. They climbed out of the car to be greeted by the housekeeper, Mrs Hudson, who ushered them inside. They entered to find themselves in an enormous, glass-topped atrium that basked the internal courtyard in light, Alexander quickly whisking them away from the feathery space to show them to their rooms. They climbed one side of a double staircase, turned left at the top, and followed the corridor to the end, where Alexander opened a door to reveal Cleo's gargantuan quarters.

'You'll be in here, Cleo. Your bags should already be waiting for you. We'll see you downstairs for supper at eight. That should give you enough time to freshen up?'

Cleo barely heard what he said. She was preoccupied with the extravagant four poster bed and view over the bay. 'Uh-ha. Yep, sure thing. See you downstairs,' she replied, not even looking at the others.

Alexander dropped Bas off in the room next to Cleo, before leading Anita over to the other side of the house and opening an understated door into a smaller, but truly beautiful room. Anita, who had thought nothing but suspicious thoughts since she'd seen the view, softened, as she took in the proportions. It was big, but not ostentatious, full of gorgeous draped fabric, and had a weightless, carefree feel to it. The ceiling to floor windows let in so much light that the room seemed to almost radiate it, and provided an uninterrupted view out over the perfectly manicured lawns that seemed to skip to the edge of the cliff and then jump off into the sea below. But the jewel in the crown was the sight of Kingdom, which seemed to almost levitate above the sea. There must be so much power in the city, thought Anita, that it wouldn't be surprising if it was suppressing its energy, causing it to lift a little off the ground.

Alexander had been watching Anita as she took in the room and the view, searching for the right words to apologise. 'Anita,' he started, almost hesitantly, 'I'm really sorry.' She turned slowly to face him, quizzing him with her eyes, but didn't say a word. 'When we arranged to come to Kingdom, I knew I had to tell you. I was going to tell you in our next lesson, but Marcus hasn't let you out of his sight long enough for me to get anywhere near you.'

Anita could see Alexander was telling the truth and could feel it in his energy, which he was making no attempt to hide, but she wasn't ready to let him off the hook quite yet. 'Why didn't you tell me when we first meditated to the cliff?' she asked, her tone neutral.

'I didn't really know how to.' He paused, looking, if Anita was not mistaken, a bit embarrassed. The impervious Alexander, embarrassed, wonders never cease, she thought. 'I thought you'd be suspicious of me if I told you, and I have no explanation for how the cliff got into your head; I have no idea why it's there. And I thought it best to keep anything personal out of our lessons. You know how Marcus feels about us spending time together; can you imagine how he'd react if he found out one of the places in your head was here?'

'How would he find out?'

'You might have told him.' He said it matter of factly, and it felt like he'd shot an arrow through her arm. Not a fatal blow, but painful none the less. He didn't trust her.

'I need time to get ready for dinner,' said Anita, clearly indicating it was time for Alexander to leave. Alexander looked for a moment like he might refuse, before whirling around and gliding back through the door, his energy suppressed so Anita couldn't read it. He opened the door next to Anita's and entered his room, resisting the urge to slam it closed behind him. He unconsciously made his way to his bed, his feet leading the way, his mind racing through replays of what had just happened as he sat down and then lay back on the fluffy duvet, running his hands through his hair and then holding them there, each one pulling on a section of his disheveled mane. You total idiot, he scolded himself. That couldn't have gone any worse if you'd tried.

*****

As eight o'clock neared, Anita left her room and went to find Cleo. She wasn't going to tell her about what had happened, but she felt like some company, so tiptoed past Alexander's room in her gold sandals and floor length goddess gown (another purchase from Temple Mews when she'd been told she would need to dress for dinner), and went in search of her best friend.

Anita got to Cleo's room just as Cleo was coming out. She looked spectacular, as always, in a floor length silk chiffon dress that wafted around her legs as she walked. 'Hey,' said Anita, 'you look amazing.'

'Thanks. You don't look too bad yourself,' she smiled back, feigning surprise.

'Very funny.'

'Ready to make our grand entrance? I think the boys have already gone down.' Anita nodded, turned around, and headed for the staircase. They made their way down the sweeping stairs and into the atrium, where the others were already sitting, sipping spectacular looking cocktails from crystal glasses. The boys stood up when they entered, and Anita thought how funny it was that getting dressed up could bring out one's best behaviour, as she was introduced to a man named Anderson.

'Anderson is a relic specialist,' said Alexander to Anita, 'and Anita is an energy specialist. She works in the Observatory with Bas,' he said to Anderson.

Anita blushed. 'I'm not sure I would quite describe myself as a specialist,' she said quickly, 'but I do work with Bas, who definitely is. But a relic specialist? How interesting,' she chirped, deflecting the conversation away from herself, 'I had no idea such a profession existed.'

Anderson looked a bit shifty. 'Well it doesn't really, not officially. The Descendants, specifically Austin, banned it a couple of years ago, not sure why, but they tend to just let me get on with it.' He smiled a smile that said 'no more questions please' and turned to introduce his wife. 'Anita, this is my wife, Arabella, she assists me with my research.'

'Hello,' said Anita warmly. Maybe she could make friends with Arabella, who could shed some light on what exactly a relic specialist did. 'It's so nice to meet you. And what great timing,' she said, quickly pressing on before someone else butted in. 'We're going to see the relic tomorrow. It's my first visit, and it would be so great if you could join us?'

Anderson looked shifty again, like he was trying to find the right way to say no, but before he could, Arabella agreed. 'Yes, of course we will. It would be our pleasure.' She knew Anderson wouldn't like it, but Arabella had heard a great deal of gossip about Anita since they'd got back to the city, so she wanted to see for herself what all the fuss was about.

After a couple more lethal-yet-delicious cocktails, Mrs Hudson ushered the group into the dining room. It was like the rest of the house; large, spacious, light and sophisticated, but not in any way grand or stuffy. The whole house felt like it wouldn't be out of place on a mountain top amid the clouds, and the dining room was no exception. Anita found herself between Alexander and Anderson at dinner and pointedly turned away from Alexander so as to shut him out of the conversation. She was still feeling hurt after the revelation earlier and had no intention of making life easy, not for a little while anyway.

The meal was delicious; whoever Alexander employed to do his cooking was extremely skilled, and when Anita overheard Alexander telling Arabella that a lot of the food had been grown in the garden, caught on the estate, or fished from the sea, she relaxed her stand against him. It was becoming hard work to keep up without looking petulant anyway.

They were just getting onto a spectacular cheese course, when Bas couldn't contain his excitement any longer, and asked, 'Anderson, if I'm not mistaken, you used to study energy, especially energy transfer. What made you change your focus?'

Anderson smiled warmly at Bas. 'Yes, I did indeed. I worked with your father at one point as I spent a great deal of time in the Observatory when I was younger. Energy transfer and destruction is a fascinating area. Of course, there's no way to truly destroy energy, you just have to find ways to hinder its transfer from potential to actual, divert it, or find ways to use it up at a faster rate, however, energy transfer is a much more delicate topic. I studied it for years. Back then, there was a great deal more interest then there is now, as that was effectively what people were doing when they transferred secret messages…'

'…hang on, what?' interrupted Cleo, annoyed that she couldn't quite keep up, especially when it was about her specialist subject. 'What do you mean people transferred secret messages? Who did and why?'

Anderson waited for a few moments, hoping that someone else would step in and explain, but given that nobody took up the reigns, he continued. 'A few decades ago, the world was a dangerous place. Peter was born into the Body bloodline and this caused widespread disruption, panic, conspiracy theories, prophecies that the world was now doomed, and crucially, powerful factions began to form. Some rallied behind the Descendants, believing they would find a way to free the world before Peter ever came to power. Some turned to the academics for answers and funded research into the relic and the energy. And one group formed with the aim of keeping the energy steady, so we could go on living normally regardless what happened with the relic. This group was called the Institution and they were particularly elusive. They took great pains to hide their work from anybody and everybody, but especially from the Descendants, for whom they had a significant disregard, thinking they weren't doing their bit to free the world.'

Anita shot a look at Alexander to see how he was taking this slight, but his face was as steady as his energy, so she turned her attention back to Anderson.

'But, as I am sure you can imagine, views questioning the authority of the Descendants were seen by many as treason, so the Institution had to operate in the shadows, passing messages carefully and without evidence between members. To do this, they used a method where they would plant a message in the brain of another, the message generally taking the shape of a brass cylinder. When the person next meditated, they would come across the brass cylinder, open it in private, and respond in the same way. This process is essentially a transfer of energy from one person to another, and nobody to this day really understands how it's possible, hence the research people are doing into areas such as this.'

Anita knew from Cleo's energy, not to mention how still and upright she had grown in her seat, that she had hundreds of questions she was dying to ask, but instead, she nodded along with everyone else, pretending to understand exactly what Anderson was talking about.

'Everything eventually settled down. I think people had had enough of living their lives having to look over their shoulders, and people started to use brass cylinders to store energy instead. Either they would store information and memories that they wanted to share with people, or information and memories they wanted to hide. The fascinating thing about this, was that if someone stole a cylinder with someone else's memories, the energy would strain to get back to its rightful owner. This breaks all the rules we understand about how energy works and is why it lures so many academics in to study it; it's truly baffling. I used to study energy transfers like this, however, I came across the idea that sending the relic home could have something to do with energy transfer, so turned my attention to the relic instead.'

'How did you come across that idea?' asked Anita, captivated like everyone else, except Alexander, who was observing Anita.

Anderson closed down as soon as the words were out of Anita's mouth and she immediately regretted saying them. Luckily, Alexander came to her rescue. 'Poor Anderson. He comes over for a friendly dinner and ends up doing a post-dinner key-note. I think it's time to take coffee and nightcaps in the library.'

Anita shot a grateful look in Alexander's direction before following the others out of the dining room. Something interesting definitely going on there, she thought, as she entered the library and helped herself to a walnut liquor on the rocks in a beautiful crystal glass tumbler.

Several hours later, after Cleo and Bas had retired to bed, Arabella decided it was time for them to make their way home. They thanked Alexander for a wonderful evening and he got up to show them out, leaving Anita alone in the library with a view out over the bay. Feeling pent up after all the talking, and, more frustratingly, skirting around the edge of some very interesting topics, Anita left the library and headed to the cloakroom, where she selected a floor length, black, hooded cloak for herself and a floor length, red cloak for Alexander. She swung her cloak around her shoulders and fastened it using the heavy, ornate broach attached to its neck before heading for the front door. Alexander appeared just as Anita got there and was about to close the door behind him, but before he got a chance, Anita threw the cloak at him and disappeared through the door and down the steps, without so much as a backward glance to see if he was following her.

Alexander stood dumbfounded for a second, watching Anita start to run across the grass towards the cliffs, weighing up his options before giving fully into temptation and flying down the steps after her, throwing his cloak over his shoulders in an easy movement as he went.

Anita could feel Alexander's energy chasing her and her energy soared as he closed in, her sky-high heels slowing her down as she sprinted. Adrenaline pumped through her, pushing her energy higher still, her cloak and dress streaming out behind her, an ecstatic smile on her lips. She had just about reached the edge when Alexander caught up, grabbed hold of her hand to slow her to a stop, and spun her around to face him. As he did it, an explosion of tingles cascaded through their fingers then raced around their bodies. They locked eyes to question and at the same time affirm that the other could feel it too. Without moving his eyes from hers, Alexander pushed his hand flat against Anita's and held it up to chest height in between them, mirroring the position with his other hand. Anita responded and lifted her free right hand to place it flat against his open left palm, feeling the tingles intensify as the energy coursed between them. Alexander half smiled then very slowly moved first his left then his right hand a few millimetres away from hers. She inhaled deeply, spellbound as the tingles continued even with a gap between them. He leaned his head forward and murmured, 'sit down,' his piercing blue eyes caressing hers. They effortlessly and elegantly sank to sit cross legged on the floor, hands and eyes maintaining their positions. His intention was clear, so she lightly closed her eyes and made her way to her Centre, where she knew she would find him waiting. Anita went through the usual flight, fall and duck through the door into the tent and she inwardly beamed when she saw Alexander's glorious, half-naked form in its usual position on the low bed in the corner.

She moved towards him, noting that this felt different to normal; she felt more connected to him, almost as though she were in his warm, protective embrace. She sat down cross legged on the bed in front of him and was about to speak when the world around her blurred and she was jolted to a new location. She looked around and realised she was on the lawn she'd just run across in the real world, so funny, she thought, that she was in the same place inside her head as outside. But whereas when they normally meditated here there was sunlight streaming down, playing on the water below, now it was night time, with the moon and stars casting only a soft, romantic glow. Anita wondered why it was night here when her Centre had still been basked in light. She looked around to see where Alexander was to ask him, when she caught sight of his toned form pelting across the lawn towards her, echoing the game from minutes before. Without thinking, Anita's body responded and she whirled towards the sea, running as fast as she could towards it, her dress, heels and cloak slowing her down as before. Alexander (also dressed as he was in the outside world) caught her, but this time, as he spun her around, he pulled her to his chest, his face inches from hers, hands moving to her hips, scared she might step away. His eyes were mesmerising and Anita felt her stomach somersault as he bowed his head and lightly pressed his forehead to hers, closing his eyes to savour the moment, breathing deeply to drink in her jasmine scented perfume. Without seeming to command it, his mouth found its way to hers, her soft lips cautiously meeting his. He placed delicate kisses on her and she responded, mouths exploring each other, movements becoming more confident. They eventually pulled apart, Alexander stealing a brief final kiss, before smiling wryly down at her. They sank to the floor to sit cross legged as they were in the world outside, although this time their knees were touching and their hands were joined.

After a few moments of silent and surprised contemplation, Anita felt guilt start to invade her thoughts, so she broke the silence. 'Why's it dark?' she asked. 'The cliff is normally filled with sunlight when we come here.'

Alexander smiled cautiously. 'Because we're no longer inside your head. We're inside mine.'

Anita was shocked, but her energy was steady, more intrigued than angry. 'This is one of the places in your head too?'

He relaxed a little. He'd been worried she would take this less well. 'Yep. But as you can see there are some differences. In my head its night time and the house and Kingdom are also here. For some reason they're not in your version, not that I'm sure how this place ever got inside your head at all.'

'But you have a theory?'

'Yes, I have a theory. But I'm not sure this is quite the right time to share.'

'Why not?' she asked, a hint of annoyance in her tone.

'Because there are so many other things to discuss.'

'Like what?' she said, Alexander's diversionary tactics successfully averting her attention.

'There isn't anything, after all the conversations this evening, that you want to ask me?' He smiled indulgently as she realised this was her chance.

'Why did Austin get rid of all the relic specialists but leave Anderson alone?'

'I don't know the whole answer to that, but Austin decided a while back that studying the relic was to be outlawed. Nobody really knows why, but he sprouted some stuff about not wanting to give people false hope. Why he left Anderson alone I have no idea, I've often wondered myself, but the most obvious explanation would be either that Anderson has something on Austin that he doesn't want to come out, or that Austin has some specific interest in Anderson's work. That's just speculation though.'

'What made Anderson connect the relic and energy transfer?'

'Again, I don't really know. I think he must have discovered something either in a book, or been told something by a scholar, or maybe he discovered something during his time in the Wild Lands. I'm pretty sure it wasn't anything in accepted academic texts or from the current academics, as there's nobody else working on the assumption that energy transfer and sending the relic back are connected. Although, even if they were, they wouldn't be able to talk about it in public, given Austin's decree. I doubt Anderson would've told anyone, except perhaps Arabella; it's not the kind of thing he'd want in the public domain. The world is much safer than it used to be, but that doesn't mean it's safe.'

'Do you think Anderson's working with the Institution?'

'No.'

'How can you be so sure?'

'Anderson hates the Institution. He thinks they were responsible for a great deal of unnecessary suffering a couple of decades back and the Institution's not entirely behind the idea of sending the relic back, which Anderson finds suspicious. It wouldn't take much for the Institution to get into bed with the Descendants and Anderson can't stand the Descendants.'

Anita laughed. 'Need I remind you that you're a Descendant and he just came over for dinner?!'

'The Spirit Descendants have always been less, uh…fundamentalist shall we say, than the rest of them. We tend to be more philosophical and less power hungry. We're more open to ideas different to our own, which means people like Anderson find us more trustworthy than the others.'

'Is he right to trust you?'

Alexander was taken aback by the abruptness of the question. 'Why wouldn't he be?'

'I don't know, something to do with you withholding information from me makes me think maybe you would do it to him too.'

'Anita, the only reason I withheld information from you was because Marcus hasn't let me anywhere near you since he found out we were coming here together. I was going to tell you.'

'You had plenty of opportunity to tell me before that night at The Island. We've been meditating together for weeks.'

'As I've said before, Marcus is a jealous person, and whether you choose to believe it or not, you'll be in danger if you two drift apart, or worse, if he thought you weren't totally loyal to him. I didn't want to get any closer to you then was needed to help you protect yourself, and I had a feeling that sharing something like a place in our minds could have that effect.'

'What do you think of the Institution?' Anita's change of tack took him by surprise. He'd expected more of an argument than that.

'Why do you ask?'

'I just want to know.'

'To be honest, I don't know. I used to be wary of them; it's what Descendants are taught from an early age. But then, their goal is energy stability, which is a noble goal for the good of everyone. But if they're willing to prevent the relic from being returned to keep the energy steady, I don't think I agree with their aim. Why? What do you think of them?'

'Would you help them if they asked?' Anita ignored his question.

'It would depend what they asked me to do. If you're asking me if I trust them, then the answer is most definitely no. I think it's best to steer clear of most people with a political agenda. Why the sudden interest? Have they asked you for help?'

'You have a political agenda.'

'Do I?' The words were a challenge, and as he said them, the mood between them sharpened. It turned wary and almost hostile.

Anita said nothing for a few moments, then raised Alexander's hand to her lips and kissed it, knowing she'd pushed him as far as he was willing to go tonight. She looked up at him. 'Doesn't every Descendant have a political agenda out of necessity?' she asked softly.

Alexander searched for words to respond but couldn't find any. She seized the moment and rocked lightly forwards, now on all fours, cat-like in front of him, her hands on his knees. She leaned in and kissed him lightly on his lips, then broke contact to wait for his response. He did nothing. His eyes were closed and his mind was racing. He knew he'd already passed the point of no return, but this was exactly what he'd been trying to avoid. If Marcus found out, who knew what would happen, but every instinct he possessed was screaming at him to kiss her.

She waited several seconds before leaning in and kissing him again. She could feel the impact she was having on his energy and knew he was fighting an internal battle, but she also knew she couldn't push him too hard or he would run away. Again, she waited, before bowing her head to kiss him for a third time. This time, as she was pulling away, she felt him respond. He pushed his lips gently back against hers, and she froze, her energy a strange mix of excitement and terror that any movement would push him away. He kissed her more assertively, pushing carefully against her warm lips. Anita moved her hands to his neck, pulling him gently towards her, their lips now parted, tongues caressing each other.

They became more confident, then more urgent, Alexander rising to his knees, his hands pulling at her lower back to press her to him before lifting her off the ground and pushing her backwards. He laid her roughly on the ground, her cloak fanned out beneath her, then followed her over and pinned her with his weight. She ran her fingers through his hair as he kissed and nipped her neck, then tugged at the clasp of his cloak, pulled of his dinner jacket, and slid his shirt free from his trousers, her fingers making their way under his shirt and greedily taking in the firm, athletic contours of his back. He kissed his way down her neck, reaching her breasts as he slid her silk dress up over her hips. Anita arched her back, pushing her body towards him as he slid his arm under her and pulled her into him. He smelt like ripe oranges and she inhaled deeply as he brushed his fingers down her spine, but as he did it, the world began to blur.

Anita opened her eyes to find herself sitting facing Alexander, palms out in front of her, just as she had been when they'd begun to meditate. 'What happened?' she asked, both confused and disappointed, moving her hands back to her lap. The tingling had stopped and all she felt now was that she had been robbed of a great deal of pleasure.

'It's likely that the guilt we were both feeling, but doing a good job of suppressing, yanked us back to the present. Our brains were caught in a dilemma, not knowing what to do, so booted us out. It's probably for the best when you think about it.'

'Why? It's not like nothing happened, and I was quite enjoying myself.'

Typical Body, thought Alexander, who, in truth, was also feeling robbed. He searched her eyes, hoping to see some sort of understanding of the danger she was putting herself in, but saw not a trace. 'I was enjoying myself too, but it's good nothing else happened, and it's best that we forget about it. I don't think Marcus would take it well if he found out.'

Anita knew she wasn't going to win tackling this straight on. He would just harp on about Marcus and the danger she was in, so she changed tack. 'There is one more thing I wanted to ask you about.'

'Yes?'

'You feel the tingles too?'

Alexander's breath caught in his throat. 'Yes,' he nodded huskily.

'And you've nudged the edge of my energy?'

'You can feel that too?'

Anita nodded. 'Does everyone feel them? I feel them with both you and Marcus,' she said, looking a little sheepish at bringing him up, 'but I've never felt them with anyone else.'

'You feel them with Marcus too?' Anita nodded again. 'Interesting,' said Alexander, pausing to consider what to say next. 'The nudges and tingles are caused when energy is exerted by one person on another, that much we think we know. They only seem to take place when the energy is intended to be pleasurable or supportive and certainly positive; there have never been reports of tingles due to negative energy. But, the problem is that it's rare to come across people who are able to feel them, and generally both parties have to be able to feel them for either to be aware of them. That's why it surprises me that you felt them with Marcus, as I had no idea he had the ability to feel them too.'

'Well I'm not entirely sure he can. He's never brought it up, nor does he ever do anything which would indicate he can feel them, and it sounds like the research is limited, so maybe it is possible for only one party to feel them? How many people have been studied?'

'As far as I know only a handful, so you may well be right. And given the nature of the situations a person has to be in to feel them, I'm sure the existing findings aren't robust.'

'Have you been studied?'

'Gods no,' he laughed. 'No Descendant could ever submit themselves to academic testing. And I'm sure there are many who feel them but are too scared to volunteer themselves; it can be dangerous to stand out when there's someone like Austin in power.'

'So long story short, nobody really knows what they are, when they occur, or what they're for.'

'That pretty much sums it up. Nudges are more easily studied, as we can learn to control them, but there's nobody who can control tingles, at least nobody who admits to being able to anyway.'

'We could try to control them? It's clearly something to do with positive energy and perhaps desire? It's lessened with Marcus now, which might have something to do with my lessened desire for him, or maybe it has something to do with the unknown? I know what to expect when I see Marcus now, whereas obviously I didn't when I first started spending time with him.'

'Lessened desire?' Alexander asked, his facial expression making Anita almost laugh out loud, and he was clearly shocked at himself for saying it.

'Only a little lessened, not entirely,' she smiled back.

'But you have slept together?' he asked tentatively.

'No,' she said stiffly. 'Not that it's any of your business.' She was shocked at his indelicate question.

'And Marcus is still following you around like a lost puppy? He doesn't suspect that you may, um, have interests elsewhere?'

'Who says I have interests elsewhere?' Anita challenged, enjoying the power of making Alexander squirm. 'And anyway, so long as he's still interested in me, he'll follow me around like a lost puppy for longer if I don't sleep with him than if I do. Marcus likes a challenge remember? And I'm his current challenge. He hasn't cracked it yet, so he'll keep trying until he does, or until something new and shiny catches his attention.'

'I thought you didn't like the Mind disciplines,' Alexander smirked.

'I don't. But Marcus does.' Anita shivered.

'Come on, let's get back inside,' he said, getting up and taking Anita's hand to help her. They both felt a shiver of energy run through their fingers and smiled as Anita got to her feet, her dress and cloak cascading to the floor. She took his outstretched arm and

151

they wandered back across the lawn, chatting about what they would do for the rest of their time in Kingdom. They entered the house and Alexander walked Anita to her room, the tension growing, the conversation more stunted as they approached. They stopped outside her door and Anita turned to look at Alexander, perplexed.

'You've spent all this time pushing me away and telling me how much danger I'd be in if Marcus changes his mind about me, or even if he thought we were friends. You've barely said two words to me outside of lessons, I know nothing about you, you normally shut down any questioning I start, yet tonight you let me ask you whatever I wanted. Why?'

Smoke filled Alexander's eyes as they played across hers. 'Because I realised life's too short not to flirt with danger when it feels like it might be worth it.'

Anita smiled, turning to open her door. 'Goodnight Alexander,' she said, looking back over her shoulder, 'it's been a most illuminating evening.' She disappeared into her room, shutting the door gently behind her.

*****

The following day, Alexander woke up early, a mix of emotions racing through his mind. He knew trying to sleep was futile so got up and headed for his grandfather's library. When he needed to think, he always found this a helpful place to go. The study was small and pokey with piles of books and manuscripts littered everywhere, along with old energy metres, works of art, and the odd piece of furniture. The room had heavy drapes across a large window that overlooked the garden, but the drapes were kept closed for fear the light would damage a priceless book or piece of artwork. Alexander had always thought somebody tripping over a stack of invaluable manuscripts was more of a risk, but seeing as he was virtually the only one that ever came in here now, he supposed that risk was small.

He turned on the lamp by the door and used its dim light to guide him to the comfortable brown leather chair in front of the large, leather-topped partners' desk. He turned on the lamp that lived in the corner of the desk, sat down in the chair, and surveyed the scene. He immediately felt more relaxed, noting how strange it was that such disorder could make him feel calm and help him find perspective. His mind raced over recent events before centring on

Anita, the Body Descendant. She hadn't taken it well when he'd withheld information from her before, so he was guessing she wouldn't be too pleased if she found out from someone else what he knew about her bloodline. Then there was all the stuff with the energy; Helena's recent proposition for him to join the Institution, and what the bloody hell Austin was playing at. He was sure Christiana's death had been about Anita, but surely something more than that was the cause of his recent stance on the energy.

Alexander spotted his grandfather's old music player in the corner and manoeuvred his way past several stacks of books and scattered artefacts to turn it on. He'd expected dulcet, classical tones to waft through the air, but to his surprise, a wistful modern melody rippled out instead, complete with smoky voice and poetic lyrics. He made his way back to the desk, but as he edged his way past the last pile of books, accidentally toppled a brass model of the world onto the floor. 'Damn,' he said out loud as the model rolled under the desk. He crouched down on all fours and followed it under, reaching around wildly with his arms to try and locate the missing artefact. After a few moments, he realised his search would be more successful with the assistance of some light, so he reached for a small lamp from a nearby table, pulled it to the floor and switched it on. Thankfully, he spotted the world near the back, and crawled further in to reach it. As his fingers closed around the model, to his surprise, he heard a soft click under his left knee, near the edge of the drawer section of the desk. He moved back out, lifted the rug covering the area he had been kneeling on, and was surprised to see a tiny panel in the floor had sprung open to reveal a small metal object inside. He reached in and fished out a tiny, simple brass key, closing the panel and replacing the rug before examining it in detail.

After a lengthy inspection, Alexander concluded that it was a normal key; there was nothing particularly special about it. If anything, it was a bit on the boring side, with no ornate head, no engraving, no suggestion as to which lock it fitted, nothing. Very disappointing and very much something his grandfather would like. He tried the key in all the locks he could find in the study; the desk, the door, the windows, the cabinets, but it fitted none of them; it was far too small. Bloody grandfather, he thought, hearing voices down the corridor and realising that everyone else must be up and eating breakfast. He pocketed the key and turned off the lights, taking one final look around to make sure he hadn't missed anything obvious. Frustrated when nothing jumped out at him, he closed the door sulkily behind him and stalked down the corridor to see his guests.

'Morning,' came Cleo's singsong voice as he entered the breakfast room, another room basked in light through enormous sash windows.

'Morning,' grunted Alexander.

Anita looked up from her breakfast, concern all over her face. He pulled himself out of his mood for long enough to send her a reassuring smile and she went back to her bacon and brioche.

'Everything alright?' asked Cleo, never one to miss out on potential gossip.

'Couldn't be better thanks,' he said with a disarming smile, whilst helping himself to a lavish portion of smoked salmon and poached eggs on lightly toasted walnut and raisin bread, covered in hollandaise sauce. He joined the others at the table and after a couple of generous mouthfuls, his mood began to lift.

'So I thought we could head straight to the relic after breakfast, if everyone's happy with that? We can send a message ahead to Anderson and Arabella and ask them to meet us there.'

'Sounds great,' said Bas. He'd been wide awake since 6 o'clock, full of excitement at the prospect of being shown the relic by an expert, a relic expert who was also an energy transfer expert no less. His excitement was almost palpable as they bundled into Alexander's car to be whisked down into Kingdom.

Alexander and Anita were, this time, sitting next to each other, with Bas opposite Alexander and Cleo next to Anita. They were giving Mrs Hudson and one of the chefs a ride as well, so the chef was in the front with the driver and Mrs Hudson sat next to Bas. Anita and Alexander's legs were touching, shivers passing distractingly between them. She pulled away, certain someone would notice their soaring energy, but the sensation continued, Anita not sure if it was a repeat of what had happened last night, or a phantom. She was pretty much certain she wasn't imagining it though when she felt Alexander send a nudge to the edge of her energy; was this flirting? If so, this was a whole new world to explore, but she did feel guilty, she had feelings for Marcus too. She made an inward promise that nothing more could happen with Alexander, in their minds or anywhere else, until she'd had a chance to work out what she wanted, and that would mean at least until she saw Marcus again. Her energy dropped as she shut herself off to Alexander's charms, and he turned to look at her, trying to hide the concern from his face as he felt the change.

He wanted to ask her if everything was alright, to convince her that it was. He knew she'd be feeling guilty, and although he didn't really know why, he hated Marcus, he felt guilty too. They pulled up at the Temple of the Spirit and once Bas, Cleo, Anita and Alexander had got out, the driver pulled away to take the chef and Mrs Hudson to the market. They made their way into the Temple, which, although broadly similar to the Temple in Empire, was on a much grander and more impressive scale. The star-clad ceiling seemed to reach up into the sky, there were more pillars than in Empire, the stonework exquisitely intricate, yet the space still felt light and lofty, and walking through it gave Anita the impression that she was balancing on the crest of an elegant wave as it curled its way towards the beach. Just like a wave crashing into the sand, they came abruptly to the closed off centre of the Temple containing Alexander's chambers; only he, or those he chose to invite inside, were allowed to visit. They circumnavigated his domain, all politely ignoring the fact they were dying to see inside and Alexander was the one with the power to make that happen, and found themselves walking directly into the courtyard that housed the relic the other side.

The relic was an odd looking piece of rock; not any particular shape and not at all pleasing to look at. It was a disappointing shade of greyish brown, with ugly ridges and edges that jutted rudely out from its core. It was a little bigger than a human head, but gave the impression that it was much heavier, like the modern metal structure that had been erected to support its weight might collapse at any moment. The relic sat under a twisted old olive tree that seemed to add to its mystery, shielding it from the real world.

The courtyard was a strange mix of contradictions, its boundaries forming a circle that joined the points of each Temple. It was open to the elements above and around the edges, devoid of Temple wall, yet sheltered by the colossal structures pointing to it. It was welcoming in that it was accessible from every angle, yet intimidating, the olive tree somehow threatening uninvited visitors. It was awe inspiring in that the relic was without doubt the main event, but also felt like a classroom, in a way mundane, with images and inscriptions on chunks of rock placed sporadically around the courtyard's edges. It felt at the same time balanced and content, yet strangely off kilter, spacious yet confined, proportionate yet both too big and too small, illuminated in places, yet dark in others. Anita felt uneasy, on edge and out of place.

'Hi,' said Arabella when she saw them, bounding over to greet them. 'Thank you so much for such a wonderful evening last night,' she gushed at Alexander, clearly not immune to his electric blue eyes and rugged charm. Anita felt a pang of, what? Jealousy? which she quickly suppressed.

'It's so great of you to show us around,' said Anita sweetly.

'It was the least we could do to say thank you,' she replied, although Anderson didn't seem to share Arabella's sentiment. He'd barely looked up from the relic to acknowledge their presence, seeming not nearly as keen as Arabella on this private lecture. But Bas, realising this was his opportunity to corner Anderson, took care of him, and Arabella started to talk the rest of them through the history of the relic.

'Of course, the relic hasn't been here forever,' started Arabella, revelling in the attention her audience were paying her. 'That is to say it's been in the world since the beginning, but we've only known of its existence for around three hundred and fifty years, since the year 1000. But I mustn't get ahead of myself; I'll start from the beginning. As you know, in the beginning, the three Gods created three worlds, and in our world they put people with skills that resembled their own. What we now know is that, at the same time, the Gods also put the relic in the world, but hid it deep within a cave system far out in the Wild Lands. Along with the relic, there were drawings and inscriptions that must have also been put there by the Gods, and if you ask me, that is the most exciting bit. People come from all over the world to see the relic and many leave again without realising the significance of the inscriptions on the walls surrounding it,' she said, making a sweeping gesture with her hand around the courtyard. 'Here,' she continued, 'you can see the image of three people around the relic. Our best academic guess is that each represents a Descendant, as you can see, there are two males and one female.' Anita wasn't sure she subscribed to this; to her they looked a lot like three smudged stick people with no clear gender, but she obviously didn't possess an expert's eye. 'Over here, we have the same three people pointing to the sky and the relic seems to be floating towards the heavens, back into the waiting arms of the Gods, depicted here by these three symbols,' she said, pointing to three shapes above where a blob of colour (the relic apparently) was stuck in the sky.

'But what are most illuminating, I think, are the inscriptions. There are three inscriptions, and again, our best academic guess would suggest that one relates to each God's line. The first, we think, relates to the Spirit discipline and says, 'look to the light', the second, we think has its origins in the Mind tradition and says simply, 'knowledge is power', and the third, from the Body, we are almost certain, due to the gender reference, says, 'she who dares will surely triumph'. We're not without doubt as to their exact meaning, however, academics are broadly agreed that they're likely to be words of encouragement to Descendants to fulfil their quest to return the relic. There's complete agreement that they must be seen as motivational in some sense or another. Anyway, as you know, the Descendants were put in the world by the Gods around the year seven hundred and seventy, around six hundred years ago, but the relic was only discovered in the year 1000. It was at this point that the true purpose of the Descendants became clear and these great Temples in Kingdom were erected in spectacular celebration. Of course, a place for the relic was designed as the centre piece, and the Crowning ceremonies were modified to include the oath that Descendants should devote their lives to freeing the world. That was the time when Kingdom really took over as the premier city from Empire. Aside from the splendour of the new Temples, it made sense for the main city to be by the sea; much more accessible that way.'

Arabella finally stopped talking as she approached the piece de la resistance. She walked towards it, creating what she was sure was a sense of awe and wonder as she went. She stopped several feet away, paused, and was just about to launch into another monologue, when Cleo chipped in. 'So who discovered the relic and who decided to move it here along with the inscriptions?' Arabella gave Cleo a piercing look and took a deep breath, contemplating how dismissive her reply should be, when Anderson answered for her.

'A group of academics discovered the relic out in the Wild Lands whilst on a research trip. They were the ones to bring the relic back with them, but they didn't think that anyone would believe them without seeing the inscriptions as well, so they extracted sections of the cave walls and brought them back. Luckily, they had a full research team with them, so this didn't pose too great a challenge; lots of people and horses to help move everything.'

'Who were the academics and how did the Descendants take it?' Cleo asked, her instinct for finding gossip piqued.

'Just a few random academics; their names escape me now. If I'm truthful, I'd be surprised if there'd been no reaction from the

Descendants of the time, but there's nothing documented anywhere, so we really don't know.'

'Nothing at all?' said Cleo surprised.

'No,' said Anderson, in a tone that indicated Cleo should move on.

Cleo knew when to drop a topic, so she nodded in defeat but resolved to investigate the matter further when she got back to Empire. There must be something in the Archives and it would be very unlike the Descendants not to react at all to a discovery of such magnitude.

Arabella spotted the opportunity to retake control, so turned back to the relic with a flourish, saying, 'and this is the much discussed relic. But Anderson is really the one who should tell you about it, he knows the subject backwards and will do it far more justice than I.' Arabella smiled warmly at Anderson, who looked as though he'd rather not, but knew the path of least resistance would be to do it; Arabella would never let him hear the end of it otherwise.

'As you can see,' started Anderson, in a surprisingly commanding voice, 'the relic is a totally irregular shape. It has no particularly unique markings and looks very much like any other piece of rock you might find in a cave, except, that is, for the fact the relic is made of an element we have not been able to find anywhere else on the planet, including in the Wild Lands around where it was found. Other than what the inscriptions tell us, we know nothing about the relic, which is why it's been a source of fascination and wonder since it was discovered, well, that, and the promise it brought with it of course. Many academics have devoted their lives to the relic, but no one has managed to make any headway with how to send it back. Of course, the Descendants are generally uncomfortable with the prospect of losing their power, so they haven't historically shown much support for our cause. We try to keep a low profile,' he said pointedly, 'attention is not good in our line of work.' With that, Anderson abruptly, and a little rudely, in Cleo's opinion, turned away from the group and got back to work.

It was clear that to stay any longer would be to outstay their welcome, so Cleo piped up, 'well it's been a fascinating morning. Thank you so much for the guided tour, we really appreciate it, but I promised my father that I would meet him for lunch, so I'd better get going. See you back at the house later,' she said to Alexander and Anita, before turning around and striding away through the Temple of the Mind.

'And we really should be heading off too. I promised Anita I would show her around Kingdom today,' said Alexander. 'Anderson, thank you so much for taking the time to show us the relic,' he said, shaking Anderson's hand, 'and Arabella it has been a pleasure as always,' he said, kissing Arabella briskly on both cheeks.

'Bas, are you coming?' asked Anita, as Bas sat down next to Anderson, making himself comfortable.

'Uh, no, I don't think so. I'll catch up with you two later. Think I'll stay and help Anderson and Arabella for a bit.' As Anderson seemed to actually perk up at the prospect, Anita just nodded and threw Bas a smile.

'See you later then,' she said, thanking Anderson and Arabella and following Alexander into the Temple of the Body.

'I've never seen him take to anyone like that before,' said Alexander when they were out of earshot.

'Well he and Bas have a lot in common, and Bas might even be able to help him. Anderson has spent a lot of time out in the Wild Lands recently, so he probably isn't up to date with all the energy developments. Given that Bas is as up to date as it comes, Anderson's probably as excited to have Bas around as Bas is to learn about the relic. I know Bas doesn't always come across as an authority, but after Alistair, nobody knows more about the energy than him.'

Alexander nodded. 'I suppose that must be it.'

Anita and Alexander walked past Peter's chambers, emerging in the main section of the Temple, and it was breath-taking; not nearly as open as the Spirit Temple, but equally pleasing. Where the Spirit Temple was one vast chamber with pillars stretching to the ceiling, the Body Temple was segmented into sections, the lines of the arches tight and pleasing. They invoked images of a ballet dancer bending elegantly backwards, off balance, yet supported by a strong, muscular partner. The sections reminded Anita of secret gardens, the kind of place she would like to have a romantic picnic, secluded but open, welcoming, cosy, stuffed full of wonderful, dusky pink flowers, and wrapped in flowing fabric. She would have liked to spend some time exploring the Temple, but Alexander was already striding towards the entrance, so she reluctantly followed.

They emerged into the crisp sunlight and meandered towards the centre of Kingdom, the conversation wandering through subject after subject. They'd been walking for a while when they rounded a corner to find themselves in a relatively secluded area with an enormous pair of bolted gates straight in front of them. Alexander stopped sharply, as though he were surprised to find himself there, then noticeably bristled. 'Austin's house,' he said, through slightly gritted teeth, nodding his head in the direction of the gates.

'Really?' said Anita, looking in wonder at the pretty-yet-imposing house that stood the other side of the gates. It was hard to work out where the buildings around it ended and it began, despite being surrounded by its own protective wall. The red brick construction had a secretive look about it, as though it was guarding a large number of highly incriminating secrets.

'It's not what I imagined,' she said, unable to tear her eyes from the building, 'not that I'm sure what I imagined really.'

'Why?' asked Alexander, doing his best to sound nothing more than conversational.

'Because it's so different to the castle in Empire. Everything about it is different. The stone, the size, the style, the proximity to the centre of the town. This seems like a wonderful home right in the thick of things, whereas the castle is a statement of power sitting above Empire.'

'Yes, I suppose so,' said Alexander offhandedly. 'Anyway, there's something else I'd like to show you,' he said, purposely moving the conversation away from Austin and also, by default, away from Marcus. 'Over here,' he said conspiratorially, taking her hand and pulling her lightly around the side of Austin's house, a jolt pulsing through each of them as their skin made contact.

'Where are we going?' asked Anita, confused, as they approached what seemed to be a solid brick wall.

'Through here,' he smiled back, leading them around what was, in fact, an overlap in the wall, concealing a small gap through to the other side. They appeared in a space that was half-room, half-tent, with stone walls and a canvas roof, but the space was full of beautiful swathes of fine silk, in a vast array of deep, rich colours.

'Wow,' said Anita, stunned, as she emerged from what turned out to be a fabric stall into a bustling street, jammed full of stalls similar to the one they had just walked through. 'I wasn't expecting that.'

'Welcome to the market,' said Alexander excitedly, not letting go of her hand. 'This is where the traders come with their goods from their farms, from the sea, or from the Wild Lands. You can get pretty much anything you can imagine here; silks,' he said, running his hand over one of the swathes at the entrance to the stall they had just walked out of, 'all manner of foods, clothes, cosmetics, precious metals and stones, brass cylinders, energy mechanisms, herbs and spices,' he said, as he gently tugged her past a stall with piles of brightly coloured powders on display, Anita's mouth wide open in wonder.

They passed a shop with early energy mechanisms chugging away in the window, brass cogs whirring around, but as Anita tried to enter, Alexander pulled her back. 'It's best not to linger for too long here. Most people recognise me and kindly leave me alone, but I don't really want to cause a scene by browsing for an extended period in an old junk shop.'

'It doesn't look like a junk shop to me,' said an indignant Anita. 'There could be all manner of treasures hidden in there, just waiting to be found.'

'Unlikely, given the number of traders around, but now is not the time to find out. Come on, we haven't got time to hang around.' Alexander finally let go of Anita's hand as they approached the city's wall, his recklessness abating a little with every person they walked past. They ducked through an opening in the wall and followed a perilous, winding stone staircase down to the sandy beach below.

'This place is like a rabbit warren,' said Anita. 'I had no idea we were that close to the beach.'

'That's why the Descendants like it so much in Kingdom. It's easy to disappear with all the passages and hidden passes; if someone follows us, it's usually fairly straightforward to lose them. And Kingdom's close to the action; if someone finds something interesting in the Wild Lands, the market is the place to find out about it.'

'It'll be a wonder if we ever get Cleo back to Empire then,' she said dryly. 'Why are you so comfortable with Anderson's work with the relic?' she asked, taking Alexander off guard, once again getting straight to the point.

'Why do you ask?' he replied, successfully hiding his surprise.

'Well the Descendants' interests run contrary to everything that Anderson's trying to achieve. If he finds a way to send back the relic, then you all lose your authority and the people decide who they want to rule.'

'Why do you think I want to rule?' bit Alexander.

'Well you are, aren't you, so you can't be dead set against the idea,' she snapped back.

'I rule because it's my duty to do so until we can find a way to return the relic, and I swore an oath to try to find a way to do that.'

'But the other Descendants don't seem to be trying too hard to free the world, quite the opposite in fact. They're doing everything they can to try to stop the world being freed, even if that means destroying it in the process.'

'And you think I'm like the other Descendants?' he said, hurt at the thought.

'Not exactly, but that's why I asked the question. Why are you so comfortable with his work, given your high and mighty position in this world?' Anita knew she was going further than was strictly necessary, but he really was being obtuse.

'I have no interest in abusing the power and authority bestowed on me because of my bloodline. I'm no different to anybody else really. I'm powerful, yes, but so are others, and I have no desire to rule in a world where people aren't happy. I told you, Sprit Descendants tend to be different to the rest. We tend to be more philosophical and less power hungry. Maybe that's something to do with the kind of skills we respect. Minds respect grand displays of mental and physical power, as do Bodies, even if the displays manifest differently, but Spirits acknowledge that it only takes one person to change the course of history. Maybe Anderson is that one person. Austin can put as many barriers in Anderson's way as he wants to, but if Anderson continues to fight, maybe he'll be the one to free the world. To a Spirit Descendant, that kind of display of power, motivated by reasons we consider more creditworthy than greed and self-interest, would be far more wonderful than the prospect of ruling for eternity.'

'But what about stability? What if sending the relic back causes chaos?'

'I think that's a bit farfetched. People are pretty good at accepting change when they have to, especially when it's change they've been asking for for centuries. And besides, as you pointed out, the world is heading for chaos as it stands anyway.'

CHAPTER 12

Helena bowed before the Great Spirit Leader, perched precariously on a small, round, stone ledge above a heart-stopping drop down the mountain to the ground below. It had been designed to put visitors on edge and let the Spirit Leader see how they reacted in uncomfortable situations. Helena had been here a number of times before, and not once had she managed to keep her energy stable. This she found extremely annoying, which meant she also had to try and hide her annoyance from the Spirit Leader, who could, of course, read her energy as though she were an open book. All in all, it was an especially stressful experience and she didn't relish her visits to the mountain.

'So nice to see you again Helena,' came the Spirit Leader's calm, even, almost bored tones. He sat in the centre of a mat, in the middle of a small pillared room, open on all sides to the elements, the wind gently toying with the fabric draped from the ceiling. He was a short-ish man, of medium build, with thick, wavy, sandy coloured hair and a voice that had a way of penetrating to the core of a person, so they couldn't help but sit up and listen. He had wise features and an aura around him of gravitas and severity, the kind of person you would always want on your side.

'The pleasure is all mine,' replied Helena, in a voice slightly louder than she had meant it to be. 'How can I be of assistance?'

The Spirit Leader chuckled. 'Typical Body,' he said. 'No preamble, just straight to the point.'

'My sincere apologies,' jousted Helena, 'how's the family?'

He snickered again, pleased to be having an effect on her. Helena had never liked being so out of control. 'Very well, have it your way. I summoned you here to see how you're getting on with Anita.' He hadn't moved a muscle since she'd got there and he stayed very still as the words hit Helena's ears like bullets, watching for any slight reaction she might show.

Helena froze. How the hell did he know about Anita? Who had let slip? Did they have a mole? She knew he would've already read her surprise, so there was no point in trying to hide it. 'How do you know about Anita?'

'There isn't much I can't find out if I put my mind to it Helena, you should know that by now.' He sent a meaningful look her way as he stood up in one, swift, seamless movement and made his way to a small stone table at the edge of the room. 'Please,' he said, indicating to the chair next to his, 'come and join me.'

Helena made her way to the seat, making a point of doing so at a dignified speed, a shock of cold hitting her from the freezing stone chair as she sat down. She always marvelled that the Spirit Leader could meditate out here all day in such unpleasant temperatures, dressed only in light robes. He somehow seemed to radiate warmth, so she'd often wondered if he cheated and snuck a hot water bottle under his clothes. She'd questioned him on it once and he'd spouted something about harnessing the power of the Mind, her least favourite discipline, so she'd left it there.

'So, how are you getting on with Anita?' he repeated patiently, more patiently than you would expect from a man so young.

'I'd be getting on a lot better if I hadn't had to take a significant amount of time out to come here and pay you a visit. I told her I'd be expecting an answer several days ago, however, I haven't exactly been in a position to follow it up, given that I've been travelling here.'

'Then I wasn't too late with my invitation. Good.'

'What's that supposed to mean?' she barked.

He fixed her with his eyes in a way that made Helena feel like an impatient school girl, before replying in a slow, even voice. 'Anita needs time. I know your natural reaction is to bully her into it, but she won't respond well to that; she's a lot like you, you see.'

'So that's why you summoned me here? To bully me into doing things your way?'

'Touché. Hopefully by the time you get back she'll have had enough time. Until next time, Helena.'

'I'll look forward to it, I'm sure,' she replied through gritted teeth, making no attempt at all to hide her angry energy.

The Spirit Leader smiled a tolerant smile as he got up and made his way back to his mat. He sat down and started to meditate, ignoring that Helena was still in his presence. As she made her way out, making sure she walked close enough to him to disturb his energy field, she marveled, as she always did, that he was so young. That he was no older than her and yet held such a position of authority was baffling. She herself had reached what most would consider dizzying heights at an early age, but he had reached the pinnacle, and she'd always been more than a little jealous. One day I'll find out how you did it, she said, under her breath, as she made her way down the stone steps to the main chambers below.

*****

Alexander sat at Philip's desk, pondering the recent developments. Anita had been distant since they'd returned to the house and he had no idea what to do about it, or indeed if he should try to do anything at all. Maybe a healthy distance between them would be a good thing, although he couldn't think of anything worse. Then there was the key he'd found that was still bugging him, mostly because he didn't know where to look next. He got up and started pacing (difficult as this was given the piles of books everywhere), to try and channel his frustration, but the books in his way frustrated him further, until he was so wound up he kicked a stack over. Needing something else to vent his anger on, he grabbed hold of the curtains and yanked them open; stupid idea not to let any sunlight in anyway. Bloody Philip, he thought, as light poured into the room for the first time in an age and the true extent of the mess became apparent. For someone that had harped on about the 'illuminating power of light' and how wise the one who came up with the Spirit motto 'look to the light' must have been, he seemed to be quite a hypocrite.

Alexander's frustration abated a little as a result of his reckless acts, so he stooped down to reassemble the pile of books, then turned to redraw the curtains; it seemed disrespectful to overturn Philip's wishes so soon after his death. As he snuffed out the last chink of light, he froze, an idea finding root in his mind that grew to become an epiphany. 'Look to the light'. Alexander reached for the lamp on the desk and turned it over; what if the key unlocked a real light? Philip had always loved it when the literal and metaphorical collided, so what if he'd taken the motto literally and the key unlocked an actual light? Unfortunately, the lamp on Philip's desk had a smooth base with no key hole to be seen, however, undeterred, he inspected all of the lights in the study. When none of them produced a result, he went to Philip's old bedroom and inspected each of the lights there, but again, nothing. Finally, he tried the garden sheds; Philip had loved his garden, but here again, no success; there were only single bulbs dangling dejectedly from the ceiling and nowhere to hide a hole for a key.

Feeling deflated, Alexander returned to the study and sat back down in his Grandfather's leather chair. 'What does the key unlock you old sod?' Alexander asked out loud, pulling the desk lamp towards him once more, hoping for some light-related inspiration. He rested it on its side and re-inspected the base, silently questioning how else a lamp could hide a keyhole. Finding no inspiration, he set it upright, however, as he was doing so, his fingers felt a tiny, almost invisible seam running around its base. He paused before turning it onto its side once more and carefully inspecting the seam. The line ran all the way around and looked like nothing out of the ordinary, except, on closer inspection, the colour of the base was very slightly different from the rest of it. He tried to slip a finger nail into the seam to prize off the bottom part, but the join was too tight, so he tried twisting instead. To his amazement, the base swung smoothly outwards from a point near the edge, exposing a second layer of brass below. Alexander's heart almost stopped as his eyes made out a perfect, key-shaped hole in the centre of the newly exposed metal. 'By the Gods,' he said out loud. He reached into his pocket, retrieved the small key and inserted it into the hole. He twisted lightly and the key turned easily in the lock, making a delicate clicking sound as a panel in the top of the lamp sprung open. He gently swung the panel cover back, noting the exquisite craftsmanship that must have been required, and delicately retrieved the piece of folded parchment that was sitting inside.

Unable to contain his excitement, Alexander quickly unfolded the paper and held it up to the light, moving his face closer to the paper to make out the words he found there. There were several lines of text, and, to his surprise, the first contained only one word, his name.

Alexander,
Remember the lessons from Philip & Fred.
Be a good scholar.
Jeffrey will help you unlock the light.
Destroy this note when you have memorised what I have said.
I have faith in you.
Philip

He felt suddenly a bit sick. How had Philip known he would find this? Why had he written it? What did it mean? And why had he gone to such pains to hide it so that it would be so difficult to find? As far as he could see, there was nothing here that could be considered contentious. Philip & Fred were nicknames that Philip had used for two famous children's authors. They'd written a book of fairy tales that Philip had read to Alexander when he was young. The stories were varied, but usually contained a moral message, similar to most other books for children. Philip's favourite story had been about a princess who'd been banished by her father, the King, as he'd gone mad when a group of powerful sorcerers had come to court. The story was about the princess' quest to retake her rightful position and rid the land of the evil sorcerers, which, of course, she did. As in every other fairy story, in the process, she found her prince and the story finished, as usual, with them living happily ever after.

Alexander stiffened as Austin's final words to Christiana came flooding back to him, 'we are the only two left that know the truth now that Philip has gone'. Philip had known the truth about Christiana's bloodline. Was that what Philip was talking about here? Could Anita be considered the princess in the story? Was that the point Philip was trying to get across?

The second line was clear enough; Philip had often used the words 'be a good scholar' and had always meant that one should question everything as good scholars do, even the facts we think we know for certain. What Alexander was supposed to 'be a good scholar' in relation to however, he had no idea. The third line was confusing. Who was Jeffrey and why, or more to the point, how, would he be able to help 'unlock the light' and what did that even mean anyway? Alexander racked his brain, but could think of no one he knew called Jeffrey, either in the real world or in a story book.

What Philip meant by 'I have faith in you' and why he wanted Alexander to destroy the note seemed to Alexander cryptic and possibly a little melodramatic, however, reasoning it was probably for the same purpose that Philip had hidden it so well, Alexander thought it prudent to follow his instructions. He picked up the note and took it to the fireplace, making sure that he both remembered what it said and that he hadn't missed anything. He then picked up a match from the mantelpiece, lit it and set the paper alight. He held onto the parchment for a few seconds before placing it in the fireplace, waiting to ensure there was nothing left but ash before turning to one of the shelves and picking up an old, worn book. This seemed a good moment to remind himself of the stories of Philip & Fred.

*****

The trip back to Empire was subdued. Cleo had, for the first time all weekend, stopped talking, and was lightly dosing with her head propped against the window. Bas was silently staring out, watching the scenery go by, and presumably contemplating all he'd learned and discussed with Anderson over the last two days. Anita was sure they'd see each other again; she'd never seen two people get on so well after such a short acquaintance.

Anita had been trying her best to avoid speaking to, looking at, and certainly being alone with Alexander. She was so confused about what she should do, what she felt for who and how she should proceed, so she too spent the journey looking out of the window, feeling a little empty as she considered her options. Alexander was desperately trying to glean anything he could from her energy, but it was as steady as a rock, not giving anything away. He was fighting an internal battle of what to do next, but now, in a car full of people, was certainly not the time for action.

The problem as Anita saw it was that she obviously had feelings for both Marcus and Alexander, her energy reacting distinctively to each of their special allures. Marcus was, for the most part, fun and care free, flirtatious and frivolous in a way that Alexander could not be. After all, Alexander was a ruling Descendant, whereas Marcus was yet to assume the heavy burden of responsibility, living instead under the ominous cloud of his power-hungry father. Alexander seemed to carry that weight around with him, possibly as he had some understanding of the perilous position the world was in, and that it was his duty to address it. Marcus, on the other hand, seemed light as a feather, as though there was nothing in the world that should be worried about with any kind of gusto.

Whereas Alexander was closed and protective of himself, Marcus had opened up to Anita, told her about his family and to some extent discussed his past. However, Marcus was a protective person who'd already become possessive of Anita and it was wholly possible that he could get worse over time; what if he did turn into Austin? At least Alexander wasn't trying to force her into a relationship with him; he was trying to do what he thought was best for her, but the way he was doing that was by staying away from her, so maybe his feelings weren't that strong after all. Anita silently pondered all the way back to Empire, but felt more confused at the end of the journey than she had at the beginning.

They arrived back in Empire and dropped Bas off first, then Cleo, Anita feeling Alexander turn to look at her when they were finally alone in the car, Alexander glad of the closed glass screen separating them from the driver, and Anita annoyed that it wasn't open. 'Is everything alright?' he asked nervously, trying to hide his uncertainty.

Anita turned to look at him and searched his glorious blue eyes. 'Not really,' she replied evenly, dropping her eyes to her lap, surprised at her honest response. 'I think I need some time to work all this out. I'm confused and have no idea what to do. I have feelings for Marcus. I feel guilty and I don't want to hurt him.' She paused and looked out of the window before meeting his eyes again. 'But I don't want to hurt you either.' A horrible thought suddenly erupted in Anita's head and her eyes widened a little. 'Sorry,' she said, her cheeks reddening, 'that is, making the presumptuous assumption that you feel anything for me...' Luckily, at that moment, they pulled up outside Cordelia's house and Anita made for the door. As she swung it open, Alexander grabbed her hand, gentle tingles spreading underneath her skin, so she turned and looked back at him.

'Your presumptuous assumption is correct,' he said huskily, whispering, so the driver, who was now unloading the bags, couldn't hear. A car turned into the end of the road, and in the twilight, Alexander recognised it as one of Austin's. He begrudgingly let go of Anita's hand. 'Looks like you have company,' he said bitterly, nodding in the direction of the oncoming vehicle. She turned to see the car stop and Marcus' long, lean body throw open the door and move rapidly in her direction. 'See you soon I hope,' said Alexander quickly, as Marcus happily reached his target and protectively took hold of her hand.

'Alexander,' Marcus nodded curtly, clearly indicating that he would take things from here.

'Marcus,' Alexander nodded back, pulling the car door closed and stealing one last look at Anita before his driver pulled away.

As soon as Alexander's car moved off, Marcus turned so his body faced hers and kissed her lightly on the lips. 'Time for you to get changed, we're going to a party.'

Anita's energy lifted immediately and she smiled up at Marcus, exasperated at his order, yet excited to see where they were going. 'Are we?' she asked, reproachfully. She wanted to make him work at least a little.

'Yes,' he confirmed unwaveringly, flashing his eyes fearlessly.

What the hell, she thought, reaching up and stealing a flirtatious kiss, before turning and sauntering towards the house. 'Then you'd better tell me where we're going so I can find something suitable to wear.'

*****

The following morning, Anita woke early and made her way to the garden for her usual yoga session, however, after a couple of minutes it was clear that her mind wasn't going to let her concentrate, vivid flashbacks of the previous night rudely interrupting. She decided to sack in the yoga in favour of something more vigorous, so donned her running trainers and headed for the river. As she ran, she contemplated, revisiting the conundrum that had been preoccupying pretty much all of her conscious thought for the last two days; Marcus or Alexander? Last night had been so much fun; they'd gone to some Councillor's daughter's 25th birthday and had danced for hours. Marcus had ignored everyone but Anita for the whole evening, much to the annoyance of all the female guests, as well as the Councillor hosting the event, who had kept trying to find reasons for Marcus to dance with his daughter. The only thing that had put a slight dampener on the evening was that Gwyn had been at the party too and had made a snipe at Anita as she and Marcus passed, not to mention the negativity that Anita could feel in Gwyn's energy towards her. Marcus was oblivious to it, and when Anita had brought it up, he'd unhelpfully suggested she was paranoid. How could men be so blind when it came to the relationships between women? It never failed to amaze Anita how they could ignore what was right in front of them.

After the party, they'd walked along the river bank back to Cordelia's house, dancing as they went and pausing every so often to kiss in the starlight. Marcus had brought up the weekend, clearly unhappy about the trip, although he'd struggled a little to find the best way to broach the issue. Eventually he'd settled on warning Anita off Alexander, saying it was bad enough she had to have lessons with him, but weekends away just went too far. At that point he'd reminded Anita of a pompous, puffed up bird, his feathers all ruffled. He'd told her that next time, she should let him show her Kingdom, as, unlike Alexander, he really knew the city and the sights to see. Anita had distracted him by saying she'd seen his home, telling him how enchanting she thought it was which, luckily, had thrown the conversation in a new, more positive direction.

The conversation had been light hearted and fun for the rest of the walk, until they'd reached Cordelia's gate, where Marcus had suddenly turned serious, kissing Anita meaningfully and hinting in every unspoken way he could that she should invite him to stay. She hadn't taken the hint, but instead had thanked him for a fun evening, given him a lingering yet firm goodbye kiss, then turned and made her way inside.

Anita snapped out of her day dream to find herself at least five miles further along the river than she'd expected, so turned around and headed back in the direction she'd come, her mind switching back to what she should do next. She felt guilty about Marcus and Alexander and knew at some point she was going to have to make a decision. Marcus would only take her seeing Alexander for so long before he found a way to put an end to their lessons, and Alexander couldn't be expected to continue as they were for an indefinite period, and it wouldn't be fair on him even if he were happy to.

The problem was that Marcus was more fun than Alexander, but Alexander was interested in the energy and the position of the world and all the things Anita was fascinated by and opinionated over. But then, maybe Alexander would lighten up if he wasn't so worried about the danger posed to her by Marcus? One thing she had decided for certain was that she didn't want to spy on Marcus for the Institution. He might not be perfect, but he didn't deserve that and the Institution sounded like an extremely shady organisation. It pained Anita to think that she would lose the opportunity to find out more about her parents, but she'd lived this long without the knowledge, so she reasoned she could probably go on living without it, and maybe some research into Helena's background would throw up a few leads. She decided to tell Helena at the earliest available opportunity. In fact, she wondered, where had she been anyway? It wasn't like Helena to be so lax about getting an answer.

Anita arrived home, showered, changed, and then headed to the Body Temple. There was no time like the present, so she went to find Helena to tell her the bad news.

As luck would have it, Anita didn't have to look for Helena at all; she bumped into her just outside the Temple. 'Anita, hi,' said a surprised Helena. 'Funnily enough I was just coming to find you.'

'Great minds think alike,' smiled Anita. 'I was coming to find you too. I've considered what you said,' she continued quickly, before Helena had a chance to intervene, 'and I've decided that I can't do what you asked. It's simply not fair on Marcus, regardless of who his father is.'

Helena paused before replying, giving Anita a piercing look that reminded her of a school teacher, before seeming to soften, her internal dialogue warning her that meeting Anita head on was not the way to go. The Spirit Leader's words came back to her, 'I know your natural reaction is to bully her into it, but she won't respond well to that; she's a lot like you, you see.'

'I'd like to show you something. Do you have time to come with me now?' asked Helena quietly, her response taking Anita off guard. It was unlike Helena to ask so nicely; she usually assumed that nobody had anything better to do than what she wanted.

'Of course,' replied Anita, an inquisitive look painted across her face. 'What do you want to show me?'

She gave Anita a frank look. 'It's better for you to see for yourself.'

Anita knew there was no point in arguing, so she nodded. 'Lead the way.'

Helena led Anita to an energy car and climbed into the driving seat, Anita taking position next to her in the front. Helena fired up the car, tutting as she noticed one of the lights on her dashboard flashing, but in her usual brisk fashion ignored it; she couldn't be less interested in cars or their various problems. Helena drove out of Empire into the countryside beyond, travelling in silence as neither knew quite how to broach the awkward subject in between them; Anita's parents.

After only a few miles, Helena turned onto a small, almost hidden track, which wound its way to a large but rundown farm house. They reached the house and Helena stopped the car and got out, swinging the squeaky door closed behind her, gesturing for Anita to join her. By the time Anita had caught up, Helena was half way across the yard, heading for a colossal storage barn. She got there and pulled the enormous door open on its runners, signaling that Anita should have a look within.

Anita peered into the relative dark inside, waiting for her eyes to adjust, but unless she was missing something, it looked like there was nothing there to be seen. 'I'm not sure I understand,' she said hesitantly, turning to look at Helena. 'There doesn't appear to be anything in there.'

'And that is precisely the point,' she replied bluntly. 'Usually at this time of year this barn would be full of grain, but since the news of Christiana's death, crops have started to fail, fishermen have reportedly found dead fish floating in the rivers and lower yields in the sea, and as you know from your work at the Observatory, we've seen no bounce back as predicted by Austin. Come with me,' she said, turning away from the barn and walking further across the grey concrete farm yard and out the other side, stopping when she reached an old wooden gate into one of the fields. 'Look at that,' she said, gesturing to a field covered in a flattened wheat crop that had turned from its characteristic golden brown to a blackish grey colour.

Anita looked gravely at the sight. 'How widespread is the issue?' she asked emptily.

'Very,' replied Helena. 'Farmers all over the world are reporting issues, some worse than others. This is a pretty extreme example; the farmer's lost nearly everything this year, his farm won't survive another harvest like it.'

'And presumably it'll push up food prices. Is it bad enough to cause shortages?'

'This year we'll probably just about survive, but if it continues into next year the story will be very different. I don't know how much prices will go up though. That could lead to protests in itself.'

'Protests?' Anita asked ,shocked. She'd heard of protests a couple of decades back, but had never in her lifetime been aware of any taking place. People didn't generally have a cause worth running the risks associated with protesting. 'I can't imagine many people will want to protest in front of Austin, and what could he do about it anyway?'

'It never ceases to amaze me how your generation have seemingly no interest in politics. We used to protest about a whole host of things that mattered. I used to protest. I remember the Institution organising a couple of protests around the Descendants not taking their vows seriously, although, of course, we didn't publicise the fact they were organised by us. But that all came to a rather abrupt halt when Austin obtained the information about us, so now we can't do anything.'

'What would you do if Austin didn't have the information about you?'

'Protest, rebel, start to make people believe there could be freedom under the relic if we overthrow the Descendants, give people hope there's a better way to live, even if the bloodline is broken, put some pressure on the Descendants to actually start to carry out what they promise in their vows, including reinstating the relic experts.' Helena was becoming more and more animated as she spoke. 'We've got to do something, we can't just sit back and take our fate if that means starvation. Can you imagine a world where you can't get food without having to fight for it? Or where you're not sure when you'll next be able to eat? You'll be alright if you stay in with the Descendants; they've probably already started to stockpile, but if this goes on unchecked, just think of the consequences.'

'But I'm sure when the Descendants find out the full extent of this, they will take action.'

Helena laughed a cruel laugh. 'You think Austin's going to come to the rescue of the people?'

'There are two other Descendants,' Anita sniped back. 'I know Alexander will fight for action, and how can Peter not join him?'

This tipped Helena over the edge. 'Open your bloody eyes Anita. Peter is spineless; he'll never stand up to Austin, meaning it's Alexander against Austin, who has Peter's silent support. That's two Descendants against one; Alexander will never win that way.'

'But Marcus has influence over Austin. I know he can make him see sense.'

'By the Gods, Anita, have you really let the fact you have feelings for Marcus cloud your judgement to such an extent? Marcus had no power with Austin; he's a puppy who follows his master around, nothing more, and the only way Marcus will ever get more power is if he becomes who Austin wants him to be. The only one who really has Austin's ear is Amber, and even then, her influence is limited. The only way to get them to listen is to take direct action and that's why we need you.'

174

Helena was back in school teacher mode and Anita didn't appreciate it. She was no longer Helena's pupil, so if Helena wanted her help, she could damn well stop trying to press gang her into it and try asking nicely. 'Tell me, Helena, why is it I should trust you? Your credentials aren't exactly what you might call exemplary. You were my teacher and mentor for years but never once told me anything about my parents, despite knowing full well I was desperate for information. You come to me representing some shady organisation that I've never heard of, talking about starting a revolution, to overthrow the rule of two of my friends, to steal back some kind of information without knowing what that information is, and worst of all, you dangle the carrot of finding out about my parents to try and force me into helping you. As I said before, I've made up my mind. I'm sorry, but I can't help you; you'll have to find another way.' Anita turned away from Helena and vaulted the gate into the field. She would walk back to Empire; she couldn't stand being around Helena for a second longer.

Anita crossed two fields that both looked exactly like the last, covered in blackened, flattened crops, so she knew Helena wasn't lying, at least about the enormity of the problem facing the world. Obviously something had to be done, but she was sure the Descendants, even Austin, would have to see sense and do something once they really knew what was happening. There was a Council meeting in a week or so; Bas was giving an energy update and she was sure they'd listen and take action then.

As Anita crossed the next field, some movement in her peripheral vision caught her attention. In the top corner of the field there was a small stone structure that she recognised as a shrine to the Body God Tatiana. In front of the shrine were two men, one holding still a struggling goat and the other holding a knife up to the sky. She couldn't hear what they were saying, but after a few moments the man with the knife lowered his hands and slit the throat of the goat in one clean movement, the animal's body losing its life and collapsing to the floor. The two men placed the carcass in the shrine and Anita stopped, stock still, shocked at what she was witnessing. She'd heard of sacrifices to the Gods obviously, who hadn't, but she'd never actually seen one. She could only imagine the desperation the farmers felt; they thought they were about to lose their livelihoods, their farms, and worst of all, that they, along with the rest of the people of the world, would starve. The men knelt in front of the shrine and started to pray. Anita moved on, she wouldn't like to be observed if their roles were reversed.

175

Helena was furious. That couldn't have gone much worse if I'd tried, she thought savagely, and worst of all, it was all her fault. The Spirit Leader had warned her about trying to bully Anita into it and she'd failed none the less. There was nothing that wound up Helena more than her own mistakes, and she hated herself for it. She beat herself up and replayed their discussion in her head, supposing what might have happened if she'd gone about it differently. Maybe she should've told Anita something about her parents, or made something up about the information they were trying to get back? Either way, Anita's faith in the Descendants, especially in Austin's desire to do the right thing, was worrying. Was she really that blind to the truth? If she was, then there was no hope of rectifying the situation, but Anita was the only way. 'Damn it,' she said furiously, pissed off at her own incompetence, 'how could you be such a stupid, blundering idiot.' She slammed her balled up fist into the roof of her car before yanking open the squeaky door, clambering in without her usual grace, and slamming the door as hard as she could behind her.

*****

Austin knew that Amber was right. If he was to prevent the loss of his son to the troublesome Anita, then he'd have to get him more involved. The problem was that there was a lot he didn't want Marcus to be involved with, or even know about, so he'd been racking his brain for suitable areas for several weeks. It had to be far enough removed to keep him out of the contentious stuff, yet significant enough that Marcus would both find it interesting and feel that he was genuinely being let in to Austin's inner circle. In the end, it was the troublesome Anita herself who had sparked an idea. Austin had overheard a conversation between Anita and Marcus where they'd been discussing her friend Cleo's new found interest in the Archives. She was on some mission to uncover something about something, not that that was important, but what was important was that the Archives would be a great place for Marcus to start, at the family vault.

Each of the three bloodlines had a vault in the Archives in which to store whatever they wanted, and given the significant security that had been installed there, the Descendants did tend to use their vaults to store some explosive stuff. Luckily, it seemed to most an unlikely place for the Descendants to store secrets, so it was one of the last places people thought to look for gossip and the security rarely had to be used. None the less, this was a place where Marcus could learn things that seemed important, where he could be let in on certain secrets, and learn about the family's history without extensive involvement in Austin's day to day business, which Marcus was not even close to being ready for yet.

Austin thought back to what he'd been like at Marcus' age. He'd been exactly like Marcus was now. Young, idealistic, hedonistic, care free and with no idea how his father really operated. If Tobias had introduced it to Austin too early, he would almost certainly have shied away, and Marcus would inevitably react the same way. This though was genius. It would seem the troublesome Anita did have some perks.

Austin opened the concealed door in the panelling under the main stair case, stooped through the gap and ran lightly down the small, cramped, flight of stairs within that took him to the castle's basement, and the headquarters of Amber's security team. Here he greeted the guard sitting behind the desk in his usual curt way. 'Keys to the archive.' The guard got up and turned to a cabinet behind him, rolling his eyes as he turned his back to Austin. He'd worked at the castle for almost five years and Austin still had no idea what his name was, let alone anything else about him, and not once in all that time had Austin asked for something nicely, or used the word 'please'.

Jerk, the guard thought as he handed a set of large brass keys to Austin, saying politely, 'there you are sir. Anything else I can help you with?'

'No, not today. I will return these later this evening.'

The guard didn't respond. He half nodded his head, waited for Austin to leave, and then sat back down again. 'You're welcome, arsehole,' he muttered under his breath when he heard the door click shut at the top of the stairs.

As Austin emerged from the basement, Marcus was coming down the stairs, having been told to meet him in the entrance hall at 10am, ready for a day of education, whatever the bloody hell that meant. Marcus couldn't think of anything worse than an 'educational day', as, in his experience, education and enjoyment did not go hand in hand, however, he was intrigued by what it was Austin wanted to show him, so he'd agreed with little argument.

'Morning,' said Austin cheerily.

'Morning. Ready to tell me where we're going yet?' Marcus asked hopefully.

'No. It's a surprise.'

'I see,' said Marcus, deeply suspicious and a little nervous about why Austin wouldn't tell him where they were going. This was totally out of character for his father and that was worrying.

'Come on. The car is waiting.'

Austin and Marcus travelled without conversing, Austin not noticing that this was strange given the circumstances and Marcus not knowing what to say to break the silence. 'Why've you brought me *here*?' asked a disappointed Marcus, as they pulled up outside the Archives. 'I've never considered myself a great historian dad.'

'And I wouldn't consider myself a great historian either Marcus, however, I find what's inside extremely exciting and I'm sure you will too.'

Marcus looked dubious. 'If you say so.'

Austin barely heard Marcus' reply, already striding off up the steps, through the front door and into the beautiful old building that housed the Archives. The building resembled a lovely country manor house, large and square with high ceilings and enormous full length windows. It had been one of the earliest buildings constructed in Empire and the stone work had a lovely worn finish that seemed to fit perfectly with what it held inside. Austin breezed past the plush reception area without pausing to say hello to the startled receptionist and made for a door leading to the staircase to the floor below, Marcus trailing in his wake. The Archives had originally all been held upstairs, however, more space had been required pretty quickly and the light the windows let in was not good for the artefacts, so now everything had been moved to subterranean levels and the vast rooms upstairs were used for hosting important events.

Austin descended a further two flights of stairs and came out onto a dimly lit floor filled with racks of books, manuscripts, letters, energy metres, brass cylinders, and a whole host of other relics of the past. He walked to the back of the room to a door separating two racks of artefacts. He checked there was nobody around, pulled out the brass keys he'd picked up earlier, and crouched down to the floor, inserting the larger key into a hole in the wall next to the door. To Marcus' surprise, this made a panel in the side of the rack to the left of the door swing open, revealing a small keypad and thumb reader. Austin quickly entered a code, then placed his thumb on the reader before the panel swung shut again, leaving no trace, or at least no trace that could be seen in the dim light anyway. Austin stood up, then used the second brass key to unlock the door as you would any other, pressed down the handle, and swung open the door to reveal a room full of artefacts similar to those outside. Marcus could not have been more disappointed. Austin had brought him here, performed a number of convoluted steps to get inside a 'vault' that was in fact a normal room, and was making a big song and dance about a few bits and pieces from the past? Great.

Austin entered the room and gestured for Marcus to follow him before closing the door behind them. 'Welcome to the family vault,' he said with a flourish. 'This is where we keep the family secrets Marcus, along with documents about our history and the sacrifices we've made to serve the world as rulers. Each Descendant family has a vault here, protected by similar security, and we use them to keep things locked away that we would rather not be in the public domain. The best thing is that nobody suspects a thing, as this is the last place anyone would imagine a Descendant would keep secrets, in such a public location. As you know, we take steps to ensure everywhere we go is secure, but over the years we've had countless raids on our properties, whereas there is yet to be a single raid here. It works really quite well.'

'And why have you brought me here?' asked Marcus, confused as to why his father was showing him this now, or indeed at all, given that he usually tried to keep him as far away from anything interesting as possible.

Austin looked surprised. He'd expected Marcus to be distracted by the artefacts and not ask questions about why he was here. 'To let you into the family secrets. To start getting you more involved in the work I do and the work you will one day do as a ruling Descendant. To bring you up to speed on our history. All of these things are essential for you in preparation for power. If you don't know our secrets, how will you ever know if someone is blackmailing you using threats with some foundation, or if they've just made something up? When you rule, you will find it beneficial to see how previous Mind Descendants have acted when faced with challenges and you can draw on their experiences to shape the decisions you make. But most importantly,' Austin softened, looking a little uncertain, 'I'm showing you this because I hope you'll find it interesting.' Austin gave Marcus what he thought was a hurt look, and although it came over somewhere between a scowl and a grimace, Marcus did feel a little guilty that he wasn't being a bit more enthusiastic. After all, this was the first time Austin had ever shared anything with him, so it was a pretty big deal, if for no reason other than that.

'It's great dad,' Marcus said with all the enthusiasm he could muster. 'So where should I start?'

Austin perked up. 'Over here I think. This is where the brief history of the family is kept. We keep a biographer on hand to document all significant occasions and events. At the end of each reign, a book is compiled about each Descendant, with a summary added to the brief history, which I'm afraid these days is not very brief. It is, however, a very good place to start. Once you've cracked that, we can move on to other areas.'

'What are those over there?' asked Marcus, pointing to a row of brass cylinders with one on the end singled out from the rest.

Austin's face pinched. 'We'll deal with those at a much later date. They're memories of important things that happened in the past. I store them here for safe keeping, but it's important you get a good grounding in our history before we touch on things like that. There is just one thing you need to remember; nothing in this room can be taken out of this room and think very carefully before letting anyone else know it exists. As I mentioned, part of the success of the vaults is that very few people know about them, and I'm sure I speak for all the Descendants when I say we would like it to stay that way. I've had your thumb print programmed in and the code is 521183. You can collect the keys from the basement in the castle any time you want to come here, the guards know to give them to you. I hope you find this room inspirational and informative, and if you have any questions about anything you find, you can always come and ask me about it. For now, I'll leave you to explore the brief history in peace, just lock the door as you would a normal door when you leave and the security will reset. See you later,' he said, handing over the keys and leaving Marcus more than a little bit bemused.

Marcus stood for a moment, wondering whether he was in some bizarre dream, then looked around, contemplating where to start. He was tempted to walk straight over to the brass cylinders, or to start rummaging around in the other piles of stuff that looked much more interesting than a not-so-brief brief history of the family, but given that this was the first time he'd been let into anything by Austin at all, he thought it best to comply with his wishes, at least to start with anyway. So he picked up the history, turned on the light suspended over one of two worn old armchairs that had been positioned next to a little sink and kettle, sat down heavily, and started to read.

CHAPTER 13

'Again, Bas, you seem to have misunderstood your brief. You are here to monitor the energy and report your findings to the Council, you are not supposed to interpret those findings in a way that is extreme overestimation and present them here as fact.' Austin was getting going now, Bas standing still as the words hit him, his face set, trying to keep his energy steady and resisting with all his might the urge to send a tirade of truths in Austin's direction. 'Frankly, Bas,' he spat the name with disgust, 'this is tantamount to scaremongering, and that is something that this Council must take extremely seriously, especially given the effect we all know something like that can have on the energy...' Austin was really starting to enjoy himself when a calm, even voice cut him off mid-sentence.

'...we can't ignore what's right in front of us Austin,' said Alexander, standing up and walking towards the lectern, clearly indicating his support for what Bas had come to the Council to present. 'Bas' report is entirely in line with reports I've been getting from farmers and fishermen all over the world. The crops are failing, fish are dying, it's only a matter of time before we start to see food shortages. I'm sure everyone in this room will be just fine; we all have means to secure food and protect it, but others, those we have a responsibility to as rulers, will not be so fortunate, and we must take action now,' he said, turning pointedly to Austin, 'or we'll have a revolt on our hands.'

Austin screwed up his face. 'This is the problem with young ruling Descendants,' he laughed, as though they were discussing a trivial matter, 'they have no experience of life, have never seen situations like this before, have never witnessed situations like this blowing over, running themselves out of steam. When everyone realises life will go on as it always has, regardless of whether Christiana or Peter is ruling, everything will go back to normal, the energy will stabilise and food will be in abundance once more. Now, I think we've had enough of these hysterics for one day. Bas, I would advise you to think carefully about what you say in this chamber during your next update, or we may have to reconsider your position here. No reflection on you of course, we have appointed you at a very young age.' Austin smirked, enjoying the power he held, Bas about to explode with indignation. The stupid, arrogant, blind, ignorant, pompous, idiot, he thought to himself.

Alexander could easily read Austin's and Bas' energy, so intervened, both before Bas did anything stupid, and due to his own indignation at Austin's arrogant stupidity. 'No, Austin, this conversation is not over. I am a ruling Descendant with as much of a say here as you, regardless of whether you like that or not, and we must take some kind of action. You cannot use the past to predict the future, especially as you've never previously encountered the situation we now find ourselves faced with. People think the bloodline has been cut, that there's no hope for freeing the world, and that isn't something people can easily bounce back from.'

'Well, luckily, we have three ruling Descendants, which comes in handy in moments like these.' Austin rounded on the unsuspecting Peter, who had shrunk so far back into his seat that he looked like he was trying to escape through it. 'Peter, we come to you for the deciding vote. More time, as the young bucks suggest, or should we move on to more pressing matters?'

Peter weighed up his options. He had no desire to piss off Austin, the cruelty that man could exact was startling, however, he did think that Bas and Alexander had a point. The energy showed no signs of perking up, and that could be the cause of untold suffering amongst the people if they did nothing, not to mention he had, after all, taken an oath. He paused to think for several moments, in the end settling on the path of least resistance. If Bas and Alexander were right, then no improvement would be seen, and at some point even Austin would have to realise action needed to be taken.

'It seems to me, that we are here weighing the merits of youthful energy versus experience,' said Peter, pausing, stealing himself, 'and I often find it best to side with experience.' Peter looked deflated as he said it and Alexander knew from his energy this was not what he really felt. Austin's intimidation tactics had worked their magic once more, but right now he had to get Bas out of the chamber before he blew his top.

'Well, I have no doubt this will be a topic we revisit time and again as the energy continues to drop,' said Alexander, walking over to stand right next to Bas, 'and when it does, we can all gain precious first hand, front row experience of the chaos that will cause. So maybe in the future, if and when this happens again, we'll have some experience to tell us how not to deal with it. For now though, I think we've all had quite enough for today.' With that, he turned and looked Bas straight in the eye, inclining his head a little in the direction of the door. Bas nodded and he and Alexander wheeled towards the doors and strode out in perfect, confident, unison, the doors opening for them as they departed. They walked quickly out through the Temple of the Spirit and almost ran straight into Anita and Marcus, who were walking towards the Temple of the Body, as they got to the entrance steps.

Anita felt them coming before she saw them, their powerful energy a strange mix of rage and comradery. 'Hi,' she said tentatively, as they marched down the steps, oblivious to everything around them, so consumed in their own thoughts. They looked up together, both of their energy reacting when they saw Anita and Marcus. Anita was glad Marcus was not a reader and almost laughed aloud at the energy change when they realised who it was. The rage in their energy was immediately directed at Marcus. Anita knew they didn't really like him, but she thought this was a bit much. The comradery was extended to Anita, who felt grateful they weren't mad with her, but this only served to further confuse her; what the bloody hell was going on? Then, to her surprise, some sheepishness crept into Alexander's energy, which he quickly supressed, although possibly this was a reaction to his reading Anita's energy spike at seeing him, which she was now desperately trying to hide. Sometimes, Anita wished she was as oblivious as Marcus now was, although even he could tell something was wrong.

'Is everything alright?' asked Anita, tentatively.

'No. Everything is not bloody alright,' fired back Bas, happy he could finally start to vent some of his frustration. 'His bloody father,' he said, throwing an accusing look in Marcus' direction, 'is an arrogant, blind, fool who is about to sink the world into chaos via starvation, whilst happily ignoring his duty to do something about it.'

Marcus and Anita looked blankly back, so Alexander stepped in. 'We've just had a Council meeting and Bas came to give an update on the energy. He reported the facts, which are, as you know only too well Anita, that the energy is showing no signs of bouncing back. In fact, it keeps falling, and the consequences of that are starting to become evident in failing crops and dying fish. It's only a matter of time before the weather starts to react as well, and then who knows what might happen to, for example, the water supply, and only the Gods know what else after that. But the Council, particularly Austin, has no appetite to accept the facts, let alone do anything about them. It's Austin's opinion that because the energy has always bounced back in the past, it will continue to do so in the future; pompous fool.'

Anita reached out and squeezed Marcus' hand before dropping it again. She didn't like Austin, but it couldn't be easy to hear others talking about him like this. Surprisingly, Marcus' energy was remarkably stable as he took stock of what he was hearing.

'So what happens next?' asked Anita. 'How bad does it have to get before they finally decide it's time to act?'

'Who knows,' said Bas, 'but the Descendants have the means to look after themselves for a great deal longer that the rest of the world, so maybe it will take starving people revolting in the streets before they finally feel the need to act. But to be honest, even if that happens, I doubt Austin would show much compassion.'

This seemed to finally tip Marcus over the edge. It was one thing criticising Austin's actions to date, but to imply he was totally heartless and would have no compassion if people were suffering, was another thing all together. 'He's only doing what he thinks is right, based on what he and my ancestors have seen in the past,' he said, pressing on, even though they'd all now rounded to face him square on. 'Dad may be many things, but to imply that he'd intentionally hurt others for his own gain is pushing it too far. He would never do that.'

'Really?' asked Alexander brashly, 'what makes you so sure?' Marcus couldn't really believe that, could he?

184

'Because I know him. He is my father after all. I know he can be quite severe and difficult to deal with, but he does genuinely want what's best for the world.'

Anita jumped in. 'But you can't possibly agree that what's best for the world now is to do nothing? To take no action? To ignore the facts in front of us?'

'What facts?' Marcus said tentatively. 'All we have are a few observations. We've had bad crop yields before; maybe this is just another bad year. Maybe it'll pick up again next year. Who really knows?'

This was too much for Bas. 'I thought Descendants were given a decent education and especially taught about the role the energy plays. It is fundamental to everything we do. It feeds into everything and everything feeds into it. A change in the levels like we are experiencing now will be having a fundamental impact on the world, and that is manifesting in poor crop yields. Who knows what will be next. Otherwise, you're hypothesising that a significant dip in the energy could have no effect on the world; something we know categorically to be false.'

'Yes, but we don't know that the energy dip is manifesting through the crop yields and fish stocks, it could be having an impact elsewhere, on something we have yet to find, and the low yields could be simply because it's been a bad year. We have had a lot of rain.'

Anita couldn't quite believe what she was hearing. 'Are you serious? It's as clear as day to see the two are linked. You're ignoring the evidence because you don't want to admit your father's wrong. Marcus, the world is on the brink of a crisis, the likes of which we have never seen. There's nothing in the past that can help with what we're currently facing; we need to interpret what we have in front of us and act on that information. Don't you think we should be taking action?'

Marcus had been backed into a corner and didn't know what he should do. To agree with Anita was to go against his father, and in essence agree with everything they were saying about him, which he obviously couldn't do. His father may be many things, but Austin took his duty seriously; he would never do something he thought would harm the world. But then again, the evidence was mounting up that they should take action. 'All I know is that dad wouldn't act in a way he thought would harm the world, which means he must know something more about what's going on than we all do. Maybe we should just trust that he's been around for longer, so maybe he has a different perspective.'

Bas and Alexander had had enough. 'I've already heard this bullshit from one member of the Mind line today, and luckily, I don't have to stand here and listen to any more of it,' Bas sniped. 'Just wait and see what happens when we take no action; you'll look like a total fool then, along with your father.' Bas and Alexander left Anita and Marcus, and stormed off in the direction of the Observatory.

Anita stood still for a second, trying to process what Marcus had just said. She turned slowly to face him and he seemed deflated, his shoulders hunched forward, his usual confident swagger momentarily deserting him. 'Did you mean that?' Anita asked slowly. 'Or were you just saying it so as not to trash your father?'

Marcus couldn't admit he wasn't sure, not in front of Anita. 'Anita, nobody's one hundred per cent sure what's going on at the moment. We've never encountered this situation before, so we can't be sure what will happen next. I don't think the right thing to do is scaremonger about disaster and destruction; that won't help anyone.'

'So we should do nothing so as not to put the cat amongst the pigeons?' Anita couldn't believe he was still supporting Austin's position.

'It's a very delicate situation. I don't think we should do anything rash.'

'Well I'm afraid what your father is doing at the moment is doing something rash. To not act at all is criminal, and you can't bury your head in the sand forever.' Anita turned away and started walking towards the Body Temple. Marcus followed her, hoping to move the conversation onto a happier topic. 'I'll see you later Marcus. I need some time alone,' she said, turning towards the entrance steps.

'You're going to let a Council debate come between us?'

She wheeled back round to face him, a look of disbelief plastered across her face. 'You're going to let some ridiculous view held by your father come between us? Open your eyes Marcus, it's a big scary world out there and daddy is number one villain.' Anita turned away, taking the steps into the Temple two at a time.

Marcus watched her go, trying to decide what he really thought and which side to come down on. His mind raced through a mix of emotions, like it wasn't sure quite which one to settle on. He was angry, confused, hurt, embarrassed, worried, and most of all had a deep sense of foreboding that this situation was not going to blow over as he would like it to. He didn't want to lose Anita; it had surprised him how much he'd missed her when she'd gone away to Kingdom, and he'd seen her pretty much every day since then. But he also didn't want to piss off his father, who had only just started to involve him in his business affairs. Nothing he'd seen so far had made him think that Austin, or indeed any of the previous Mind Descendants, had ever done anything out of line with their duty. However, now he came to think about it, it was a little strange that nobody had ever put a single foot out of line. Maybe he was being lied to? Everyone was terrified of Austin, but up until now, Marcus had assumed that was because he had a powerful position and an unpredictable temperament, but he would never purposely hurt someone without good reason. Would he?

Anita reached the top of the stairs feeling like she was going to explode; how could Marcus be so stupid? She could feel that he'd been fighting with his emotions, but he'd sided with Austin when deep down he must have known that some kind of action needed to be taken. He'd sided with Austin when he could've quite easily sided with her once the others had gone. She understood the political setting; Marcus couldn't publically trash his father, especially in front of another Descendant, but surely he trusted her enough by now to tell her what he really felt? Anita felt hurt and frustrated. Not only had he not trusted her, but he'd also let her down in front of the others, so now she looked like a fool for being so close to him. She wanted to punch something.

'Anita?' came a voice from behind her, startling her that anyone had managed to get so close without her feeling their energy. She whirled around to see Helena standing next to a pillar, a strange look on her face, like she was almost nervous.

'I'll do it,' said Anita, surprising both of them equally. Action needed to be taken by somebody, she reasoned.

Helena walked forward. 'Er…what we discussed the other day?' she said the words cautiously, 'you'll do it?'

'Yes,' she said, holding her breath, wondering if she was really doing this.

'I think we should go for a run. We don't want to be overheard,' Helena replied in a low voice.

Helena led Anita to a small cottage around the corner from the Temples, pulled out a key and let them in. 'Here, I'll be back in a minute,' she said, throwing some running tights, a t-shirt and trainers to Anita before making her way up the small spiral staircase to go and get changed.

A few minutes later they were running in the direction of the river, Anita relishing the opportunity to vent her frustration, so she pushed the pace faster and faster, her energy lifting higher and higher. By the time they reached the river she felt really quite good; it still took her by surprise that something as simple as a fast run could make her feel so invigorated. They paused by the edge of the river, stretching and watching the lively water ripple its way down stream.

'So what made you change your mind?' asked Helena, pleased to see that Anita was a great deal more relaxed now than she had been earlier.

'I realised the Descendants aren't going to act any time soon. Austin's too determined to make sure they don't, but somebody has to do something, and you've offered me a way to help. I would be as bad as they are if I didn't act either.'

'And what about your relationship with Marcus?'

'If all goes well he'll never know about it, and we can carry on as we are, which is in a tense fashion at the moment.' A shadow played across her face before she pushed it away. 'What exactly do you need me to do? Where will I find this information that needs to be retrieved?'

Helena took a deep breath. 'We don't know. That's part of what you're going to have to do. All we know is that a memory was stolen from me. I obviously can't remember what it was, as it was stolen, but it was something about the origins of the Institution, something that could be used to undermine us if we ever challenged Austin. It was stolen a couple of decades ago; that's why the Institution went quiet around that time and we've had to stay that way ever since. All I know is that it's stored in a brass cylinder, alongside but slightly set apart from other brass cylinders. We only know that much because Amelia, Marcus' mother, managed to get inside Austin's head once and find out. It was just before they separated. Unfortunately, Austin realised something was wrong before she could find out where the cylinders were stored and steal the memory back.'

'So you need me to find out where Austin stores his memories, which Marcus may not even know, get him to take me there, then somehow steal the cylinder, which is easily identifiable as it is set apart from all the others, and therefore someone will notice as soon as it's gone, sneak the cylinder out of wherever it's stored, without Marcus noticing, and bring it to you, presumably without taking a peek inside?'

'In a nutshell.'

'Sounds like a piece of cake,' Anita said sarcastically.

'Of course, you may have to find a way to tap Amber and Austin for information on its whereabouts, or maybe some of the security guards, because as you say, Marcus may not know.'

'Great,' she said quietly. 'So, just out of interest, what do you think will happen to me if they catch me?' She said it flippantly, but she had to admit, if only to herself, that the thought was worrying.

'I shouldn't get caught if I were you. One thing I can guarantee is that it won't be pleasant for you if you do. They probably won't kill you, as you mean too much to Marcus, unless of course they find a way to do it so it looks like a genuine accident, but either way, probably best to try and avoid it. Amber can be most unpleasant.'

'I'll bear that in mind. Anything else to mention before I jump into the fire?'

'No, I think that pretty much covers it. I think it'd be best if we have as little contact with each other as possible. I don't want anyone to get suspicious. If and when you succeed, find a way to send me a message and then, as promised, I'll tell you everything about your parents.'

'That's not why I'm doing this.'

'I know. But surely you want to know about them?'

'Not if you tell me something I don't want to hear,' she fired back confrontationally. 'Of course I want to know. I've wondered my whole life, but I don't want to think about that until I've done this, focusing on reasons entirely separate to knowing about them; focusing on taking action against a Descendancy that's going to let the world's population starve. When I've done that, I would very much like to hear all about my parents, but not as payment for what you're asking me to do. I'm doing this because I want to, not because it's part of a business transaction.'

'Understood,' Helena replied unthreateningly, 'I just want that cylinder back in our safe hands so we can start to work on restabilising the energy. I'd love it for you to help us do that too, if you want?'

'Let's not get ahead of ourselves. I could end up in Austin's dungeon for the rest of time if I'm not careful. One small step at a time for now I think.'

'Right you are. In which case, I'll look forward to your message. Good luck.'

'Thanks. I'll probably need it.' Helena ran back towards Empire. Anita headed in the opposite direction, found a place to cross the river, and set off for the castle. As ever, there was no time like the present.

*****

Anita had reached the castle at the same time as Marcus arrived back from Empire. She'd suggested they take a walk to the cliff where they'd danced before the ball. They'd made up, neither one really apologising and neither one adapting their point of view; Anita thought he'd be suspicious if she had. They accepted that their opinions differed on this subject, which would inevitably happen from time to time, so they agreed to draw a line under it and move on.

For a few days after that their relationship had been tense, but that wore off and it soon went back to how it had been before. Regrettably, there now seemed to be a silent agreement between them that Anita would no longer see Alexander, although that made her feel even more guilty about him. She hadn't seen him, apart from bumping into him outside the Temples, since they'd got back from Kingdom. She'd been avoiding him as she didn't know what to say, and now she was working for the Institution, it wasn't the best time for Marcus to have something to be jealous of. She put off arranging any more Spirit lessons and spent more and more time with Marcus instead.

Marcus seemed to relax a little when he realised Anita wasn't seeing Alexander any longer and their relationship strengthened as a result, however, he was also becoming more controlling as the days went by. He wanted to know where Anita was going and who she was seeing, and he tried to go with her practically everywhere she went. The only saving grace was that she could go to work at the Observatory, which gave her some much needed space. However, even this was unpleasant for a while, Bas appalled that she was still with Marcus. Luckily, Bas couldn't stay mad with Anita for very long, his distain wearing off after a couple of weeks, but Anita found herself on the roof, lying on the largest energy receiver (who cared about the readings, there was still no improvement), much more often than usual. She needed time to consider what she was doing, whilst enjoying some coveted time by herself.

The quest to find Austin's brass cylinder was going in much the same way as the quest to find the one in her head had; nowhere. There were no clues anywhere and Marcus didn't let her near Austin and Amber, or any of the security guards, for her to be able to probe them for information. She'd seen a guard emerge from an invisible door in the panelling under the stairs one day. This had taken her by surprise, but that the castle stretched down into the ground wasn't in itself surprising or suspicious, much to her disappointment. Although it wouldn't be remarkable if that were where Austin kept his secrets, with nothing more than that to go on, Anita was not doing very well so far.

To compound her problems, Marcus now wanted to meditate with her as well. He kept harping on about how she'd meditated with Alexander, so it was only fair that he should be allowed to meditate with her too. She kept putting it off, but knew that would only fly for so long without him becoming suspicious. The problem was, she worried they might accidently find the cylinder in her head. What would happen then? She needed advice from Alexander before they meditated, but Marcus barely ever left her side, so she was finding it tricky to think of a way to get some time alone with him, without Marcus knowing. Eventually, Cleo saved the day.

Anita had been skirting around the issue of the possessive Marcus on one of her rare evenings out without him, when Cleo had mentioned that Marcus was spending a lot of time in the Archives when Anita was at the Observatory. She had no idea what he was doing there, as she only ever saw him coming and going, and was wondering if Anita knew. She'd replied honestly, saying she had no idea, although it did seem a bit strange, then had changed the subject to see if Cleo had found anything interesting in her research; she was looking into the relic discovery and the reaction of the Descendants, but hadn't yet found anything. This wasn't surprising given the Descendants controlled the Archives, but she was sure it was only a matter of time until something cropped up.

*****

The following day, Anita had gone to the Observatory as usual, allowing Marcus to drop her off in his car, but twenty minutes later, having received a message from Cleo that Marcus was safely in the Archives for the day, Anita left the Observatory and headed for the river. Cleo had delivered a message to Alexander to meet her in the trees next to where she'd first learned to supress her energy.

191

Unusually for Cleo she hadn't made a suggestive comment or questioned why. Maybe it was something in Anita's worried face that had put her off, but Anita had been extremely grateful.

She reached the river full of anticipation and could feel Alexander's powerful energy in the trees waiting for her. Her energy soared when she felt it and his did the same when he sensed her presence. He hung back in the shadows, just in case Marcus had someone following her, or in case somebody happened to be passing by and spotted them. She stepped into the trees, her heart soaring as her eyes took in his beautiful, rugged form. It took all the self-control she possessed to prevent her from running to him and throwing her arms around him; she hadn't realised until now how much she'd missed him. He was fighting a similar battle, straining against every instinct he had to reach out and pull her to his chest. She stopped a few feet away from him, feeling a nudge at the edge of her energy, and without hesitation sent one back. He closed his eyes until the sensation had passed, a pained look on his face when he reopened them, his electric blue eyes sad as they looked hopefully into hers.

He searched for something to say but didn't know where to start, instead standing silent, taking in the contours of her face, Anita doing the same to him. She finally broke the spell. 'I've missed you,' she said hesitantly, his stomach flipping as she said the words. He took a step towards her, reaching out to place his hands either side of her face and pull her to him, the familiar tingles starting to shoot through his body before their skin made contact. When his fingers met her cheeks, the shock was so strong he worried they might be fusing together, his eyes boring deep into hers, confirming she felt the new intensity too. He closed his eyes and placed his forehead against hers, his brow furrowed as he fought desperately to get his boiling energy under control. Anita finally managed to steel herself, using every ounce of control she possessed to pull away from him, the aroma of oranges swirling around her, filling her lungs, screaming at her to kiss him. 'I need your help Alexander,' she breathed breathlessly, forcing herself a safe distance away from him to focus on what she had come for. She sat down on the trunk of a fallen tree and waited as he took deep breaths, recovering from the physical effect her touch had had on him.

'Of course, anything,' he said, shaking his head to concentrate on her words, moving towards the tree trunk, his body seeming to pull him unconsciously towards her.

Anita put her hand up to stop him. 'Please don't come too close,' she said. 'This is difficult enough as it is.'

'What's wrong?' he asked, his face full of concern.

She looked dejectedly at the floor; meeting his hypnotic eyes wasn't a great idea right now. 'Aside from the confusion I feel every time I see you, Marcus wants to meditate with me. I've put him off so many times already, it's only a matter of time before I'm going to have to do it, but I'm worried that he'll find out about what happened between us, or that we'll stumble across the cylinder in my head. I don't know why it's there or what it contains, but I know I don't want him to know about it.'

Alexander was relieved; his energy losing its panicked edge. This was nowhere near as bad as the things that had been running through his imagination. 'It's always risky to let someone into your head, but there are ways to control it. In the same way that I made sure we only ever meditated to places in your mind until that night in Kingdom, you can keep the meditation in Marcus' mind, which will protect you.' He paused for a split second, pushing away the flood of memories of what her lips had felt like on his and the feel of her skin under his fingers. 'Marcus will probably buy some story about you wanting to explore his head because you're fascinated by him, or something similar.' Alexander stopped himself from going any further. Anita was obviously shaken; he didn't want to add to her troubles by criticising Marcus.

'All you need to do is think of your energy pushing into Marcus' head when you start to meditate and that should take you into his mind. You may need to be quite forceful as he might try to do the same thing to you, but you should be stronger than him; you've had much more practice recently. The Gods only know when Marcus last meditated; the Mind Descendants don't think it's a necessary skill to maintain. Just make sure you keep the pressure up for the whole time so you stay in Marcus' head and he doesn't find a way into yours. It's a lot like when you supress your energy downwards, but instead of pushing it down, push it into Marcus. If he insists that you should visit somewhere in your head too, go for the boat on the sea. It's the place you're least attached to and it has a lot of Mind in it. Marcus will feel comfortable there and you're likely to quite easily be able to push him back into his head from somewhere like that. Avoid your Centre if you're worried about divulging information, and it goes without saying that it'd be best to stay away from the cliff in Kingdom. Even though the house isn't there, Marcus will instantly recognise it, and I wouldn't want to bet what he'd do then.' Anita was calmer than when she'd arrived, but was clearly still worried. 'You'll be fine,' he said reassuringly, 'you're a natural at this stuff.'

'And he can't get into my head unless I'm there too when we're meditating? There's no way for him to keep me occupied in his head and then sneak off into mine?'

Alexander supressed a smile at the thought of someone as blundering as Marcus being capable of something as complex as that. 'It is possible, but I very much doubt someone like Marcus is able to do it. I can do it occasionally and there are a handful of very skilled Spirits who have practiced for years who can too, but you should be safe with Marcus.' Alexander hesitated before adding, 'you should be more worried about him getting into your head when you're asleep though; that anyone can do.'

'Well that's less of a problem,' she said, looking directly into his eyes, her face neutral, 'as I haven't recently been asleep in his presence.' Alexander couldn't hide the uplift in his energy and Anita smiled inwardly. 'I really do miss you,' she whispered again guiltily, averting her gaze.

'I miss you too,' he breathed, wanting to rush to her once more, to gather her into his arms, but instead respected the distance she had placed between them. 'Why don't we start up lessons again?' he asked desperately, 'nothing will happen between us, I promise.'

'The problem is I don't promise. We don't even have to touch any longer to be able to feel tingles between us; can you imagine what it's going to be like if we meditate together?'

She did have a point. 'Well what about drinks with Cleo and Bas some time? Drinks in a crowded bar with other people can't be anything to worry about?'

Anita laughed. 'There's no way Marcus would let me have drinks with you without him there and I'm finding it difficult enough to be close to you at the moment, I don't want to have to deal with Marcus being there too.'

Alexander was frantically searching for ideas. It was so unfair that Marcus, stupid, naïve Marcus, could spend time with her, but that he was being denied that pleasure. 'Then leave Marcus and be with me,' he said urgently, catching her off balance as he swiftly closed the gap between them. 'I'll look after you,' he said, grabbing her hands and kneeling down so he could look her directly in the eye, surges of energy shooting through them again, 'Austin won't try to hurt you if you're under my protection.'

Anita looked like she might cry, bowing her head, a knot of desire growing so strong in her stomach that it felt like it might explode. 'I can't,' she choked, 'at least, not yet anyway.'

'Why?' he asked, in gentle disbelief, reaching his hand to her face, lifting her chin so her smoky grey eyes met his, urging her with every fibre of his being to change her mind, 'and what do you mean 'not yet'?'

'I can't go into it now,' she said, resigned, her eyes begging for forgiveness as she placed her hands on his shoulders and pushed herself to her feet, ripping herself away to put a safe distance between them once more, 'but I'll tell you as soon as I can, I promise.'

'When?' he asked, standing up but not invading the space she had once again placed between them.

'I don't know,' she said, shaking her head, tears pooling in her eyes. 'I have to go. It's too dangerous to stay any longer. I need to get back to the Observatory.'

'Ok, but if there's anything I can do, come and find me, or send Cleo, or do something, but I'm here if you need me.' As Anita turned to leave, a realisation dawned on Alexander; he wouldn't, he hoped silently to himself, but not too deep down, Alexander knew that Marcus would.

'What is it?' asked Anita, noticing the change in Alexander's energy.

He hesitated for a split second. 'Nothing. Just let me know if there's anything you need.'

She smiled a weary, thankful smile at him. 'Thank you Alexander, and I'm sorry it's all so secretive. I promise I'll tell you everything as soon as I can.' She reached out and touched his arm as she passed him to leave, causing an eruption of tingles so strong they almost stopped her in her tracks. She said nothing and nor did he, both using all their energy to keep away from the other. Anita left, Alexander feeling her energy ebb away. That bastard had better not hurt her, he thought, but it would be better that she didn't know what was coming her way.

CHAPTER 14

Anita returned to the Observatory just in time to see Marcus' car pull up outside. She hadn't been that long, had she? 'Hi,' she said, walking over and planting a kiss squarely on his lips as he climbed out of his car.

'Hello,' he said provocatively. 'Where have you been? Slacking off work?'

Anita laughed easily, if you only knew the half of it, she thought smugly. 'Just went for a quick walk. You know what us Body types are like, if we stay still for too long we get antsy.'

'That is true,' he said smirking, then pushed her back against the car and kissed her deeply. 'I got bored, so thought I'd come and see if I could persuade you to bunk off work for the afternoon.' He flashed her his most charming smile and Anita went with it; it would be easier that way.

'Alright, let's go,' she said, leaning in and whispering in his ear, so Marcus' driver couldn't hear, 'I think I feel like meditating this afternoon anyway.'

Marcus' energy soared and he looked at her like a child in a sweet shop, a mix of excitement and awe but with some concern that the promise of sweets could be withdrawn before the transaction was completed. She laughed, nodding her head. 'So are we just going to stand here all day?' she asked in mock frustration.

'Or are we going to go?' They climbed into the back of Marcus' car, his excitement contagious, and he held her hand tightly all the way back to the castle. When they got there, Marcus burst out through the door, pulling her along in his wake, Anita giggling uncontrollably at his unrestrained delight. They raced each other up the stairs, taking them two at a time and, unusually, Marcus won, Anita still trying to control her laughter. They entered Marcus' room and he pinned her against the door as he closed it, kissing her enthusiastically, reminding Anita of an excited puppy when he took a step back. His unbridled joy had lifted her energy, but Anita made an effort to get herself under control as he led her to a rug in front of one of the full length windows, preparing herself for the concentration she would need to ensure they stayed in Marcus' head.

Anita sank down and sat cross legged on the rug, expecting Marcus to sit opposite her, but he shook his head. 'I think it's fitting that we practice the love pose today.'

'The love pose?' asked Anita, confused and a little apprehensive.

'You don't know what the love pose is?'

'No,' she said honestly, looking at him like he might be losing his marbles.

Marcus' energy rose even further as he realised that Alexander and Anita had never practiced the love pose; maybe Alexander wasn't trying to steal Anita from him after all. 'The love pose is the only pose practiced lying down and the only pose where you touch the person you're meditating with. It gives you a sense that the meditation is all encompassing; it's a deeper, richer experience and has a more profound effect on those doing it.'

'So what do we have to do?' Anita asked, a little nervously.

'Lie down on your back, or on your side, and turn your head to face me.' She obliged, lying on her side as this felt less vulnerable than lying on her back, and Marcus lay down next to her, also on his side. 'Now we intertwine out hands.' He took her hand so the back of it was close to his lips and vice versa. 'And now we meditate as you would normally. See you on the other side,' he said, smiling broadly, kissing the back of her hand lightly and then shutting his eyes.

Anita was trying to take in everything Marcus was telling her, while at the same time focusing on pushing her energy into Marcus' head when she closed her eyes. Immediately the meditation felt different to normal, although this was probably to be expected, as the only person she'd ever properly meditated with was Alexander. It didn't feel more intense than usual either, if anything it felt less so, but she pushed the thought aside as she focused on keeping her energy towards Marcus.

Anita found herself in thick woodland when the meditation settled. She looked around but couldn't see Marcus anywhere, so started walking in the direction that felt best. She soon hit a small stream with sunlight spilling down through the trees, illuminating the water and moss-covered floor. She leaned against a tree, watching the trickling water as she waited for Marcus to find her.

After a few moments, Marcus' voice pierced the silence. 'Over here,' he beckoned, drawing her towards a small wooden cabin with a veranda overlooking the stream.

'It's beautiful here,' she said as she reached him, taking hold of his outstretched hand. 'Where are we?'

'I don't know exactly,' he replied. 'I've been meditating here since I first had Spirit lessons, but to this day I have no idea where it is. Funny that, don't you think?'

'Yes, I suppose. I wonder how these places get inside our minds, places we've never knowingly been.'

'Some think they're inherited through our bloodlines,' Marcus said as Anita sat down on one of the large rocking chairs on the veranda. 'I don't know if I believe that though. Mind you, dad would never divulge something as intimate as the places in his mind to me and I can't even remember my grandfather, so obviously I don't know what his were.'

'What about your mother?' asked Anita, hoping Marcus wouldn't mind her probing further, 'would she tell you about the places in her mind?'

'She might do, but I'd never ask her about it. Something like this is very private, and many minds would see it as a weakness for others to know something as intimate and unique as that about them. What about the places in your mind? Do you know where they all are?'

Anita hesitated. 'Not all of them. There's one where I'm in a boat on the sea but I don't recognise anything about it. I've been sailing many times, but I don't recognise either the boat or the coastline. I have no idea at all how it got there.'

'Can we go there?' he asked hopefully.

She paused, but her instincts were telling her she should let him in. He'd be suspicious if he'd let her into his mind but she hadn't let him into hers. 'Sure,' she said, before concentrating all of her energy on the boat, and moments later, she and Marcus were sitting on the deck as it sailed itself in the gentle breeze. Marcus' face instantly darkened.

'Is this some kind of joke?' he spat, looking nervously around.

'What do you mean?' she replied, startled.

'You expect me to believe you have no idea where we are? I'm not that naïve Anita.'

'Marcus, I honestly have no idea what's wrong. Where are we?'

The next thing Anita knew she was back in Marcus' room lying on the floor, Marcus yanking his hand away from hers and jumping up, putting what he considered a safe distance between them. 'Anita, that was my Grandfather's boat, Aphrodite.'

'What? Which grandfather?' Anita was shaken by the news.

'Tobias, my dad's dad.'

'How's that possible?' she asked, drawing her knees to her chest and hugging them to her. How could she have something like that in her head? 'But Tobias must have died when I was only three or four and I'm pretty sure I never even met him. How can his boat possibly be in my head?'

'How am I supposed to know? But that was definitely Tobias' boat; I saw a picture of it in the Archives only yesterday.'

'Why are you shouting at me?' she said, losing it, flying to her feet and storming towards him. If he was going to yell at her, she could play at that game too. 'You said only minutes ago you have no idea where that place in your head is. What if that's somewhere my grandmother has a connection to? Do I get to round on you then? Look at you in an accusatory way and suppose you're up to something underhand? Don't you trust me at all?'

'Well how do you explain it?'

'I can't,' she stressed the words, standing inches from him and looking up as though he were truly stupid, 'in exactly the same way that you can't explain how that place got into your head.' At that moment something in Anita's brain fell into place and she replayed what Marcus had just said, '...I saw a picture of it in the Archives only yesterday...' Why was he spending so much time in the Archives anyway? He hated history and he wasn't researching anything that he'd told her about, yet he was looking at things that had belonged to his grandfather. He shared every other waking thought with her, much to her irritation, yet he hadn't even mentioned the Archives, where he was spending time every day. Why? She needed to get him to take her there, which meant she'd need to do something radical to get him back on side. There was nothing for it. Anita and Marcus stood, faces inches apart, tension building, eyes clouded with fury, when Anita's intention changed from rage to furious passion. She tilted her head upwards, lifted her hands to Marcus' shirt and pulled him to her, her angry lips meeting his with fervour.

Marcus responded immediately, kissing back with equal force, lifting his hands to her face, drinking in her urgent kisses. He pushed her back against the wall, pinning her like she were his prey, holding her there with his hips. He released her long enough to pull her dress over her head before lifting her off the ground to pin her back against the wall. She wrapped her legs around him as he kissed her neck. She clawed at his shirt, pulling it out of his trousers, but unable to get it any further, his hands busy unclipping her bra. Marcus turned, easily holding Anita's lithe body in place, as he carried her to his bed and threw her roughly down on it. He bent down and removed her lace knickers, discarding them onto the floor, Anita's athletic body now lying totally naked in front of him. She sat up and pulled Marcus' shirt off over his head, enjoying the ripple of muscle on his torso as his arms came back down to find her. She stood up, relishing the sensation of Marcus' hands running down her back and over the contour of her behind, resting there as she reached for his trousers, urgently ridding him of his remaining clothes. She succeeded, then spun him round and pushed him back onto the bed, climbing on top of him like a cat and kissing her way seductively from his navel, to his torso, to his neck, to his lips.

Marcus retook control, no longer able to restrain his desire. He grabbed her waist and rolled her sideways off him and onto her back, following her over, pinning her to the bed, Anita wrapping her legs around him once more. He pushed into her, intense shivers of pleasurable energy running unexpectedly through them, Anita pushing her hips up to meet him, grabbing his hair with her hands and pulling his mouth to hers. They moved faster, tension building, loud gasps of pleasure escaping unnoticed from their mouths until Anita could take no more and felt the tension burst inside her, convulsions racking her body. Marcus collapsed on top of her, finding his release.

He rolled off her and turned his head to look into her sated eyes. They smiled indulgently at each other before Marcus pulled Anita's back to his chest, wrapping a protective arm across her, holding her tightly to him. He used his other hand to pull her hair back off her neck, planting light kisses on the exposed flesh. She played her fingers across his arm, then lifted his hand to her lips, kissing the palm gently.

He ran his teeth over her ear, 'sorry,' he whispered, so quietly she could barely make out the word. 'I may have overreacted a little. I was just so shocked that my grandfather's boat was in your head, especially after only so recently seeing a picture of it.'

Anita recognised this as her chance. 'Why were you looking at a picture of it?' she asked innocently.

'Because I've been learning about my family. Dad recently introduced me to some family history that I never knew existed, so I've been spending time at the Archives looking into it further. It's been fascinating. There's so much I never knew about the Mind line and there's so much more to learn.'

'Can I see the picture?' asked Anita quickly. As soon as the words were out of her mouth she regretted them; way too forward, surely that would scare him off.

'Why do you want to see it?'

'Because I'm as intrigued as you are about how Tobias' boat found its way into my head and why it's there, and there may be some kind of clue in that picture. How would you feel if I had a picture of the wood in your head? Wouldn't you want to see it?'

Marcus couldn't argue with her there. If Anita had a similar picture, he would most definitely want to see it, but he'd promised Austin that he wouldn't tell anyone about the family vault. 'The problem is I can't take the picture out of the Archives,' he said slowly.

'But we can go there,' she said tenderly, not conceding that this might be a problem. 'I'd love to see your family vault. Your family's had a profound impact on the history of the world; it would be an amazing privilege to see some of the artefacts.'

He took a deep breath. 'Ok,' he said resignedly, kissing her shoulder, 'let's go now and we can go for a walk afterwards. The sun will be setting by then and the archive gardens look beautiful at that time of day.'

'Thank you,' she said, rolling into him and gently kissing his lips.

*****

They arrived at the Archives and Marcus led Anita down the three flights of stairs. Half way to the back of the room, they bumped into Cleo, who looked a little shocked to see them there.

'Hey,' she said, giving Anita a quizzical look, 'I don't think you've come here more than twice in your entire life have you?' she laughed, mocking her best friend, 'what are you doing here?'

Marcus looked uncomfortable. 'Nothing much,' Anita replied. 'Marcus spends so much time here I thought I'd come and see what all the fuss is about.' Anita threw Cleo a look pleading her not to ask any more questions, and thankfully she took the hint.

Marcus relaxed a bit, realising this could in fact work in his favour. Cleo could keep Anita occupied whilst he unlocked the vault, that way she wouldn't see the security, which meant he could downplay the extent of the family secrets contained within. 'Anita, I'll come and get you in a minute, there's something I have to do.'

'Ok,' Anita agreed without hesitation, not wanting to put him off now they'd come this far.

*****

Austin descended the stairs to the basement and asked the guard for the keys to the Archives. He'd seen Marcus leave earlier with Anita, so now would be a good time to remove a couple of choice artefacts before Marcus explored too widely. 'Keys,' he barked at the security guard, who looked back blankly.

'I'm afraid Marcus came and collected them earlier sir.'

'What? You gave them to him when he was with Anita?'

'He was with Anita? It was only Marcus who came down here.'

Austin's fuse had been lit and if this were not resolved to his satisfaction extremely quickly, then he would explode and no one in the castle would be spared his wrath.

'Amber,' he bellowed.

She appeared at her office door, immediately knowing something must be wrong. 'What is it?' she asked concerned.

'This blundering employee of yours has given Marcus the keys to the family vault when he was with Anita.'

'Are you sure?'

'I just saw them leave the castle together.'

Amber reacted instantly, barking orders back into her office and at the guard behind the desk. 'I need a team of four people, now. Bring round the cars. Alert the Archives that they're not to allow Anita to leave until we get there. Are you joining us Austin?'

'Of course I'm sodding joining you. Let's go.'

Marcus walked off and Anita realised that Cleo being here could work to her advantage. 'I need your help Cleo,' she whispered conspiratorially.

Cleo looked intrigued, loving nothing more than a conspiracy. 'What do you need me to do?'

'Distract Marcus. He's about to take me into a separate room and I need you to come snooping around just after we enter. He's showing me a picture, but I need you to buy me some alone time in there so I can have a look around.'

'Anita,' called Marcus, striding back towards her. 'Are you coming?'

Cleo nodded at Anita. 'I'm in,' she said happily, in a low voice.

Anita walked towards Marcus, who led her through a very normal looking door that interrupted the rows of shelves housing a wide range of seemingly randomly categorised artefacts. The room looked very average and housed artefacts that resembled those on the shelves outside, all very boring, until Anita spotted a row of brass cylinders on the far side of the room, with one cylinder set slightly apart from all the others. Her stomach lurched and adrenaline flooded her blood as she turned back to look at what Marcus was showing her. 'As you can see, Aphrodite is definitely the boat in your mind,' he said, marvelling that it could've found its way into her head.

'By the Gods, you're right,' she said, genuinely shocked. Although her focus here was now on something altogether different, she was fascinated by the picture and concerned about how the boat had managed to end up as a place in her mind. Anita took the picture from him and scanned every inch of it, although there was nothing that gave any clues as to why it was in her head. At that moment there was a light knock on the door and the colour drained from Marcus' face. This was exactly what he'd wanted to avoid; the nosey Cleo finding out about the vault would not go down at all well with Austin. 'Go and keep her occupied,' said Anita, 'I'll be out in a minute; I just want a bit more time with the picture.' As he turned, she made a big show of sitting down and studying the photo as though engrossed. Seeing this, Marcus decided it was safe to leave her alone and went to deal with Cleo.

As soon as the door clicked shut behind him, Anita abandoned the photo onto the desk and made for the brass cylinders at the back of the room. She picked up the end cylinder and felt the smooth, cold metal in her hands. It was heavier than she'd expected, but as she placed it in her coat pocket, something curious happened; it started to shake. Anita turned to make for the door, not wanting to stay for a moment longer than she needed to in Austin's treasure trove of secrets, but as she was about to push down the door handle, the conversation she'd had with Anderson in Kingdom came back to her. He'd said, 'if someone stole a cylinder containing someone else's memories, the energy would strain to get back to its rightful owner'. If that were the case, she had the wrong memory. This had only started to strain when she'd stolen it; it had been quite still and quiet before that. She looked back at the shelf to see which cylinders were straining so she could select one of those to take with her, but they were all standing entirely still, none of them seeming at all uncomfortable where they were. She looked around to see if she'd missed another row of brass cylinders, but there were none to be seen.

Anita had a horrible moment of clarity. Helena had lied to her. She wasn't here to take back one of Helena's stolen memories, she was here to steal for the Institution something of Austin's. Anita hurried back across the room and put the cylinder back in exactly the same place she'd taken it from, slightly set apart from the others. However, as her hand left the cylinder and it reverted to a still, lifeless object, the door flew open and Amber, Austin and four security guards came hammering in. Amber took in the scene and reacted instantly, running forward and grabbing Anita by her arms. Anita countered instinctively; she was, after all, an adept Body, and used Amber's forward momentum to flip her onto her back, causing her to release Anita's arms. Anita valiantly fought her way through three of the four body guards, however, as she reached the fourth, the others, including Amber, had recovered, and collectively wrestled her to the ground, two of them pinning her down with all their weight.

Marcus appeared at the door, aghast as he took in what he found. 'Leave her alone,' he ordered, starting towards the pile of humanity in the centre of the floor, but Amber intervened, placing her body in his way.

'She was stealing from your father,' she said smugly, her words like poison.

'No she was not. She was here looking at a photo of Tobias' boat.'

'Then why, when we came through the door, was she reaching for that brass cylinder?' Amber asked triumphantly, gesturing towards the cylinder on the end that moments before, Anita had held in her hand.

'I was just having a look,' Anita spluttered, gasping for breath to speak again, finding it difficult to breath with such an immense weight holding her to the ground. 'I've never seen cylinders so delicate before, so I just wanted to see them up close.' She felt faint as she desperately tried to refill her lungs with air.

'Do you really believe that?' laughed Amber, looking at Marcus as though he were a stupid, naïve child.

'Yes, I do,' he spat back, turning to the so-far-silent Austin, who was weighing up what to do in this unusually delicate situation. 'She was looking at this photo of Aphrodite,' he said, picking up the picture of the boat and waving it in front of his face. 'What's wrong with that?'

'Aside from the fact you brought her here at all, Marcus, and that you left her alone to explore to her heart's content, and that we found her reaching for one of my brass cylinders, nothing, I suppose.' His sarcasm was chilling. 'And why exactly did you feel the need to show Anita this picture?'

Anita silently prayed for Marcus not to tell Austin about their meditation, or that the boat was a place in her head. She had a feeling that Austin would not think this was a redeeming factor. 'Because we got talking about boats and sailing and I told her I'd just come across a photo of the most exquisite boat I'd ever seen. Anita asked me to show it to her, so I did.'

'You expect me to believe that someone as manipulative as her came here just to see a photo?' Austin laughed cruelly, exchanging a look with Amber that was clearly a commentary on his son's incompetence.

Marcus' temper flared. 'What makes you think Anita's manipulative? I tried to teach her Mind skills and she's useless at manipulation.'

'Don't be so stupid Marcus. How else would someone from Anita's background get so close to someone like you if not by manipulation? She was probably feigning ignorance to reinforce the ruse. Don't you think it's time to open your eyes and see who she really is?'

'Don't treat me like a child. Anita is not who you paint her to be, now let her go and stop being so melodramatic. There was no harm done. I'm sure if Amber calls off her guards, Anita will apologise for the confusion and we can all move on from what is an embarrassing misunderstanding.'

'Marcus, you have a lot to learn,' said Amber, enjoying patronising him. 'Boys, take her back to the castle and put her in a cell for questioning.'

'No,' Marcus ordered, 'let her go,' but everybody ignored him, Austin turning to leave the room, followed by Amber, then the guards, dragging Anita between them. She threw Marcus a last pleading look and mouthed the words, 'I love you,' to him as they took her away. Austin, it would seem, was right about one thing; these days Anita did have a manipulative side.

*****

Cleo hid, crouched down behind a rack of artefacts, watching them take Anita away. Luckily she'd managed to drag Marcus to the other side of the room, saying she wanted to show him something. When they'd got there, she'd acted as though she'd misplaced whatever it was and started to rummage through a pile of papers. Marcus had lost patience at this point and said he needed to get back to Anita, but that if Cleo could give them some space he'd appreciate it. She'd let him go, thinking Anita would have had long enough to explore a bit, but when Marcus had got about half way back towards the door, Austin, Amber and four large guards had burst onto the floor and run towards the door, reaching it before the startled Marcus.

Cleo hadn't been able to hear what happened inside, however, had watched, appalled, as her best friend was dragged roughly up the stairs towards the entrance, a furious, flapping Marcus in tow. He kept appealing to Austin, saying, 'dad, please, don't do this,' but Austin ignored his son's words entirely, carrying on as though nobody was uttering a sound. The only time Marcus' words had any effect was when he had said, 'dad, I love her, please don't do this.' At this revelation, Austin and Amber had rounded on Marcus, each fixing him with a terrifying stare. They'd said nothing however, knowing this was neither the time nor the place, so turned back and followed the guards up the stairs, Marcus following in their wake.

Cleo stayed where she was for a full fifteen minutes after they'd gone, terror and shock fixing her in place. When she was convinced they weren't coming back, she cautiously climbed to her feet and made her way out of the building, making sure nobody saw her leave. The last thing Anita needed now was for the only person who knew she'd been taken to be spotted by one of Austin's informants. Once she was free of the Archives, Cleo ran back to town, heading directly for the Temple of the Spirit. The only person she could think to tell was Alexander and she hoped desperately that he was there, as she had no idea where else to look if he wasn't.

As she reached the Temple, Cleo raced to the circular slab in the centre of the floor, got down on all fours and started pounding the stone, hoping that Alexander would be able to hear her. To her amazement, within seconds, the slab in the floor began to slide aside, Cleo scrambling out of the way in time to see Alexander ascending the stairs.

'Cleo, what is it?' he asked, concerned.

'It's Anita,' she garbled. 'Austin has her.'

'What? What do you mean 'Austin has her'?' Alexander looked around, noticing the few people in the Temple beginning to take an interest in what was going on. 'Come on, we should talk downstairs.'

Normally this would be a source of great excitement for Cleo, after all, nobody else she knew had ever been to one of the chambers below the Temples, but right now she was just grateful that Alexander was here and might be able to help. They quickly descended the spiral staircase and came out into Alexander's study. He sat Cleo down in one of the large, brown, leather chairs and made her a cup of hot, sweet tea, saying, 'tell me what happened,' as he did it.

Cleo recounted what had happened and Alexander looked drawn and worried when she finished, sitting down opposite her and pausing to consider what she'd just said. 'There's one more thing,' said Cleo, looking down into her tea, struggling to find the best way to say it. 'As they were leaving and Marcus was trying everything to get Austin to free Anita, he told them that he loved her. They rounded on him and looked like they might have locked him away too, but didn't say a thing, they just carried on and Marcus followed them out.'

Alexander looked pained, but in reality, something like that might be the only thing that would keep Anita alive. It would be dangerous for Austin to kill Anita knowing that Marcus loved her, however, he wouldn't easily be persuaded to let her go.

Once Cleo had left, Alexander carefully considered his options. He considered contacting Marcus to try and work together to break Anita out, he thought about storming over to the castle and demanding she be released, he even briefly considered killing Austin, but quickly put that one aside. In the end, Alexander reasoned it was most important to maximise the chances that Anita would be kept alive, and the best way to do that was to let Austin know that Alexander, along with others, knew she was being held by him. That way, Austin would probably think it too risky to kill her outright and it would buy Alexander some time to work out a way to get her freed.

Alexander got his driver to take him to the castle, the light from its windows blazing out into the now pitch black sky. He walked up to the imposing front door and pulled the handle that rang the bell. Amber answered and looked at Alexander suspiciously, 'why are you here?' she snapped, sounding surprised.

'I have something important that I need to discuss with Austin.'

Looking at Alexander as though it were ludicrous that he'd not already told her, she said, 'and that important topic of conversation is…?'

'…none of your business,' he replied severely. 'And since when have Descendants had to explain themselves to the likes of you?' This was the kind of thing Austin would say, so Alexander hoped it would resonate with her.

She looked petulantly back at him. 'Fine, come in. I'll see if Austin is available.'

A few minutes later, Alexander was standing in front of Austin's desk, Austin pretending to have no idea why he was there and making a point of not offering Alexander a seat. 'Austin, I have something of a sensitive nature to discuss with you.'

Austin raised his eyebrows in mock surprise. 'Oh?' he said. 'How can I help?'

'It would appear as though you have one of my students detained at present and I would very much appreciate it if you would release her into my custody.'

'Which student is that?' he asked casually, sipping honey coloured whiskey from a tumbler.

Alexander replied evenly. 'I think we both know I'm referring to Anita. She's very close to your son, is she not?'

Austin's nostrils flared. 'Tell me, why is it you think I should release someone who tried to steal from my family vault into your custody?'

'As I said, she's one of my students, which makes me partially responsible for her. I should like to resolve this quietly and as a matter of urgency, so there is no embarrassment for any party involved.'

'I see. Well I'm afraid I can't do that. I'm yet to finish questioning her and it's important we conduct a thorough investigation into what happened. I'm intrigued as to why she tried to steal one of my memories, for example.'

'What could Anita possibly want with one of your memories?' Alexander laughed, although the laughter never reached his eyes.

'I don't know, Alexander. That's what I intend to find out.'

'And when you've found that out? Will you release her into my custody then?'

'That all depends on what I find,' he said, threateningly. 'I might decide its best to lock her up for a couple of years instead.'

'Well let's all hope that is not the case,' Alexander said, turning to leave. 'I can't imagine Marcus would like that very much.'

Alexander left the castle with mixed emotions. He'd never expected Austin to hand Anita over, and now at least he was unlikely to kill her, however, the spiteful look Austin had had on his face was not something to be taken lightly. Anita was in for a rough ride.

*****

Amber stood over Anita, whose hands and feet were cuffed together and tightly attached to the uncomfortable wooded chair on which she sat. They'd given her no food or anything to drink since they'd tied her up, and after twelve hours of sitting in the same position, her muscles were cramping and her mouth was dry.

'You're quite the trouble maker,' Amber said slowly, threateningly, circling the chair like a shark would its prey. Amber was looking forward to drawing this out, so she took her time as she walked, her high heels clipping menacingly on the slabs of stone with each step. 'And let's not forget that you're quite the manipulator from what we've seen so far. It would seem you've caught the attention of not only Marcus, but Alexander as well, if our reports from Kingdom are anything to go by. How do you think Marcus will feel when he sees pictures of you and Alexander holding hands in such a public location?'

Anita didn't say anything. What could she say? Deny she was manipulative? Justify the photos? Anita knew Amber would say anything to try and elicit a reaction. Amber's powers of manipulation surpassed anything Anita could display, but the important thing now was to stay calm. And even if Marcus saw the photos, she was pretty sure holding hands was a minor offence in comparison to what Amber and Austin were doing to her now. She was sure such innocent pictures wouldn't change his mind about her; he'd said he loved her, so it would take more than that to turn him against her.

'Not answering are we?' Amber said, pausing directly behind Anita and bending over to whisper ominously in her ear. 'Don't worry, I wouldn't want you to, not yet anyway. That would be too easy. So, tell me Anita, why were you trying to steal one of Austin's memories?' Anita kept silent, looking obstinately forwards as Amber circled round into her peripheral vision. Out of nowhere, Amber raised her hand and swiped it as hard as she could across Anita's face, making a slapping noise that seemed to reverberate coldly around the hollow room. Anita's head whipped to one side, her face immediately throbbing from the impact. 'I can't tell you how long I've wanted to do that for,' Amber purred, continuing to circle, 'and I'm sure you'll be pleased to hear it was everything I'd hoped it would be.'

'So, let's try a different question. What do you hope to achieve through your relationship with Marcus? Was it just about getting access to the vault, or do you have something else planned? Maybe you're working with someone else? A group of academics? The Institution maybe?' Anita kept looking forwards, so didn't see that Amber had picked up a whip from the back of the room and was advancing darkly towards her. 'I'll give you one more chance to say something,' she said, 'and if you do, I promise to go easy on you. It will ruin my fun, but I like to reward good behaviour.'

Anita said nothing. She knew there was nothing she could say that would really help her. Amber paused for a couple more seconds before raising the whip high into the air and cracking it down onto Anita's unsuspecting legs. It too made a sickening noise on impact that bounced around the empty, grey, windowless room and Anita let out an involuntary gasp of pain as Amber struck again, this time on her stomach, then a third time across her upper arms. Apart from her cries of pain, Anita uttered not a single sound, nor did she start to sob. She felt empty, detached from her skin that was now singing from the impact of the whip. She felt like she was floating above her tied-up form, neither connected to what was happening, nor fully detached, her energy the lowest it had ever been, feeling powerless, like there was nothing she could do to influence her fate.

The questioning and torture went on for hours, Austin joining Amber for the later stages to see if Anita would break; he was pretty sure she would. By the end, Amber was furious that she'd managed to extract not a single word from Anita, indeed, the only signs she was still alive were the whimpers of pain she now uttered at every new injury inflicted. Anita's body was covered with wounds; the whip had cut her flesh, she had several broken ribs, a black eye was starting to form, but still, she wouldn't talk.

'I think you're losing your magic touch Amber,' Austin taunted. 'I wouldn't have thought this one would be a hard nut to crack.'

Austin's ridicule drove Amber over the edge and she rained a number of blows down on Anita with such ferocity, that by the time she'd finished, Anita had been knocked unconscious. 'Stupid bitch,' spat Amber, regaining her composure, turning towards Austin and smoothing down her pencil skirt. 'Can't we just kill her?' she pouted.

Anita stirred but kept her head down, listening to Amber and Austin talk. 'Alas, no,' replied Austin, sternly, holding Amber's chin and kissing her dangerously on the lips. 'Marcus being in love with her complicates matters somewhat, as you well know. And it would seem Alexander has somehow got wind of the fact we have her. He requested that we release Anita into his custody, as she's a pupil of his. Killing her, I am afraid, is off the cards.'

'By the Gods, she gets around a bit. We should've tried to recruit her when we had the chance; manipulation skills like hers are really quite rare, especially for someone with such profound Body abilities. We missed a trick.'

'Indeed, but that doesn't solve the problem of what we should do with her, given that killing her isn't an option.'

'Say she confessed to stealing on behalf of some group or other and lock her up for a few years. Marcus and Alexander will soon move on.'

'A nice idea, but I'm not sure that's going to fly. Marcus has never been truly interested in any other girl and I can't recall Alexander ever having a girlfriend for very long. I don't think this is just going to blow over as we might like. Locking her up seems pretty likely to lead, if anything, to more profound problems.'

'Then what? Let her go?'

'Maybe. But I think we should get Marcus to question her first.' Amber and Austin turned and left the room, closing the heavy grey door behind them, Anita hearing the key turn in the lock and the bolt clunk home. No escape through there, she thought, and no escape anywhere else either. There were no windows and only tiny ventilation holes in the wall to let air in. Even if she could get out of her cuffs, there was no way to escape.

*****

Austin climbed the stairs, photos in hand, and knocked lightly on Marcus' door. The door swung open and Marcus looked at Austin with disgust. 'What you do want?' he sneered.

'I want to talk to you about Anita and then I'd like you to question her for us.'

Marcus laughed coldly. 'And why do you think I'd do anything to help you after the way you've treated both of us. You've hauled Anita off like some common criminal whilst totally ignoring both my wishes and my judgment. I've been trained just like any other Descendant to identify deception and deceit and I can assure you Anita showed no signs of either.'

Austin handed Marcus the pictures of Alexander and Anita holding hands in Kingdom. 'No deception or deceit at all?' he asked triumphantly.

Marcus took a long look at the photos before casting them aside. 'What exactly are you trying to show me? All I see is Alexander dragging Anita through the streets of Kingdom, during a visit that happened several months ago, before we were properly seeing each other. Alexander and Anita are friends; she had lessons with him in the Spirit disciplines. What do you expect me to do,' he smirked, 'fly into a jealous rage because Anita's holding another man's hand? Show me pictures of them kissing and then maybe I would react differently, but this means nothing at all.' Inwardly Marcus was jealous, very jealous, but that could be worked out later. First he needed to concentrate on getting Anita free. 'But I'll question her for you, so we can clear this whole thing up and let her go.' Marcus pushed past his perturbed father and made his way to the basement, Austin following him, trying to keep up whilst maintaining a dignified pace.

Marcus burst into the basement, snapping, 'where is she,' at Amber. Amber looked to Austin, who was coming down the stairs behind Marcus, nodding his approval.

'Right this way,' said Amber sardonically, leading the way down the corridor and unlocking the cell that held Anita inside. 'Just knock when you want to come out,' she said, standing aside and motioning Marcus through the door. Marcus saw Anita's slumped form and rushed past Amber, hearing the door shut and lock behind him as he sank to his knees in front of her and lifted her head with his hands.

'By the Gods, what have they done to you?'

She looked at him through her swollen eyes and smiled weakly. 'They beat me up.'

Marcus was relieved to hear they hadn't managed to rip every shred of her apart and marvelled that she still had any semblance of a sense of humour. 'I'm so sorry Anita, this is all my fault. I should never have left you alone in the vault.'

'Don't say that Marcus. I should learn to curb my curiosity.'

'What were you even doing anyway?' he asked softly.

'The cylinders caught my eye as they're exquisitely made. All the energy recording equipment we have at the Observatory is made of brass and needs to be very precise, so, crazy as it sounds, I appreciate beautiful brass work!' She laughed, but immediately stopped, the pain in her chest confirming that all of her ribs had not survived the beating intact. 'I've never seen such fine cylinders, so I wanted to examine one close up. I was about to pick one of them up when Amber, Austin and the cronies burst in, saw me reaching for the shelf and assumed I was about to steal something. The rest you know.'

'I'm so sorry Anita,' he repeated, not knowing what else to say. 'I'll get you out of here, I promise. You haven't done anything wrong, so they can't keep you here.'

'I'm sure they'll find a way if they want to,' she said in a low, cynical voice. 'They've kept me for this long and have beaten me up for no reason.'

'I'll find a way,' he whispered, placing a gentle kiss on her cracked and swollen lips. 'I have to go now, but I promise I'll be back before too long and I will get you out. I love you,' he said meaningfully, before placing a protective kiss on her forehead.

'I love you too,' she said, in a voice so small it was barely even a whisper.

CHAPTER 15

Marcus left the castle without stopping to talk to his father. Much as he hated him normally, it was time to work with Alexander. He did, after all, have power as a ruling Descendant that Marcus did not, and he possessed a fairness that his father seemed to think unnecessary. He made his way to the Spirit Temple and rapped on the stone covering Alexander's chambers, not having to wait for very long for a response. 'Marcus? What are you doing here?' said Alexander as the stone slid aside.

Marcus stood silently for a moment, not quite believing he was about to say what he was. 'I'm here because I need your help to free Anita. I saw you arriving at the castle earlier, so listened in to some of your conversation with dad. I know you want to free Anita too and I can't do it on my own. You have power as a ruling Descendant that I don't and the only way we'll get her back is if we force dad's hand.'

'Marcus, I went to the castle earlier to try and make sure they keep her alive. You know that your dad and Amber would kill her if they thought they could get away with it?'

'I, uh,' Marcus wasn't sure what to say. He'd had his eyes opened when he'd seen the state of Anita, so he supposed there was no reason to assume what Alexander was saying was incorrect, but he couldn't believe his father would murder someone without good reason. 'All I know is that Anita is a total state. Amber didn't show her any kindness when she was interrogating her, and she seems to have a couple of broken ribs along with wounds everywhere else.'

'That bitch,' Alexander blazed. 'What are they accusing her of?'

'They think she was trying to steal a brass cylinder of dad's. It contains some memory or other. Anita's story is that she wanted to take a closer look at the brass work; she said she appreciates it because of her work at the Observatory. I'm not sure dad will buy that though.'

'So how do you suggest we go about freeing her if they won't believe her story?'

'I think we need to use your power as a Descendant to threaten dad. The one thing he cares about more than anything is his reputation. If you threaten to embarrass him publically, for example, at a Council meeting, then he may opt to let her go instead.'

'And what do you suggest I use to embarrass him?'

'Luckily, I've been spending a lot of time researching my family history recently, and there's a lot that I've cross referenced with other sources to get the real story, including what happened that caused mum and dad to separate, for example.'

Alexander perked up; this sounded as though it might actually have legs. 'Go on.'

'It turns out that dad was having an affair.'

'With who?'

'I'll only tell you that on a need to know basis. It should be enough just to threaten him.'

'Ok, I'm in. How do you want to play it?'

'I'll go back to the castle, tell dad I think Anita's innocent and explain the misunderstanding. When he says he thinks I'm naïve and don't know what I'm talking about, I'll tell him that you're willing to blackmail him over the affair if he doesn't let her go. Hopefully that should be enough, especially given that keeping her locked up indefinitely presents a serious problem when it comes to me. If not, then we have to go through with it, and we keep digging up embarrassments until he's willing to set her free.'

'You would do that to your own father?'

'If he keeps Anita locked up, yes. I love her, and she hasn't done anything wrong. It's my fault she was in the vault in the first place; I've got to get her out. Anyway, dad will recover, he always does.'

Marcus went back to the castle, stood outside Austin's office, took a deep breath, and knocked sharply before entering, without waiting for an answer. He entered to see Amber and Austin sitting on a sofa drinking whiskey and laughing about something in a way that made Marcus feel cold.

'Marcus,' said Austin, surprised that his son, who usually waited obediently at the door after knocking, had waltzed straight in. 'Join us for a drink,' he said, covering his surprise.

'No thank you. I have something I want to talk to you about privately,' he said, looking Austin straight in the eye.

'That sounds ominous,' said Amber contemptuously, getting up to leave. She walked past Marcus, then turned and shot Austin a knowing look before reaching the door. If Marcus had been ten minutes later, who knew what he would have walked in on. It would be a good idea to lock the door from now on, she thought, although how Marcus could be so blind as to not see what was going on between them anyway, she had no idea.

'Dad, please let Anita go. She's done nothing wrong; she was looking at the brass work on those cylinders, nothing more. You yourself must know how rare it is to find such well-crafted cylinders and she has an interest in brass work as everything at the Observatory is made in equally well-crafted brass. If you want to punish anyone, then punish me. I was the one that took her to the vault and then left her alone. If I hadn't, this would never have happened.'

'And why did you leave her alone?' Austin asked, realising he was yet to find this out.

'Because we bumped into Cleo at the Archives and she was snooping around, which isn't exactly unheard of for her. I went out to ask for some privacy and walked her to the stairs. She went back upstairs to where she'd been working and I started to walk back to the vault. I stopped to look at an artefact on the way and that's when you burst onto the floor.' His story wasn't entirely accurate, however he didn't want to get Cleo into trouble too, so it was probably best to downplay that she'd wanted to show him something. Marcus was sure it was all innocent, but Austin would be unlikely to see it that way.

'And you think it's a coincidence that Cleo happened to be at the archive when you took Anita there?'

'Yes. Cleo's at the Archives almost every day and has been since before you showed me the vault. I would've been surprised had she not been there. Anyway, it was an impromptu visit by Anita and I, and Anita couldn't have got a message to Cleo to meet her there without me knowing.'

Austin had to admit this part of the story checked out, especially given that her spending so much time at the Archives had been what prompted Austin to introduce Marcus to the vault in the first place. 'So you want me to simply let her go? You know I can't do that. She's a manipulative person Marcus, why can't you see she's using you for some reason and we have to find out why?'

'Why do you see a conspiracy theory everywhere you look? Couldn't it be that Anita just likes me for the same reasons that I like her? We have fun together and have a lot in common. Most people either suck up to me or are terrified of me, but Anita's just normal; it's refreshing. Unlike you, I don't want people to treat me differently.'

'Marcus, you're acting like a naïve child. Why can't you just trust that I know best?'

'Because you don't always know best and one day I'll be a ruling Descendant, so I can't stay in your shadow forever.'

'You're not even close to being ready to rule,' Austin scorned. 'You're a lost boy who's been led astray by a girl and you're not even able to admit you might be wrong when she was caught stealing red handed from your family vault.'

This was the point of no return, but Marcus knew that to get anywhere with his father he had to fight fire with fire, it was the only way to win his respect. 'If you don't let her go then Alexander will expose details of the affair you were having just before you and mum separated.' He said it then stopped dead, the air around them seeming to crackle as Austin took in what his son had just said.

'What affair?' he asked, testing Marcus' resolve.

'Don't play with me dad. You know exactly what I'm talking about.'

Austin looked at his son and was impressed. Indeed he was stepping out of the shadows. 'You would do that to your own family? Bring embarrassment down on yourself at the same time as me?'

'You're trying to play the family card when you locked up Anita, who I love, ignored my wishes to set her free, beat her up, and then refused to listen to her perfectly reasonable explanation of what happened? Do me a favour dad and come up with something better than that.'

Marcus' resolve was impressive. Austin saw a look in his eye that reminded him of his father, Tobias, and it filled him with pride.

He knew now that Marcus had it in him to enter the family business, if he was happy to blackmail his own father, then only the Gods knew what else he was capable of. However, it was important, now that Marcus had found his teeth, to keep him on side and bring him firmly under his wing. Amber would have to start taking orders from him; she wouldn't like that, but he had to see incremental benefits, or there was a danger that Marcus would defect, and much as it pained him, Anita would have to be set free. He could easily deal with her at a later date, after he'd managed to drive a wedge between her and Marcus. Austin was confident that wouldn't be difficult to do, not now that Marcus had shown his true colours.

'Alright, consider her freed. You can go and get her and take her home if you want.'

Marcus froze, holding his breath. Was he dreaming, or had that really been so easy? Austin laughed. 'Son, I'm proud of the way you've dealt with this. You've leveraged a piece of delicate information to your advantage; I couldn't have done it better myself. The only thing is, does Alexander really know about the affair?'

'He knows there was one, but he doesn't know who it was with. I said I would only tell him that if he needed to know.'

'But you know who it was with?'

'I guess we'll never know now, will we,' Marcus said smugly, turning for the door. 'Come on, I'll need you to call off your dogs.'

Austin laughed again. 'I think we should tell Amber it's time for her to start taking orders from you now too. Just let me have a word with her first, I have a feeling she won't like it very much. Amber is a one boss kind of girl.'

They made their way quickly to the basement, Marcus still not totally convinced he wasn't dreaming. A part of him worried that Austin was playing some cruel joke and was about to change his mind. They reached the desk where Amber was talking to one of her guards and Marcus said, 'Amber, please come with me. We're setting Anita free.'

Amber laughed insultingly. She was about to rattle off a tirade of abuse, telling him he was living in a dream world if he thought she'd go against Austin's wishes and set Anita free. But when she looked up, she saw Austin standing behind Marcus, nodding, a smile playing about his lips, waiting with interest to see what she would do next. Amber narrowed her eyes, throwing a furious look at Austin; he would be deriving no end of enjoyment from this, but she could take that out on him later.

'Of course,' she replied through gritted teeth. Marcus was trying to keep his expression even, but couldn't totally hide his amazement. Who would've thought that blackmailing his father could have such positive effects? He followed Amber to the cell Anita was being held in and watched whilst she uncuffed her hands and feet. Anita looked worried, unsure what was going on and what torture she could expect next.

'Dad's letting you go,' said Marcus, in a gentle voice, helping her to her feet, but as she tried to put weight on her legs, they gave way. She would've fallen to the floor if Marcus hadn't scooped her up into his arms and carried her out of the room. He didn't stop for a second on the way to his car, still concerned that something could be done to stop him. Anita said nothing, resting her head limply on his chest, full of relief to be out in the cool night air. Marcus placed her cautiously on the back seat, trying to be as careful of her broken ribs and bruised flesh as he could. He sat down opposite her and took her hand as his driver set off towards Cordelia's.

Anita said nothing for the whole journey, her energy not responding as she would have expected to freedom. She still felt empty and drained, and although she knew she should be thankful to Marcus for getting her out, she felt nothing but numbness. They arrived at Cordelia's and Marcus picked Anita up again, pushed the gate open and walked to the back door, ajar as usual, not stopping as he made his way inside, calling for Cordelia as he entered.

'Hello?' he said urgently. 'Cordelia? Are you here? I need your help.'

Cordelia came rushing out of the sitting room, where she'd been sitting with Cleo by the fire. Cleo had told her everything, knowing she would, by now, be beside herself with worry at Anita's sudden disappearance. 'By the Gods,' she said, seeing the state Anita was in, 'what've they done to you?'

Cleo had followed Cordelia out of the sitting room and burst into tears at the sight of her best friend. She was barely recognisable, the strong, confident Anita nowhere to be seen. 'Bring her in here,' said Cordelia. 'Cleo, clear the sofa so Marcus can put her down.'

Cleo did as she was told and Marcus placed Anita on the sofa, then knelt on the floor and took her hand protectively. Cordelia rushed to the kitchen to get a glass of water and a sponge; they needed to rehydrate her and Anita wouldn't be able to sit up and drink normally in her current state. Anita was aware of all the activity going on around her but she still felt detached, her energy had deserted her; it was an effort to even breathe. All she could do was lie motionless and let them fuss around her. She knew she'd be alright; the wounds would heal with time and the emotional scars would fade, however, right now, that didn't seem to matter, all she could do was wallow in her own stupidity. How could she have been so brainless as to not work out what Helena was up to? She had deserved to be locked up given her foolish, reckless actions and now she had to reconcile her self-loathing alongside people fussing endlessly around her, trying to make sure she was alright. She deserved the pain she was in and she wished they would just leave her alone.

After Cordelia had managed to feed her some sugary water, Anita drifted off to sleep and Marcus, Cordelia and Cleo discussed what to do next. They'd been debating it for some time when Cordelia put her foot down. 'It's simple,' she said finally, shutting down any further conversation on the matter. 'She will stay here, being looked after by me until she is better. There will be very few visitors in that time and even you two can't be here all hours. She needs to rest, recuperate physically and spiritually, and come to terms with what has happened to her. She cannot do that with people around her twenty four seven. Do I make myself clear?'

Cleo and Marcus wanted to argue, but they could tell from Cordelia's body language that to do so would not get them anywhere, so they nodded their silent agreement.

'Good. I'm glad. Now thank you for your concern but I will take it from here. Come back tomorrow, and if Anita wants to see you, I will let you in, if not, you'll just have to wait until she's ready for visitors.' Cordelia could see they were gearing up to argue again, so fixed them with a look that made them think twice.

'Ok,' said Cleo, sensing that Marcus wasn't happy with this arrangement and thinking it best that she intervene. 'Come on Marcus, I should think you've got some recuperating to do too, and there's nothing more we can do for Anita at the moment. Cordelia has it under control.'

'Alright,' he said in a strained voice, 'but I'll be back early tomorrow to see her.'

'As I said, that's fine, but I will only let you in if she wants to see you too.'

Cleo took Marcus' arm and gently but firmly steered him out of the house. 'See you tomorrow Cordelia. Let us know if there's anything at all we can do.'

Marcus and Cleo said goodbye when they reached the gate, Marcus climbing back into his car, Cleo resisting the temptation to ask for a blow by blow account of what had happened. The car pulled away, Marcus slumped in the back seat looking tired and drawn. This couldn't have been easy for him either, Cleo thought, as she made her way to the Temples to tell Alexander what she knew.

Alexander had rushed to Cordelia's as soon as Cleo told him what happened. He couldn't quite believe that Marcus' plan had worked, but he was relieved that it had. Cordelia, surprised to see a second Descendant on her doorstep, had reluctantly let him in, but only after he agreed that under no circumstances would he do anything to wake her up. She reasoned that while Anita was sleeping, she wouldn't know about the visit anyway. Cordelia left them alone, satisfied that Alexander would keep his word.

He entered the sitting room and took in Anita's battered body, lying lifeless on the sofa, her energy so low that it was barely recognisable as hers. He walked slowly, silently to her side, crouching by her head and delicately moving a strand of hair off her swollen face. There were no tingles now, no excitement at his touch, but Alexander felt her energy lift a little at the contact, or at least he told himself that's what it was. He sat by her side for an hour, not moving a muscle, willing her energy to start to recover, but it stayed where it was, with no movement at all. Eventually, he got up, brushed his lips lightly against her forehead and left, thanking Cordelia and saying he would be back in the morning to see how she was. As he was leaving he paused and turned back to Cordelia. 'Her energy is dangerously low. We have to do this at her pace. Don't let Marcus force her into doing anything more quickly than she wants to. She's going to need a great deal of time.'

Cordelia nodded. 'Goodnight Alexander. I will no doubt see you tomorrow.'

*****

The following morning, Anita woke up and immediately sat bolt upright, the pain hitting her like an express train. She hadn't been able to feel it the night before, but now it was so strong she felt like she might faint. She froze and waited for the pain to abate a little before more gingerly swinging her legs onto the floor and carefully standing up, testing that her legs would take her weight before fully committing. Another shot of pain stabbed at her chest,

221

but this time she was expecting it, which somehow made it more bearable. She hobbled to the door and made for the stairs, but Cordelia heard her footsteps and headed her off before she could reach them.

'Good morning,' she said. 'I'm glad you feel well enough to walk, but what exactly do you think you are doing?'

'I'm going to my bedroom,' Anita said weakly, it was taking all the energy and concentration she could muster to make it to the stairs.

'May I ask why, when you have everything you need down here?'

'I want to be alone,' she said, now tackling the stairs, one painful upward step at a time.

'Alright. I'll bring you some water and some breakfast. You need to get some food in you.'

Anita didn't answer, she knew it would be futile to argue and was more concerned with reaching the top of the stairs on her own than with Cordelia bringing her food. She reached the top and paused to let the pain lift a little before pressing on to her room. Luckily, given the size of the cottage, this didn't present too much more of a challenge. She reached her bed and climbed carefully on top of the covers; it seemed like too much effort to crawl under them. She curled up, bringing her knees to her chest and began to cry.

Anita stayed in her room, refusing to see anyone but Cordelia for a full week. She fluctuated between sobbing uncontrollably and staring blankly into space for the first two days, the sobbing doing nothing to help the pain in her ribs. When she slept, she had flashbacks of Amber torturing her and Austin's cruel face seemed to loom in the back of her consciousness. When she was awake, she was consumed by her stupidity at not seeing through Helena and her guilt at having lied to Marcus. She didn't love him, not yet anyway, and Amber had been right, she had been manipulating him. She heard Marcus and Cleo downstairs demanding to see her, but Cordelia sent them away day after day, saying they had to do this at Anita's pace; they couldn't force her to do things she didn't want to do. Alexander's visits were different, instead of demanding to see her, he asked if she wanted visitors and asked questions about what she was eating and if she seemed to be getting her energy back. Anita's energy was coming back slowly, however it was nowhere near its normal level. She heard Alexander explaining to Cordelia that it would probably take a while for her to recover, given that she was a Body and currently unable to exercise, something that would normally lift her spirits. He suggested to Cordelia that she could encourage Anita to meditate instead, as this may help with her psychological healing.

Cordelia was careful to always speak to those who came at the bottom of the stairs, so Anita could hear what was said if she wanted to listen. That way, Anita would know what was going on and could decide for herself what she wanted to do and not do. Taking Alexander's advice, she began to mediate after a few days and it did start to help clear her mind, her anger at herself fading and becoming less consuming.

After a week confined to her room, Anita ventured out and headed downstairs to the kitchen, the pain in her ribs having mellowed, the cuts and bruises starting to heal, and the swelling in her face gone. She made herself a sandwich and took it to the sitting room, where she sat down by the fire. As she finished, the first whole meal she'd eaten since she'd been freed, there was a knock on the door and she heard Cleo's voice calling to see if Cordelia was around.

'Cleo,' Anita called out, her voice cracking as she spoke. Cleo heard her and came rushing in, embracing Anita when she saw she was alright. 'Ouch,' said Anita, Cleo a little overzealous with the pressure of her hug.

'Sorry, but I'm so happy to see you up and about. I've been so worried about you, we all have, Marcus, Alexander, Bas, Cordelia, Alistair, everyone. How are you feeling?'

'I've felt better, obviously, but I'm getting there. My energy seems to be properly picking up now. That's been the worst thing really, I just haven't had the will to get out of bed. Until this morning I felt either totally empty, or full of anger and loathing, but for some reason, today I woke up and started to feel a bit better. It's really good to see you Cleo. Thank you for all your help, it must have been terrifying trying to get out of the Archives.'

Cleo laughed. 'Probably not as terrifying as being tied up and tortured,' she said frankly, then, realising what she'd said, quickly followed it with, 'sorry, didn't mean to bring that up quite like that.'

Anita laughed. 'It's alright. It is what happened after all. So, what've I missed in the last week?' she asked, changing the subject. 'Fill me in on all the gossip.'

'Well, to be honest, everything pales into insignificance next to what happened to you, but Marcus and Alexander seem to have kind of made up, or at least they can tolerate spending time together now, so that's good I suppose. A couple of Council kids had a party and trashed their dad's three hundred year old energy metre; it was a particularly fine piece apparently. Austin and Amber have gone to Kingdom and everyone's speculating as to why, sorry, didn't mean to bring them up again.' She paused. 'To be honest Anita, I'm more concerned with how you're doing and if there's anything I can do to help?'

'Not at the moment. I need to work out what to do about Marcus and Alexander, but I can't face them at the moment. You could come for a walk with me though? I'm dying to get out of the house and do some exercise.'

Cleo jumped at the offer; she'd felt entirely useless for the past week, desperately searching for something she could do that would be helpful, so she wasn't going to pass up an opportunity like this.

CHAPTER 16

Anita spent the next couple of weeks building her strength both physically and mentally, going for long walks with Cleo and spending hours meditating in the garden. However, she refused to see either Marcus or Alexander until she was feeling more like herself and had had time to think about what to do.

She'd told Cleo everything; how Helena had approached her asking for help and that Helena had known about Anita's parents all along. She thought Cleo deserved to know after everything she'd been through. Anita had expected Cleo to react badly, to tell her that she was stupid to have gone along with someone as dubious as Helena without really knowing what she was getting herself into, but she didn't. Cleo had said she totally understood. She'd said Anita was the kind of person who felt the need to act if everyone else was shying away from action and as Helena had offered her a way to do that, it wasn't surprising that Anita had taken the bait. Cleo said if it'd been her, she wouldn't have turned Helena down the first time; she would've bitten off Helena's right arm to have found out information about her parents. Furthermore, when Anita was beating herself up for having believed Helena's story, Cleo told her that everyone makes mistakes, that nobody's perfect, and that as far as ruses went, Helena's was pretty believable, so she shouldn't be so hard on herself.

After a couple of weeks, Anita started to feel more like herself again and decided she was ready to start letting people back into her life. The time was fading the scars, Anita was starting to forgive herself, and she turned her attention to what she should do about Marcus and Alexander. They both still came to visit every morning, having settled into a routine of who arrived when, so as to avoid being there together. Cordelia turned them away every time without fail, saying that Anita would let them know when she was ready to see them. She'd had a couple of near misses, where one of them had altered their visiting time for some reason or other, and once Anita had had to duck behind a tree to make sure that Alexander didn't see her. Of course he would have felt her energy and known she was there, however he'd respected her wishes, continuing into the house to see Cordelia as normal, returning, again without stopping, a couple of minutes later.

After a great deal of consideration, Anita decided it would be best to see Marcus first. She was supposed to be his girlfriend after all, he'd been the one to rescue her, and although he didn't know it, she had deceived him. She owed him at least that much.

The following morning, Anita sat in the garden at Marcus' normal visiting time, on a bench near her usual yoga spot, and waited for him to arrive. She heard and felt him before she saw him and steeled herself as the sound of his footsteps disappeared onto the grass. As he rounded the corner of the cottage, he saw Anita and stopped dead, blinking a couple of times to make sure his mind wasn't playing tricks on him. When he was sure it was really her, he flew across the lawn to where she sat and dropped to his knees in front of her, hugging her around the waist and pulling her head to his shoulder.

'Anita, thank the Gods you're alright. I'm so, so sorry. How are you feeling?' he garbled into her hair, still not totally convinced this wasn't some cruel mirage.

She pulled back and smiled at him, running her hand down the side of his face. 'Marcus, this wasn't your fault. It was mine. I should've respected that you took me to a place of great importance to your family and should've known not to pry. I was extremely privileged that you showed me the picture; if anyone should be sorry, it should be me.' Tears of guilty regret welled up in Anita's eyes before they burst free and trickled down her pale cheeks.

Marcus couldn't believe what he was hearing. Austin had locked her up and tortured her when she'd done nothing wrong, and she was sorry? He moved to sit next to her, pulling her into his

arms, softly stroking her hair, willing her to come to her senses.
'Anita, please don't blame yourself. Dad's reaction was crazy, it was
unforgiveable. I'm just happy you're still able to stand the sight of
me.' His kindness caused the tears to flow vigorously and she
pulled herself closer to his chest, Marcus wrapping his arms more
tightly around her, bowing his head forward to kiss the top of her
head. The flow of her tears finally abated and Marcus helped Anita
up, taking her inside. He made them a pot of tea and sat them
down on the old, worn sofa next to the fire, Anita cuddling up to
him and Marcus gently calming her, stroking her hair. They talked
intermittently, sitting for periods in silence, just enjoying the contact
with the other, until Marcus told her quietly that he had to leave.
She sat up and kissed him, his lips soft and comforting. She felt
protected with him there; she didn't want him to go.

'Can't you stay?' she asked, willing his answer to be yes, her
forehead furrowed with distress. 'Just for a little bit longer.'

Marcus faltered, his heart breaking at the prospect of leaving
her, but he really had to go, he'd be late as it was. 'I've got to go,
but I'll be back as soon as I'm done, I promise.'

'Where're you going?' she asked, hoping to find some logical
argument as to why he didn't really have to leave her.

He hesitated, fighting a battle over what to tell her, but
reasoning lies had no place in their relationship, especially at the
moment, and she'd find out eventually one way or another. 'I'm
going to meet dad,' he said sheepishly.

'What?' Anita breathed, her mind muddled at his words, her
body sending a shot of adrenaline through her veins, her heart
starting to race.

He looked guilty and embarrassed, but continued honestly.
'Since I blackmailed dad to make him release you, he's developed a
new found respect for me. He's starting to get me more involved
with his business activities and Amber even has to take orders from
me now. The relationship is far from a good one with both of
them, but I'm learning so much that'll be invaluable when I'm a
ruling Descendant.'

The little colour she'd had drained from Anita's face. She felt
like she was in some kind of nightmare. After everything Austin
had done, how could Marcus be working with him? How could
Marcus be closer to him now than he had been before? She felt
cold and started to shake, Marcus trying to pull her back towards
him, but she pushed him away. She felt numb, just wanting him to
go. Whereas moments before she'd felt safe in his embrace, now

she was scared. 'I'll see you later,' she said, pulling her knees up to her chest, clearly indicating it was time for him to leave.

Marcus looked hurt. He wanted to say something to justify what he was doing, but he really had to go; Austin didn't take kindly to having to wait around for anyone. He'd explain everything to her later, even if he couldn't tell her what Austin had been getting him involved with. 'Ok,' he said, resigned. 'I'll see you later. I'll be back as soon as I can.' She nodded and he placed a soft kiss on her lips but she barely responded, she was like a different person from the girl who'd kissed him just moments before. He got up and made for the door. She'd come round with some more time, he hoped, as he left the room, Anita's energy plummeting as he went.

As soon as Marcus left, Anita got up and headed for the door. She needed to get out and do some exercise. She needed some space to think. She started to run as soon as she left the house, not thinking about where she was going, ignoring the dull pain in her chest. She couldn't believe it; was he choosing Austin over her? After everything they'd been though? After she'd been beaten to within an inch of her life?

Anita halted abruptly as she realised she'd run to the Temples, the ancient buildings climbing majestically into the sky ahead. She ran straight past the Temple of the Body and headed to the Spirit Temple instead, feeling like meditation may help her. She settled down at the back of the Temple, in the place she and Alexander used to meditate, and closed her eyes.

When she returned, she felt calmer and more composed. The news from Marcus had taken her by surprise, but when she thought about it, it would be both difficult and dangerous for Marcus to cut all ties with Austin straight away. Maybe he hated his father too and was stepping closer to him only because it would work to his advantage in the long run? Or maybe he was just doing it to make sure Austin didn't come after her again? She'd overreacted to the news as it had taken her by surprise. She'd never, even for a second, entertained the thought that Marcus would go back to work with Austin; she hadn't really even entertained the thought that they'd speak again. She'd thought they might have a similar relationship to that of Austin and Amelia, with them avoiding each other. But she should at least give Marcus a chance to explain what was going on before jumping to judgements.

Anita was about to get up to go back to Cordelia's, when she felt Alexander's powerful energy enter the Temple. She closed her eyes and pretended to meditate, not ready to see him yet, especially as she was so confused about Marcus. Alexander saw Anita and paused, leaning against a pillar and watching her rise and fall as she breathed long, slow breaths. He toyed with the idea of going and sitting down opposite her, joining her meditation, but aside from that being a total invasion of her privacy, he knew he had to respect her wishes; she'd talk to him when she was ready.

He made his way quietly to the Temple's centre and descended into his chambers, Anita watching his graceful, flowing movements as he went. She had such strong feelings for him, but after what she'd put Marcus through, it wouldn't be fair to push him away now, especially now he seemed so vulnerable to his father's influence.

*****

Marcus was waiting for Anita when she got home, his face full of relief when she didn't appear to be angry with him. 'Are you ok?' he asked, concerned.

'Yes,' she smiled, 'I just needed to do some exercise, so ran to the Temples to meditate. How did it go with Austin?' There was no point in tiptoeing around the topic, so Anita just dived in.

'It was fine. We had to visit a farmer that owes us rent. We have several of those at the moment, so we're working out what to do with them.'

'The poor things must be having such a tough time.'

Marcus nodded in agreement. 'We agreed he could give us two of his goats to cover the shortfall. He seemed grateful.'

'What?' she said, shocked. 'The farmers are having the worst year ever, obviously because of the energy, something which is entirely beyond their control, and you're making them pay rent they can't afford?'

'We were kind to them,' he said defensively, not understanding her reaction. 'Instead of money we accepted goats; we didn't have to do that.'

'And what are you going to do next time he can't pay? What if he has no goats left to give you? What will you do then?'

'I'm sure it won't come to that. We're just having a bad year. I'm sure very soon everything will return to normal and the farmers will be prosperous again.'

'And if it's not that simple? If it is to do with the energy and we have bad season after bad season?'

229

'Then the farmers will have to diversify and find a different way to make a living, like everyone else. We run a business Anita, not a charity.'

'You have a responsibility to the people of the world as their rulers to look after them, not suck them dry. You should be charitable; Gods know if anyone can afford it, it's you.'

CHAPTER 17

The next few weeks were difficult for Anita. She wanted to make things work with Marcus; how could she do anything else given what he'd done to get her out, but he was coming under more and more influence from Austin, his views becoming more radical and more entrenched. The time she spent with Marcus was tense and she felt guarded in his company. In stark contrast, she felt calm and safe when she was meditating in the Spirit Temple and she started going there every day. Every day she felt Alexander's energy watching her from afar. He never came over, not wanting to invade her privacy or push her into something before she was ready, but she had to hide the spike in her energy whenever she became aware of his presence.

It was a beautiful Autumn day, the sun sparkling low in the sky, the air crisp and sharp, the ground covered in leaves that crackled under every footstep. Anita was lost in her thoughts as she walked to the Spirit Temple for her usual meditation, wrapped up warm with only her face exposed to the wind, but as she was approaching the Temples, she looked up, feeling powerful energy ahead. She caught sight of Helena descending the steps from the Body Temple, conversing animatedly with someone she didn't recognise. Anita froze, her energy turning to hatred, feelings of anger at Helena and disgust at herself flooding back. She pushed the feelings aside and looked around for somewhere to hide; she wasn't ready to face Helena yet. Given the limited options available, she selected a large oak tree and managed to scramble behind it before she was spotted. Helena passed, not seeing Anita, or at least not letting on if she had, and disappeared, still deep in conversation with the man she was with.

Anita had been wrestling with what to do about Helena. She'd considered confronting her, to find out what she'd been playing at, telling her she knew it was one of Austin's memories that Helena had been trying to steal and demanding to know why. In the end, she'd decided the best course of action was not to do anything. Knowing Helena, the thing that would piss her off the most would be not knowing what had happened. No doubt she'd heard on the grapevine the rough story, but not to hear it straight from the horse's mouth would be killing her. Helena had no problem with confrontation, in fact, she enjoyed it, but she hated being kept in the dark, so Anita decided that was exactly what she should do. She still wanted to know what the memory was about, but there was no chance Helena would tell her willingly and she'd have no way to tell if Helena was lying or not, even if she did.

Anita waited to make sure she was definitely gone before proceeding to the Temple of the Spirit and sitting cross legged in her normal spot. She didn't have to wait long before she could feel Alexander observing her and she smiled, today not making any attempt to hide the effect he had on her. His energy rose in response and without stopping to think, she sent a nudge to the edge of his energy field. He responded immediately, striding over to where she sat, sinking down in front of her and taking her hands gently.

'I've been so worried about you,' he said softly. 'How are you feeling?'

She smiled. 'I'm getting there,' she murmured, enjoying the close up view of his face, especially those glorious eyes. 'How are you doing?'

He looked at her indulgently. 'How am I doing? In comparison to what you've been through I've had a walk in the park, I'm fine.'

Alexander dropped her hands, sensing others about to walk into the Temple. 'I don't think we should talk in such a public place,' he said, 'I don't want Marcus to find out through other people, especially now he's working more closely with Austin.' Alexander chose his words carefully, he didn't want to be too negative about Marcus given the circumstances, however, it was a real threat and they shouldn't ignore it. Anita nodded and Alexander led her to the centre of the Temple, the stone above his chambers sliding aside and they descended the steps, Anita excited to see under the Temple for the first time.

They entered a room that housed Alexander's desk and several worn leather chairs. It was crammed full of books and pictures, but had a warm, cosy feel to it, with a lit fire in the corner that reminded Anita of home. 'It's amazing,' she said, wandering around looking at the contents of the shelves.

'I'm glad you like it,' he smiled. 'I can't take credit though I'm afraid, I've hardly touched it since I took over from Philip. All this stuff belonged either to him or previous Descendants. I've barely even started working my way through everything; I'm trying to work out what kind of treasure trove I'm sitting on.'

'A happy task,' she said, spotting a rare energy book and taking it off the shelf to flick through the pages, 'and quite a significant treasure trove if this book is anything to go by,' she said, putting it carefully back on the shelf. 'So, what do you know about what's going on between Marcus and Austin?' she asked abruptly, taking him off guard.

There was no point in trying to sugar coat it, she wouldn't respect him for it if he did. He took a deep breath and told her everything he knew. 'From what I can tell, Marcus is being brought further and further under Austin's wing. Since he managed to convince Austin to free you, their relationship has changed; Austin seems to respect Marcus now, in a way that he didn't before. He's even making Amber take orders from Marcus, not a move he would've played lightly; it's probably to make Marcus feel like he has some degree of control. In reality he has no control at all. Marcus is being groomed to follow in Austin's footsteps, in exactly the same way that Austin was by Tobias. No doubt Marcus feels he's learning invaluable lessons that'll put him in a more powerful position. He may even have some naïve notion that he'll be able to bring Austin round, so he'll do something about the energy if everything gets really bad. In reality, Austin has Marcus exactly where he wants him and all he has to do now is get Marcus so involved in his 'business' activities that he can't get out. He'll probably encourage him to do things of an incrementally more dubious nature, so each action is only a small step further from what he's done before. Eventually, Marcus will be forced to make a choice, to do something so bad that he passes the point of no return, and at that point, Austin will have won. Marcus will no doubt hate himself for a time and wonder how he's got so entangled in such a web of deceit that there's no way back, the only hope of a way out being to go further into the clutches of the trap. You may still have influence over him, but you'll have to be careful how you use it. For the first time in his life Marcus' father is treating him like he's worth something, like the Mind line is lucky to have him. Marcus has wanted his father's acceptance for a very long time and it'll take something significant to make him give that up.'

Anita sat down in one of the leather arm chairs and paused to digest Alexander's words. 'Do you think an ultimatum would work?' she asked carefully, avoiding his eyes.

Alexander couldn't hide his shock, nor the stab of loss he felt imaging a world where Anita had bound herself to Marcus in such a way that they could never be together, not to mention the risk that if Marcus did subsequently follow Austin anyway, she could have cause to blame herself. And what if Marcus chose Austin over Anita? Then all influence would be lost and there'd be no hope of ever prising him away from his father. 'No,' he responded, happy that he wasn't just saying it for selfish reasons. 'The worst way to deal with Marcus at the moment is to force his hand; he'd feel as though he were being backed into a corner and not like he was making a real choice by himself. He's unlikely to want to give up Austin totally at the moment, especially now he finally feels he's getting somewhere.'

'Then what should I do? His views are already more extreme; he can't see that some of the things he and Austin are doing are totally wrong. They're forcing farmers, who are scared of losing their farms, whose crops are failing, who feel responsible for the impending food shortages, into paying their full rent regardless. They're taking their livestock as payment for Gods' sake and he can't see it's wrong. They have a responsibility to the people of the world and all they seem to care about is collecting what they're owed.' She stood up and started pacing, her agitation evident.

'All you can do is suggest there may be an alternative way. Every time you take him head on he'll go defensive, he'll try to justify his actions rather than think about the logic behind what you're saying. Showing how others are being more compassionate is more likely to work. That way he'll come to the conclusion by himself, feeling like it's his idea, not like he's been railroaded into it by you or anyone else.'

Anita nodded, she knew what Alexander was saying made perfect sense. She struggled with such a round-the-houses approach, but she knew she'd have to try.

'Anita, regardless of what happens, it won't be your fault.' She turned away, tears filling her eyes. He closed the space between them and put his hands on her shoulders, the familiar tingles returning and gently flowing around their bodies. 'Austin's been setting this up since Marcus was born and you can't expect to bring him around on your own.'

Anita turned to face him, standing so close she could feel his breath skip across her face. She met his electric eyes with hers, heady at their proximity, her energy responding, as did his. Anita bowed her head, stepped forwards and wrapped her arms around his chest. He pulled her tightly into him, Anita feeling secure with his muscular arms around her, Alexander resting his lips on the top of her head and closing his eyes.

They stood, each enjoying the touch of the other and neither wanting to pull away. Eventually, Anita pulled back, looking up at Alexander. 'Will you meditate with me?'

'Of course,' he said simply, as an idea came to him, 'I want to show you something though. There's somewhere special I want us to meditate.'

Anita looked up at him, intrigued. 'Where?'

'Just come with me,' he said coyly, taking her hand and pulling her further into his chambers, into a room with an enormous, luxurious looking bed. She faltered as he pulled her towards the bed, grateful and surprised to see the shelves next to it swinging towards them, revealing a secret passage behind. Alexander stuck his head through and looked both ways to check there was no one there. The passage was dimly lit with lanterns along the ground and Anita wondered who maintained them, surely not the Descendants, as Alexander pulled her gently forwards.

They made their way through what seemed like a maze of tunnels, pausing only once, when Alexander thought he heard something. He'd explained it was probably just someone up above; there were vents all through the tunnels, serving the joint purpose of ventilating the chambers and enabling the Descendants to spy on those above to their hearts' content. They finally arrived at a large, ornate door and Alexander turned to Anita, smiled indulgently as he pushed its heavy baulk open, and stood back to let her enter first. She walked through and looked around. Here too there was only a dim light from the same candle filled lanterns, so it took her a few moments to take in what she was seeing. She'd stepped into a columned space that seemed to circle around something in an open area in the middle. She could hear the soothing sound of running water, and, as she stepped forward, through a beautifully constructed archway, she finally twigged, spinning around violently to confirm she was where she thought she was.

Alexander laughed. 'It took you a while.'

'We're directly below the points of the Temples?'

He nodded. 'I've always thought it a shame more people don't get to see it; it's really quite beautiful down here.' She looked around. He was right, it was. There was a raised pool in the centre, under the points, which was somehow surrounded by lush green grass. There were climbing plants trailing sweet smelling flowers as they wound round the columns and reached for the ceiling. There were rose bushes blooming with enormous white flowers, not the tight, uniformed variety, but the looser, freer kind. And there was a tiny pin hole in the ceiling, that, by some trick, let in enough light to illuminate every inch of the pool's shimmering surface. The pinhole had been added by the Temple's designer to connect the sacred pool below to the Temple points above. The point directly above the hole was inside the Council chamber, the area no one was allowed to walk over, however, the designer had also installed a magnificent skylight in the chamber's roof, with a tiny hole in its centre, so the pool was always connected to the outside world. 'Like it?' he asked.

'It's incredible,' she replied. 'It feels so calm, like the energy is totally even, without even the smallest ripple.'

'It is even,' he said, 'in the same way that the pool under the Observatory absorbs the energy 'noise' in the area there, this pool does the same thing here. It has a more potent effect here though as there's less background energy to start with and the place has a special balance being under the points of the Temples. Nobody can explain exactly why; it just does.'

'We're meditating here?' she asked excitedly.

He nodded. 'I want so share something with you and here seems like the best place to do it.'

'This isn't what you want to show me?' she asked, astonished.

'No. I want to show you something inside my head.'

She smiled. Alexander was so private; she loved it when he let her in. She moved so she was standing right next to the pool and lay down on her back; she didn't feel at all vulnerable with Alexander. He hesitated, 'Anita...'

She turned her head and sent him a calm, level look, '…sush,' she said, stopping dead any further words, placing her hand beside her, ready for him to hold. He moved to her and lay down easily on his back, placing his arm down by his side and taking her waiting hand. He turned his face to look at her, curved his head forward so their foreheads touched, and they both closed their eyes, Alexander controlling their destination, Anita relishing the trust she had for him, letting him take her wherever he wanted to go. The intensity was astounding; it felt like there was so much energy coursing between them that it might try to escape, ripping them apart as it went. She felt powerful, like she could do anything, like she was floating off the ground and Alexander was floating with her, supporting her, lifting her up.

The meditation settled and Anita looked around, confused, wondering if something had gone wrong. 'Hey,' said Alexander, 'everything ok?' Alexander had never felt anything like this before either. He'd practiced the love pose only a handful of times before, and never with anyone he actually loved. It was incredible the power that was flooding between them and he savoured the sensation, forgetting that Anita would be full of confusion.

'Yeah, I have literally never felt better. The power's unbelievable; you can feel it too?'

Alexander nodded. 'I've never felt anything like it; it's extraordinary.'

Anita sat up a little to make sure she wasn't missing anything. 'The pool is a place in your head?' she asked cautiously.

Alexander sat up on his elbows, making sure he kept hold of her hand; he'd forgotten all about where they were given all the excitement. 'It's more than just a place in my head,' he explained softly. 'This is my Centre.'

'This is your Centre?' she repeated, stunned, trying to work out what this news meant. 'Why?' she asked; the best she could come up with.

'Why is anyone's Centre what it is?' he laughed. 'I've looked into all the research there is, but there's nothing concrete about what causes our Centres to be what they are. There's speculation it's inherited from parents, but I don't know what my parents' Centres were and Philip would never go anywhere near the topic, so I couldn't ask him. Given most people don't even know how to meditate properly, the research is pretty limited, and those who do know usually consider it a sign of weakness for others to know the places in their heads. You're the only one that knows any of mine,' he said, looking down self-consciously.

She turned her head to look at him, rolling her body towards him so she could place her free hand on the side of his face and gently turn it back towards her. She looked into his blue eyes, seeing there a reflection of the longing she felt, and dipped her head to kiss his stubborn lips. As their lips touched they felt a jolt of energy like nothing either of them had ever felt before, so strong it was almost painful. They responded instinctively, Alexander rolling his shoulders towards her, wrapping one arm around her, pulling her to him, his other hand grabbing a handful of her hair, locking her lips to his. He rolled her gently backwards, lowering her lightly to the ground, pining her there with his weight. The world around Anita seemed to swirl. She had no idea if she was sitting, lying, standing, floating; she was lost in his mouth, his smell, the hard contours of his body. It was like she was both grounded, supported by the grass pushing up against her back, and at the same time suspended, drifting in the air. Alexander pulled back, his breath ragged, looking hungrily down at Anita's serene figure on the grass. He leant back towards her, planting soft, slow, heavy kisses over her face, Anita running her fingers playfully across the exposed skin at his neck. He bit her lip, exquisitely, seductively and Anita's stomach clenched. She took a deep breath and pushed him gently away, sitting up to face him.

'I think I love you, Alexander,' she said huskily.

He looked ecstatically back at her. 'I think I love you too.' He pulled her to him, folding his arms protectively around her, caressing her back, not quite believing he wasn't in a dream.

'I think it's time to wake up now,' said Anita. 'It's so perfect, what I'm about to say isn't allowed in here.' Alexander pulled them abruptly out of the meditation, not sure he wanted to hear what she had to say. They woke up to the feeling they were falling, their stomachs lurching upwards as they landed on the ground with a heavy thump.

'What was that?' asked Anita, alarmed.

Alexander looked astonished. 'I don't believe it,' he said, delighted.

'What?'

'We were floating, when we were meditating. I've heard about this happening, but only ever at the Spirit Temple in the clouds and never without extensive practice. I just can't believe it,' he said, grabbing her and pulling her into a rough, excited embrace. Anita had never seen Alexander so animated, so went with it, clearly this was a big deal. A couple of seconds later, Alexander let her go, remembering why they'd left the meditation so quickly. 'What did you want to talk about?' he said quickly, bracing himself for the worst.

Anita took a deep breath. 'I love you Alexander, but I owe it to Marcus that nothing more happens between us until I've had a chance to end it with him first.'

'Is that all?' Alexander asked, relieved.

'Yes! What did you think I was going to say?'

'I don't know, that we couldn't be together, or something equally horrible.'

She took his hand. 'Alexander, when I meditated with Marcus it was also in the love pose. I'd never even heard of the pose, let alone practiced it; you stayed away from it for obvious reasons, but when I meditated with Marcus, the feeling was less intense than when you and I meditate normally together. I thought maybe that was just because Marcus is a Mind and you're a Spirit, but after what I just felt, I know that can't be all it is. I don't feel for Marcus what I feel for you,' she said hesitantly, 'it's as simple as that, but I don't want to cheat on him; I can't do that to him after what he did to get Austin to let me go.'

'I understand,' he replied. 'You've been through a lot together.'

'I just hope me leaving him won't push him further towards Austin.'

'It might,' Alexander said truthfully, 'but Marcus and his choices are not your responsibility. He has to account for his own actions and you have to account for yours. To stay with him when you don't love him wouldn't be good for either of you.'

'I know,' she said. 'I've made up my mind; I just need to talk to him. Come on, let's go, the longer we're alone together the more likely my resolve is to break,' she flirted.

He smiled as he got up and took her hand to help her to her feet. They left, Alexander firmly closing the door behind them before taking Anita's hand and leading her back the way they had come.

Neither of them noticed Gwyn hiding in the shadows, watching them leave, her energy supressed as low as she could make it go. She'd been in the tunnels earlier and had heard Anita and Alexander coming towards her. She'd ducked into a side tunnel and supressed her energy, hoping they wouldn't see her, but she'd kicked a lantern as she went, a muffled scraping noise floating to their ears. They'd paused at the sound, however, when nothing followed, they'd carried on, Alexander explaining to Anita that it was probably someone from above.

Gwyn had silently followed them to the pool, and watched as they'd entered and closed the door. She couldn't follow them inside; they would have heard the door open, not to mention that Alexander would have definitely detected her energy. Instead, she waited until they came out, seeing if they would give anything away. To her great disappointment, they moved silently back towards Alexander's chambers, but they were still holding hands and Gwyn reasoned that was suspicious enough for Marcus to want to know about it. If her boyfriend had been down here with another girl, she would want to know, and anyway, she didn't like Anita, so it would give her great pleasure to cause her some pain.

CHAPTER 18

Gwyn went straight to the castle, telling Amber she had something she urgently needed to discuss with Marcus when she got there. Amber let her in and told Gwyn to go up to Marcus' suite and knock on the door; she was still bitter about having to take orders from him, so she was damned if she was going to go and ask him if this was a call he wanted to take.

Gwyn climbed the stairs and knocked on his door, Marcus surprised to see her when he answered. 'Gwyn?' he said hesitantly. 'What's up?'

She hadn't stayed long, just long enough to tell him what she'd seen, twisting the knife a bit by adding an embellishment here and there. Marcus had remained composed, which had surprised her; she'd expected a jealous rage. He thanked her and showed her out, not quite sure of the best way to handle the information. He tried to stay calm, however, couldn't think of a single legitimate reason for them to be at the pool together, especially not holding hands. He decided the best thing to do would be to talk to Anita about it, so he barked for Amber to get him his driver – bossing her around was never going to get old – and headed to Cordelia's to see what she had to say.

Anita had just got home, still on a high from what had happened with Alexander. They hadn't kissed when they'd said

241

goodbye, respecting Anita's wishes to tell Marcus first, and this had only served to add to the tension. She was replaying their most recent meditation kiss in her mind when Marcus' voice pierced her daydream, his footsteps following his call.

'Anita? Are you here?'

'Hi,' she said, a little off balance. Why was he here? 'Good day?' she asked, trying to buy herself a bit of time to get back on kilter.

'There's something I need to discuss with you,' he said tersely, trying to keep his tone as even as he could, but irritation plain to read on his face.

'What is it?' she asked, concerned. The only saving grace was that this couldn't be about what had just happened with Alexander.

'Tell me,' he said abruptly, 'how is Alexander?'

Shit. 'He's very well, I've just seen him in fact,' she replied rigidly, trying hard not to escalate the situation.

'Really?' he said, feigning innocence. 'Why did you see him?'

'We're friends, it was good to catch up, we meditated together. As you know, I've found meditation very helpful recently.'

'I think it would be best if you don't see Alexander any longer,' said Marcus, as though this were a perfectly normal thing to drop into conversation.

'I'm sorry, what?' Anita spluttered in shock, half laughing. They'd had an unspoken understanding that Anita would stay away from Alexander before, but the words had never actually been said, and she'd only obliged as she'd been working for Helena and hadn't wanted to do anything to piss him off.

'I think it would be best if you don't see Alexander any longer,' he repeated, condescendingly.

'Yes, I heard what you said; I'm just in shock that you think you can dictate who I'm allowed to see.'

Marcus was a little taken aback; he'd expected her to reluctantly agree with him, seeing the logic behind what he was saying. 'But I think it's for the best, don't you?'

'What does that even mean? Why would it be for the best for me not to see one of my friends?'

'Because I'm uncomfortable with you holding hands with your male friends,' he said venomously. Anita went cold. How could he possibly know that? 'It's not like this is the first time you've been caught holding Alexander's hand in public.'

By the Gods, how had he found out? Surely not from Alexander? 'Marcus, I hope you realise what you sound like. You

242

sound exactly like your father. You can't order me around, or force me to do things I don't want to do, whether you think it's for the best or not. I'm an adult, quite capable of making my own choices and I choose to spend time with Alexander.' She paused, steeling herself for what she was going to say next. 'And, in fact, I choose not to spend time with you anymore.'

The colour drained from his face. 'What?' he whispered, looking lost. 'You can't break up with me. I love you.'

Tears pricked at Anita's eyes. She didn't want to hurt him, but there was no other way. 'Marcus, since,' she paused, taking a deep breath, 'since you convinced your father to set me free, you've changed. Austin has let you into his inner circle and you're obviously happy about that, but I don't like the person he's turning you into. He's closing your eyes to what's really going on in the world, he's making you kick people when they're down, and above all, he's turning you into someone like him.'

Marcus didn't know what to say. Anita was wrong, he was nothing like Austin, he was doing what he was doing to put himself in a position of strength, so he could protect them both from Austin in the future. 'You're wrong,' he stuttered, 'I'm not turning into him, I'm making sure I can protect us.'

'You think Austin isn't cleaver enough to see through that? He's immersing you in his shady world so that one day you'll be so far in that you can't get out. I don't want to be a part of that,' she said, the tears overflowing, 'and I don't want you to either. You are an amazing, genuine person Marcus. You take life at face value and that suits you, it makes you fun and daring and carefree, it's what drew me to you when I first met you, but I can't be part of this any longer; you need to work out who you want to be on your own. If you want to be like Austin, then carry on as you are, if not, then you need to get out before you're so far in that your trapped forever.'

Marcus felt like she'd ripped a hole in his chest; he'd never loved anyone like he loved Anita. 'I thought you loved me?' he choked, thinking maybe this would remind her that she really did want to be with him.

'I do Marcus, but I don't want to be under your control. If the way you try to show me you love me is by trying to stop me from seeing my friends, then it's not a relationship I can be in with all my heart. It may just be Alexander now, but what if you decide you don't like Cleo, or Bas, or you think that someone looks at me the wrong way? I can't live like that. I don't want to live like that. I'm sorry Marcus, but it's over.' She said it as gently as she could whilst conveying the finality of her decision, wiping away the tears still trickling down her face.

Marcus couldn't believe this was happening. He kept hoping he was about to wake up from a bad dream, Anita lying by his side, but he didn't. He turned to leave; there was no reason for him to stay any longer, his mind racing as he left the room.

'I'm so sorry,' Anita said softly as he left, sinking to the sofa and pulling a cushion towards her, unable to stop the tears that just kept coming. She'd known it wouldn't be easy, but that had been a lot harder then she'd expected. She felt horrible and hated to think what Marcus might do now. She just hoped it didn't push him further towards his father, that some of what she'd said had gone in.

'Hello?' called a voice from the corridor, Cleo appearing at the door and rushing over to her best friend when she saw her tears. 'What's wrong?' she asked, her concern palpable as she put her arms around Anita and pulled her in. 'What happened?'

'I just broke up with Marcus,' she sobbed, 'and he didn't take it very well.'

Cleo pushed Anita away so she could look at her face. 'You did what? Doesn't that put you in a bit of a dangerous predicament?'

'I don't care about that. If Austin wants to come after me then he'll come after me, but he was just so hurt, I feel horrible.'

'Why did you do it?' Anita had never acted like this before; she'd always been so tough. Cleo wasn't sure how to handle a teary Anita.

'Because I realised that I love Alexander.'

'I see,' said Cleo, her tone turning firm. 'So, you're sitting here, sobbing into a cushion like some silly girl, when you broke up with Marcus because some other man wants to be with you? Please get it together.'

Anita looked at Cleo, shocked at her lack of compassion. 'I feel like a total bitch for hurting him,' she said defensively.

'Well I'm sure you'll get over that as soon as you're back looking longingly into Alexander's beautiful eyes. Bloody hell, some people,' said Cleo cattily, getting up and pacing across the room.

Cleo's reaction had a sobering effect on Anita. Maybe she was being a little melodramatic; it wasn't like her to let things get to her like this. 'Is everything ok Cleo?' Anita asked, wiping away the last of her tears and putting aside the offending cushion.

'No, everything is not bloody well ok. It's alright for you, Miss 'I've got two men chasing after me, but boo hoo I've just had to tell one of the Descendants I'm not interested because I'd rather shag the other one,' but for those of us living in the real world, men are total shits who don't turn up for dates when they said they were going to.'

Anita realised that because of all the drama going on in her own life, she'd been totally neglecting her best friend and everything going on with her. 'Sorry Cleo, I've been horrible recently, what's going on?'

Cleo looked relieved she had a chance to get her story off her chest and sat back down on the sofa. 'Well, you know I've been seeing that Councillor's son off and on, the one I went to the ball with?'

Anita nodded. 'Of course, Henry.'

'Yes, Henry. Well, we've been seeing quite a lot of each other recently and it's been going really well, but he was supposed to be taking me to Bas' concert tonight…you're coming too, right?'

Shit, she had forgotten all about it. She needed to pull it together on the friend front and stop being so self-obsessed, she thought, nodding to Cleo. 'Of course.'

'Anyway, Henry was supposed to pick me up earlier. We were going to go for dinner and then go on to the concert, but he stood me up. I walked into town, thinking he must have just lost track of time or something, but as I walked past Temple Mews, I saw him all over some other girl outside the flower shop. I went over to him and tapped him on the shoulder and when he saw it was me he turned away dismissively and said he would see me later. I slapped him, obviously, a little melodramatic perhaps, but it made me feel better, and then I stormed off; I didn't want to make a proper scene. Stupid arrogant arsehole,' she said, feeling much happier just to be replaying the story to someone else.

'What an idiot,' said Anita, 'the Councillors' children always seem to think they're something special and they're really not.'

'Well anyway, I won't be seeing him again. Pity, the sex was good.'

Anita smiled indulgently. 'Come on, we'll be late for Bas' concert, and you never know, you might find some fresh meat.'

'Let's hope so,' she said frivolously.

'Cleo,' Anita said, stopping before they left the house.

'Uh huh?'

'I'm really sorry I've been so self-absorbed for the last few weeks. I promise not to be from now on.'

'Don't be silly, you've had a lot going on. I forgive you, just don't do it again. That includes the getting kidnapped bit as well.'

Anita laughed. 'I'll do my best. Nice touch with the slap by the way.'

'Thanks, I thought so.'

CHAPTER 19

Anita and Cleo arrived at the clearing in the woods by the river where the gig was being held just as Bas' Indie Rock band was taking to the stage. Thank the Gods, thought Anita, she was really glad they hadn't missed his band, she didn't want to have something else to apologise for. They sat down in a spot at the back, near the treeline, and listened as Bas' raw, melodic voice filled the air around them.

They listened silently for a few minutes before Cleo introduced herself to the group of guys next to them, who, incidentally, were absurdly good looking. Good luck to them, smiled Anita as she lay down, closed her eyes, let the music flow over her and thought about what had happened earlier with Alexander. She replayed their meditation again and again, her lips tingling at the memory. Bas' fourth song finished, the crowd clapped raucously and Anita felt a familiar, powerful energy all around her. She opened her eyes and looked up to see two electric blue eyes looking down at her, her energy lifting as she remembered she and Marcus were no longer an item.

'It's rude to sneak up on people without giving them any warning,' she flirted up at him.

'It's rude to be so grumpy when someone comes to find you especially,' Alexander flirted back. 'Come we with,' he said, offering her his hand and helping her to her feet. 'It's probably best not to be seen here for too long so soon after your break up with Marcus.'

'How have you heard already?' she asked, astounded and a little bit annoyed.

'News travels fast around here; you should know that by now.'

'Hmmm,' she said poutily, 'we can talk about that later. Let's go.'

Alexander led Anita into the woods, heading further up the river. When they were safely out of sight of everyone at the concert, he reached out and took her hand, a spark of electric energy flashing between them as their flesh met. They laughed excitedly, elated by their new found freedom.

'How did it go with Marcus?' asked Alexander. He knew it must have been difficult for her after everything they'd been through.

'It could have been worse,' she said truthfully. 'He came to see me because he somehow knew that we'd been to the pool together. Someone told him they'd seen us holding hands and he told me I wasn't allowed to see you anymore.'

'Oh.'

'So, as I said, it could have been worse. He reaffirmed that it was the right decision and it gave me a chance to warn him about getting too close to Austin's business transactions. I doubt he'll listen, but at least I tried. I feel guilty though, after what he went through, and I think he really does love me. I'd be lying if I said I didn't have feelings for him too, but they're nothing in comparison to what I feel for you.'

Alexander looked at her happily as they rounded a sharp bend in the path that exposed a graceful waterfall, the path coming to an abrupt halt by its side, the water cascading into a deep plunge pool, throwing up a fine white spray. 'I'm very glad to hear it,' he said, as she took a step towards him, the mood between them altering as she reached for his lips. 'Wait,' he said, turning away. 'Anita, there are some things I need to tell you before we take this any further. I don't want secrets between us; it would be too easy for us to be pulled apart if there were.'

Anita felt robbed; she'd been fanaticising about their first kiss in the real world for a very long time, but she had to admit, what he said made perfect sense. She nodded, 'I know. There are some things I need to tell you too, but I have one condition,' she said, looking up at him seductively.

'Name it,' he replied, matching her tone.

'That you kiss me first. If you hate me after what I have to tell you, or I hate you, I want to at least have kissed you first.'

Alexander said nothing, instead, he swiftly closed the gap between them, lowering his face so it was right next to hers, Anita looking up at him, entranced. He placed his hand on her stomach and pushed her backwards, her body complying without hesitation to his rough touch. She met the rock behind her, the cold stone halting her movement and holding her in place. He moved a hand to her face and ran his thumb down her cheek, caressing her cheek bone, before closing his beautiful eyes and slowly lowering his lips so they hovered just above hers. He touched his nose to hers, breathing deeply, relishing the tension that stretched at breaking point between them, breathing in her jasmine scent and savouring the contact of their skin. Their mouths finally met to a shower of tingles, Anita forgetting everything but Alexander as his lips caressed hers. He pushed his body into her, kisses more demanding, Anita's hands clawing at his back, holding him to her. Alexander broke away, pulling back a little, turning his head from hers, his brow furrowed, breathing deeply to get himself back under control, strengthening his resolve, before returning for one last gentle kiss. 'I hope we can both forgive whatever sins our secrets hold,' he breathed, moving his face back dangerously close to Anita's before pushing himself away, leaving both of them a little shaken, wanting more.

'I couldn't agree with you more,' she said, a deep sense of loss welling up inside her, trying desperately to regain some composure, her energy going crazy, her instincts urging her to demand more. Who really cared about secrets anyway?

Alexander sat on the grass next to the plunge pool, just out of range of the spray. Anita sat down next to him, leaning on a rock, her legs out straight in front of her, toes still tingling a little with energy from the kiss.

'Shall I go first?' she asked. She wasn't sure she really wanted to hear what Alexander had to say, so she may as well get her bit over and done with.

'Sure,' he said, taking her hand, 'fire away.'

Anita told Alexander everything. She told him that she'd been approached by Helena and had said no to start off with, but after the Council meeting and Marcus' views on the energy, that she'd agreed to help. She told him about the cylinder with Austin's memory, about being beaten up and about how she'd felt for the past few weeks.

Alexander's energy remained calm the whole time. He stroked her hand when she told him how empty she'd felt when she'd been set free, about the self-loathing and how stupid she'd felt. When she finished, Alexander simply said, 'you thought you were doing something to help. You had no idea Helena was lying to you. We can only make decisions based on the information we have in front of us and you chose to do something rather than sit back and let the world suffer. I would probably have done the same in your situation, especially if the proposal had been from someone I trusted.'

'But I should have known not to trust her. She's been lying to me for years about my parents.'

'Anita, things look different with the benefit of hindsight; you were just trying to help.'

Anita took a deep breath, she didn't want to talk about it anymore, although she was glad Alexander knew the truth. 'Alright, your turn,' she said, smiling. 'Make it quick, we have better things to do.'

Alexander stalled, pulling her towards him to kiss her temple, his chest feeling like it contained a whole aviary full of birds, all flapping their wings furiously inside him. 'Okay,' he said. 'When we first arrived in Empire, we came because Christiana was ill and she wanted to find someone before she died. Austin agreed to it because he thought she just wanted to see the person, to make sure life wasn't treating her too badly, but Christiana had other ideas; she wanted to tell her the truth about something that happened a long time ago, that Christiana had regretted ever since. It would seem that they altered the bloodline so the relic could never be sent back. I have no idea why, or what their motives were, but Christiana thought it was wrong for them to play God and the girl had to be told what had happened.' Alexander paused, took a deep breath and steeled himself. 'It would seem that the most plausible candidate for who that girl is, is you Anita.'

His words hit her like a hammer. 'What?' she laughed. 'Have you hit your head or something? How could I possibly be a Descendant?'

'You've got to admit you're powerful. You're probably the most adept Body I've ever met.'

'But I also have a significant Spirit influence; I wouldn't be a reader if I were the Body Descendant.'

'Christiana was a reader.'

'I'm not a Descendant.'

'Really? Why not? Who were your parents?'

'Bloody hell Alexander, that's a bit much don't you think?'

'I'm sorry, but just entertain the idea for a second before you dismiss it, and there's more.' Alexander told Anita about the conversation he'd heard between Alistair and Peter, confirming she was the Descendant, about the note from Philip, and that Austin had killed Christiana to keep her quiet. The bit Anita was most surprised about was that Alistair was involved. He had always looked after her, but surely this couldn't be the reason why?

'It all fits perfectly,' said Alexander, 'I'm just sorry I didn't tell you sooner.'

She sat numbly for a minute, processing his words. 'It's going to take a bit of time for me to get my head around this,' she said slowly. 'But I still want to kiss you,' she smiled, reaching up and placing a quick, flirty kiss on his lips. Alexander looked relieved and pulled her playfully into him, wrapping his arms gruffly around her and holding her in place.

'Good, because I want to kiss you too,' he said, kissing the top of her head. Anita fought her way out of his arms, tickling him mercilessly to make him let her go. He threw his hands up in defeat and let her wriggle round to face him, pulling herself up onto his torso to kiss him squarely on the lips. She pulled away and got to her feet. 'Come on,' she said, 'I think we should go somewhere more private.'

Alexander smirked. 'I'm not going to argue with that,' he said, getting up and putting his arm around her, pulling her close to him as they made their way back towards Empire. They walked in silence, full of blissful content, neither one believing this was actually happening, each looking at the other every now and again to check it was real.

They emerged from the woods onto the track that led back to Empire and waited for the energy van that was coming down the road to pass by. However, to their surprise, as the van pulled level with them, the back door opened and four balaclava-clad men dressed all in black jumped out and bundled them inside, where another four men were waiting to restrain them. They struggled wildly and Anita tried to scream, but a gloved hand covered her mouth, stifling her cries. They quickly realised that to struggle was futile, so they stilled. There were eight men against two of them and they already had hand cuffs clamped around their wrists; there was nothing to do now but wait and see where they were being taken.

The van travelled for what seemed like forever, the path it followed winding this way and that, nobody saying a word, Anita and Alexander forced to sit with their backs to one another, so they couldn't even share a reassuring look. The van stopped abruptly and the door opened, two men dragging Anita out and two dragging Alexander. The others flanked them as they walked, presumably in case they tried to make a bid for freedom. Although it was pitch black, the place felt familiar to Anita, like she had been here before, but she couldn't quite place it.

They were dragged roughly into a barn, then towards an open hole in the middle of the floor, which they were forced to jump into one at a time. It wasn't deep and they each landed lithely on their feet, several more guards ready to collect them when they landed, the hole's cover replaced as soon as they were in. They were shoved along a rudimentary corridor and into a small, box-like room, the guards forcibly pushing them down onto wooden chairs, their hands and feet cuffed to the struts, Anita reminded disturbingly of her time spent in Amber's basement, wondering if Austin was behind this too.

The men filed out of the room as three new figures entered. Two of them Anita didn't recognise, but the third she knew only too well. Helena? Why would she do this? They'd been gagged, but their eyes flew wide with surprise.

'So good to see you both,' she said. 'Sorry about the unfortunate circumstances, but it was really the only way.' She sat down, taking her time, making herself comfortable before speaking again. 'Now, Anita, let's have a little chat about that cylinder in your head.'

If you enjoyed Legacy of the Mind, why not write a review on Smashwords, Amazon or Goodreads. Reviews are the best way for readers to discover great new books and authors really appreciate your feedback.

ABOUT THE AUTHOR

Harriet was born in Germany in 1987, the family returning to the UK, to Dorset shortly afterwards. She lived there until she was 5, her grandfather teaching her the basics of cheating at cards and swindling chocolate, her mother starting to instil a (some would argue) unhealthy relationship with cake, and the neighbours demonstrating that some people don't understand cherry blossom is there to be picked, mixed with mint and water and sold as perfume.

Then there was Scotland; stealthy guinea pig breeding, riding horses, advanced cards, more cake, then to Devon and school in Exeter. She loved maths in the early years, but by the time she got to A Level, Sociology was her favourite subject, opening her eyes to things she'd never before considered, namely, nobody is really right, nobody is really normal and primary socialisation has a lot to answer for.

At the age of about 12, Harriet started rowing for Exeter Rowing Club. This quickly took over her life and before too long she was clad in lycra, training 6 days a week and competing at events around the country.

After finishing her A Levels, Harriet went to university in St Andrews, studying Philosophy for two years, then switching to Management. She was particularly interested in the 'people' elements of her course and especially the areas concerning how people create and react to change. After four very civilised years by the sea, she ventured to London, to foray into the strange world of insurance (surprisingly, more interesting than you might think). She worked as a Project Manager on large change programmes before founding her own consultancy in 2015.

Harriet now lives in Hertfordshire with her husband Chris and daughter Atia. When she isn't, writing, editing, eating, running around after her toddler, or imagining how much better life would be with the addition of a springer spaniel, she occasionally finds the time to make hats.

CONNECT WITH HR MOORE

For more information about HR Moore and the journey she's been on whilst writing and publishing The Legacy Trilogy, check out her website and blog:
http://www.hrmoore.com/

You can also connect with HR Moore by:

Following @hr_moore on Twitter

See what the world of Legacy looks like on Pinterest:
http://pinterest.com/harrietjr/the-legacy-trilogy/

Like HR Moore's page on Facebook:
https://www.facebook.com/harrietrmoore

Follow HR Moore on Instagram
https://www.instagram.com/hr_moore/

DISCOVER OTHER TITLES BY HR MOORE

The Legacy Trilogy:

Legacy of the Mind

Origin of the Body

Design of the Spirit

Printed in Poland
by Amazon Fulfillment
Poland Sp. z o.o., Wrocław